I0588680

THE KINGDOM WE DON'T

Copyright © 2022 by Halle Clark

All rights reserved. No part of this book may be reproduced in any
manner whatsoever without written permission except in the case
of brief quotations embodied in critical articles and reviews.

First Printing, 2022

The Kingdom We Don't

HALLE CLARK

IngramSpark

Dedication

This book is dedicated to my own Nana, an avid reader, one of my biggest supporters, and someone who always encouraged me to write and read. While she was two weeks too late to see my first book printed, she made a huge impact on the creation of this series. So, this book is for you Nana, and it is written with all my love.

Map of the Continent

Map of Dolma

CALVINE
ANDALUCA
ADELACE
EXPERION
CASIMONIUS
AGREMERRE
VASPELLO
ROAD TO
NEVREHERRE
"BORDER TOWN"
ASMEZREL
DUEGLE
OHMEHEV
DOLMITE ISLANDS
AGREMERRE
ISLAND
OF NOR

Contents

PART ONE

Chapter 1

The Familiar Journey

The carriage jostled slightly as we rode below the bright green canopy. It was a beautiful day, the sun was shining, birds chirped as they flew across the clear blue sky, startled by our movement, and the sweet smell of trees wafted across my skin from the open window. You'd never have known we were in a drought, with all the life that surrounded us right now. Although the roads that passed through the border of my home country, Nevremerre, and our neighboring allies, Agremerre, had always been given extra care, this road showed the strength between our two countries. So it was important it was always maintained. And yes, the roads were beautiful and green, and animals trying to avoid the effects of the drought found much-needed shelter here.

One would be forgiven for assuming, in all this nature and sunshine, that my traveling companions and I were merrily chatting as we moved between the shining trees. Instead, the atmosphere of our party was stifling. Not one word had been spoken since we left Nevremerre, and now, several hours later, the silence was more than a little uncomfortable. Not even the knights riding beside us spoke. They simply solemnly followed Sir Galileo as he led us towards Vierage Castle, the home of Lady Lucy, the only member of my party that was not yet traveling with us. At just 21, Lady Lucy, my future Lady-in-Waiting, had graciously offered for us to stop at her familial home in Agremerre after our first day of travel. Being a Nevremerre native, I would have thought Sir Galileo would have had to ask directions or confirm our location with one of the Agremerrians in our party at least once, but there hadn't been as much as a whisper throughout our entire journey.

Honestly, I probably could have endured the silence if it weren't for my ever-growing suspicions that the silence was maintained solely for my sake. I felt an unheard sigh fill my body as my maid, Ana, snuck another, less than subtle, glance towards my direction. This was about the hundredth time I'd caught her staring at me, and I had to fight my eye roll at the behavior. Far more subtle, but still painfully obvious was Sir Abel's occasional glances at me. It took longer for me to notice his actions, as he was far more successful at pretending to be looking elsewhere when our eyes did meet. The first two times I caught him, his impression of a vacant stare had me totally fooled, however by the third and fourth time I caught him, the jig was up.

There was no respite to be had from outside the carriage either as Mateo, my good friend and knight, would quite literally bend over on his horse to look at me through the carriage window. Each time we saw each other his face would go a little red, and he quickly sat back up. His embarrassment didn't stop him from repeating this behavior though. I really did appreciate the concern, well at least early on, but as the morning continued, I started to get more and more annoyed.

I mean what exactly are they expecting? Sure, I had just said a painful goodbye to my family, and we were currently traveling to a country I had never been to, so I could move there and marry their Crown Prince, whom I had never met or even seen, but it wasn't like I was about to collapse. Not to mention everyone here should be well aware that going to Dolma was my choice! In exchange for aid for both Nevremerre and Agremerre during the drought, we would support Dolma in their next war, and I would marry the Crown Prince. What a marriage had to do with receiving aid was beyond me, but Dolma had insisted and I wasn't about to let my people starve. It was my decision, and, frankly, the constant concerned gazes of the three people in this party I was closest to were not helping. It made me feel like I was weak or indecisive in their eyes, and it was driving my anger and frustration to the surface. It was becoming quite the battle not to snap at them for their behavior.

It was especially annoying considering that I was not the only one who was leaving their home country today. Abel, Ana, and Mateo were, too! Not to mention Sir Galileo and Sir Leonard, whom I didn't know quite as well. Surely, if we had to be giving out concerned looks, I shouldn't be the only one on the receiving end. Plus, although I knew we were in Agremerre now, in just four days, we would cross the border into Dolma, and then all the members of my party would have left their home country for someplace entirely new.

Another glance from Ana finally broke me as I breathed out into the silence, "Please stop staring. I really am okay." I was proud of myself for keeping the large amounts of frustration I felt out of my voice and maintaining a steady tone.

Ana blushed violently, but determinedly pressed on, "Are you really? That was a big goodbye you just had, and you just left Nevremerre for who knows how long. We just want to know that you're okay." A pang of sadness tore through me at her words, as I thought about the places in Nevremerre I never got to say goodbye to.

"It's okay to be upset, Princess," Abel said kindly, compassion filling his dark eyes. His words hit me, in a way that perhaps nothing else could as I was suddenly, painfully, and clearly aware that I had just left behind all those who could freely and easily call me by my name and nickname, Ava. Of course Abel had permission to do so in private, but he could hardly call me as such in front of others. In Nevremerre, the use of one's title was the highest form of trust and gratitude for the role that person fills. To not use another's title in a public setting was considered extremely rude, the only exception to this was if the person you were talking to was your family.

And, I had just left all my family behind.

Tears filled my eyes as I stared back at Abel. "Well, I was fine until now" I cried out, accusingly as hot tears started falling down my cheeks. My breath got caught in my chest and my shoulder started heaving up and down. My mouth felt tight and dry as I tried to silence my forthcoming sobs.

"Oh, Princess!" Ana's voice called out somewhere beyond my tears. I felt her arms wrapped around me, and I surrendered myself to her willowy grasp. The part of my mind that wasn't overwhelmed with emotion noted the astonishing presence of Ana's own tears falling onto my shoulders; her usually stoic demeanor breaking as she clung to me in the swaying carriage.

After a few minutes, my breath began to even out, and I carefully extracted myself from Ana's hug. My emerald eyes met her clear blues, and instead of saying "Thank you" like I'd planned, we both collapsed yet again into a pile of tears. I don't know if there can ever be words to describe how we both felt, although I'm quite certain we both felt the same. It was a curious mix of sadness at the loss of what we knew, the excitement of going someplace new, the nervousness of living someplace we'd never been before, and the eternal gratitude of not having to go alone. All of these emotions collided and crashed inside of us, having nowhere to go but leave through our tears. And so, we could do nothing else but cry, loudly, obnoxiously, and unendingly as we pushed further into Agremerre.

It wasn't long before I realized that Ana and I weren't alone in our tears. There wasn't a single dry eye among us Nevremerrians. Sir Leonard was loudly sobbing, making a sound akin to a honk with each breath that was likely scaring off all the local wildlife, or, possibly, attracting some swans. Even some of the Agremerrians weren't immune. I noticed Sir Hugo crying opposite Mateo on the other side of the carriage. He was doing his best to hide the tears, with the occasional swipe of his hand over his face, however, it wasn't really working. Sir Challa, on the other hand, mirrored Sir Leonard's approach, his massive shoulders shaking as he roared out his tears. The liquid making his black skin shine in the late morning sun. Sir Oberon and the woman who would become my other maid, Miri, were driving this carriage and the one behind us, filled with our luggage, so I had no way of knowing if they too were caught up in our crying madness.

"We can't all be crying!" I exclaimed, trying and failing to quell my own tears.

Ahead of us the hardened voice of Sir Galileo called out. His words cracking with his own emotion, "You're quite right, Princess," he hiccuped, "but I fear there is no - hic - no - no stopping them now. As you know, - hic - you weren't the only one who had to say goodbye today." His voice broke on the last word, causing a heart wrenching sob from all of us. I look back at the crying faces of those around me. Tears streamed down the faces of everyone in sight.

"I know," I cried back, before crashing into my tears once more.

And that's how my party of some of the strongest and bravest people in both Nevremerre and Agremerre wound up at Vierage Castle, completely exhausted, with red and puffy eyes. At the very least, we had exhausted all of our tears, but, needless to say, we were probably not the best company for Lady Lucy and her parents Marquis Elyan and Duchess Amanda.

If they were in any way shocked by our emotional appearance, the Marquis and Duchess did not show it. They kindly welcomed us all into their home, and I noticed Marquis Elyan slip a silk handkerchief into the hand of a, still sniffling, Sir Leonard. "Lucy is still packing," Duchess Amanda explained as she walked with Miri, Ana, and me towards where we would all be staying for the evening. "Last I checked, she was trying to fit the whole library into her suitcase. I did try to inform her that books exist in Dolma as well, but I'm not sure if she believed me." Duchess Amanda waved a hand towards a long stone hallway, "And this is where you three will be staying. Crown Princess, I have set you up in the middle room. The rooms for Ms. Miri and Ms. Ana on either side, with connecting doors for ease of movement. Please take your time unpacking, dinner will be in two hours."

"Thank you," I smiled as she turned away.

"Should we call you Crown Princess too then?" Ana questioned, still watching Duchess Amanda's retreating figure.

"I - well-," I stuttered. Technically, I was not a Crown Princess until I married the Crown Prince of Dolma, Thomas, but I also still remembered the parting advice of Queen Anora of Agremerre, one of the few people in my acquaintance who had actually been to Dolma. She'd advised me to start acting like a Crown Princess even before I had received the title, certainly a change in how my party addressed me would be a part of that. However, the title still felt a little awkward to hear.

"Yes, yes we should," Miri interjected before I could come to a decision. "Shall we go in, Crown Princess," Miri continued, walking towards the middle room, and holding open the door.

"Ah, yes, thank you," I started, in slight awe of her certainty as we moved into the large room. In a slightly surprising turn of events, the guest room I'd walked into was larger than my bedroom at the Nevremerre Royal Palace. We entered into a comfortable sitting room with fluffy green rugs, and three large velvet sofas were around a dark table. A massive unlit fireplace was located right near the door, and beautiful paintings of various natural wonders in Agremerre took over the expensive stone walls. Beyond the sitting area was a massive bed and another fireplace that opposed it. Tucked away in the far corner on the other side of the bed was a large window surrounded by two even larger bookcases and another forest green sofa.

"I guess that's that then," Ana nodded as she followed us inside, "Shall we run you a bath now Crown Princess?" Now that my title had been agreed upon by others, I felt a small shiver of satisfaction and delight at hearing it. After all, while I may not have intended to become the Crown Princess of Dolma, I did want the title.

"Most of Agremerre has communal baths as well as individual baths, correct?" I asked.

"Yes, Crown Princess," Miri replied. "I believe I can find Vierage Castle's communal baths quite easily, should you desire."

"Yes, let's do that. It's been a long journey for everyone, and I'm sure we could all use the hot water." With that we all headed to the communal baths. True to her word, Miri did find the baths easily. She directed us there, weaving through the many hallways and rooms as if she'd been here many times before. A shiver ran through me as my mouth opened on its own accord, "You were never a domestic spy, were you?"

Miri laughed, "No, no Crown Princess, Agremerre doesn't spy on its own people, or its allies. I'm just following the pipes," Miri stuck her short wrinkled hand into the air where I looked up to see a series of copper tubes lining the stone ceiling. "Communal baths take a large amount of water, so really all you have to do is follow the second biggest pipe. The biggest being for the main water supply of course. It's easy to find when people have open plumbing like this."

"Oh," I replied, slightly embarrassed by my outburst. Miri's pipe theory proved to be correct when two turns later we entered the communal bath area. Grabbing towels, we headed towards the female pool. Ana and I stripped down quickly, greedily pouring some water over our traveled skin before sliding into the almost too hot pool. The heat seeped into my muscles and moved its way through the knots in my back and neck resulting in an involuntary sigh escaping my lips. I heard Ana respond similarly before I turned towards where Miri was, and I watched in awe as she pulled out an increasingly large pile of weapons.

I shouldn't have been surprised, really, after all Miri was a spy - or at least a former spy... probably a former spy. Father and Anora had encouraged me to take her as essentially another bodyguard, and as a tool to get critical information in Dolma if I could not get that information myself. She should have weapons, she should be able to hide them so that even I can't see them, and yet, the thought of it all made me wildly uncomfortable.

I already knew myself to be lacking in any of the skills required for being cunning, or performing espionage, and I knew that in politics and in ruling both those skills could be necessary. However, there was just something about the idea of sneaking around in the shadows and going behind people's backs that made my skin crawl and my stomach constrict painfully. I couldn't help it, I just didn't trust Miri, at least not just yet. I could only hope that that would change in time. So I beat my discomfort down and watched as she joined us In the bath.

Obviously devoid of my lack of trust, Ana swam happily in the large bath, wringing out her hair, and washing it with a water jug sitting on the side of the pool. "Shall I wash your hair too, Crown Princess?" she asked as the last bit of dirt left her now blonde hair.

"I doubt I could ever say no to that," I laughed as Ana moved over to work on my hair. "Are you not washing yours, Miri?" I asked, noticing she'd wrapped a towel around her brownish gray hair.

"Oh no, Crown Princess, a bath like this would wash out the dye," she smiled in what I interpreted to be a kind manner.

"You dye your hair?" Ana exclaimed, her hands pausing, still wrapped around my own hair.

"Of course!" Miri replied, "The first rule of espionage is that no one can describe you if they don't know what you look like."

Ana laughed, "So what color is it naturally?"

"Even I don't know that at this point. I've gone through so many colors over the decades, I couldn't possibly tell you how it would look now." Ana laughed once more, but I felt my unease grow. We continued to talk about hair and dyes for a while as Miri regaled us with secrets of dying one's hair a variety of colors. I had to admit she was quite fascinating, even if I was still slightly unnerved by her. Miri's knowledge of herbs rivaled my own, although my knowledge was more medically inclined. All in all, it was a peaceful time that was far too quickly interrupted by the need to change for dinner.

The Duchess, Marquis, and Lady Lucy were already waiting for us when we arrived in the dining room. Sir Galileo and Matteo were also there, although the rest of my knights and Sir Abel were nowhere to be found. "Crown Princess!" Lady

Lucy greeted me with a smile and a perfect bow. "How was your journey?" she continued, pulling out chairs for Miri and Ana before directing me towards the seat near hers.

"Very emotional," I admitted, "but the road was very smooth and the birds were chirping, so overall not too bad."

"I can imagine, poor dears," Lady Lucy said, sitting down once more, her straight black hair swinging behind her. "You'll have to forgive me if I'm the same way tomorrow."

"Of course! There's no shame in tears," I encouraged.

"Do you miss your family already?" Lady Lucy pushed on.

"Well yes, I suppose so, but of course, I will also miss the land and the people around me."

"Oh yes, of course, but what about your family do you miss the most?" Lady Lucy pressed. I was a bit taken aback by her direct and focused line of questioning. While our five days of intense training on all known Dolmanian etiquette left little time for us to really get to know each other, I hadn't pegged Lady Lucy as being this... direct in her communication.

"Mostly their love and support, I suppose, but fortunately, even if they are not physically here, I still carry their feelings with me," I answered diplomatically.

"Perfect answer, Crown Princess," Duchess Amanda beamed at me.

"Yes, it really was," Lady Lucy agreed. "You must know, Crown Princess, that when we enter Dolma there will be people who will try to control you," Lady Lucy continued, her voice suddenly becoming serious, and her dark eyes were sharp and confident as she looked into my own. "In Nevremerre, you were known, you were a beloved Princess, who could some-day become Queen. Your power, strength, wisdom, and values were marked down and discussed since King Edgar found and adopted you. In Dolma, you'll begin as a foreign Princess. They will not know your strengths, but there will at least be a few foolish people who will try to control you and the power you wield. They will try to do this through any means necessary. So, when I asked seemingly innocuous questions like "What will you miss?" give them nothing that they can try to replace. If I may, Crown Princess, I'd like to introduce myself once more?" I nodded, and Lady Lucy stood up, her thin yellow dress swishing across brown skin. "I am Lady Lucy of Agremerre, and I promise to do all in my power to get you the strength and loyalty you require in Dolma."

"Thank you Lady Lucy," I said back, just a tiny bit over-whelmed by her both informative and intense speech.

"Please just call me Lucy when we are among friends, Crown Princess," Lucy smiled. "I'm sorry to have questioned you like that, Crown Princess, but I need you to see how you were able to handle things. I will probably interrogate you more like this over the carriage ride to Dolma. I mean no offense, but I wish to prepare you for anything we might face. Queen Anora said Dolma is very different, so I believe it's best we prepare for the worst."

"I agree," I said seriously. Despite the persistent approach, I had no doubt that Lady Lucy was right to train me in this way, and I could see the logic and importance of all she was suggesting. "In that case, Lucy, I will be in your care," I smiled back at her.

Lucy smiled back at me before turning towards the rest of the party. By now, all those who had been missing had finally appeared. "The same goes for everyone else here. We can't have any weak links when it comes to the Crown Princess." There was a chorus of agreement, and my entire party nodded seriously as they responded to Lucy's order.

"Don't scare them too much, Lucy dear," the heavily accented voice of Marquis Elyan broke through our conversation. "I'm certain that everyone here is just as dedicated to the Crown Princess as you are."

Lucy opened her mouth, potentially in protest, before thinking better of it, and simply nodded her head. "We're quite grateful to you, you see," the calm voice of Duchess Amanda interjected as she smiled at her husband and daughter. "This family in particular is grateful to not have to go to war, especially against Nevremerre." I jolted in my chair, having nearly forgotten that Agremerre's first solution to the drought was to declare war on Nevremerre. For Duchess Amanda, whose father was a Nevremerrian Prince, and whose sister, Duchess Amber, still sat on the Nevremerrian Council, war with Nevremerre meant fighting against her sister and her cousin, my father. It hit me all of a sudden what war with Agremerre could have become. Beyond the loss of thousands, if not hundreds of thousands of lives, the open border relationship our two countries had shared for centuries meant that, if war were to occur, there would be many having to fight against friends and relatives.

"I am just glad I could do something to prevent it," I said earnestly.

"We shall help by sending you off with a good meal, a comfortable bed, and our brightest daughter," Marquis Elyan grinned playfully at me. "Let's eat" he declared as food was brought out.

"Really, I'm the brightest child," Lucy whispered to me as we started eating, "but since Ender is taking over the role of Marquis they can't just go around saying I'm smarter." I laughed at her words, and my party finally began the easy process of learning about each other. We talked late into the evening, before we called it a night. Only seconds after Miri and Ana put me to bed, I fell soundly asleep.

Chapter 2

The Arrival in Dolma

The next two days riding through Agremerre passed in a blur. Lucy did cry when she left her home, but not nearly as long and hard as the rest of us had the day before. We were all quizzed on etiquette and given lessons on how not to leak information from Abel and Lucy respectively. We played games, got to know each other, and hypothesized about Dolma and my future husband. Lucy was dying to know what he might look like, and Ana was quite interested as well, but I didn't want to have any expectations when I met him. So, instead, Lucy and Ana made increasingly preposterous guesses at his appearance to Mateo, Oberon, and Galileo and hoped their reaction might give something away. I did learn that my betrothed did not have bright purple hair that stood straight up, as after Ana suggested it Oberon laughed so hard that he nearly fell off his horse. This, however, was the only confirmation we got.

As we got closer and closer to Dolma the more nervous and excited I became. All these emotions rumbled in my stomach, and they made me feel rather ill whenever the carriage ride was too bumpy. It was an odd sensation, after a life of roaming around Nevremerre, I was never one to get carriage sick. Yet, now, it felt like one wrong turn would send my last meal hurtling towards the other side of the carriage. As long as I could distract myself with conversation or games, I was fine, but left alone to my own thoughts, I was a mess. Abel sensed my discomfort, and could often calm me down. However, it would never last. No amount of ginger tea could soothe my stomach, and no transitioning session could quench my aching desire to learn what life would be like for me in Dolma.

The truth was, for all my words otherwise to Ana and Lucy, I was dying to know what Dolma was like, what my betrothed was like, what he looked like, how his voice sounded, was he smart, was he kind, was he strong, would we get along? All these questions burned through my mind. They consumed my soul and enthralled me with every breath, and as we got closer to our destination, they got louder and stronger inside of me.

To be very clear, I was neither looking for nor expecting a great love. I mean, honestly, how can you fall in love with someone you just met? But, come love or disinterest, this man would be my partner, someone I would rule with, someone I would grow with, and someone I would be with for the rest of my life. I was dying to know just who he was, and what my new home and country would be like. And, maybe, I wasn't the only one because as the carriage finally crossed over the border to Dolma, another tense silence filled the air. It seemed like even the animals didn't dare to breathe as we rolled into our new home.

If it hadn't been for our own manufactured stillness, the actual transition would have been rather mundane. After all, the forest is still a forest, even if humans put an imaginary barrier there. Despite this, our self-imposed silence carried on for another hour as the forest rolled into farmland. Miles and miles of unbroken wheat fields replaced the greenery of the forest from the Agremerre border. It was mesmerizing at first, until a realization set in that caused a pit in my stomach which lodged itself so firmly in my core, it took decades to fully come undone.

"That's wrong," I said loudly, clearly, and confidently into a carriage of silent, scared people. I could hear the movement of their heads, as they turned to look towards me. Even the knights riding outside turned my direction. However, my gaze was locked onto the field in front of me. "All these farms, they all grow the same thing. There are absolutely no barriers between them other than a fence. The only type of agriculture we have seen in the past hour has been monoculture."

There were quiet sighs all around me. "Well maybe they just have a different farming technique in Dolma," Abel soothed.

I shook my head, "No, you don't understand. "The Experiments of Historical Farming" address this type of farming, even in just small portions of a country, it's not sustainable."

"Dolma has produced enough food for three countries, Crown Princess," Lucy pointed out, "They probably just found a way to make this style work. Maybe we can learn something new."

Frustration rang through me. I quickly tried to calm myself as I reasoned that not everyone would have been educated on agricultural disasters like my brothers and I had. No one else in this party would have ever been trained to manage and rule over an agricultural region, so it was okay for them to be ignorant of the impending disaster. My body stopped for a moment. Should I maybe just leave them in ignorance? They could stay happy and excited about what was to come. Perhaps I could solve this problem quickly and easily, and they wouldn't even have to know about the danger. I glanced around at the faces watching me, patiently waiting for a reply. I couldn't keep them in the dark, I realized. I needed their help to fix this problem, and I still felt the sting that had come with not knowing about Nevremerre's drought. I would not put my people through that.

I took a deep breath, and I looked back at those in the carriage. "Pay attention, all of you, because this is vital information, and I need you to understand the gravity of the situation," I commanded. Those in the carriage moved to sit up straighter, and the knights riding by our side moved closer. I waited a moment to ensure I had their attention before I began, "'The Experiments of Historical Farming' is an agricultural guidebook to avoid extreme farming disasters. It details every major disaster since the rise of King Dormian. It includes explanations of what each disaster looks like, all possible causes, all possible solutions, and is revised every five years." I pause for a moment remembering Azar's groan every time a new edition came out, and all royal children had to reread the entire thing. I couldn't deny that by just the second read it was quite the chore. My parents had to reread it as well, so we had turned it into a game, a race of sorts, to see who could get through the new manuscript first. Al won two years ago taking less than two days to read it all. Azar still swears that Al cheated somehow.

With some effort I pulled myself away from my happy memories to focus back on the task at hand. "One of the biggest disasters happened about 300 years ago. It was called "The Dust

Out". Most likely you all learned about this in school as it had very dramatic social consequences," I paused to look around as my companions tried to remember their school days.

"I remember it," claimed Leonard as Mateo, Lucy, and Galileo nodded in agreement. Everyone else agreed that they had probably heard of it, but couldn't remember all the details.

"The general result was about five to ten years of economic instability and a nationwide food shortage. Fortunately, we had Agremerre to provide aid. Arguably less fortunately, we conquered the once-nation of Camulonia, now the province of Champagina, and used a lot of their resources. However, we were also able to house and feed their entire population. That said, war is always a controversial choice, it was likely not the most morally correct decision at the time-"

"The Dust Out, Crown Princess?" Abel questioned, kindly preventing me from going on a tangent.

"Yes, thank you. Because of its huge effect, researchers almost immediately flocked to the affected land to develop theories and find solutions. They found the cause of the Dust Out was the shallow-rooted plants used all over one specific area without any natural barriers. The use of plowing in these areas created lots of loose dirt that wasn't held by the natural vegetation, which had deeper roots and was accustomed to the wind. As a result, there were a few years of extremely abundant crop yields followed by a massive windstorm that picked up so much loose dust it completely covered the sky, blocking out the sun, and making it impossible to grow anything for several years.

The conditions of the fields in this area of Dolma are the exact same conditions as just before the Dust Out. They have the same climates, and even the same crop, wheat. The solutions identified by the researchers were crop rotations, natural barriers, especially with trees, and farming with methods other than plowing, or some combination of these three. Dolma, from all we have seen so far, is doing none of these.

Also, even if they were somehow using a long-rooted wheat, a plant which does not exist to our knowledge, they are still likely experiencing the deficits of a monoculture, including, but not limited to, less rich soil - leading in decreased crop production, an increased presence of plant-eating insects (and potentially other animals as well) - leading to decreased crop production, and a lack of pollinators - leading to decreased crop production. In the best-case scenario, with zero intervention, a few decades down the road, Dolma will have extremely low wheat harvests. In the worst-case scenario Dolma goes into their own Dust Out at some point next year. Either way, their method of farming is not sustainable, and could lead to the death of their citizens."

There was a silence throughout the carriage and outside as everyone processed my words. I watched as the grim realization sunk into each of their faces as my message finally got through. "Dear Gods," Abel said in shock. "What can we do, Ava?" His worry causing his propriety to slip.

"Crown Princess, Sir Abel. We must maintain decorum under stressful times," Lucy scolded.

"It's fine Lucy, it's just us here," I responded in Abel's defense.

"No, Lady Lucy is right. We cannot be seen to dishonor you, Crown Princess, especially in Dolma. Even more so when we must bring such important news. So, what can we do?" Abel said seriously.

"Sir Abel, you and I should meet with the King, Queen, and the Crown Prince once we arrive. They likely do not know of the potential consequences of their actions. Tree transplants will help break the window flow in the short-term, and then we can start re-fertilizing the soil and implementing crop rotation to fix long-term issues. Luckily this can all be solved, but we should speak with the King and Queen as soon as possible. Perhaps we could also get them a copy of "The Experimental History of Farming", so they can check on the other crop and farming areas they have. They might even have something similar and we can share ideas and improve everyone's crop quality," I said, trying to sound hopeful, and even though all I said was accurate, for some reason, the pit never left my stomach.

We stopped a few hours later at a town where we would spend our first night, and the pit in my stomach only grew. It was the smell that hit us first, rancid and putrid, it assaulted our noses and ravaged our carriage. Inside the carriage, we quickly jammed the windows shut and covered our faces with our clothes. Outside, my knights were forced to endure the stench, and we gave them all pitying glances as they braved the outside air. When we finally stepped out onto the streets, we learned just what that smell was - the outside streets were littered with the urine and feces of its residents.

"I don't need a book to know this can't be healthy," Ana said, looking around in disgust.

"It most certainly isn't. This might be another thing to mention to the King. I'm surprised Queen Anora hasn't mentioned it before," I agreed.

"I believe she's tried," Oberon responded, "but I don't think they listened."

"These poor people," Challa said, burying his nose into his shirt.

"Agreed," I commented. "Shall we go inside then," I said, pointing to the nearby inn. There was a rush of nods, and we moved towards the inn, leaving Miri, Leonard, Challa, and Hugo behind with the horses.

We moved quickly, excited to get out of the street, although the inn itself wasn't too much better. Built with a combination of wood and stone, there appeared to be several layers of rotten floorboards, along with a thin layer of dust that covered just about everything. In the corner, a group of men were sprawled out at a table, clearly drunk. Although they looked more morose than cheerful as they quietly mumbled at each other. None of them even bothered to look up as we entered. However, the teenage girl behind the bar certainly did. She gasped loudly as we walked in. Her eyes widened, her mouth gaping as we shuffled into the bar.

"Hello. I'd like to inquire about some rooms for my companions and myself," I said politely.

"Here?!" the girl gasped, her dark curls bouncing atop her head as she looked between us. It was the same texture as Mother's hair whenever she let it out of the strict confines of her braids, although this girl wasn't nearly as dark as Mother's.

Still, I found myself growing partial towards her all the same. "You can't stay here!" The girl finished with a little bounce and a wave of her hand.

"Why ever not?" Lucy asked, "This is an inn, is it not?" she teased.

"Oh, well yes," the girl responded frantically, "but the noble District is further down!"

"The noble District?" I questioned.

"Yes, well-"

"What are you doing, girl!" an angry voice called from somewhere in the back, causing me to jump. A large round man came barreling forward, pushing the black haired girl to the side. She stumbled slightly into the bar, and a quiet fury overtook me as I stared at the man above me. His clothes stank of sweat and alcohol as he grinned at me, showing a large array of missing teeth. "So I hear you want to stay at my inn. I assure you, it's a fine establishment. Best prices in town too, just 20 gollups each."

My mind went blank for a moment as I tried to comprehend the nerve of the man in front of me. We'd been briefed on Dolmanian currency before we arrived, so I was well aware that 20 gollups (Dolma's highest valued coin) was an unbelievably high price for an inn like this.

"Why you -" Mateo started, quick on the mathematical uptake, but I held out my hand to stop him.

"20 gollups is quite the price indeed, and you're saying that's a bargain around here?"

"Indeed it is," the loud man confidently boasted.

"Ah, I see. And you, my dear," I said, turning towards the girl, "how much is your salary then?"

"Why you asking her that?" the loud man interrupted.

"I wasn't talking to you," I said coldly, looking back at the girl.

"Now listen here! Who do you think-" the loud man raged at me, moving closer towards me. He was quite expertly cut off by Mateo and Galileo's swords at his throat.

"You will not speak again unless spoken to," I commanded, staring directly into his little blue eyes. My tone was icy and my voice sure. The man gulped, but did not say a word. Even the drunk men were watching now, silent in their corner. Turning back towards the girl, I repeated my question. "How much does he pay you?"

"I - I get 5 bollups a month," she replied back. It was now my turn to shut up as I contemplated the measly sum. Anger boiled up within me. Five bollups (Dolma's lowest form of currency, with 100 bollups equal to one gollup) would be barely enough to buy food for a month in Nevremerre, never mind anything else. A gasp from Mateo indicated that he'd come to the same conclusion as myself, this man was trying to overcharge us while severely underpaying his employee.

Unfortunately, I didn't yet have enough of an understanding or power in the Dolma legal system that would allow me to do anything to this criminal, but I did have the ability to help the girl. "Would you rather work elsewhere? I can offer you free accommodation, and a much higher salary, if you're interested. Although, we are heading to the capital, so it will mean a move. You'd travel with us, assuming your parents agreed, of course."

"I - my parents are dead. What would I do?" she asked.

"You'll be my maid," Lucy chimed in. "Don't worry, we will teach you everything you need to know."

"I have a younger sister," the girl said, hesitantly.

"Bring her too, I'm great with kids," Lucy replied easily. While Lucy was a nice person, I'm not sure I would have trusted her with children up until this point, but I wasn't about to stop her from getting this girl and her sister out of this situation.

The girl nodded, "Yes, I - I would like to go."

"Wonderful! I'm sure you'll be an excellent addition to the team," Abel replied, "Why don't you come with me towards the carriage, and we'll get everything figured out." Together Abel and the girl walked out of the inn, Abel gently consoling her along the way.

"Now you," I turn back to the loud man, "to overcharge one's customers and underpay one's employees is the lowest form of business, and clearly," I said, obviously looking over the broken inn. "It isn't working very well for you, so I'll offer you this advice: stop drinking, clean your inn, pay your employees a livable wage, and don't overcharge your customers. I promise you it's actually a rather good business plan. Really, I just recommend that you do better. Everyone, let's go."

"Just who do you think you are?" the loud man bellowed as we were leaving.

"Oh, that's easy, I'm your future Queen," I said before walking out the door.

Chapter 3

The "Border" Town

"You know, Crown Princess, I was expecting a bit more insults at the end," Oberon commented as we made our way back to the carriage.

I blushed a little at his comment, "To be honest, I'm not really good at insults. The only people I've ever really had to insult were my brothers, and even then, those insults were highly tailored to what would have been most hurtful to them. I don't think "You're an incompetent hammerhead" would work out too well here."

"Probably not," Oberon agreed.

"We might want to teach you some," Galileo commented, raising his eyebrow at me.

"That might be good," I said awkwardly before quickly getting into the carriage. "Miri, can you get me the name of this inn, and the owner's name? When the time comes, I'd like to charge him with breaking labor laws."

"As you wish, Crown Princess," Miri nodded approvingly.

"Now," I said, finally getting into the carriage and turning towards the girl, "I am Princess Avalynn of Nevremerre. I'm currently in the process of moving to Dolma to marry your Crown Prince. If you wish, I'd be very happy to hire you and support your sister if you choose to move to the capital. However, if you prefer living here, I will help you secure other employment. Which would you prefer?" I stared at her patiently, taking in her overall appearance. Her clothes were covered in a light sheen of dirt, and there were small holes in the hem of her overly long and rough-looking skirt. What was supposedly a white apron, was covered in mysterious brown stains. There was also a strange stench that seemed to be a mix of sewage and rotten food wafting from her general direction. I made a mental note to get her some new clothes and a place to bathe this evening.

A few minutes of silence passed by, as I waited for her response. I was hoping that she was using this moment of silence to think about her move and how it would impact her life and goals. However, based on the way her brown eyes were staring at me with her mouth hung wide open, it seems more likely that she was in a state of shock. Sensing this, Abel moved forward, touching her lightly on the shoulder, "Solista, my dear, are you quite all right?" Abel said, his low voice rumbling soothingly as he spoke.

This seemed to work, although perhaps not in the way Abel had hoped, as instead of responding to any questions that had been posed to her, Solista threw herself on the floor of the carriage. Her body was bent in an almost cat-like way, her chest hugged her knees, but her arms were thrown straight out in front of her. "Your Highness, please forgive me for my rudeness," Solista pleaded.

I shared a startled look with everyone around me, all of them now giving Solista similar stunned expressions to what she had given me moments before. "I - it's - er, Solista, you haven't done anything rude, so please get up," I said, trying, and failing, to understand what was going on. Solista slowly rose from her crouched position. She did, however, remain kneeling on the carriage floor.

"I truly apologize, Your Highness, I had not realized you were royalty," Solista said, staring at the floor.

"How could you possibly know I was royalty? I just arrived today. Also, please get up, and sit on the cushions, the floor can't be comfortable," I reached out my hand, to help her up.

"I couldn't possibly, Your Highness!" Solista responded, "This is my place."

"No one's place is on the floor," Challa chimed in from outside the carriage window.

"He's absolutely right, Miss Solista," I nodded, "Please sit comfortably and we can discuss what you want for your future." Still looking a bit startled, Solista finally grabbed my hand, allowing me to pull her up and direct her to her previous seat.

"Good," I nodded when she was seated, "now obviously, if being a maid is not something you're interested in, I will support you in other careers as well, and your sister, of course.

However, at the current moment I'm not sure what positions are used or what I will need in the Royal Palace of Dolma, so, if you choose to come with me, we may need you to start as a maid before moving on to other opportunities. However, it is completely understandable if you would prefer to stay here. Since I was the one who encouraged you to leave your job, I will be happy to provide for you here until you can find another opportunity with a far more fair boss and better labor conditions. What option best fits your idea for a happy future?"

Solista looked at me oddly, but did respond after a few moments, "I... I think going to the capital would be best for me, Your Highness."

"That's wonderful! I'm so glad you decided to join us!" I smiled. "Now why don't you direct us to where you live, so we can pack, and we can pick up your sister. Will it take much to get out of your house? Will you need help selling it, or is it a rent based accommodation?"

Solista directed us to her home, and told us her home was rented. Although she said she didn't even have a renter's contract which managed her accommodation, which caused so much confusion for the rest of us in the carriage that it dominated the 15 minute ride to Solista's home, and would likely have gone on longer had we not reached our destination.

"Are you sure we are in the right place?" Leonard asked, a bit sheepishly.

"Yes, of course. This is a fairly standard home for people like me," Solista commented, gesturing towards the line of similar structures down the dirt road. I was pleased to note that Solista's confidence has grown tremendously in our short journey, even if the location she'd led us to left much to be desired. In Nevremerre, I learned from my father many lessons on leading and on life. Father encouraged us to be open and understanding towards all people and cultures. However, he also instilled in us an idea that our country was only as strong as its poorest citizens. This is what made it so difficult to stare at Solista's "house", which was barely more than a wooden shack, and not start judging Dolma very harshly.

Solista happily moved inside, with Ana and Lucy following hesitantly behind her. I, however, couldn't stop staring at the "house" in front of me. "Perhaps Dolma it's not as wealthy as Nevremerre, this home after all, it's better than nothing," Abel said from behind me, obviously trying to soothe my frown.

"If that was the case, they should have requested money instead of a Princess during negotiations. Or maybe builders," I answered, unimpressed.

"Perhaps they simply do not know," Abel tried again.

"How can they not know! It's their country!" I hissed back. Anger and sadness roared through me at the place I had come to.

"Ava," Abel said calmly, moving in front of me, "We don't know what goes on in this country, we don't know their finances, their problems, or their governing style. This is just one town, clearly, some of the people here need assistance, but not all of the governments of this world are prepared to provide that. When we get to the capital, we can share our knowledge of this town's problems with the King and Queen and help brainstorm solutions that will work with the resources we have. We cannot judge until we understand. Even for Nevremerre, a nomadic rule just came about in the past century, so it's very possible that Dolma's King and Queen just haven't seen a town like this in several years. You must step back and breathe Ava, we will not know anything for sure until we reach the capital."

"You're right of course," I smiled at him, reveling in the calmness he could bring to my racing mind and scattered emotions, "and, when we know more, we will do what we can to help these people."

"Right you are, Crown Princess," Abel smiled at me.

"See, this is why renters need contracts," Lucy said loudly as she exited the "house" carrying a brown sack in one arm. She was followed by an utterly bewildered looking child who practically stumbled out after her. "I mean the wood was rotting and the roof was leaking and you say you'd have to fix that by yourself? Incredible!" Lucy finished her tirade by carefully placing the sack she was carrying into the carriage filled with all of our luggage.

"But what are you going to do if your contractor overcharges you, or if there's an emergency and you have to leave?" asked Solista who had just come out of the house with Ana, each carrying another brown sack.

"That's where it becomes the government's job to step in and ensure the contractors follow fair terms and abide by the rules outlined by government relief funds. Although, I suppose it does make it harder to leave as quickly as we did just now," I replied thoughtfully, trying to abide by Abel's no judgment lecture earlier.

After I finished speaking, there was a loud squeak before the child who was following Lucy threw herself on the ground like Solista had several minutes ago. "Gracious child!" Lucy exclaimed. "Don't just go throwing yourself on the ground like that! You'll get all dirty!"

"But, the Princess..." the girl stumbled glancing at me as Lucy dragged her back on her feet.

"The Crown Princess," Lucy corrected, "does not need to be acknowledged by people throwing themselves on the ground. In Nevremerre and Agremerre a simple bow would do. In Dolma, we've been told most women curtsey. Like so," Lucy said primly, gathering her flowing skirt in one hand, tucking one leg behind the other and bending her knees in a flawless curtsey, complete with a lowering of her head.

Solista's younger sister tried to mimic this motion, and nearly toppled over as a result. Fortunately, her fall was prevented by Mateo who caught her quickly. Her dark cheeks took on a pinker shade as Mateo set her right once more. "We'll work on it," reassured Lucy, causing the child's cheeks to get even pinker.

I walked over to her with a smile. "Don't worry, that's just about how my first attempt went as well. Although, Sir Mateo just let me fall," I said, sending a playful wink towards Mateo.

"A truly terrifying mistake on my part, Crown Princess. I should have learned how to teleport, so that I could get to the other side of the Agremerrian ballroom to prevent it," Mateo said with a mock sincerity, causing me to giggle before he smiled once more.

"Now, why don't you get into the carriage and I'll introduce everyone, and you can tell me about yourself," I said to the young girl.

We did just that, and Solista directed us to the noble District. We learned that her sister's name was Chantel, or Chanti for short. She was just 13 years old, and while she was almost the same age as Ari, I couldn't help but see her as much younger. Perhaps it was the fact that Ari already towered over me, but Chanti had yet to have much of a growth spurt. We learned Solista was just 16, and thereby shocking our party once again as it seemed far too young to work a full-time job. Abel helped us come to our senses once again by pointing out that by Nevremerre standards, I, at just 19, was far too young to get married. Lucy and I still agreed to give Solista plenty of time off though.

As we rode through the town, both sisters became much more comfortable in our presence, and soon we came to the noble District. I noticed the difference as soon as I stepped out onto the clean, well-lit street. The buildings here were built with stone and brick, reminiscent of buildings in Nevremerre and Agremerre, were it not for the incredible amounts of ostentatious gilding and marble that decorated each building. The one we stood in front of looked particularly elaborate, with golden statutes adoring the roof. I looked at Abel, begging him to make sense of the appalling difference in this area compared to where we'd stopped before.

"This, I cannot defend," Abel said to me. "However," he whispered in my ear, "I still recommend learning more before we come to any judgments."

"I'm not sure what explanation could defend this," I whispered back, "but, I will heed your judgment."

"I told you this is where you should be," Solista smiled at us, obviously proud of her advice. "Oh, you should make sure they know you're a royal. I'm sure you'd get better treatment that way, Your Highness."

I frowned a bit at this, but not wanting to disappoint the obviously excited Solista, I smiled once more. "I'm sure you're right," I said. "Now it's getting late, we should go and get settled." Everyone nodded in agreement. The once bright sky was quickly falling into a shade of lavender above us, and the cool night's breeze slipped along our skins providing a pleasant chill.

Abel, Galileo, Oberon, and I went inside the intricately carved wooden doors, pulling on golden handles to find a sparkling marble entryway with high vaulted ceilings painted with colorful scenes of nature and children playing. Even though I had yet to announce my title, our clothes must have spoken for us as we were instantly greeted by a member of staff who ushered us to a marble desk where he asked what he could do for us.

"I am Princess Avalynn of Nevremerre, and I'm looking for rooms for my staff and me, as well a stable for my horses, and a place for my carriages this evening."

"Princess!" the man helping us exclaimed, "Let me just get my manager!" The man quickly ran off to a back room, leaving us alone in the empty hall.

"I wonder if they have enough decor," Abel said casually into the silence, causing snorts of laughter from the rest of us. The room was indeed packed with paintings, sculptures, pottery, flowers, and other trinkets littering every open space. It was all a bit loud for my personal taste, and it seemed like my thoughts were shared by those around me. We weren't left to take in the intense decor very long, however, as shortly after another man in a dark suit came out to greet us.

"Princess," the man bowed, taking my hand and kissing it. "It's a great honor to have you here, it was announced that Your Highness would be coming to marry His Highness the Crown Prince, but I never thought that you might stop here!" The man said, genuine enthusiasm pouring out of him as he kept his head bowed down.

Although his excitement was no doubt sincere, I still felt an odd feeling of revulsion wash over me, and I pulled my hand quickly out of his clammy grasp. "Yes, well I need a place to stay for this evening. So if you can kindly find my party and me some rooms, that would be most appreciated," I replied, trying to remain polite.

"Oh of course!" The manager squeaked, moving back around towards the desk. "And, how many Lords and Ladies are traveling with you?"

"Just myself and one other lady," I responded, not really sure why that was relevant.

"Ah," the manager said, looking a bit disappointed, "so you'll only be needing two rooms then. Well not to worry, we'll take care of everything and will direct your staff to some other local inns."

"I'm sorry, there appears to be some mistake. I asked for rooms for my whole party. That includes my knights and maids. While traveling we've made do with seven rooms total, ah, but we did just hire some new staff, so I suppose we'll need eight rooms tonight."

The manager and the boy who we first met stared at me blankly, "Oh, you must mean for your knights!" The manager started, smiling at me once more, "Yes, yes, I've heard how you people value war, of course you must want your knights treated well. It's no matter, we could, of course, accommodate them. Just send your servants to the back then, and will direct them to the proper servant's quarters."

It was my party's turn to stare dumbfounded. Only starting back to reality when the large wooden door opened once more revealing the rest of my party. There were several things I took issue with in the manager's most recent statement, but I dealt with the most pressing issue first. "I think you are still misunderstanding me," I said coolly, "So I'm going to say this very clearly this time. Listen closely, so you don't miss anything. I require eight rooms. One for me, one for Lady Lucy, one for Sir Abel, the new Ambassador for Nevremerre, three for my knights to share, and two rooms for the maids of myself and Lady Lucy. Have I made myself clear?"

"Rooms, here, for your servants?" The manager squeaked.

"Clearly it must be different in Dolma," Lucy interjected. Walking slowly and deliberately towards the desk, her head high, as an aura of authority and condescension rained down around her. Her voice was cold and steady as she eyed the man in front of her. I tried to hold back my surprise. The bright and loud person I'd come to know on the journey had transformed into the perfect visage of an arrogant noble. The ability to adapt her personality to fit with her desired outcome was one of the reasons I had hired her, however, it was a bit uncanny to see the change in person. "You see, Nevremerre and Agremerre are rich enough to afford the highest quality of living for all those who work for us. Who would have thought the nobles of Dolma would be so poor?" Lucy finished, her tone becoming one of false innocence.

The manager turned red before us, "I - no we - that is I mean to say," the man paused once more tugging nervously at his shirt, "The nobles of Dolma are very wealthy, it's just that, being a border town as we are, we don't often see as high-ranking nobles such as yourselves. I will of course get you those rooms. Albert, go get the keys, and make sure to grab the suite keys for her Highness, Lady Lucy, and the Ambassador."

I was liking this man less and less by the second, which was an impressive feat considering the disgust I felt within seconds of his first words to me. "Good. Now I believe you suggested that your staff would be taking care of us this evening? I expect them to take care of all of my people. We should have hot baths drawn for everyone, as well as a hot meal delivered to our rooms. We will dine separately this evening, but have breakfast together at about 9 tomorrow morning. I will also need two new dresses for Lady Lucy's maids, Solista and Chanti. They will need two dresses each, and my maid, Ana, will help you with the specifics. I understand if any alterations cannot be done by the morning -"

"Oh don't worry, Princess. We will have that done by tomorrow!" the manager interrupted. I frowned at his rudeness, but was pleasantly surprised at what must be incredibly efficient tailoring skills in Dolma. In Nevremerre, tailoring would take at least two days for a full outfit. Dolma must have different techniques or possibly machinery. I was curious to look into it more, but it had been a long day and I was ready to turn in for the evening. "That's good. Now, please show us to our rooms."

The manager agreed, and hurried off, presumably to find Albert and get the keys. "Well he's rather rude," Lucy huffed, her voice going back to normal. "And, the staff might be too, since they kept trying to direct us to a different inn. Frankly, a rather poor business model if you ask me. Also I have to object to the idea of a border town that's at least a four hour carriage ride from the actual border."

I smiled at her. My mood, which I had not recognized having fallen, rose at her antics. "It is rather odd, and they truly are awfully pretentious. Although perhaps that's to be expected when you compare this inn to the first one we went to."

"Just because it's expected doesn't make it right," Lucy said sagely.

"No it does not," I agreed. "It seems we will have a lot of work to do once we get to the palace."

"No one here is afraid of hard work," Galileo said, his voice strong and determined. "Especially not if it means helping the people outside of the noble District." Around him the rest of the knights along with Ana and Miri nodded. Solista and Chanti looked a bit confused, but I knew that they would understand with time.

"Good," I responded simply, smiling at those around me.

Not long after, the manager returned with the keys, and we were all shown to our rooms. Mine was by far the largest, complete with two sitting rooms, and a large sleeping area. There was also a large bathroom which, thankfully, had the plumbing the last inn, and probably Solista's house, had lacked. A quiet looking group of maids came in, bringing along my luggage. There were a lot more of them than I was used to, with five women in total, and still the head maid apologized for their being so few of them. I was too shocked to inform them that in Nevremerre, even my father only had a maximum of three man servants, so I just nodded at them as they hurried into the room. They moved efficiently around the space, not bothering to introduce themselves as they got to work.

I was quickly undressed as my bath was prepared, and I wondered what exactly all these maids were going to do. The answer, as it turned out, was to stand around silently as I bathe. After about 20 minutes of awkward silence as I waited for one of the women in front of me to do something, I finally got fed up and asked them to leave. However, instead of going back to their rooms or a servant's hall like I had intended, when I finished my bath, I found them all waiting for me in the first sitting room. All of them, just standing by the wall. As soon as I came in they fluttered around me, directing me to a comfortable sofa where one maid began brushing and braiding my hair. Each of my hands were massaged by a different person, while the head maid went off with the final maid to get my dinner. I had to admit to feeling quite pampered and relaxed by the time dinner arrived.

My relaxed mood didn't get a chance to linger though, as all five of the maids stood once more, watching me eat. While it's true that during large dinners in Nevremerre there would be one or two servants lingering in the hall to ensure everything went smoothly, when it came to smaller dinners, a servant would only be by every 15 minutes or so, and there was never anyone watching you when one dined alone. It felt incredibly uncomfortable to be sitting alone while five people stood around me watching me eat. I felt the pervasive need to start a conversation, but my energy levels felt completely drained from the past day.

"Thank you for everything, but I can handle myself from here. Please enjoy the rest of your evening, and wake me up at 8 tomorrow," I finally said.

For the first time this evening my maids looked at each other uncomfortably. "We can't just leave you here alone, Your Highness," the head maid said. "We still need to clear away your dinner and dress you for bed."

"Well, I can always call one or two of you to clear up after I'm done, and fortunately, in my 19 years of life, I have learned how to dress myself."

"But Your Highness, we're supposed to serve you," that head maid said nervously.

"And you've done a wonderful job," I said wondering why they weren't just leaving, "but now I can serve myself. Surely you all would enjoy more free time tonight?"

"But we have to serve you!" one of the maids, possibly the youngest if I was just looking at appearances, burst out. She got hard looks from the rest of her colleagues.

"Apologies, Your Highness," the head maid cut in.

"It's not a problem." Turning into the young maid, I asked, "Why do you have to serve me?"

"Well..." the girl said hesitantly, anxiously eyeing her other co-workers.

"Whatever it is, it's fine, please just tell me," I said, trying and probably failing to keep my frustration out of my voice.

"Well if we come back too quickly, Mr. Laderdell will think you were dissatisfied, and we will get in trouble," the young maid rushed out.

"Even if I was the one who sent you down?" the maids nodded. I sighed, leaning my head on the back of the couch. I knew I didn't like the manager, and everything I had heard about him did nothing to improve his image. Clearly, I couldn't send the maids back now, but I was exhausted and my tolerance for people in my space was wearing thin. "Okay, here's what we'll do," I decided. I got up and grabbed the basket of bread that had been brought with my meal. "Everyone follow me," I said, marching into the other sitting room, the maids scrambling behind me. "Sit." I ordered, gesturing to the chairs and sofa.

"Your Highness we can't-"

"Yes, yes you can," I said, anticipating their words. "I'm telling you that you can, so please just sit." Mercifully, the maids complied. "Thank you. Now here's the plan. I am going to eat, alone, then get ready for bed. I will then call you to take the dinner away, and then one of you will bring me a pitcher of water and a glass. Then I will go to bed and you can safely retire for the evening. While I eat, you will all sit here, rest, and enjoy this warm bread." I placed the basket on the table in front of them. Looking at it pitifully placed on the table, I had to recognize my rudeness in this abrupt order and my frustrated tone.

With a deep breath, I calmed myself once more, before apologizing. "I am sorry I can't offer you more in the way of food and drink, and I am also sorry if I've been a bit snappish. It has been a very long day for me, not that that justifies rudeness on my part, but I hope it lends to some understanding. Please rest and be comfortable here, I will finish eating, and when I leave tomorrow I will be sure to tell Mr. Laderdell that you all served me very well, which is the truth. Does this work for everyone?"

There are a series of startled nods from the maids, all of whom were staring at me with wide-eyed shock. I internally berated myself for my rudeness once more. "Please enjoy the rest of your evening then," I said before walking back towards my own food and closing the door behind me. I sunk on the couch with a dramatic exhale. My first day in Dolma was filled with far too many problems for my liking. I was struggling with this new culture and my thoughts were plagued by the troubles with housing and farming that I'd already seen. There was a pit in my stomach that wouldn't quite leave. But, the food was good, and the room was now blissfully quiet. I tried to comfort myself that this was just day one, and I would adjust to the culture and I could help fix the problems I saw. After all, I had the solutions for them. These thoughts only partially worked, and I instead relied on Nana's old reminder that sometimes the world isn't nearly as horrible if you just go to sleep. With that thought, I called back in the maids to clear up as I wrapped myself in the giant velvet comforter that adorned my bed, and quickly fell asleep.

Chapter 4

The Journey Continues

This time, sleep was only a partial cure. While my energy levels were replenished, there was an anxious cloud that still swept over me. It enveloped me, pulling at my stomach, harassing my head, demanding to be seen, heard, and felt to the fullest extent. Despite my pounding heart, I reasoned that my nerves were far more favorable than the dread I had experienced when we first entered Dolma. So, I chalked up my nervousness to just being two days away from arriving at the capital and meeting my future husband. Even still, it took several minutes of breathing alone in my room before I found the strength to ring for the maids the inn had assigned me.

The rest seemed to have done them well too, as instead of the awkward silence I had endured the night before, the women that worked around me today were loud and chatty. I learned their names, their reasons for working there (some of which were quite surprising, and I had to make a mental note to look into why several had suggested it was their only work option), and their favorite of my dresses.

"I've never seen dresses like yours, Your Highness," Hannah, the young one from the night before gushed. "Why, there are even trousers in here!"

"Oh, can I see?" Mary, another maid, crowded over.

"That's enough, both of you," Allison, the head maid, scolded.

"Sorry Your Highness," the two girls apologized.

"It's no matter," I commented, confused as to why they were apologizing. Back home, that is, back in Nevremerre, Charlotte and Ana had spent hours fawning over my clothes, even pushing me to do several fashion shows, as well as trying on some pieces themselves. I saw little wrong with people getting excited about new or different clothing items.

"However, Your Highness, it is a bit odd to have trousers. They are rather a brutish style," Coraline, another maid said, a bit snottily in my opinion, but after so many years in the public eye, and dealing with nobles, her tone didn't bother me. "You know they're for men," she continued.

I had to laugh at this. "Are you trying to imply that all men are brutes?" I chuckled. "I think there are many who might take offense to that." Coraline turned red and mumbled something I couldn't quite catch. Moving on, I turned back to Hannah and I continued, "Are trousers not in fashion for women in Dolma? If not, I might need to start a new trend. They can be very comfortable and very easy to style," I smiled at the room, which caused a few more faces to go red, although I couldn't quite understand why.

Allison cleared her throat, "It's almost 9, Your Highness, I believe it's approaching your requested breakfast time. Do you wish to go down?"

"Oh yes, thank you for the reminder." I jumped off from the large bed I was sitting on, my green silk dress flowing behind me. I moved to where my crown was sitting, and placed it on my head. Although it was definitely something the maids could have done for me, ever since Father had given me my gold crown to signify my becoming a Crown Princess on the day of my departure to Dolma, I had taken great pride in being the only person to touch it. It was, perhaps, a silly notion, but I was still so in awe of the intricate piece of gold that I couldn't bear to let it be held in anyone else's hands just yet.

I gave the request to have my things packed up, and went downstairs for breakfast. When I arrived, Abel and Galileo were the only ones there.

"Morning, Crown Princess," Abel smiled at me. "I trust you slept well."

"Oh yes," I replied, "the bed was very comfortable."

"I've been talking with the other knights about the last leg of our journey," Galileo jumped in looking serious. "With only one full day of travel left, and the largely unfamiliar territory we now find ourselves in, we think it's best to try and cover as much ground as possible today. We also think that it would be best that, when we get close to a good stopping point this evening, we send a few runners ahead to avoid any mishaps like the inn last night."

I frowned slightly. "I would like to see more of the land and its people before arriving at the palace, and, if there are more inns like the one we saw yesterday, I should like to know," I fought back.

Galileo shot Abel a tentative glance. Abel gave him a smile, and then looked at me. His dark eyes were filled with kindness, and he gave my hand a gentle squeeze before speaking once more. "Crown Princess, I know of your desire to help others, and I know you wish to create quick change -"

"It's not that I want quick change," I interrupted. "It's that I know how to fix it. When you have a solution, change comes quickly. The speed of change is merely just a byproduct of having an answer."

"Either way," Abel continued, giving me an amused smile, "it's not wise to make changes without a better understanding of the situation you are trying to change. Beyond that, there are other things we must focus on. You are now in Dolma, you will become this country's next Queen, and, in a little over a day, you will ride through the capital where a large part of this country will see their future ruler for the first time. I trust I need not tell you how important that moment will be."

"No, no you do not. I understand what that moment means," I conceded

"Good," Abel smiled at me. "There will be time to fix the problems you see. You have the rest of your life to rule Dolma and fix the injustices and problems you observed yesterday and in the future."

"Mhmm yes, and while I wait, people suffer."

"You could potentially cause more suffering if you move too quickly, Crown Princess," Galileo advised, "or you might lose a chance to solve an even bigger problem. Action is important, but using caution can be very wise."

"You are right, of course," I finally agreed, "and I did promise Queen Elenore that I would learn about Dolma's history and structure before I made any changes." I sighed, "I just wish I didn't have to let people suffer in the process."

"If there were easy solutions to the problems of human suffering, then anyone could rule," Abel said, sagely.

"I'm sure you're right," I agreed as the rest of our party slowly shuffled into breakfast.

Galileo told the others of the plan, and we were soon ready to leave. I went up to the manager for what with any luck would be the last time, and prepared to pay our bill. "Thank you for your service. Your maids and manservants received good reviews for my entire party, and myself," I told him honestly. Apart from the sleazy manager, and setting aside the idea that the maids in Dolma apparently had to stay at your side until you fell asleep, I truly had no complaints with the staff.

"Of course, Your Highness," the manager bowed, "We are happy to serve such an illustrious person at our humble inn." It took everything in my power not to snarl at him in disgust as an unpleasant shiver ran down my spine.

"Yes, well how much do I owe you?" I asked, probably a bit too curtly. Fortunately, the manager didn't seem to notice, although Mateo did. He gave me a slight raised eyebrow from his place beside me. While only a simple gesture, it did bring a genuine smile back to my face as I waited to hear from the manager.

"Good, good, the total today will be 500 gollups," the manager said with an excited smile.

My smile fell instantly. Beside me, Mateo looks similarly unimpressed. "I seem to be getting a strange sense of *deja vu*," I said flatly towards Mateo, "I could have sworn we've had this conversation before."

"That we have, Crown Princess," Mateo responded. His words were calm and measured, but his golden brown eyes flash murderously at the greedy man in front of him.

"Is there a problem?" smiled the manager. I couldn't decide whether this man was an idiot, or if he simply was so self-absorbed that he couldn't see anyone else around him.

"Yes, yes there is a problem. The problem is that you are substantially overcharging us," I said pointedly.

"Oh, but Princess, you made such a show of declaring Nevremerre and Agremerre such wealthy countries, surely you can afford such a measly sum," the manager said with a predatory smile. He looked almost triumphant, like he'd won some grand prize with this rebuttal. He was egregiously confident in his cheating me out of my money - out of the country's money.

Any leftover politeness left my face. My blood went cold, and I glared at the smug man who had unknowingly made himself so little in my eyes. "You're right, Nevremerre and Agremerre are both incredibly wealthy countries, and we stay that way by not falling for underhanded tricks of con men who lack the sense to make profit without resorting to cheap and obvious tricks. Now for hotels about this size one room, generously, would cost about 15-20 gollups a night, including breakfast and service for ourselves and our horses. Now we also purchased four dresses with expedited tailoring feet, depending on the dress quality and factoring in the rush time frame, that's about another 10 gollups. Again, being generous that totals about 170 gollups, but tell me, why should I be generous when you chose to belittle and scam me? I will pay you 100 gollups-"

"100!" the manager cried out indignantly. Mateo's sword was at his throat in less than a second, and for the first time the man in front of me's eyes widened. It seems he finally understood the gravity of the situation.

"Put the sword down, Sir Mateo," I said calmly as the sword moved away. "We cannot go around attacking every scumbag we see. I'm beginning to think we might never put our weapons away. Now, as I was saying, you will receive 100 gollups. This is enough to justly compensate the actually competent staff that you have here and nothing more. In fact, this money won't go to you at all. Excuse me mister," I called out to a manservant who was staring at us wide-eyed by the main hall. The man quickly hurried my way. "Can you ensure this gets evenly distributed amongst the staff here?" I said handing him the 100 gollups.

"Ye- yes, Your Highness," the man said before throwing himself on the floor like Solista and Chanti had done the other day. Although it was now the third time I've seen it, it was still a rather startling form of greeting.

I turned back to the manager. "The name of this inn is "Gilded Border," your name is Gadrion Laderdell," I said, recalling my discussions with the maids here. "I know where this inn is located, and I will be keeping an eye on you. I will hear of the way you "run" this business, and, if word were ever to reach me about scamming your clientele, or if I learn that you've taken the money I've given to your staff, I promise you I will punish you to the fullest extent of the law. If Dolma is lacking in laws that would justly deal with your crimes, I will simply create them. My title is Crown Princess Avalynn of Nevremerre, future Queen of Dolma, and you do not have my permission to call me less than that. Have I made myself clear?"

"Yes Your Majesty, the Crown Princess," the manager said, also throwing himself at my feet.

Now, I've never thought of myself as an intimidating person. It's rather hard to be intimidating as the only short person in a family of giants, but as I watched the manager shake on the floor below me, I felt intimidating. I felt almost powerful... almost. If I ignored a small part of me, I could easily get swept away in this power. I could revel in seeing this man tremble before me, to do whatever I asked of him. I could see the fear in his eyes after he had insulted me so. I could fly away on this power, and see nothing more. But, there was this other small part of me. The part of me that said that what I was feeling wasn't real power. That had I had real power, this never would have happened in the first place. That this man would never have tried to trick me. Real power would have laws in place so that this man couldn't trick anyone. Real power did not come from groveling on the floor and fear, but rather from trust and support. As I sat with that small part of me, it grew in size, taking over the egotistical mirage power that held me before. Shame and disgust swelled through me, aimed at my own actions. I couldn't regret fighting back against the scammer in front of me, but I did not want to rule with fear. My goal was never to swing a sword and force others to their knees.

I squatted down and held out my hand to the man in front of me. "Please get up," the manager looked a bit bewildered, but took my hand to stand up. "You have a nice inn and excellent staff. You do not need to go to such lengths to make money. You could do quite well on your own. It would also be wise to not underestimate the intelligence of your clientele. Today was a warning. Do better, I will not be so forgiving a second time."

"Thank you, Your Majesty," the manager bowed normally this time.

I nodded, ignoring that technically I should have still been addressed as Your Highness, "Mateo, we should be on our way." I turned towards the exit. I had just gotten to the door when I was stopped by another person speaking.

"I must say that was a rather impressive display," the voice spoke. I turned to see an almost blindingly dressed nobleman in front of me. His white suit was laced with layer upon layer of embroidery, and jewels adorned almost every finger and piled on his neck. "I greet her Highness the Crown Princess," he bowed, a full head of blond hair flopping over. While he was more than a bit ostentatious in his appearance, this man at the very least addressed me with the correct title and did not throw himself at my feet. "I daresay that fat old men need to take him down a peg or two."

I frowned at his wording, "I'm not sure what being heavy or old has to do with it, but hopefully he will learn," I responded.

The shining man laughed pleasantly, "Lord Whimely Matherion Casimonius, but you may call me Whimi. I won't hold you up on your journey, but I did want to introduce myself to our future Queen and say that I look forward to getting to know you better. No doubt an opportunity will arise shortly as the current King and Queen will surely wish to hold a ball honoring your arrival in the coming weeks," he bowed once more.

"Yes, I shall see you there, I suppose" I responded, not entirely sure what to make of this odd man before me. "Sir Mateo," I said, moving outdoors and doing my best to drive Mateo with me.

"Any problems, Crown Princess?" Lucy questioned.

"Too many," I said, getting into the carriage, "but none that I'd like to discuss at the moment. Oh, but Miri," I called, sticking my head out of the carriage window, "please keep an eye on this inn like you did the last one."

"Yes Crown Princess," Miri responded, and I noticed her hair was now a shade of auburn.

"Did you dye your hair?" I asked pushing myself further out the window to have a better look at her atop the second carriage. Miri just winked at me before signaling to Galileo that she was ready to depart.

"Did this man try to scam you too, Crown Princess," Lucy hummed, annoyed as I sat back down in the carriage.

"Yes, do you think this is a common occurrence in Dolma?"

"Well," Solista jumped in, a little nervously, "many noble-men will pay greater prices just to prove they can."

"What a terrible way to manage your money!" Lucy said in astonishment, and I nodded my head in agreement.

"That's not something we need to worry about right now," I said as we began to roll forward. "You two are looking quite well today," I said to Solista and Chanti.

"Yes, the tailoring was rather well done, I think," Ana said from her spot next to Chanti. "I really must learn what they do to get it done so quickly."

"Agreed, but what about the two of you? Do you like your new dresses?" I asked.

"They're remarkable!" Chanti said excitedly, "They feel so smooth against my skin."

We settled into a comfortable rhythm, chatting about fashion and clothes, and speculation on what the capital of Dolma would be like. Chanti and Solista confessed to never having been to the capital, so it was just as new for them as it was to us. We learned more about the two girls, and I became more and more relieved they were leaving the "border" town behind. Occasionally one of the knights or Abel, who had decided to ride today to give us more space, would jump in with their thoughts on Dolma, fashion, or the capital.

Mateo told everyone about Lord Whimely, and this prompted a large debate over the amount of jewels one would have to wear in the capital. The ride was peaceful and comfortable, and it almost felt like home. I assured myself that Dolma would feel like home in time, and reminded myself that "almost home" was good enough for now. The day passed quickly enough, and finding lodgings went far smoother with Oberon and Hugo riding ahead to find nice accommodations. There was, again, a moment of shock when I informed the owner I wanted rooms for all of my staff, but there was much less bumbling compared to the manager at the last inn. I let their staff attend to me in the evening, but when I rose in the morning only Ana and Miri were there.

Chapter 5

The Long-Awaited Entrance

I got a bit of a shock when Miri walked in with silvery gray hair, and displayed more wrinkles than I remembered her having. When I commented on it, she just smiled at me and told me it was time to get ready. Ana was giving her an odd look, but said nothing as she helped me prepare for the day ahead. Before my departure from Nevremerre, a great deal of thought had been put into this day, my arrival to the Royal Palace of Dolma. It was not just speculation on my never-before-seen betrothed, but mostly a discussion with Queen Anora, Father, Mother, Mama, Nana, and all my brothers on how to make the best possible entrance to the Royal Palace.

"You must appear strong, confident, and unshakable," Anora would argue. "Give them no reason to look down on you."

"Better still, she should look wise and strong, as if she could solve all the problems that come her way," Mother would counter.

"Would it perhaps be better if they saw her as someone gentle, willing to listen and adapt to this new place? She can then show her strength only when required," Al would suggest.

"Would it be better for her to ride in the carriage or ride a horse? Here royals always ride into town, but in Dolma they seem to prefer the carriage. Would it be better for her to keep with our traditions or show consideration towards theirs?" Father would ask.

"Dress or pants?" Mama would call out.

"Should she carry her sword?" Azar would ponder.

"Can't we all just go with her?" Ari would plead.

"Silence, all of you. What you should do is easy. Simply be yourself, Songbird. You will shine the most brightly when you are wearing and entering in a fashion that is comfortable for you," Nana's wise voice would carry over the room. All eyes would turn to me, and I would promptly forget any original thought that I had ever had, thus prompting the discussion to repeat itself.

Finally Nana, fed up with it all, brought me outside and had me close my eyes and listen to the rustle of the trees around me. "Now feel, Songbird. You are confident, you are happy, you are excited for what is to come," as Nana spoke I felt the emotions she named simmer within me. Confidence filled my being, with safety and love sweeping out to the ends of my fingertips. Joy jumped in my stomach, bashing into excitement exploding across my chest and through my heart. "Can you feel them all?"

"Yes, Nana."

"Good. Now picture yourself, flowing with all these emotions. What do you look like? What is around you?"

"I am in a gown, my crown is on my head, but I am in a field, the wind is blowing my hair, and there are flowers on all sides of me. The wind catches my hair and my dress, almost carrying me away, but it does not frighten me. It just makes me excited to see what comes next."

"How could my Songbird's joy not come from her flying away," Nana smiled.

"I didn't actually leave the ground," I pointed out, opening my eyes and turning towards her once more.

"Hmm," she said stroking my hair, "I'm not so sure, but, either way, I think we have figured out your entrance!"

"We have?"

"Oh yes, just leave it to me, Songbird we'll have you soaring into Dolma like the Queen you will be."

As Ana laid out my outfit for today, I had to confess that all Nana had prepared did seem to match my personality. Yet, I couldn't help but feel nervous as Ana and I finished packing away the rest of my things. Miri was intricately braiding my hair, expertly weaving handcrafted flowers into loose strands. When that was finished, Ana brought over today's outfit. She tucked my night clothes away, locking up the clothing trunks before turning back to me. She then helped me into a dress of Nevremerre purple and gold. It had a tight, high neck top, which exposed my shoulders before cascading down to my arms and legs in a pretty purple cotton. Gold silk was embroidered around my neck and waist. The true genius of the dress, however, was the built-in pants that reached about my calf and would allow me to ride astride Kholassi, my horse, without any discomfort.

I was adorned with gold jewelry, and, thankfully, my jewelry wasn't anywhere near as much as Lord Whimely had been wearing. No, just a few rings, bracelets, and a pair of earrings made their way onto my body. Last, but not least, I lifted my Golden Crown onto my head. Miri and Ana moved to fix my hair under the weight of my crown. "You look beautiful, Crown Princess," Ana said, her voice a little above a whisper, but nearly deafening in the silent room. I took a step back and looked at myself in the full-length glass.

A small gasp overtook me as I stared at my own reflection, scarcely believing the image before me. I couldn't understand what changed, I had worn fancy dresses my entire life. I'd even worn a crown! Although, it had been silver as opposed to the gold I wore now. Yet, I looked different. I felt different. My nerves from before had all but faded away, and the person I saw before me... well, I look like Mother. Not physically, of course, Mother was dark in every possible aspect, and, even if I was much more tan than the red-haired members of my family, I could still pass as a ghost next to Mother. No, I looked like Mother in the sense that I looked like the most elegant and powerful person in the room. Even if she stood by Mama and Father, two of the greatest warriors Nevremerre had ever known, Mother always managed to look so much more indomitable than those around her.

Somehow, without even trying to achieve it, I had matched Mother's perfectly regal air, and I could feel that unbreakable spirit push and flow inside of me. Was this what Nana had meant about shining most brightly when you are comfortable? Probably, I could hardly remember a time when Nana's advice was anything less than accurate. Something she assured me came from decades of experience. However, perhaps the reason didn't matter. All that really mattered was that for the first time since embarking on this journey I felt truly ready to be in Dolma.

"Is everything ready?" I asked, turning back towards my maids. I smiled at them both, and waited for the response. A small bit of pride filled me as they both needed a moment to compose themselves before they could respond.

Ana spoke first, a brilliant smile taking over her face. "We are all set, Crown Princess. The inn staff will take the luggage down while we finish breakfast."

"Perfect, shall we head down then?"

They both agreed and we moved out the door. This inn was slightly larger and more full than the previous inn, so it wasn't really a surprise that several wealthy individuals were already dining when we entered. What was surprising was the complete and utter hush that fell over the hall. I was once again reminded of Mother and her uncanny ability to silence any room simply by walking into it. It was with her in mind that the room's sudden silence didn't bother me. I just moved purposely along to the table where the rest of my party sat.

As I approached, Abel stood, bowing deeply before saying, "I greet the Crown Princess." There was a rush of movement as not only the rest of my party, but the rest of the dining-room followed Abel's lead. For a brief moment I felt flustered by the response of the people in the room. My party was one thing after all, they knew I was a Princess, but the people of Dolma knew as much about me as I did about their Crown Prince, meaning just a name. They had no way of knowing if I was really their new Crown Princess or just some random stranger playing a joke. I composed myself quickly though, and I waved for all of them to sit down, taking my own seat as well.

"If only Betty could see you now, Crown Princess" Abel said, his eyes glowing as they met my own, "She would be so proud." My cheeks grew warm at the compliment, and I smiled back at him gratefully.

"Who's Betty?" asked Oberon, sending confused looks towards me and Abel.

Abel laughed, winking at Oberon, "It's the nickname of The Dowager Queen Elizabeth."

"Are you allowed to call The Dowager Queen by her nickname?" Challa asked, looking scandalized.

"You forget that Dowager Queen Elizabeth married into the royal family of Nevremerre. There are many people who knew her before she was a Queen, and they have her permission to call her as such," Leonard said.

"You say that like you weren't just in shock the first time you heard Sir Abel address the Dowager Queen," teased Galileo. "The only difference between you and Challa is that you've had time to adjust in Nevremerre."

"Did you really know Dowager Queen Elizabeth before she was Queen?" Lucy said, turning back to Abel excitedly.

"Indeed I did," Abel smiled.

"That's incredible! She's an icon!"

"Thank you," I smiled at Lucy, "I think so too." The conversation continued around Nana, and it was satisfying to hear Nana spoken about so well, and to have her described so favorably to a curious Solista and Chanti. It was also a nice distraction from the continuous glances we received from the tables around us. I then paid, a finally reasonably offered price, for our rooms, and set off on the final part of our journey.

It was only a two-hour journey from this most recent inn to the capital. To satisfy Ana's fears that I might somehow ruin my dress before we even arrived at the capital, I agreed to ride in the carriage for the first half of our journey. It wasn't really cramped. It was a carriage designed to comfortably fit six people after all, and with Abel back inside the carriage we met that number perfectly. However, I suspected that the mix of excitement and nerves felt in some combination by everyone in the carriage made the space feel awfully small.

There was a thrilling sort of buzz in the air that made one feel like they were dying to talk about something, but just couldn't put their finger on what. It was amplified by the agonizing pace we took that was both far too quick and not nearly fast enough at the exact same time. Knights, maids, Ladies, and Princesses alike were all fidgeting in our seats when finally Galileo called out, "There it is! The capital of Dolma, Ohmehiu."

Everything rolled to a halt. Those of us in the carriage raced out to see the sprawling city laid out below us. Ohmehiu was located near Dolma's largest ports, and buildings stretched as far as the eye could see. In the distance, the glimmering sea sparkled. Similar to Nera, the royal palace sat slightly off to the side of the city. Unlike Nera, however, the Dolma royal palace looked positively massive, even from up where we were. I could tell that the palace would cover several city blocks and was quite a bit higher than any of the buildings surrounding it.

We stood in awe of the city for a few moments. "I've never seen the sea before," Chanti's voice broke through our stunned silence.

"Well then we'll have to take you!" Ana smiled at her. "It really does wonders for your soul."

"We have to get there first," I reminded her. "Come on every-one. Not long now!" I watched everyone meander back to the carriage chattering happily about our arrival, and I went to get Kholassi. The time had come to make an entrance into Dolma, and I was feeling confident and ready. I quickly mounted Kho-lassi, his black coat sparkling in the late morning sun. With his height, and sturdy body beneath me, I felt my confidence grow. The sun added a gentle heat, and an early fall breeze tickled my exposed skin. Ana came around and adjusted my dress behind me, before giving me a bow and saying, "Your Highness."

I gave her a soft smile and waited for her to ascend back into the carriage before turning back towards my knights. They looked at me with bright faces, their heads held high, and their backs straight. "Everyone ready?" I asked, feeling warm and safe and proud. Proud of myself, proud of the people who had changed their lives to come with me, and proud of all that we have done and will do. Perhaps it was just my own feelings overwhelming everything else, but I swore I saw my pride and confidence reflected back in the eyes of those around me. I felt so sure in that moment that we could handle anything we might find in Dolma. That there was no challenge we couldn't overcome.

Looking back on that moment, I suppose that feeling wasn't wrong, per se, but it certainly wasn't as easy or as certain as it felt at that time. Regardless of what was to come, the first step is always to keep moving forward, so, with the agreement of my party, I gave the command to head-on into Ohmehiu.

Chapter 6

The Wedding Negotiations

It was like the whole city paused as we passed. People froze mid-task, mid-step, even mid-bite as they watched us move through the city. There were furious whispered debates on whether they were supposed to bow, who I might be, and what we were doing in Dolma. Some people skipped the discussion entirely and threw themselves on the ground beside us. I briefly wondered if it would be incredibly rude of me to change this strange type of bowing or if I would just have to get used to people throwing themselves on the ground before me for the rest of my life. Occasionally, the whispers would break free of their confines and find their way to my ears, pushing for with phrases like "Who is she?", "Could she be the new Princess?", and "Just shut up and bow!" I didn't bother addressing any of these whispers, any questions would be answered soon enough, but I did smile at all who I passed. I hoped to show them that I would be a kind Queen, willing to help those in need and whoever asked for it.

I was so focused on the people, I forgot to look around me, so it came as a bit of a shock when I found myself at the gates to the Royal Palace. A guard in a blue and red uniform hurried out before us. It was, frankly, a rather garish ensemble, and I wasn't sure the combination of colors was flattering on anybody's figure. However, I recognized the pattern as what was supposed to resemble Dolma's flag, so I tried not to judge the unusual pattern too harshly.

"Name and information please?" the guard spoke. I guess he was trying to be intimidating in his stance and words, but I noticed his feet were planted right next to each other and his sword was obscured from his reach by some rather large golden tassels. While I've always found it wise not to judge an opponent by their physical appearance, every fighting bone in my body was screaming that I could knock this man down with little more than one kick. Everything from his stance to his outfit told me that this man would lose a fight to a child. It seemed glaringly obvious that Dolmanian Royal Palace guards were in no way ready for any sort of combat, and I briefly wondered if the King might just let me take over all knight and guard training. This did seem unlikely though since I was still a foreign Princess. Perhaps, I could start leading them after my wedding.

Pulling my thoughts back to the matter at hand, I announced, "I am Princess Avalynn of Nevremerre. I have come, as requested, as part of the treaty between Dolma, Agremerre, and Nevremerre. I'm arriving with my party of six knights, one Lady-in-Waiting, the new ambassador from Nevremerre, and four maids."

The guard bowed, "I greet the Princess Avalynn," he said politely. "We had information that you only had two maids you were bringing along, but that was clearly a mistake on our part."

"No, it was not," I responded, kindly. "I was originally only bringing two mates for myself, but along the way we hired two more maids for my Lady-in-Waiting, Lady Lucy." It didn't seem reasonable to go into the details of Solista's and Chanti's positions in my household, so I tried to keep the explanation brief. For some reason, however, the guard looked awfully confused.

"Forgive me, Your Highness, but you say that both you and your Lady-in-Waiting only have two maids each?"

"Yes. Is that an issue?" I asked, a little confused myself at this point in time.

"No, no!" the guard hurried to assure me. "Don't worry, I'm sure it'll be handled at the palace," he smiled. "If you could please wait here a moment, I will let the attendants know you're here," he bowed once more, and then proceeded to stay in that position.

"Thank you," I said, still a little confused. There was a silence for a moment as the guard stood bowed before me. "Er, is there a reason you have not left yet?" I asked after several minutes.

"I am waiting for you to dismiss me, Your Highness," the guard replied patiently.

"Oh, well I'm not sure that's necessary, but you are dismissed Sir - sorry, I don't believe I ever asked your name."

The guard gasped a little. "It's Sawyer Aberforth, Your Highness!"

"Right, well then you are dismissed Sir Sawyer," I said, and the man quickly scurried off.

"Well, he seems nice, if a little odd," Leonard commented.

"Perhaps, but he doesn't seem like a well-trained guard," Galileo observed.

"He can be taught though. A few proper lessons will make a world of difference," Hugo chimed in.

"Lesson one will have to be to fix that stance. Honestly, surely he must know that standing with your feet together just makes it easier for you to lose balance," Challa said with an exasperated sigh.

"Well the good, or I suppose bad news since we live here now, is that the knights here aren't much better. I only saw them briefly on our last trip, but many made several rookie mistakes," Oberon said pensively.

"We could have seen beginners last time," Mateo said in an attempt to remain positive, "Although, what they were doing wouldn't have been the best way to train them."

"It's no matter," I said. "They have us now, and hopefully, with some time, we can retrain them all."

"I do think I understand why King Edgar wanted you to have six knights, Crown Princess," Leonard said. "If the castle security is this weak, it could pose a significant safety threat to all its inhabitants."

"While I would never attempt to comment as to the inner workings of King Edgar's mind, I do not think the poor palace security was the only reason for our presence. Nevertheless, we must use this information as a reminder to stay vigilant with protecting the Crown Princess and all those under her care," Galileo stated.

"Yes Sir!" came the chorus of knights around me.

"Do remember that all six of you fall under the category of those under my care, so please look after yourselves and each other as well."

"Yes Crown Princess," the chorus called again, and I felt a rush of warmth at their words. We waited only a few minutes longer before Sir Sawyer came running back towards us.

"They are ready for you, Your Highness," he bowed, "The gates will open shortly."

"Thank you, Sir Sawyer," I said politely. His face went curiously red after this, but I had little time to ponder his reaction before the golden gates before us were pulled open. We rode through a long road, with large green trees on either side. This road went on for what felt like an hour, but was probably closer to 15 minutes before we finally saw the true palace entrance.

The Royal Palace of Nevremerre was a large palace. With three stories and a couple of towers, as well as large gardens, a big ballroom and a dining room that could fit all of Nevremerre's nobles. There were more than enough bedrooms to fit the entire Council and my whole family and still have rooms to spare. Agremerre's Kings and Queens had been nomadic for centuries before my Grandfather took up the trend, but the Royal Palace of Agremerre was also a large and spacious building. Dolma's Royal Palace, however, was downright enormous. The building stretched five, maybe six stories into the air, and the walls stretched for miles and miles on either side. It seemed like one could fit a whole city inside this building, were they inclined to try.

It was, as I moved my eyes from the building to the crowd of people gathered by its entrance, entirely possible that Dolma was trying to create a small city in their palace. To my right stood row upon row of people dressed in suits of black and white. To the left a slightly smaller crowd of people in elaborate outfits, each sparkling in a dazzling array of jewels that I could only hope I would not have to emulate. Finally, in front of two large, golden doors stood a row of about 12 people, leading them was the royal family of Dolma.

I halted my party, dismounted Kholassi, and made my way towards the King. Remembering all that Anora had taught me, I pushed my knees out into a curtsy. "Princess Avalynn of Nevremerre greets His Royal Highness, King Harold Whimeriner Augustine Varrelion Raginer Carleon of Dolma, Her Royal Highness Queen Priscella Aripoza Magnolean Marie Carleon, His Highness the Crown Prince Thomas Rayforth Ecardio Davenforth Carleon, and Her Highness Princess Ollifele Analise Elliayah Carleon," I said, sending a silent thank you to the Gods that I had successfully remembered all the many names of the Dolmanian royal family.

"Welcome Princess Avalynn," said the King. I stood up as he spoke, finally taking a real look at the leader of this Kingdom.

The King was a reasonably tall man, probably still a good half foot shorter than Father, but that was to be expected. He had curly white hair and a thick, but short beard, and his eyes were light brown. There was nothing inherently unfriendly about his smile and open arms, but my instinctive reaction was not to trust this man. I didn't necessarily feel like he would purposely harm me, but rather I felt that if I stopped being useful to him, he wouldn't hesitate to throw me away.

Here and now, however, I was useful and that would have to be enough. As if sensing that I had finished my perusal of him, the King grabbed my hand and spun me towards the crowd on the right. "My Lord and Ladies of the Court, it gives me the utmost pleasure to present to you the Princess Avalynn of Nevremerre, the woman who will marry Crown Prince Thomas Rayforth Ecardio Davenforth Carleon and become the future Queen of Dolma." The sea of people around us sunk into bows and curtsies as they chanted their greetings of welcome. "Now, I believe you have others to introduce us to," the King said loudly, looking back at the carriage, where my party now stood.

"Yes, Your Majesty," I said, gracing the court with a smile. "May I introduce Sir Abel, ambassador of Nevremerre, and my Lady-in-Waiting, Lady Lucy of Agremerre. I also bring my knights, Sirs Galileo, Oberon, Mateo, Leonard, Challa, and Hugo. As well as a few trusted maids, Miri, Ana, Solista, and Chanti." As I said their names, each person bowed or curtsied towards the King. I smiled as everyone managed to do so perfectly, even Chanti and Solista. Although Chanti looked as though she may faint.

"Yes," the King mused, "it's such a quaint custom in your parts to introduce all who travel with you."

I didn't miss the derision in his voice as he spoke, but today I was unshakable. I looked directly into his eyes and said, "Thank you for your understanding of our "quaint" custom. We find it shows appreciation for all who travel with us, and all that they have done for us along the way."

The King raised his eyebrow at me, but didn't miss a beat as he said, "Well Dolma always strives to accommodate our esteemed guests, and soon-to-be family. As such, I am pleased to announce that in celebration for the arrival of our future Crown Princess, and those who follow her, a grand ball will be held in two weeks time where we shall introduce Princess Avalynn to all of Dolma." Applause filled the courtyard at the King's words. "Yes, yes," the King called out, silencing them all. "Now, Princess Avalynn, in honor of your first day here, please allow me to escort you into the palace."

"Thank you, Your Majesty," I said, taking his offered arm, and laying my hand upon the mound of gold and white velvet that covered his body. I moved with the King into a massive marble entryway, with gold etched between each wall, beautiful murals of Ohmehiu's skyline covered the ceiling, and beneath my feet, shining tiles clicked against my shoes. Behind us came the thunderous clacking of hundreds of feet, following us inside.

"If you have not yet eaten, Princess Avalynn," the King said, and although he was facing my direction, he projected his voice out to the whole hall of people. "I would like to invite you to join the royal family for lunch."

Although I was unsure of the need for the performance, I projected my voice like the King had when responding to him, "Thank you, Your Majesty, lunch would be lovely."

The King smiled at me, and gave my hand on his arm a quick pat. "Good, this way please," he projected once more before leading me down another large hallway. This time, however, the footsteps behind us were far fewer. We made it part way before the King stopped us once more. "We allow one knight per family member at family meals, which of your knights should we call?"

For a short moment, I tried to imagine what my family meals would be like if we'd had knights present as well. Not that Nevremerrian knights weren't lovely company, but they would make family time slightly uncomfortable. However, now was not the time to examine this oddity, "Sir Galileo please," I said. If I were really honest, I would have preferred Mateo. Even though I had gotten closer to all of my knights on this journey, Mateo had been my friend since before this adventure, and he was the first knight to swear his loyalty just to me. I suspected, however, that by asking me this question away from my knights, the King was attempting to suss out any particular loyalties I may have. In that respect, and considering that Galileo would likely want to keep an eye on me in the early days of navigating this new and large place, my head knight was obviously the better choice.

"Go fetch him," the King said, nodding at his own knight. We continued down the hall in silence for a while before we heard the slightly rushed footsteps of Galileo and the King's knight as they echoed behind us. The King kept walking, however, causing the two knights to rush to make up lost ground. We continued to move forward, twisting and turning through so many halls that I began to believe I'd never be able to find even the entrance way again without a map.

Finally we stopped in front of two large wooden doors. The King and his family waited patiently for two servants in black to open the doors for them. Then the King led us all inside. There was a very large granite table surrounded by fine wooden chairs set with blue cushions. There was a long blue strip of fabric lining the middle of the table, held down by three evenly distributed candelabras. At the end of the table there was a large window overlooking a small garden. The King moved towards said window towards where four plates were set up on either side of an overly large wooden chair placed at the head of the table.

The King sat at this larger chair, and placed me at his right. Around me, his family filled in the empty chairs. For the first time, I got a chance to observe my future in-laws, and my betrothed. The Queen moved directly across from me, she was a thin woman with light brown hair which was peppered with streaks of gray. She had icy blue eyes that stared at me, judgingly, as she sat down. My only saving grace was that it seemed she had yet to make a judgment on my character. Next to her, sat a small girl, who couldn't have been much older than Ari. She must be the young Dolmanian princess. She was quite lovely, if perhaps a little too thin and a little too pale to be considered healthy in Nevremerre. Her long wavy hair hung freely around her face; it was an incredible shade of light blonde that looked almost white against the afternoon sun that peered through the window. Her eyes were the same color as her father, but lacked the shrewdness I'd seen and his gaze earlier.

Then, on my right side sat him, my future husband, Crown Prince Thomas, although he'd yet to give me permission to address him as such. He was handsome, thankfully. He had the same light blond hair of his sister, and the icy blue eyes of his mother. He was tall and lean, likely around the same height as his father. He was not breathtaking, or even close to the most beautiful man I've ever met, but something about him reminded me of a piece of art. There was something about the way he looked that was frozen in time, classic, like he was a painting or sculpture. As if he was something to be admired in museums and galleries. To me, it seemed like he fit right in with the grandeur of the Dolmanian Royal Palace. It was, honestly, a bit of a relief, not that it would have mattered either way, but if the worst came, and I was incapable of carrying on a conversation with this man, at least I could look at something nice.

The Crown Prince didn't even look in my direction as he sat down, staring instead rather determinedly at the wall in front of him. What was so interesting about it, I could not fathom a guess. Perhaps he was a bit slow, or this was another strange Dolmanian custom. Perhaps there was a rule about never looking at those who join you for lunch. I was a bit disappointed to learn that my betrothed was perhaps a bit dull, but there were other important traits, and perhaps he might give me more ability and power to change the issues that I had already seen. Although, intelligence can be rather important in a future ruler. Hopefully, it was still too soon to judge.

I turned my attention away from the man beside me and towards the King. "So, your knight Galileo," he inquired rather open-endedly.

"Yes, this is my head knight, Galileo. He was appointed by King Edgar and Queen Anora, and has served me well on my journey over," I said smiling at Galileo behind me.

The King frowned slightly, but didn't let the thought bother him too long as he smiled again and said, "I hope you had a pleasant journey."

"Yes, Your Majesty, it was-"

"No need for formalities when we're all alone, child. Just our lesser titles will do here," King Harold said waving his hand. I had several problems with the statement, first the room was filled by not just the royal family and myself, but also five knights and at least seven servants. So, I'm not quite sure how King Harold defined the word alone, but his definition certainly did not match my own. Second, it was rather rude for the King to declare that I could call him and his family less formally without even asking the other people at the table. However, given that there were no objections from said other people, I could probably let this grievance slide. Thirdly, and probably most pressingly, I had no idea what a lesser title was.

"Forgive me, but there is no such thing as a lesser title in Nevremerre, may I ask you to clarify what that is," I asked, trying to maintain my composure.

There was a snort from across the table, that Queen Priscella failed at attempting to hide in a cough. This was an incredibly rude thing to do to anybody, and felt even more obnoxious to do to someone who had only arrived in your country two days ago. I looked at her a bit incredulously, wondering why someone her age felt the need to be so immature in her response. Something in my face must have gotten through, however, as she then explained, "A lesser title is your rank and your first name, Princess Avalynn. For example, mine is Queen Priscella."

"Thank you for the explanation," I said wondering why she hadn't just said that from the beginning instead of laughing at me. King Harold gave his wife a funny little smile. I couldn't quite place what was off about it, but it almost seemed as if he was smiling at Queen Priscella instead of in support of her. Soon lunch was served, and I turned back to King Harold to try to discuss the problems I'd experienced on my way to the Palace.

"I noticed, King Harold and Queen Priscella, that the outer farm lands of Dolma use monoculture farming. I must ask if you have managed to find a way to counteract the effects high soil turnover has on dust storms and poor crop survival. We once tried this method in Nevremerre, only for a rather disastrous result," I began, keeping in mind Abel's suggestions that perhaps Dolma was not in as much trouble as I had thought.

"What, like a drought?" Queen Priscella said, haughtily.

"Well yes, among other things, although this was several hundred years ago," I said. I was still perplexed by the Queen's attitude. I hadn't gotten the sense that she actively disliked me, although it was clear she felt superior to me somehow. It was almost like her rudeness was rehearsed, or even automatic. Other than to confuse me, her comments had yet to injure my pride, so I simply let it go. After all, I felt quite certain that she was looking more the fool than I at this particular moment.

Moving back to the topic, King Harold merely laughed at our exchange, and said, "An interesting question, Princess Avalynn, it would be best to ask one of my advisors, however. For now, let's put the matter of ruling aside and enjoy our first lunch together."

It felt wrong. This was a problem, a problem that potentially needed a quick solution. Inside, I was screaming that we shouldn't just let this topic go. But, rationally, I knew that this was not a bad move. I had promised to understand all that was involved before I acted, and I knew in the core of my being the understanding was what led to the wisdom required to rule effectively. So, with only a small internal sigh, I conceded, "As you wish, King Harold."

"The wedding will take place in three months' time," King Harold announced, nodding at me. "I believe this should give us the time to prepare an appropriate celebration, as well as not overly prolonging the engagement period. The date will be announced at your welcoming ball."

"That seems appropriate," I agreed. "My family and friends from Nevremerre will wish to attend. Is there a limit to how many people I should invite?"

"As many as you wish, Princess, but do give us a list of those attending as soon as possible. Weddings in Dolma are a grand affair, so large groups of people are to be expected."

"Thank you. Now, I'm happy to incorporate any major Dolmanian traditions into the wedding, however, I hope there is room for some Nevremerrian traditions as well, for example-". And so lunch progressed, with King Harold and me negotiating over wedding details... with just King Harold and me negotiating and going over wedding details. For, during the over hour-long lunch, no one else offered any opinion on the wedding. No thoughts from the Queen, no little comments from the young Princess, and not even a single word from the groom! If I wasn't required to be fully engaged in the battle of wits and negotiations that the shrewd man in front of me had started, I would have said something to them, maybe even demanded that they have some opinion–about anything. Instead, they simply sat and ate, almost mechanically, seemingly unbothered by their own silence.

When the wedding negotiations were over, King Harold announced the end of lunch, and the Queen and Princess simply stood up and left. It was honestly astonishing. I had never seen such an odd and quiet family meal before. So as to not seem too flustered, I stood to leave as well. Before I even made it to the door, my arm was grabbed by my future husband.

"I will never love you," he hissed at me. From his tone, and the way his fingers dug into my arm, I got the sense that this was some kind of threat or a warning perhaps. But, despite his imposing height compared to mine, and the coldness of his tone, I found not even the slightest fear at the sight of him.

Instead the growing confusion I'd felt at the way the lunch had gone tumbled out of me as I stared back at him and replied, "I don't believe I ever asked you to."

The hand on my arm dropped, and the Crown Prince's eyes grew wide at my words. Before anything else could be said, however, another voice called out. "Wait here, please, Princess," King Harold's voice rang out. At the words of his father, Crown Prince Thomas abruptly left the room, leaving King Harold, a bunch of servants, knights, and myself in the dining room. This time, however, it appeared the knights and servants were being counted, as the moment Crown Prince Thomas had left, King Harold ordered, "Leave us alone now." The servants filed out, and Galileo informed me that he would be right outside the door if I needed him.

Then the room really was empty, save the King and me. "Do you drink, Avalynn?" King Harold question, dropping my title.

"Not usually, Harold," I answered both honestly and impertinently.

"No, no, no. I am still King Harold to you," King Harold scolded, pouring himself a drink.

"Then, it's Princess Avalynn to you," I said unflinchingly.

King Harold threw his head back with laughter and sat back down at the head of the table, gesturing at me to sit in the seat the Queen had once occupied beside him. "All right, call me Harry then," he decided.

"Ava," I agreed, sitting down.

"I must apologize for my family, Ava. You see, they don't know what I do. In fact, there are precious few in all of Dolma who know the value that you bring." To an outsider, this may have seemed like a compliment. However, even after only being here for a few hours, I knew better. While possibly still, in some sense, a compliment, King Harold's evaluation of me was not a judgment of my character or person. Rather he was evaluating me as an object, as a shiny new jewel for his collection.

"Tell me, Ava, and do be honest, what do you think of me?" Harry continued.

"I've known you for only a couple of hours, Harry. How could I possibly make a judgment on your character?"

"Nonsense! Everybody makes initial judgments, especially people in our position. We have to, it's the only way to survive in a role such as ours. So go on, tell me your thoughts. I can hardly kill you for your opinion. No doubt I'd have two nations worth of armies on my hands if I did."

"Funnily enough, you murdering me wasn't my first thought when you asked the question," I deadpanned.

"Because you made a snap judgment about me! So go on, let it out."

"I suppose so," I conceded, "but I'm not sure making quick judgments about people is the only way to survive a crown."

"Meh," Harry hummed, waving me off.

I eyed him before giving my observations, "I think you are a shrewd and cunning man. I think you are demanding and particular, but you are not wholly unreasonable. I believe you are intelligent and a keen judge of character. However, I also believe that you won't hesitate to shun or dispose of me if I were to no longer hold any perceived value for you."

Harry laughed once more. "You are quite right, Ava, about it all. I am an old greedy man, Avalynn. I am not sure I would do as well in a country like Agremerre or, no doubt, Nevremerre, which value truth and hard work."

"That is an oversimplification of our values," I said, feeling the need to clarify.

"Either way," Harry said, waving me off again, "the point is, I am a greedy old man, and I have no intention to change that about me. However, I am also smart - not always a guarantee when you gain a throne the way I did - and that intelligence has served me well. It allowed me to see what my father and grandfather could not: Agremerre thrived where Dolma, in all its extravagant opulence, could not. The same was true of Nevremerre, when we looked into your country as the enemy of Calvine. And then there was this drought, and, I confess, it was a grand opportunity for someone like me. You see I could gain you, someone who had been trained to rule a prosperous country and who could apply that knowledge here. And, you could still inherit the Nevremerre throne. You who could combine both of our lands and give Dolma greater power than we've ever known. You, dear Ava, was all that I was trading for."

A chill ran through me as his words smacked me in the face. I was the true object of the treaty with Dolma. The weapons sales, the trade deals with Agremerre, those were all just smoke screens for my arrival here. It was both overwhelming, and suddenly underwhelming as well. After all, Nevremerre and Agremerre still needed aid, my decision would not change, even if I had known I was the target since the beginning. "You know I'm not guaranteed the Nevremerre throne," I said, as I digested his words, "In fact, in two years, I may even relinquish the throne all together."

"Yes, yes you may," Harry said, suddenly solemnly. "But, as I've said, you do have other benefits than just the land," he said, perking up once more. "Even still, Ava, this place will not be easy for you. The people here, even my own son, won't know you are still a possible heir to the Nevremerre throne. They won't understand a "merit-based" succession system. You're not the right gender, or the right-aged sibling, to inherit if you were born here. I've watched the people here belittle and mock the people of Agremerre and, more recently, of

Nevremerre. Totally blind and ignorant to the prosperity and abundance your two countries reap, a prosperity the nobles here are dying to replicate. They will not respect you as a potential heir to multiple thrones, not unless you tell them of your status, and, even then, most will not believe you. And, I will not help you with this, nor will I publicly support your agendas. I am a greedy old man Ava, and I will get far too much pleasure watching you turn them all on their heads to even dream of interfering. No, in that regard you are on your own. I will, however, get you the information you require about our agricultural style and about anything else you wish to change in Dolma. If you make a compelling enough argument, I will help you make the changes you see fit."

I stared at Harry for a while, weighing his words before I spoke, "Thank you. I will review the documents in question and prepare a response for you as soon as possible."

Harry smiled at me, "Come talk to me like this again soon, Ava. You are a worthy conversationalist, but always remember your first impression of me. I keep nothing in my life that isn't of the highest quality and value."

"Of course, Harry," I smiled back at him before he waved me out of the room.

Chapter 7

The Accommodations

Galileo stood waiting for me on the other side of the door, anxious lines carved into his face. "How'd it go?" he asked upon seeing me.

I smiled at him, "You needn't look so worried."

"It was your first meeting with the King of Dolma. I remember when King Edgar first met with him. He called him a cunning character, and a devious man. Also he was the one who demanded you come to Dolma in the first place!"

I'd never seen Galileo look so nervous. The usually stoic knight was now a bundle of nerves in front of me, and what had caused this transformation? A still teenaged girl meeting with her future father-in-law. Even if he was not a paragon of strength at the moment, I felt very supported by the man beside me. I gently placed my hand on his muscular forearm before saying, "All that is true, and King Edgar's words were certainly correct, but it did not go poorly. We will be alone in facing the court and nobles of this land, but the King will listen to our thoughts on their farming. So, we can still do some good for the people."

"That's a relief," Galileo sighed.

"Not exactly, there is still a lot of work to be done."

"You can do it, Crown Princess. You held your own very well against the King for your wedding. I'm sure you will do the same for your plans to help this Kingdom."

"And, yet, you were still worried about me meeting with the King?"

"I am your knight," Galileo said defensively. "It's my job to worry about you."

"I know," I smiled at him. "You know, I actually quite like him, the King," I said, whispering conspiratorially into Galileo's ear. "I don't trust him in the slightest, but he's an interesting character."

"I'm not sure that's a good combination," Galileo said, a little scandalized.

"Perhaps not," I laughed a little. "Now," I said, turning towards the staff that still lingered in the hall, "does anyone know how we can get to our rooms?"

Galileo and I followed a manservant through the numerous halls of Dolma. I was, frankly, astonished that the servant was able to find anything, as I myself was completely turned around. After what felt like an hour, we finally approached a large set of white doors. Blue and red flowers were carved into the painted wood, and a golden plaque read "Princess Avalynn," on the right hand side.

"These will be your chambers, Your Highness, until your wedding with His Highness the Crown Prince. From then on you will live in shared accommodation."

"Thank you, Mr. -?"

The manservant looked at me in surprise, "I'm only a commoner, Your Highness, I only have one name."

"Well there's nothing wrong with that, no one in Nevremerre has more than one name. It has the added benefit of no one running out of breath when trying to introduce themselves. So, your name is? Mr.?" I responded.

"It's Stanley, Your Highness," the man said, looking at me with wide eyes.

"Will thank you, Mr. Stanley. I won't keep you from your duties any longer."

"Thank you, Your Highness, please let me know if you need anything at all!" Stanley bowed, before turning and heading off in the opposite direction.

"Why does everyone we meet in Dolma look so surprised by us?" I asked, watching Stanley run off.

"I cannot say, Crown Princess," Galileo responded, also watching the hallway Stanley went down, "It happened when

King Edgar was here too. At the time, I attributed it to our sudden arrival, but that's clearly not the case this time."

"Perhaps it's something that will change in time," I said, finally turning back to the door in front of us. I stepped forward and walked through the heavy doors. The chamber was massive. Just the entryway was large enough to fit a small house. There was a grand sitting room that stretched probably two stories above us, with big vaulted ceilings. Similar to the dining room I had just left, there was a large glass window that took up one entire wall, with a view into a pretty courtyard, filled with a variety of plants and flowers that bloomed with their end of summer buds. The room itself was filled with crisp white furniture, and a lot more gilding, but it was not as over-the-top as I had seen at the first inn we'd stayed at. It was nice. It felt peaceful and comfortable, even if it was overly large. Galileo seemed to have come to the same conclusion, as he was nodding approvingly at the room.

"Crown Princess!" came Chanti's delighted yelp from across the room. There was a flutter of movement as Ana, Solista, and Lucy appeared from the doorway. "You must come see! It's beautiful!" Chanti continued, happily running towards me and grabbing my hand.

"Chantel!" Solista exclaimed, "You can't just grab the Crown Princess's hand like that!"

"It's quite alright," I said, giving Chanti's and squeeze. "Why don't you show me around?"

Our rooms were in fact more of a block than just a room. We had all the rooms that surrounded this courtyard. Apparently, the first two floors belonged to me and included, among other things, a bathroom, a bedroom, a closet room, four sitting rooms, a music room, an office, and a, currently empty, library. The floors above me held the rooms of my knights and Lady Lucy. Lucy had her own two-story lodging, although it only wrapped around half of our little square. My knights each had their own bedroom and bathroom on the third and fourth story. As Chanti ran us through our little corner, I noticed several of my knights already unpacking in their chosen room. They gave us cheery waves as we passed by, and assured Galileo they'd saved the best room for him. Galileo didn't look convinced by this, but informed everyone to get ready to meet in my chambers for a group meeting in a couple of hours.

We finished on the top floor. There was a noticeable difference between this floor and the ones below it. For starters, there were no painted walls or colorful furniture, There were also far more rooms crammed together and only four rooms with a combined bathroom. The other rooms seemed to share joined bathrooms at the end of two long hallways. The floor was also divided by two thick doors with large metal locks. "Isn't it wonderful?!" Chanti explained, throwing herself onto a bed inside one of the rooms. "And look! Both Listi and I get a bed!" she said pointing to the other side of the room.

"Beds are important," I agreed, thinking of the shack she and her sister shared beforehand. "but it does look like there is some work to be done here, some more color on the walls for a start."

"Maybe a couch on this side," Ana suggested.

"Plus, surely you would like your own room," Lucy chimed in.

"We can't have our own rooms!" Solista explained, "What of all your other servants, Crown Princess?"

"That will be up to Ana," I said. "This place is larger than anticipated, so it'll be up to you, as my personal housekeeper, to be in charge of managing the area," I smiled at her.

"I told you there were housekeepers in Dolma," Ana winked at me. Getting serious once more, Ana continued, "When he brought us here, a butler gave us documents regarding your personal budget, we can review those once we get you settled and I'll see how much staff we need versus what we can afford."

"Sounds logical," I agreed. I turned back to Chanti and Solista, "I will not force you, if you'd rather share, but I'm certain we can give you both separate rooms should that be what you desire, at least for the next three months."

"Why only three months?" Lucy asked.

"That is when the wedding will be. Apparently we will be switching to joint rooms with the Crown Prince after that," Lucy nodded.

"You're getting married so quickly!" Chanti said, "Shouldn't engagements be at least a year?"

I smiled down at her, before taking a seat on the bed she was lying in. "I came to Dolma to get married. With my wedding, I will become the future Queen. It's not shocking for things to move this quickly. I would not have been surprised if the wedding had happened immediately upon arrival. I'm just glad now that my family will be able to attend. Speaking of which, I must write to my family and inform them of my safe arrival. Also, where is Sir Abel? And, have you all eaten yet?"

"Yes," Lucy nodded. "There are a few private dining rooms for our use right next to the rooms on our side. The palace staff is serving us for now, but I do believe the idea is to hire our own help. The housekeeper who led us here suggested the Queen would assist you in the hiring process. Sir Abel was taken to a living area with all the other ambassadors."

I was suddenly greeted with the mental image of a calm, serene Abel turning a bunch of ambassadors on their heads as he tricked them into evaluating all of their life choices and becoming more confident and positive people. "I suspect he will quite like that arrangement. Now, here's the plan. Galileo, you should get some food and start unpacking. Everyone else should do the same, minus the food. We will all meet in the main entryway for a couple of hours to discuss all I've learned so far. I will also take this time to write to my family and review the budget the King has granted me. If you could please spread the word to everyone, and does someone think they might be able to find Sir Abel?"

"I can," came Miri's voice by the door, causing me and everyone else in the room to jump. "I have found maps!" she said, waving an arm full of scrolls around triumphantly.

"That is a good find!" Galileo agreed.

"We should try to replicate these for everyone." I said, nodding encouragingly.

"Leonard and Hugo are both good artists," Galileo added, "We could get them to make copies."

"It will take awhile, even with the three of us working on it," Miri said. "There are 6 wings of the palace, and each wing has five floors. That's 30 maps total, times 13 that's 390 maps to copy."

"360 if we can use the ones you're holding," said Lucy.

Miri shook her head, "It's best we return these to their original owner. "

"Did you - did you perhaps steal these?" I asked, a little uncertain.

"No, no. That wasn't required this time. Some nice girl took pity on the poor little old lady lost in the big palace and let me borrow these," Miri responded.

Fair enough, I thought to myself as Ana asked, "How old are you exactly?"

"Good question," said Miri, and she did not elaborate further. "I think we should start with the ground floor maps," she continued instead. "From what I gather, the ground floor is where most of the events are held anyways, and all ground-floor rooms are labeled, which gives me time to fill in the blank rooms on the other levels."

"Right. That sounds good then. Everyone will meet back in two hours, and I think Miri would be the best choice to find Sir Abel."

"That I am, Crown Princess," Miri agreed, and we all moved in our separate directions.

Like most people, I assume (or at least I had assumed prior to the oddly silent lunch I had just this afternoon), I had spent many hours talking with my family. It was easy, usually, to speak with them, to tell them what was on my mind, to share with them my observations about the world around me, and yet here I sat, a blank piece of parchment in front of me and an unused quill in my hand, with absolutely no idea how to start this letter. How was I to describe the problems I had experienced on the way here? How should I discuss my disappointment that my betrothed might be... a poor conversationalist, to say the least? How was I supposed to describe how Solista and Chanti lived? Was it even possible to mention that the King supports me, but will not help me transition into this new space? Not to mention trying to inform them that I was King Harold's grand prize in the treaty. That fact, at least, could likely be left out.

In the end, I wrote to Anora first. I asked for advice related to the state of the streets and buildings I had seen, and the curious mix of support and abandonment from King Harold. Reading it over, it did read more like a cry for help as opposed to a report on Dolma's current situation, but I trusted Anora to give me the support and reinsurance I sought.

The letter to my family went as follows:

Dearest Family,

I have arrived safely in Dolma. There is, as we suspected, going to be a steep learning curve for me and those traveling with me. Dolma Is a very different place. I do think there is a lot of good I can do to help the people living here though.

I've not had the time yet to get to know the royal family here, other than King Harold himself. As such, I have scarcely said more than a few words to my betrothed, but I suppose there will be plenty of time for that later. I have, on the other hand, spent a sizable amount of time with King Harold. He is an interesting man. I had a rather intense debate with him over wedding details. I'll have you know I won all the demands we decided on before I left, so don't worry Mother, your negotiation lesson did not go to waste.

Speaking of my wedding, it will take place in three months time. King Harold said that I can invite as many people as I wish, so please get together a list of everyone who can come. I'd love to see all of you, and as many knights, nobles, and friends who wish to come. I'll send you more details once I have them.

The palace is far bigger than I could have imagined. We've also been given a whole section of the building just for our own personal use. It's still all very new, and I've only really been here for a few hours, so it's hard to make any solid judgments yet.

Until I can see you again, know I am safe, healthy, and eager to learn more about this new world around me. I miss you all, very much. I send you all my love from Dolma.

Love,
Avalynn

I did not lie in my letter, but it wasn't exactly an honest representation of my thoughts about Dolma. Still, I wasn't ready to trouble my family with my worries so soon upon my arrival.

Instead, I sealed both letters and turned to the documents Ana had received from a castle butler. The contents were truly shocking. I was still staring at them, when Ana came to get me for our group meeting.

"Did we not get a lot?" Ana I asked, looking worried as she approached my desk.

"No, no, I can safely say that too little money is not the problem," I said, snapping out of my reverie and handing her the document.

"200,000 gollups!" Ana yelped.

"Per year," I added.

"And this is just for your personal use?" Ana asked in astonishment. "You could feed and house a small city with this kind of money! Well, at least you know that Dolma is rich."

"With this kind of discretionary funds, it makes me wonder why Solista and Chanti live the way they did."

"Oh," said Ana, looking back at me with wide eyes.

"No matter," I sighed. "We will have to investigate some more, but the money will be useful, for now. I haven't worked out salaries for everyone yet, I was distracted by the amount we were given. It won't take long though, so please tell everyone I'll be down in fifteen minutes."

"Yes Crown Princess," Ana said, returning the papers to my desk and moving out of the room.

I took slightly longer than anticipated to write down the budget, and then to write it out three more times so that Lucy, Galileo, and Ana could each have a copy. I hurried as best I could and soon I was grabbing my makeshift budgets and the letters and heading downstairs.

"Okay, as Ana may have already told you, we have been given an incredibly large budget," I said as soon as I reached the large sitting room. "As such, I've made everyone salaries just a little higher than they would have been in Nevremerre."

"Thank you, Crown Princess," Mateo smiled at me.

I gave him a quick smile back before continuing, "I made copies of all the salaries I am willing to pay, as well as your specific salaries, and beyond that, I have written a budget for you three," I said, handing a copy to Lucy, Ana, and Galileo. "For Ana, this is my estimated annual expense for managing the household and staff. You should have budgets for wages, food, supplies, repairs, decor changes, and an overflow in case of emergency. This was done with my thoughts about the household size, so if you need more funds, please let me know where my calculations were short, and by how much."

"This all looks like more than enough," Ana replied, going over my report.

"Still, let me know if that changes."

"Yes, Crown Princess."

"Moving on-"

"Wait, Crown Princess!" Solista cried out, "I think you're making a mistake!"

"Oh, did I not give enough money to something?" I asked, looking through the papers in my hand.

"No, no – my salary! It's too much!"

"That is a terrible thing to say to your employer," Lucy clicked. "You should take as much as is offered to you, and demand more if you deserve it."

"She's right,"I said. "Your past employer was woefully under-paying you. As a lady's maid to Lady Lucy, 150 gollups per year is a perfectly reasonable salary."

"But, I think even the palace butlers get paid less!" Solista argued back.

I had to smile. It was a testament to how comfortable she felt with us that she even argued at all. "I'm sure that can't be right. If the palace has the funds to give me 200,000 gollups a year, then it has enough to pay its butlers a competitive salary. Either way, that is your salary and I will not pay any person in my employ less than they deserve."

Solista stared at me before whispering, "Thank you, Your Highness."

"Of course. Now on to Galileo, for the knights' budget-" I continued with my description of the budget for my knights and Lady-in-Waiting, making sure my initial calculations ap-peared accurate for all of their needs before I begin with my budget related conclusions.

"I will have a 2,000 gollup discretionary budget and I plan to give Chanti a gollup a month for her discretionary spending and of course hiring a tutor for her as well. That leaves-"

"Chanti's getting money too!?" Solista asked.

"Yes, and a tutor," I said, wondering if I'd skipped a sentence in my previous speech.

"But you're already giving me a salary!"

"Yes, of course, you work here."

"But that's too much!"

"Sweetheart, you really need to stop turning down money when people who can afford it offer it to you," Lucy sighed. Solista blushed at her words.

"It is as she says," I said kindly to her, "I have more than enough money. One gollup for your sister is something that I can easily afford."

"Okay then, Your Highness," Solista said, still blushing from Lucy's words.

"As I was saying," I moved forward in the conversation, eager to get to my next point. "After all the budget allocations, we still have a remainder of 158,160 gollups. I would like to use this amount to support projects and charities to help the people of Dolma. Obviously, I will have to do some research as to where this money can be of best use, but I would appreciate it if you all could keep an ear to the ground about possible projects or charities we can help build or strengthen."

"Yes Crown Princess," said the chant of the people around me.

"Good, now I just want to briefly touch upon my meeting with the King, and the relevance to all of you." I shared with them the current details of my wedding and the proposed wedding date. Although he most certainly wouldn't need it, I also shared with Abel my observations about the King's personality. In return, Abel told us about the many ambassadors he'd met and his block of accommodations. I was right in thinking he would be thrilled by his set up. He said he was "simply fascinated" by the ambassadors he'd met so far. And remarked that they all had their own "unique and original" thoughts on life, themselves, and Dolma. I could see in his eyes he was excited by the prospect of getting to know them all. And, since Dolma bordered many more countries than Nevremerre, there were a great many people to get to know.

After work was out of the way, we spent the rest of the afternoon chatting casually about the palace, the King, my betrothed, the ridiculous number of rooms, and other mundane nonsense. I gave Ana my letters to mail, and soon it was time to change into dinner clothes and prepare for another meal with the King. Unlike in Nevremerre, where noble banquets happen only once or twice a week in the summers, in Dolma, the whole Court gathered together for dinner every single night throughout the year. I can't say it was an event I was really looking forward to, and Oberon agreed it wasn't much fun when he recalled my father's journey. Still it was something I was required to attend as the new, or soon-to-be new, Crown Princess.

Before we could leave, Galileo reminded everyone that, from this night forward, whenever I left our rooms I was to be escorted by at least two knights. It felt a little overbearing and a tad ridiculous, but I knew better than to argue. This was, after all, one of the few orders that Father and Queen Anora gave before my departure. Tonight, Oberon and Mateo would guard me. Lucy and the other knights would join the banquet as guests. With that all decided, I let Ana and Miri take me to my bedroom to prepare for the evening ahead.

Chapter 8

The Jobless Nobles

I should have been nervous. I should have been terrified as Ana slipped me into a flowing gown of blue and gold, and Miri let my now curly hair flow loose behind me. I should have been quaking in my golden slippers, but I wasn't. Cowering in fear had never been my style. Perhaps, if I had been weak, fearful, and quiet, as many thought I ought to be, my time in Dolma would have been easier. But there is never any long-term joy to be found in being something you're not. So, I was confident, proud, and self-assured as I followed the palace servants to the Grand Banquet Hall. For me, this was no different than being in Nevremerre, after all, I had attended a great many noble banquets before. Perhaps it should have been obvious; perhaps I should have realized it from that first initial knot in my stomach; or perhaps I should never have come at all, for after that first evening, it was very clear that Dolma wasn't like Nevremerre in the slightest.

The Grand Banquet Hall was marvelous as Mateo, Oberon, and I walked in. Marble columns decorated the sides with gilded ceilings and baseboards that sparkled in the candlelight of hundreds of golden chandeliers. Between the gaps of the marble columns stood beautiful paintings of people, buildings, nature, or all of the above. These paintings stretched from the floor to the ceiling. The beauty of it all caused me to gasp as we walked in, and I thought to myself that I could spend all night just staring at these paintings and enjoying this wonderful room. Then, my gaze turned toward all the people. Hundreds of eyes turned my way burning holes into every part of my body. I was used to the stares. People stare at royalty in every country, but, as I looked out at this massive sea of people, there was not one friendly face, not one kind eye, or even one reassuring smile. For the first time since coming to Dolma, I felt alone. I felt removed from the rest of the room, as if a glass wall was placed between us, and there was no hope of ever breaking through.

For just a moment, it sent a chill down my spine and held my breath hostage inside of my chest. They just don't know me yet, I soothed myself. Breathing deeply before smiling at the waiting crowd. I moved into the room, and waited. By this point in the halls of Nevremerre, I would already be surrounded by nobles, all of whom were eager to engage in any sort of conversation with me. Father had told us that should we become the Crown Prince or Princess, this crowd would only grow. Now, in Dolma, I was curiously alone. No one approached me, but they all still watched me, whispering to each other.

It was uncomfortable, but, as Mother said, a ruler must always adapt and overcome. With this in mind I walked up to the nearest group of people and introduced myself. "Good evening, I am Princess Avalynn. May I ask your names?" I smiled at the group of gentlemen before me, just now realizing the curious lack of women in their group. In fact, as I did a quick glance around the room, I noticed that the groups were all segregated into groups of just men or just women. This would make things very difficult for the ungendered, I thought in passing. In front of me, the gentleman bowed.

"Princess Avaynn," they said before announcing their names and titles. Lord Bertram Wimberly Knotsen, Lord Amerton Cassiel Ramberry, and Lord Marxton Kneebly Eloriamen, I was told. I had to run the names through in my head several times in order to commit them all to memory. I really did not want to judge, but the sheer amount of names the people in Dolma had was beginning to get just a tad tiresome. Still, I smiled at them and tried to carry on a conversation.

"It's a pleasure to meet you, my Lords. Which regions in Dolma do you rule over?" Lord Amerton snorted into his wine.

"We are courtiers, Princess Avalynn," Lord Bertram supplied haughtily. "We don't rule over any land," he finished, rather condescendingly.

I, however, was not raised to be rude, so I simply continued my line of questioning, "Oh, I see, and what is your role in court then?"

"We are courtiers, that is what we do, Princess Avalynn," Lord Marxton said, looking a little confused.

"Yes, I understand that, Lord Marxton Kneebly Elotiaman. I am attempting to ascertain what the job of a courtier entails."

"It's to be a courtier. What else is there?" Lord Bertram responded again, still in his same condescending tone of voice. I briefly marveled at the ability to sound so superior after having just given such a stupid answer.

"My lords," I said, trying not to let the frustration leave through my voice. "What is it that you do at court each day? What is your job? And please don't say to be a courtier."

"We are nobles, Princess Avalynn," Lord Amerton said. "We don't have jobs, those are for the common folk." His voice also reeked with superiority and entitlement. It was, without a doubt the worst conversation I've ever had, yet, foolishly, I pushed forward, needing to address the insane claims of Lord Amerton. There was so very much wrong with his statement, it took me a second to decide where to start.

"Lord Amerton Cassiel Ramberry, what do you think the King does if not a job?"

"The King is a title, obviously," Lord Amerton laughed at me.

"A title that comes with responsibilities. Does the King not have to guard the land, command armies, manage the country's finances, negotiate treaties, and look after the best interests of its citizens? Is that not work?" The three Lords stared at me for a while. Identical looks of surprise on their faces they thought over my words.

"Well he can't have a job, he's the King," Lord Bertram said, recovering first. "Jobs are for commoners."

"But he does manage the land, and he does make treaties," Lord Marxton said, still looking a little dumbfounded as he thought, "and he must manage money too as he pays us and the palace staff."

"Marx!" Lord Amerton exclaimed, "the King does not have a job!"

"Excuse me, but Lord Marxton Kneebly Elotiaman just said that you get paid by the King, so wouldn't that mean you have a job as well?" I asked, and the three of them just stared at me once more.

"No, no, we are paid to be courtiers, that's not a job," Lord Bertram declared confidently.

"And he pays the butler to be a butler. I'm not so sure I understand the difference," I said.

"But we don't know what a butler does!" Lord Amerton declared.

"Well yes, of course, because your title isn't butler, it's courtier." Although I was still unsure of what exactly a courtier did. "The King pays for the butler to be a butler and for the courtier to be a courtier, and they are both jobs."

"But we are nobles! Nobles don't have jobs!" Lord Bertram said frantically.

I stared at him in disbelief. "Lord Bertram Wimberly Knotsen, there is no law in Dolma that says nobles can't have a job. The King, as well as any nobles that manage an area of land, have responsibilities and tasks they must do, and you, and the other courtiers, get paid to fill a role at court. These things are the very definition of a job. Having a job is a very important thing in any community, so I am unsure why you would so adamantly deny being in a position to bring so much value and good to the Dolmanian society." I finished with a small encouraging smile. I honestly did hope that they would understand that they must have some job and that jobs were very important, but there was also a part of me wondering why these gentlemen were at court. The King did not seem like the type of man who would easily suffer the company of idiots.

The three men continued to stare at me for a long while. Thankfully, some laughter behind me caught my attention, and I was able to excuse myself from the still silent men. I turned instead to a group of laughing women. "Good evening, I am Princess Avalynn." One of the women snorted as I said my name. "Might I know what's so amusing?" I asked, genuinely curious. There was laughter amongst the women once more. They all glanced around at each other before one stepped towards me. She had light red hair that seemed to be peppered in with some blond. Her hair was wrapped in an elaborate sort of updo, but, while it looked nice, it looked awfully heavy. A small part of me was worried it was simply going to fall off her head.

"Well you see, Princess Avalynn," giggles came from around her companions once more. "We were just wondering what you might have done to startle all your companions so much. My theory is they finally realized that you've come down in your nightdress." Laughter peeled from the ladies around her, before they hid their faces behind a sea of hand fans. The occasional giggle peeking through.

It took me a few seconds to realize what they were talking about. Of course, I knew they were trying to be rude, but as I looked down at their outfits, I couldn't find it in me to be offended. If I had to wear their overly large dresses, I was sure to be annoyed too. The ladies in front of me wore massive dresses with large puffy sleeves and even larger skirts. In fact, the women had to space themselves several feet apart because their dresses wouldn't allow them to get any closer together.

It had to be terribly difficult just to have a conversation. As seemed to be the norm in Dolma, the woman all appeared to have a whole chest of jewelry on each of them. I could hear Mama in my head clicking her tongue and pointing out that they would have a very hard time moving if they were ever attacked.

"I see, well in Nevremerre, we value comfort and mobility in our clothing. If you would like to try one on, I will be happy to have one made for you." I thought this was a rather nice offer, but they all looked a little disappointed at my words. Probably because I didn't respond to their taunts, I realized belatedly.

"Right. Well, Princess Avalynn, we should introduce ourselves. I am Lady Sabine Rosella Countenberg," the red-haired woman said. The rest of the ladies followed, each with their own equally long name.

"It's a pleasure to meet you," I said, again rehearsing everyone's name in my mind. I was about to ask what their jobs at court were, but, fearing a repeat of my last conversation, I stopped myself.

Fortunately, unlike my last companions, the women in front of me were more than happy to continue the conversation. Or, more accurately, the lady in front of me, as Lady Sabine was the only one of the group to do any actual talking. "You know, Princess Avalynn, it is so weird that you have just one name. Here in Dolma the higher in status you are, the more names you have, so the only people with just one name are," she paused to let the laughter of the other women be heard. "commoners!" she finished, her delighted smile showing on her face for just a moment before she hid her mouth with her fan.

Again, I was sure this was an insult, the tone of her voice in the laughter of those around her confirmed it, but, once again, I couldn't understand what the insult was. I was also a little dismayed by the number of nobles who seem to be belittling commoners, as if they would be able to maintain any semblance of nobility without them. To be honest, I could find no insult in her words, so I simply said, "Thank you for that information. I did not know that piece of Dolmanian history. I can understand how my single name would be odd to you."

Lady Sabine frowned once more. I got the sense that she was growing angry at my lack of response. I couldn't for the life of me figure out why she wanted to insult me in the first place, but I also didn't really care. After all, there's not much you can do about people who dislike you before they even get to know you. I decided my next step would be to leave the conversation, however, right as I was about to move to do so, I saw Lady Sabine's opposite hand move. In her other hand, she'd grabbed a glass of wine that she was clearly intending to throw at me. However, I was trained to be a knight, trained by, very possibly, the best knights in the continent, and I was wearing a very movable dress, so I simply just stepped aside.

The red wine fell onto the floor with a loud splash. Lady Sabine looked shocked as her wine failed to hit any target. "I had assumed that manners were something that were taught in Dolma. Apparently, I was wrong, so I will tell you this, Lady Sabine Rosella Countenberg. It is very rude to throw wine at people," I didn't say this condescendingly or harshly. I simply gave her this information casually as one would tell you about the weather or their second favorite kind of pie.

Nevertheless, Lady Sabine looked infuriated, and she stormed right up to me, or as far as her dress would allow.

"You'll never be good enough for him. Thomas will never choose you! You're nothing more than a foreign Princess," she hissed at me.

"That doesn't really seem like a problem though," I said, a little confused. Lady Sabine gave a frustrated scream before storming off, stepping into the puddle of red wine, and successfully drawing the attention of those few in the room who were not already looking at us.

"Getting into fights already, Crown Princess?" came the joking voice of Sir Abel.

"Apparently, but to be honest I'm not really sure what I did." Oberon snorted behind me. I turned around to find both him and Mateo struggling to contain their laughter. I smiled at them both and gave a little eyebrow wiggle, which caused both of them to lose their composure and let out hearty laughs.

"You both better not be abandoned in your duties or goofing around," came the stern voice of Galileo. Oberon and Mateo shot up to attention, although they still let out a few stray giggles.

"It was a deserved laugh," Oberon insisted, although he looked far more serious now.

"Just make sure your focus is on the Crown Princess," said Galileo, "and I look forward to hearing about the cause of your laughter later." It was a bigger relief than I could say to once again be surrounded by the familiar smiling faces of my friends, but Dolma was not a place where we could walk and talk freely, and we all had duties to attend to. My duties came in at that moment. The royal family was greeted by the bows and curtseys of all of the guests. They made an impressive sight as they all walked in together, although I can't say any of them looked very happy.

King Harold walked my way and announced that dinner was ready. He escorted me to where several large tables had been set up. Ours was a smaller table that bridged two large ones, leaving us in the center of the Grand Banquet Hall. When we reached the table, Harry whispered in my ear, "You'll be seated by my son tonight, Ava, but I'm looking forward to hearing your thoughts on everything tomorrow." I smiled and nodded as he showed me to a seat at the far end of the small table. To my left sat Crown Prince Thomas, then Harry, then Queen Priscella, and finally Princess Ollifelle. There was no one to my right. In fact, now that I was sitting down, the one sided table at the head of the room where we sat was wildly uncomfortable; it gave way for every other soul in the area to stare at us unhindered. It also meant that my only talking companion was Crown Prince Thomas, and I wasn't all that convinced of his conversational skills.

Soon enough, food was brought and it was time to eat. Somewhat reluctantly, I turned to my dining companion, and started a conversation. "I don't think I've had the formal chance to introduce myself yet. I am Avalynn."

Silence.

"I hope that we can get along well."

Silence.

"I noticed this afternoon that you didn't appear to have any thoughts on the wedding. Are you sure that you don't have any preferences about how or when we get married?"

Silence.

"Are you perhaps hard-of-hearing?" I guessed.

"What, no! I was ignoring you," Crown Prince Thomas replied quickly, whipping his head around to look at me.

"Er, why?"

"Because I don't like you," he said, turning his face forward once more.

"I'm sorry I was under the impression that you were 21 or older."

"I'm 23," he responded a bit indignantly.

"Then why are you behaving like you're 8?"

"What?!" he said, whipping around to face me once more.

"Well the silent treatment is rather juvenile, don't you think? I've always been taught that adults communicate with words. The last time I used the silent treatment I was, maybe 12?" Crown Prince Thomas stared at me, so I just kept talking, "It's fine if you don't like me, but we still are getting married, so we should at least be able to communicate with each other in a civil manner." As seemed to be the theme for Dolmanian men this evening, Crown Prince Thomas just continued to stare at me.

Finally he spoke, "But, I don't want to marry you."

"You're not exactly my first choice either," I deadpanned. "So I'll tell you what, if you can manage to convince your father to accept the treaty with Nevremerre without having us marry, I will happily go back home, but since that seems unlikely to happen, we should probably try to get along, Crown Prince Thomas."

There was another long silence, and I had just about resigned myself to a quiet evening when a soft voice spoke from beside me, "Thomas, you can just call me Thomas."

"Then let's get along, Thomas," I smiled at him. Thomas nodded.

"Princess Avalynn," Harry's voice rang out from next to Thomas. "You will need to meet with the Queen tomorrow to go over staffing options."

"Thank you King Harold, I've already set aside a budget and I look forward to getting Queen Priscella's input." Harry's eyes sparkled and a rather sinister look came over his face.

"I'm sure you will," he said with a rather disconcerting smirk.

I filed this look away, leaning across the table to speak with Queen Priscella. "When and where should I meet you tomorrow, Queen Priscella?"

Queen Priscella huffed, "Around 10 at my rooms, I should think. Yours may be a bit too small for my taste."

"All right then," I smiled. "I appreciate your help in this matter."

Dinner was a large affair, with no fewer than 12 courses and wine refilled constantly. I watched as the court got drunker and drunker until the room looked more like an extravagant party as opposed to a meeting of the most powerful people in the country. The only sober people being the royal family, my party, and, rather noticeably, the group of foreign ambassadors at the far end of the table. A queasy feeling hit my stomach as I watched the foreign ambassadors. Dolma had many neighbors, and from my discussions with Queen Anora, it seemed like very few, if any, would be considered close allies. It seemed very dangerous to let nobles indulge in such excess, right where their potential enemies have planted people waiting to expose their secrets. But, no one in the Royal family seemed very concerned, choosing instead to eat their meal in relative silence, ignoring the increasing ruckus of those around them.

Soon King Harold stood and signaled the end of the banquet. However, this was apparently not the end of the evening as a large crowd of nobles moved instead to another set of large rooms filled with more alcohol and tables filled with cards and other games. A Gambling Hall, I realized. Anora had told me it was a common pastime in Dolma, but I had never seen one before. Both Nevremerre and Agremerre had strict rules about gambling, so Gambling Halls were few and far between. It was overwhelming, the decadence that surrounded me as nobles filtered into the rooms, sitting down at the tables with large bags full of gollups, getting glasses of colorful cocktails, and picking up plates of sweets that towered above the wandering people.

"You don't have to stay here," a voice said beside me. I turned to see Thomas standing next to me. "In fact, father has a rule that we aren't allowed to stay longer than an hour, and you'll never see him in here. Although I suppose he hasn't given the same rule to you. Be warned, most nobles will stay all night," with that, Thomas walked into the room.

I stood in the doorway a little longer before turning to leave. Behind me I heard Mateo and Oberon walking. "I'm sorry, you didn't get a chance to stay, but I'm not sure I could have stayed in there for very long," I said, wandering through the empty halls.

"You forget, Crown Princess, we've been here before. We've already seen the Gambling Hall. It was not something we were interested in," Mateo said reassuringly, moving to walk beside me.

"Yes, it's hard to forget those "The Dark Side of Gambling" lectures from school," Oberon agreed, also moving to my side.

"In Nevremerre, those were called "Gambling's Moose," Mateo said.

"Moose is a term in gambling that refers to a bad hand," laughed Oberon, "Your lecture title was a pun!"

"Yes, it was actually King Edgar's idea to change it," I smiled as I thought of my father, "He thought learning should be more fun."

"Those lectures were about how gambling masters used to cheat people out of all their money and leave them starving and homeless out on the street!" Oberon exclaimed.

"Yes, but they had a very fun title," Mateo said, causing us all to laugh. We walked in silence for a little bit longer before I stopped and looked at my guards.

"Does anyone know where we're going?"

Chapter 9

The Good Gossip

They did not, and we spent the next ten minutes aimlessly wandering before we found a maid who was able to point us in the right direction. It took another 30 minutes, but we did, eventually, find our rooms.

When we entered, Galileo and Abel were already sitting on the couches, telling an excited Solista, Chanti, and Ana about the evening. "How can anyone eat that much food?" questioned Ana, as Chanti said, "Oh how magical!"

"I have no idea," I responded to Ana. "I was full by the second course. And the hall was beautiful. You'll have to go see it sometime, but make sure to take one of us with you so you don't get lost."

"It's a wonder they aren't all rolling around," Leonard commented, walking in with Hugo.

"They can't eat like that all the time," I said while Galileo asked, "Where is Lady Lucy?"

"She's with Challa. She said something about wanting to get more information, but I'm sure she'll be back soon. I'd be surprised if anyone could stay in the Gambling Hall for long," Hugo responded.

Meanwhile, Mateo turned to me and said, "I don't know, Crown Princess, they ate like that when King Edgar was here as well. It may be normal for them."

"That sounds like such a waste of food!" said Ana.

"They're nobility," Solista shrugged as if that explained everything.

"So? That's no reason to be wasteful," Ana said.

"According to the Crown Prince, some nobles stay there all night," I said, circling back to Hugo's statement.

"You spoke with the Crown Prince!" Solista and Chanti said.

"What did you think of him?" Ana asked anxiously, and all eyes turned to me.

"Well," I said, not entirely sure how to describe my weird truce with Thomas. "He doesn't seem unreasonable. He doesn't seem very fond of this arranged marriage, so that makes it difficult to begin any sort of relationship. But, we will have plenty of time."

"Oh," said Chanti, looking disappointed, and, though I wasn't looking for anything from Thomas, I felt her disappointment in my heart as well. It would have been nice if Thomas and I had a better start. However, I cheered myself up, this was not necessarily a bad start; I had, after all, gotten him to talk to me in the end. Perhaps we could grow a solid friendship. And, if not, hopefully we would have a neutral relationship where everyone was heard and neither would have a chance to get hurt.

"I have news," Lucy called, flinging the doors open and leaving a rather panicked Challa rushing to follow her.

"What's your news?" I asked, smiling. I sat down on one of the sofas and took off my shoes.

"Prepare yourself, there's a lot," Lucy said, falling down next to me and throwing her feet on my lap.

"Don't get your dirty shoes on the Crown Princess' dress," Ana scolded, moving to remove Lucy's feet from my person herself. Lucy groaned, but righted it herself and took off her own shoes before she began.

"Let's start with the obvious, the Dolmanians - wait - what are you still doing up? Shouldn't you be in bed?" Lucy paused, looking at Chanti.

"She's 13, and it's our first night here. It'll be fine for one night, now finish what you were saying," I said, urging her on.

"Fine. As I was saying, the Dolmanians are quite rude, and seem to have a rather inflated sense of self," Lucy said seriously.

"Well that comment seemed rude as well," I pointed out.

"It's the truth, you can't say it's rude when it's true. You can't tell me you haven't noticed it," Lucy argued.

I couldn't really say anything because I had most definitely noticed it. "The staff are, in general, pretty nice," Ana said thoughtfully, and Solista and Chanti nodded in agreement.

"True," Lucy agreed. "The courtiers then. From what I learned, all the nobles here at the palace are courtiers, and none of them have managed a territory."

"Did you ever find out what a courtier does?" I interrupted. "I know they get paid by the King, but I had the hardest time figuring out what their job was."

"From what I can tell their job is just eating, drinking, and gambling," Lucy said, wrinkling her nose.

"That's not a job," Leonard pointed out.

"Exactly, I'll have to look into it more," Lucy agreed. "Anyways there's a definite variety of people at court, although visually, they all look the same."

"How so?" Ana asked.

"They're all white," Lucy pointed out. I was startled to realize that this observation was completely true. I noticed Galileo, Leonard, and Hugo all look slightly shocked by the announcement as well.

"I hadn't even noticed! That's insane," I pointed out.

"How can you possibly manage to get an all-white group of nobles?" Leonard asked.

"To get this many people to look the same, it had to have been partially a deliberate choice," Abel I said seriously. "Crown Princess, as you make your changes, of which I now believe many will be required, please keep this lack of diversity in mind."

"Yes, I promise," I said earnestly.

"Don't be too worried about it, Crown Princess, there are many here who won't give you the opportunity to forget about the lack of diversity," Lucy said with a smile. "Now, as I was saying, while there is little variety in looks, there's a large variety in intelligence levels. Many of the Dolmanian courtiers seem rather stupid."

"I noticed that," I said thinking back to the Lords I spoke with this evening.

"Yes, but, importantly, not all of them are that way. I think I'll put together a list of the more cunning ones," Lucy said, more to herself than any of us. "Now," she said, her voice directed at us once more. "Most of the court believes that the Crown Princess has no power. This is for a multitude of reasons. The first being, as the Crown Princess said this afternoon, they do not know or believe the Crown Princess is still a competitor for the Nevremerre throne."

"This is no longer true for the ambassadors. They did originally believe this to be the case, but were corrected by the Agremerrian ambassador as well as myself," Abel interjected.

"Be warned, Crown Princess, I believe many will try and approach you."

"Thank you, Sir Abel," I said, thinking quietly to myself for a moment. "I don't believe we should inform anyone else about my contention for the Nevremerre throne just yet. I'd like to know more about Dolma before we get into discussions about the possibility of my ruling over another country. I don't mind people discovering it, or the ambassadors knowing, but I don't believe it's information we should be giving away just yet," I said after awhile.

"Yes Crown Princess," said a chorus of voices within the room.

"I agree with you, Crown Princess, although for slightly different reasons," Lucy said, nodding at me, "but, that's not the only reason they believe you are powerless. Apparently, the rooms given to us are smaller than what would be expected for a Crown Princess. As such it is believed you don't have the King's favor." I nodded, now understanding the Queen's comment from dinner. "They also have assumed that you received a "standard Princess's salary" of 50,000 gollups. Of course your actual salary is the same as the Crown Prince. They take your assumed "lack of funds" as another sign you have no power."

"How is 50,000 gollups considered a lack of funds?" I asked in astonishment, well aware that even 50,000 gollups would more than cover my household budget, and a good part of Lady Lucy's budget as well.

"I agree," Lucy smirked, "and even that is far more than what any of them make. Although many seem to gamble their money away. I'll have to look into that more too," she mumbled to herself again. "But, Crown Princess, I don't think you should disclose your funding either. It's fine if the court discovers it on their own, but I believe it's best to keep this to ourselves for now."

"All right then," I replied, not having any arguments against her idea, and trusting Lucy's judgment.

Lucy smiled at me, "Now, finally, for the last bit of gossip. The Crown Prince has a lover!"

"What?!" came shocked voices from various parts of the room.

"How could he?!" Chanti asked, "He's supposed to be marrying you, Crown Princess!"

"It's an arranged marriage," I said, smiling at Chanti. "He'd never met me before today, so it makes sense that he could have already been in a relationship with somebody else." And, I added mentally, it would make more sense as to why he opposed the marriage his father had arranged.

"Queen Anora was adamant that it's illegal for you to have a lover," Mateo said, looking upset, "How can he have one?"

"Perhaps because we are not yet married, or perhaps because it's a rule that's not really enforced. It is awfully difficult to control one's heart after all. I will never begrudge him for having loved," I said honestly.

"Hmm, still Crown Princess, I would hold off on a lover of your own until we know more," Abel said, looking grave.

"Sir Abel, you yourself had said how much work needs to be done in Dolma, when am I supposed to find the time to gain a lover?" I asked. Abel just shrugged, but his smile took over his face once more. "Anyway, did you get any information on who his lover is? It would be nice if we could all get along," I said, looking back at Lucy.

"That might be difficult, Crown Princess, I've heard you've already met her. It's Lady Sabine Rosella Countenberg."

"Her!" Mateo and Oberon explained at the exact same time.

"Well that explains a lot," I said simply.

"She was awful, how can the Crown Prince possibly like her?" Mateo questioned with a bit of disgust.

"She was probably just mean to me because I am marrying the man she loves," I said, dismissing his words.

"You're far too nice, Crown Princess," Oberon said, shaking his head.

"Nice is a good thing!" I insisted. A look passed through my party and they all seem to come to some unspoken agreement. I gave a little huff of annoyance at them before turning back to Lucy. "How did you manage to get all of this information in just one evening?" I asked, impressed by her detective skills.

"Oh it was easy!" Lucy said with a smile. "After all, once they got drunk they would just tell me whatever I wanted to know!"

"Which wasn't always a good thing," Challa jumped in, "some of them were extremely rude."

"Yes, yes, it was probably a good thing I had one of the knights there, but I did get a lot of good information," Lucy said triumphantly, apparently unfazed by the rude remarks she had received. "You should try interrogating drunk people sometime, Crown Princess, you learn a lot."

"I'm not sure it's really my style," I confessed.

"That's true," Lucy agreed. "but that's why you have me!" she beamed at me.

"Speaking of alcohol," Galileo jumped in. "I will not try to crush your enjoyment of your free time, but do remember that everyone here represents and has confidential knowledge of the Crown Princess. If you choose to drink, please be cautious of the location and the quantity of your drink."

"Yes Sir," came a chorus of voices around me.

"Right, with that all done, I think it's time for bed," I instructed, moving to get up. "I need to be up at 8:30 tomorrow to be at the Queen's residence by 10," I said to Ana.

"Yes Crown Princess," Ana agreed.

"Hugo, Challa, you will escort the Crown Princess tomorrow," ordered Galileo, "The rest of you will be training with me."

There were nods from the surrounding knights, "I will probably be too busy tomorrow, but I will join you for training someday soon," I informed Galileo.

The older knight brightened immediately, "That would be wonderful, Crown Princess!" he said, while Mateo and Leonard nodded.

I smiled at them all. "Sleep well everyone. Sir Abel, do you need a room for the evening, or will you be all right to find your room again?"

"I can go get a servant to lead you back to your room if that's what you desire," Solista offered. In the end, that's what Abel decided to do, and we all went off to our new rooms. Ana and the newly arrived Miri got me ready for bed. Miri, like Lucy, also arrived with news, but we agreed it could wait till the morning. I was soon sliding into my new bed, bidding my maids goodnight.

It was a long day, so I fell asleep quickly. I woke in the morning, and, in a half asleep state, was convinced that I was back in my bed in Nevremerre. That I'd open my eyes and see my brown brick walls, my wooden bed, my table and dresser, Ana's and Charlotte's smiling faces. That I'd walk down stairs to my family at breakfast. I opened my eyes with a smile, only to find that I was not in Nevremerre at all. There was an ache in my chest I've never felt before as I looked around an unfamiliar room and remembered just how far away my family was. It was easy enough to push away those feelings as I got myself out of bed, but it still haunted me, like an echo in my soul that threatened to return with a vengeance should I ever allow it. I, however, was far too busy to ever let that happen.

Miri was the first to come in that morning, apparently she'd let Ana sleep in as an apology for not being around much yesterday, but I suspected she was also looking to have a more private chat with me. My suspicion was correct as Miri immediately launched into a detailed description of Dolma's current financial state. It was grim, to say the least. The palace, at least, was not missing any funds, however, the nobles were drowning in debts. It seemed those Gambling Hall events were more destructive on the nobility than even I had expected, and had left many in debt. Miri had also discovered that the King had recovered many losses left behind by Dolma's previous rulers, however, he rarely invested it back into the general public. Miri described it as doing the bare minimum to avoid revolts. She also said the palace staff was being significantly underpaid by Nevremerre standards, but that the staff didn't seem to realize. She attributed it to the fact that many of them were paid discreetly by courtiers and nobles to spy on other courtiers and nobles.

"Gods Miri, how could you find all this out in just a day?"

"Little, sweet, harmless, old ladies get all the gossip. Not to worry, Crown Princess, with me in your corner you will never be out of the loop." I wanted to point out that she was none of the things she just mentioned, at least to my knowledge, but I did have to admit she was currently doing a rather impressive imitation.

"Between you and Lady Lucy I'm sorted," I said with a smile.

"Not so," Miri responded seriously. "You could still use a few more people like us, but we'll take care of finding them for you. For now, just tell me what information you need, and I'll get it."

"All right then," I said, a little taken aback by the extensive spy network Miri believed that I required. "To begin with, King

Harold is getting me information about Dolma's agricultural system, can you make sure I'm getting a complete and accurate agricultural budget, as well as information on the current agricultural Minister, if Dolma has such a thing?"

"Of course, Crown Princess," Miri beamed at me.

"Am I asking for too much?" I asked, suddenly unsure of myself.

"Oh no, Crown Princess. In fact you can even ask much more of me, but you will learn more of this in time," Miri responded, and I was suddenly struck by the sensation of being a child taking classes with Mother once more. I could only nod in response. "Crown Princess," Miri continued "I will be there to serve you in the mornings, when you prepare for dinner, and to get you ready for bed in the evenings, but I will best serve you and other places during the time in between."

"That's understandable," I nodded. "Do what you need to, I will hire another maid to assist Ana in the meantime."

"Crown Princess," Miri said, looking straight into my eyes, "it is vital that you allow me to do background checks on all the staff here before you invite them into our area."

"I - of course, if you wish it," I said, caught off-guard by her intensity.

"I do, now turn around, I have to finish your hair." Again shocked by the abrupt change of tone, I simply did as she asked. While I trusted her information and loyalty, I didn't really feel like I had a solid grasp of Miri as a person quite yet.

Chapter 10

The Dueling Knights

Breakfast was served in the dining room that was enclosed in my section of our little square. Most everyone joined, and I happily chatted with Lucy, Ana, Solista, Chanti, Hugo, and Challa over eggs, sausages, and scones. Miri had disappeared after dressing me, something which I now understood would be a regular occurrence. Galileo was taking the other knights for what had promised to be a rigorous morning training session. Both Hugo and Challa expressed secret relief that they had managed to avoid such a fate. Soon enough, I was being guided by a now map-equipped Hugo and an "entirely unhelpful commentator," Challa.

"I think you took the wrong map," Challa said, in a falsely helpful tone.

"I did not take the wrong map!" Hugo snapped back. "See we just have to take this hallway here, and eventually we'll pass Lord Segren Sorful Taserbee's room and the Queen's rooms are just a little beyond that," Hugo continued panting slightly as he purposefully strode down the never-ending halls, his map held out in front of him.

"But isn't Lord Sergen Sorful Taserbee's room down here," Challa asked, pointing to another spot on the map.

"What?" Hugo exclaimed, stopping so suddenly I nearly crashed into him. "No it isn't! Challa, that's not helpful!" Hugo said with ample frustration.

"Apologies," said Challa with a smile that suggested he was anything but apologetic. Hugo sighed and hurried forward once more. "He's usually so unflappable," Challa said to me with a smile, "How can I not tease him when he gets like this?" I laughed a little at this, but soon we were rushing after Hugo once more.

"There," said Hugo triumphantly, a little while later, "the rooms of the Queen."

"And we were only fifteen minutes late!" smiled Challa.

"Then next time, why don't you navigate," Hugo said, pushing the map back at Challa.

"And miss the show?" Challa asked, "Never!"

"Gentlemen," I called, as Hugo opened his mouth to argue back. "We really mustn't keep the Queen waiting any longer." This shut them both up as we turned to face the intricate painted wood door in front of us, beside it had a gold plaque like the one on my own door engraved with the Queen's many, many names. I did, however, note that she had one less name than the King, which I found curious given Lady Sabine's revelation that in Dolma name length equated to power.

Still, now was not the time to ponder as I knocked on the door, internally preparing apologies and excuses for my tardiness. Turns out I needn't have bothered, as when the footman answered the door he informed us that the Queen was still asleep, and escorted us to a nearby tea room. Unsure of what I was meant to do, I simply followed the man into the tea room and sat on the couch. The man gave a bit of a gasp when Hugo and Challa sat down with me, but he must have recovered quickly enough because when he came back in a few minutes he had three tea cups and was followed by a group of other footmen carrying trays of cakes and pastries, along with different varieties of teas. Each set down the tray on the table before us, carefully preparing each of our teas to our preference, before standing in front of us in a straight line, looking just above our heads.

It was unbelievably awkward, and eerily reminiscent of my first night in Dolma. Beside me, Challa picked up his tea trying his best not to spill anything, his large hands working carefully against the smaller cup. He took an echoing sip in the silent room before setting the tea down on his saucer with a large clatter. Hugo, on my other side, just looked terribly confused at the men standing before us. His tea stuck halfway between his saucer and his mouth.

"So," I said, clearing my throat in an attempt to break the silence, "what are your names?" I asked the row of footmen. There was a long silence. As the silence lengthened, some of the footmen would shoot curious looks down at me or at each other before staring back at the wall above us. Finally, the first footman we met spoke.

"Begging your pardon, Your Highness, but were you speaking to us?"

"Well yes," I said, once again questioning the Dolmanian education system, "I already know the names of my knights." The footmen jumped to give me their names before lapsing into another silence. For the next hour or so one of my knights, or I would try to break the silence with another question, the footmen would struggle to answer, and then we would lapse into silence once more before the cycle would repeat itself. Finally, the Queen joined us. I believe everyone in the room was relieved at her entrance.

"Why are your knights sitting down?" the Queen asked in lieu of greeting. We all stood up to bow and curtsey, but Hugo and Challa looked hesitant about sitting back down.

Personally, I chose to stand with them, asking the Queen curiously, "Why shouldn't they sit down, Your Majesty?"

"Because they're knights, of course!" Queen Priscella said, sitting down.

The three of us just stared at the Queen for a long moment, "They - they are still people," I finally stuttered. "and it's not physically healthy to stand all day."

"But they are knights," Queen Priscella said dismissively, "That's what they are trained for."

"Your Majesty, many studies have shown that consistently standing for hours on end can be detrimental to a person's back and joints. My knights are expected to guard me all day, which means it's my duty as their employer to see to it that they get appropriate amounts of rest whenever they are able. From a purely selfish point of view, it also means that my knights are more alert and less likely to injure themselves, if they have to move quickly and defend me, which is the purpose of keeping knights with me, is it not? Furthermore, while it is understandable that my knights would be required to stand while in your presence, if you so desired, you were not here, so it's perfectly reasonable for my knights to sit by me."

The Queen gave me a curious look, "Are you saying my knights may not be equipped to defend me since they stand all day?" Around her stood four tall men, each sparkling in full armor. It was not the first time I've noticed Dolma's penchant for keeping their knights in full armor all of the time, all members of the royal family did so. I couldn't help but find it a terribly poor defense plan.

"Forgive me, Your Majesty," Hugo interjected, giving the Queen a low bow, "but if you truly believe that you knights are unaffected, then perhaps you would agree to a duel, Sir Challa and myself versus all four of your knights."

The Queen raised her eyebrow at him and gave him a small scowl, but looked curiously at her knights. "Very well," she agreed, "but we have to do it now. It wouldn't do to give you extra time to prepare."

"Of course, Your Majesty," Challa bowed. With that, Queen Priscella made a sweeping motion with her hand and we all followed her out of the room. I was giddy as Queen Priscella expertly guided us through the halls. There was nothing like a good duel, and I was beyond excited to see the match. Queen Priscella's knights had fallen behind, forcing Queen Priscella and me to the front of our group. However, Queen Priscella made no attempt to talk with me as we made our silent march to the training grounds.

Like everything in Dolma's Royal Palace, the training grounds were huge. It wasn't a stretch of the imagination to say that one could train a whole army here and still have room to spare. However, despite the ample space, the grounds themselves were fairly empty, in fact, the greatest movement came from just four very familiar people. Around them about six or seven Dolmanian knights trained quietly on their own, or simply watched the rest of my knights train.

"Crown Princess!" Galileo called as we approached, halting the fighting, "and Her Majesty the Queen," he added with a bow mirrored by the rest of the people on the grounds.

"Hello!" I said, smiling at Galileo, "The knights look good!"

"Oh yes," Galileo replied, "it will be interesting to see where Hugo and Challa line up, but Oberon fits right in with the rest of us from Nevremerre. I'm thinking this area will be great for distance and endurance training, which is always a plus."

"And you found everything you need?"

"Absolutely. The training grounds are well-stocked, many of the supplies look to be in brand-new conditions, and the staff put all of our stuff away neatly and in easy to find places," Galileo nodded approvingly.

"Your sword is just there," Mateo smiled at me, pointing in the direction of the armory. I gazed in that direction longingly, wishing I had the time to train with them myself.

"Shouldn't we be getting along with it then," Queen Priscella said sharply behind me.

"Of course, Your Majesty," giving the confused Galileo and Mateo a smile.

"Clear the field then," Queen Priscella ordered, and my knights moved to the side lines. Beside me, Hugo and Challa appeared, swords already pulled from their belts.

"Don't worry, Crown Princess," Challa whispered to me, "We won't lose this fight."

"I never imagined you would," I said with a smile. "Be safe, keep your guard up, and use their armor to your advantage."

"Yes Crown Princess," they said as I walked towards Queen Priscella. She gave me a brief nod as I moved to stand next to her. The knights moved into position, four of the Queen's fully armored knights across from my two knights, who were armed with just their swords.

"Begin," Queen Priscella called out, her voice clean and crisp in the early fall air. The first clang of metal rang out, and the battle began.

Truth be told, the Queen's knights were not bad. Their movements were practiced and the basics were all there, with more consistent training, they all had the potential to become great knights. It was very clear, however, that they had no consistent training. The armor they wore made their movements slow and heavy, their attacks were uncoordinated and sloppy, and they may have had the very basics of technique, but they failed time and time again to follow through on any of their attacks and defenses.

Challa and Hugo, on the other hand, look like a well-oiled machine. They moved so fluidly and connectedly, you could be forgiven for thinking that they were reading each other's mind. Hugo's keen eyes picked up on the weaknesses of each opponent, and exposed them so Challa's raw strength could knock them down flat. They were experienced, collected, and strong, even outnumbered, they dominated the Dolmanian knights. Only 15 minutes later, all four of the Queen's knights were flat on the ground, and Challa and Hugo didn't even have the grace to look winded.

"Your knights have potential," I said to Queen Priscella, "but they could use some more training. My head knight runs a training session every morning. If you send your knights to him, he will improve their skills for you. I also don't recommend wearing full armor constantly." Queen Priscella stared at me, her mouth hanging slightly open.

"This is bullshit!" a voice came from behind me. I turned to see one of Queen Priscella's knights throwing his helmet at the ground. The knights around him looked at him in surprise as they picked themselves up off the ground. His face was pinched in frustration, a smattering of freckles covering his scowl, and an array of brown hair shot off in random directions as a result of his helmet. He stormed up to Challa angrily, forcing his way into Challa's space. "The only reason you won is because you're from some bullshit savage warmongering country that's never heard of civility a day in its' life. No doubt you are all just a bunch of filthy peasants only playing at nobility. You rotten bastards!" he yelled, spit flying into Challa's face.

I saw red. "How could anyone even dream of calling themselves noble when they can barely string together a few words without a curse, or a knight when they cannot act graciously in defeat?" I asked, stalking up to the man in question. "Also, "savage" countries and people would not have even granted you the luxury of standing back up after a fight. There are a million other things desperately wrong with what you have just said, but I'll focus on one. If you really believe that you only lost because my "warmongering knights" were just playing at nobility, then I will be your next opponent. And if you cannot beat a five foot four, 19 year old, Princess in a dress, then you will get on your hands and knees and beg for my knights' forgiveness and pray to all the Gods above that they, especially Sir Challa, forgive you for your behavior."

"What?" the knight said, stupidly.

"My sword, Sir Mateo."

"I can't fight a girl!"

"Then you can get on your knees and beg," I said, looking pointedly at the ground below us. The knight said nothing, and I felt Mateo hand me my sword. "Then prepare yourself."

The knight scowled at me, "If you're so desperate to play with the big boys, Princess," he scoffed, spitting out my title with contempt as he pulled his helmet back over his head, "then I won't go easy on you."

"Good," I said simply, waiting for him to get in position. "Now begin."

When I first debuted my fighting style against Mama, I was only eleven years old, and I could barely last five minutes against her. I was no longer a young girl though, and in the past eight years I had become a well-trained fighter who could consistently beat Mama, Al, and Azar in a duel. I was by no means perfect, but there had yet to be a knight who could defeat my unique style of fighting. After all, to win a fight one must first be able to land a blow.

The man barreled towards me the first chance he got, obvious in his movements, and blind in his fury. I really only had to step slightly to the side to dodge his blow and whack him sharply behind the head with the butt of my sword. A satisfying clanging sound rang through the training grounds. Perhaps I was blind and my anger too, for instead of knocking him to the ground as he desperately tried to recover from his shaking helmet, I simply waited for him to right himself so I could humiliate him all over again.

It was cruel, I realized 15 minutes later, watching him desperately try to swing at me with a crooked helmet and in the absolute wrong direction, light peels of laughter coming from the surrounding knights as he floundered, while I stood there without even a smear of mud on my emerald dress. Enough was enough, I decided, tripping him and sending his sword and helmet sprawling towards the other side of the training ground.

"Since you're already on your knees," I said, pointing my sword at the back of his head. "I do believe it's time to apologize."

"I'm sorry, Princess," he mumbled to the ground.

Fury ran through me once more. I grabbed his head and pulled him to his knees. "Not to me," I commanded, "to them," I finished, pointing at Challa and Hugo.

There was a bit of dazed fear in his eyes, that did manage to invoke a bit of my pity, but did not stop me from watching him turn towards Challa and Hugo, fold himself on the floor, and say, "I apologize Sirs for behaving badly and insulting you and your country."

I looked at Challa and Hugo waiting for their response. "Just don't do it again," Hugo shrugged.

Challa took a bit longer. "I will forgive you, provided you come to me once every three days for two months and dutifully study all that I teach you about Nevremerre and Agremerre." The knight stared at him before nodding slowly.

I turned back to Queen Priscella, who looked not to have moved since the first duel, still standing there with her mouth slightly open. "You will see to it that he attends, correct, Your Majesty." I said, rather than asked her.

This seemed to be enough to shake her out of her stupor, as she nodded back at me in the affirmative. "Yes, yes I will."

"Sir Galileo, see to it this knight gets seen to by a doctor," I sighed, before turning back to the Queen once more. "Shall we return to your rooms, Your Majesty?" The Queen nodded, and we walked silently back through the halls of Dolma's Royal Palace.

It was still silent as we walked back into the tea room we had been in before, however, the Queen did instruct all the knights to sit down. This was a minor victory. In truth, I had begun to feel guilty about lashing out at the knight before. I didn't regret fighting him, but I should have ended it immediately instead of waiting for him to get up. Mother had always said that the longer an attack lasted, the more chance for you to get hurt. Revenge attacks are usually not the best long-term strategies.

Going over staffing with Queen Priscella was fairly mundane compared to the battle we just participated in, but it was important. Soon we had given ads to the Queen's butler to post to the castle staff and around the capital looking for applicants. The Queen was surprisingly vocal during these instructions and freely gave her opinions on qualities I should be looking for in each position. Approximately one hour later we were finished with her instructions and I was told to report to the King's rooms for lunch. Before I could leave, however, the Queen pulled me to the side. "You are lacking in your knowledge of Dolma's edict and culture. I will send you some books to read on the subject and you will come here every other morning to learn from me."

"Thank you, Your Majesty," I said, a bit shocked that she was helping me.

"See, you don't need to say that. King Harold already told you you can be informal around us. So when no nobles are around you can greet me informally, and you shouldn't say the full names of nobles who rank beneath you. Only use their lesser titles," Queen Priscella scolded.

"Yes, thank you Queen Priscella," I said wondering why only nobles would require us to be formal.

"And they will be there tomorrow," Queen Priscella continued, as she walked me to the door.

"Who?" I asked dumbly.

"My knights! They will be there tomorrow to train," Queen Priscella said stiffly.

"Oh, that's great! I believe sir Galileo starts training at 8 a.m.," I responded.

"I'll make sure that they are there," Queen Priscella said. I nodded and moved to walk out the door but a soft hand on my arm stopped me. "Do you - would you - could perhaps, Ollie - Princess Ollifelle's knights join too?" the Queen implored me.

"Of course!" I said earnestly, squeezing the hand on my arm. "Anyone is welcome as long as they honor Sir Galileo, my knights, and their teaching style."

Queen Priscella gave me a quick smile, "I'll make sure of it," she nodded, looking serious once more before she all but pushed me out the door saying I'd be late for the King.

Chapter 11

The Busy Day

Challa, Hugo, and I stood staring at the door for a moment before I regained my senses and asked Hugo where the King's rooms were. It took a few minutes for Hugo to find it, but soon enough we were moving through the palace again. "Your fighting style was amazing, Crown Princess!" Challa gushed as we walked through the halls. "Where did you learn it?"

"I came up with it with the Dowager Queen Elizabeth," I said with more than a little pride.

"Well, if it was the Dowager Queen, no wonder it was so incredible," Hugo said, still focused on the map. Logically, I knew this was meant as another compliment towards Nana, although why one would give her sole credit for a fighting style when she had never learned to fight was beyond me. However, I was a little offended that Hugo didn't include myself as part of the reason why my fighting style was so impressive. I let it slide though as we stopped in front of King Harold's rooms.

When I knocked on the door to the King's rooms there was instantly a different atmosphere than Queen Priscella's. First, before the footman could even speak, King Harold's gruff voice broke through. "Is that Ava, send her in, send her in man!" The footman hurried to open the door and pointed me down a hallway towards another slightly open door. I followed his gesture and entered a large study - a large study that was an absolute disaster. Books were scattered all around and papers were sprawling all over several wooden desks.

"Ava!" Harry said, a delighted smile taking over his wrinkled face from where he sat partially hidden by a pile of books. "I've been waiting for you, for this. Sit, sit, and tell me what you thought about the wonderful courtiers we have here."

"Well, I have to admit I'm a bit confused about what their job is," I said trying to find a place to sit amongst the scattered papers and books littering the office, "I understand you pay them, but I can't seem to find out what for." I went on to describe the conversation I had with the three Lords from yesterday. This brought Harry immense joy as he started cackling maniacally from behind his desk.

"Ah, I assumed he talked to you. Lord Marxton, that charming fool, came in today asking me if he had a job, and, if so, what was he meant to do for said job. It was honestly perfect timing as we have lots to do in preparation for your wedding, my dear. I put him in charge of flowers, something even he should be able to manage. Still, if you could convince more of my nobles to start working, that would more than repay the effort it took to bring you here."

"So the courtiers don't work?" I asked, ignoring the fact that I had never asked him to bring me here in the first place.

"No. No, the most they do is sit on their asses and lose money in my casino. Mostly they're a rather useless lot."

"Then why do you pay them!" I asked, astonished.

"It's simply the way things are done," Harry said dismissively.

I stared at him with awe. In my previous encounter with the King, I had thought him to be a wise and cunning person. How then, could you let slide the utter idiocy of wasting government funds on people with no job, and no need of the money! It was ridiculous. It was a huge waste of money, and it was completely useless. I couldn't fathom ever running a country in agreeing to such an expenditure. Certainly no wise ruler would do so.

As per usual, my astonishment must have appeared on my face because Harry laughed a little at me and said, "This has been a tradition that has been in place for hundreds of years. It's not something that can just go away. Change doesn't happen easily after all."

"That's such a lie!" I blurted out. Harry looked a little shocked by my outburst, but I pushed forward anyway. "Change happens without us even trying. It will come no matter what we do. It's the only constant in life. Change is the easiest thing in the world. It's only when you resist that the change becomes difficult."

Harry stared at me for a long moment. "I wonder what you'll actually accomplish if you choose to plow your way through it like that," he muttered, it seemed like he was talking mostly to himself, but his tea brown eyes were locked on to me, and his gaze was cold and calculating. It pierced into my body, and rolled over me with the passionate detachment of a scientist observing an animal he is researching, but is required not to interfere. "Still," he continued, his face changing so rapidly, one might be inclined to believe his dissecting gaze was nothing more than a figment of my imagination. That is, I could have thought this, if I had not vividly imprinted the shiver his cool gaze had triggered to my memory. "You should keep that outlook," Harry smiled. "You will need it if you wish to improve this country of mine."

A roar of anger pushed through me as I took in Harry's words. He was acting as if he was nothing more than an outsider in his own country. As if he weren't the King! As if the ability to change Dolma didn't rest primarily in his hands! But, instead of doing any of his own work, he was pushing all of the responsibility onto a girl from a foreign country. It was irresponsible, and undoubtedly, a little cruel. I breathed, calming my raging spirit. After all, this wasn't exactly news. Harry had never made any move to hide his personality from me. Even when we spoke yesterday he had made his intentions known. And, one could argue that he was doing what he thought was best for the country. There were already many things I believed I could help improve. Still, I realized, his support was only silent, and I was still dreadfully alone in Dolma.

"Your country will improve," I said firmly, staring determinedly back into his eyes. "It doesn't even matter if I'm here, although I will do all in my power to make a positive change, but my presence might only serve to speed up an inevitable process. The only way to go is forward. It may take time, and it may not always be a linear progression, but, at the end of it all, corruption is not sustainable, and the world will become a lighter place, by whatever means necessary."

Harry stared at me once more. "The royal family of Dolma has exclusive access to a library containing all records of Dolma's economic, political, and diplomatic history, though I doubt anyone in my family has used it other than myself. I will get you a key. The agricultural records will be brought to your room by the end of today. Show me this change you say that is inevitable." It was an order, but it was also a desperate plea. Harry's voice was solid, but his eyes held mine begging. You would think that he was some sort of prisoner or a starving man, for whom I held the key to release all pain and suffering. It was terrifying. All I could do was nod, and excuse myself back into my own rooms. Encompassed by the heavy silence broken only by the clicking of my knights and my shoes along the deserted hallway.

"He asks too much of you," Challa said, his deep voice echoing along the marble walls.

"He asks no more of me than he believes I can give," I said impassively, looking towards the blankness before me.

"Just because he believes you can give it, doesn't mean you actually can," Hugo said quietly from my right.

"We have no knowledge of what I can or cannot give. We have no idea of my limits as we have not even begun to test them."

"And what happens when you push those limits too far?" Challa asked gravely.

I stopped, and turned to look back at both of them. "Is that not why you are here, to catch me and protect me when I fall?"

A warmth filled me as I smiled at them both. My warmth was met by determined looks from Hugo and Challa.

"We will support you in any way we can, Crown Princess!" Hugo confidently claimed. His voice rang out in the hall, as if to raise the spirit of Challa's grave echo from before.

Challa responded with a vigorous nod, "We will never let you fall," he agreed.

I knew these claims were a tad ridiculous, even a perfect knight couldn't protect me from everything. Nevertheless, Challa and Hugo looked dead set on keeping their word. And, even if logic wasn't on their side, I felt safer with them. In the end, that feeling of safety was more important. The belief that you are safe is what allows people to take the biggest risks, and allows one to get the most wonderful of rewards. The risks need not even be thought about, and sometimes, boldly is the only way forward.

For about two weeks my life was as follows: my mornings were spent alternating between learning endless amounts of etiquette (most of which seem to me to be quite insane) and memorizing the names and positions of what felt like thousands of nobles, but was probably closer to several hundred. In the afternoons I poured over Dolma's records in the royal families library, and became increasingly upset by the growing number of problems that burden primarily the country's poorest citizens. In the evenings, I would attend Noble banquets where I would attempt to talk to the courtiers or my future husband with seemingly decreasing levels of success. It seemed that Thomas was choosing to ignore me after all. So, finally, I ended almost every day by fighting my knights on the training grounds while the rest of the court wasted away in the Gambling Halls. If I'm really honest, it also served as a way of making me tired and busy and unable to dwell on the ever pressing longing and loneliness that came with having to leave my family behind.

Then it was the day I was to meet the nobles, or rather, the nobles who actually ruled the territories in Dolma, and the day my engagement was to be announced, and also happened to be the day the first letters from my family arrived.

The thing about really any emotion, but especially homesickness, is that you can only hide from it for so long. It's difficult to describe the sensation of homesickness, it's not like anything else I'd ever experienced. See, for two weeks I was swept up in the newness of it all. The new location, the new people, the new food, the new style of talking, the new culture, the new weather, the new buildings, and everything else. Then, the newness wears off, and it just becomes unfamiliar and different. When that happens, you can't avoid the feeling anymore because there's no escape from the reminders. Everywhere you go, everything is different, so you have this constant pressing at your heart reminding you that you are not home. That you are an outsider here, that everything you know is somewhere far far away.

But, there's nothing to do about it. There's no cure other than time. The only way to fix it is to go home, but I'd made my choice. Dolma is where I live now, and despite my struggles, I didn't regret my choice. People in Nevremerre and Agremerre weren't going to starve, and there was so much I could do to help Dolma too. Going home wasn't something I would choose, so the feeling stayed, throbbing inside of me with every step I took. It felt like, maybe, I could just lay in bed for days on end staring at the ceiling, and waiting for this feeling to go away.

That wasn't an option though, there were things that had to be done, so I simply had to keep plodding through.

And, I was doing it, I really was. I was pushing my way through life in Dolma ready to make changes and learn the ways of this new place. Then, the letters from my family came. I opened them excitedly, sending my maids, knights, and other friends to enjoy their own letters, or to deal with other business. The content of my letters was simple. There were no complaints, no hidden messages, nothing unexpected, just the love and genuine curiosity of my family, each presented in everyone's distinctive handwriting and their own distinct voice.

It was a new sharp and exacting form of torture.

It was excruciating. It was a reminder, a strong, demanding, and unignorable reminder of all I had left behind. And it killed me. It really did. Pain, tears, frustration, and futility crashed through me, collapsing me onto my office floor in a puddle of inconsolable sobs. And that was how Queen Priscella found me, who knows how long later. "Good Gods, girl! This can't happen! Not today of all days! What in the continents do you think you're doing?"

She was right. This was not exactly an ideal time to lose my senses, but I couldn't seem to find it in me to stop my tears. I really did try, but I just kept hiccupping noisily on the floor. "What in the name of all that is sacred has made you like this?" Priscella screeched, sounding thoroughly irritated. I managed to weekly point the letters, now scattered around me. Priscella scowled and picked them up. It wasn't long before her expression changed, however, as she glanced through my letters.

"Tilt your head back," she said, her voice was softer and more gentle than I'd ever heard it. She gently grabbed my chin, pulling it up so it was pointed towards the crease between the wall in the ceiling. "Good, now take big slow breaths. Nice and deep," she continued, placing a feather light hand on my upper back, "and pinch right here," she finished grabbing my left hand and pinching the skin between my thumb and forefinger. I moved to follow the motion and she quickly stood back up.

Only a minute or so later, my sobs ceased, now, the room was only filled with my occasional sniffle. I was exhausted. I felt drained and tired and oddly cold even next to the crackling fire. Still, I looked back at Priscella and said, "Thank you." My voice was weak and scratchy following my tears, but Priscella still nodded in acknowledgement.

"Remember that trick. It will stop even the worst tears relatively quickly, although it'd be best if you didn't cry at all," Priscella's voice sounded distant from where she now stood on the other side of the room. Her words hung in the air, and I was sure they were meant to be a reprimand, but they lacked any of her usual heat. "Don't read any letters from home on the day of big events. At least not for a few years or so. Read them in the morning when you have nothing to do, or in the evening after you come home from a noble gathering, where you have the rest of the night alone to process," She said in her same distant voice.

"Yes," I agreed, slowly nodding my head.

"In the beginning, it's sometimes easier to just not write or read any letters at all," she said, her voice only just above a whisper. Only the silence around us permitted me to hear her words.

"You've been through this before." It was not a question; it did not need to be; I already knew the answer.

"Dolma's tradition of arranged marriages has occurred for far longer than you or I have been around," Priscella scoffed, before her face softened once more. "I, perhaps, had it a little easier than you. Three of the five countries surrounding Andaluca choose to do treaties through arranged marriages. Although, it is not the culture for us normally, my sisters and I have always known that one out of the three of us would have an arranged marriage. I suppose there's something in Harold choosing me over my sisters, although I do not know if his choice was due to my virtues or my failings."

I stared at her from my spot on the floor, watching her as she spoke and silently urging her to continue. "Fine," she sighed, moving to sit on the sofa opposite my desk. "I guess we have time to kill anyway, as no one should see you as you are now." This, I thought, was a bit dramatic, especially as most of my people had already seen me cry in the carriage on the way here, but I stayed silent, eager to hear more of Priscella's story. "And off the floor with you! You are a Princess, not a scullery maid!" she snapped, gesturing at the opposite couch. I pulled myself up, and moved to the couch. I had to admit, it was far more comfortable than the floor.

Priscella closed her eyes as she began to recall her story, keeping me in silent anticipation before her ice blue eyes opened and she began. "Andaluca is a beautiful country. The north has a wonderful chill in the air, and you can see snow on the mountains between us and Maychula all year round. My childhood was peaceful, although I was never really aware of how much effort it took to maintain that peace. Andaluca has never been a weak country, but with five neighbors, including a war prone Calvine and the inordinately wealthy Dolma, diplomacy was always the most important job for any Andalucian King. That's why it's written into the law that once every generation, a Princess or Duchess of Andaluca must marry into a foreign country to secure treaties with our neighbors.

I was the youngest of my three sisters, and, with the birth of my twin brother, my oldest sister was no longer the future Queen. It was easy to assume that one of my elder sisters would be the ones who would have to leave, even if there was only a two-and-a-half-year difference between me and my eldest sister. My parents had married for love, it hadn't lasted, but mother always maintained that love had made everything easier in the beginning, and by the end they could just stay on opposite sides of the castle. So, I confess, I was rather unprepared for when the then Crown Prince, Harold, requested my hand in marriage.

Still, I was a Princess. There was no other choice. So, I never fought the decision. I was never close with my parents, and Andaluca was not so far away. Our cultures are not so different from Dolma. I assumed I would be fine. It did not take me long to realize I was wrong. Nothing felt familiar, and I was very alone. The people I had brought with me soon left to go back to Andaluca, and I couldn't find it in me to stop them from doing what I so longed to do.

The people here don't like what they don't know. Everything must be done the Dolmanian way. Even now, despite being their Queen, despite changing my hair, my clothes, and learning all their very many societal rules, I am still an outsider to this land. I watched my sisters and brother marry in joyful ceremonies filled with smiles and promises of everlasting love.

Each one hurt more than the last. Each letter, no matter my previous relationship to the sender, was a reminder of how alone I was. Several remain unopened to this day. Thomas was the first thing to help. He was something to love and to ground me to this place.

Gods willing, you will have your first child soon, and you will understand; however, in the meantime, events like this are vital! You must show no sign of weakness. You must show them you are not the uncivilized savage they believe you to be!"

"The what?" I interrupted.

"Exactly! Now come along, we must prepare you!" Priscella said, moving determinedly towards the door. I hurried to follow her, not wanting to appear rude, but not entirely convinced by her arguments. Why should I change myself for people who are never going to accept me even if I did? Especially if it meant having to wear the outrageously large dresses and hair that was frequented by the women in Dolma.

Queen Priscella moved determinedly forward, barking orders at Ana, as well as to Katy, and Louisa, my newly hired maids. Her presence must have startled the group as Katy and Louisa nearly tripped over themselves to obey. Ana, on the other hand, calmly moved to my side and gave me a concerned glance which I soothed with the gentle smile before she moved to complete her duties as well. I was pulled and pushed and quizzed for the better part of the afternoon before Priscella decided I was "as good as we're going to get." I was under no Illusion that had she had the materials, she would attempt to put me in the Dolmanian fashion. I mentally prepared myself for the day I'd have to say no to her style choices.

As the afternoon wore on, I was growing steadily convinced that Priscella's nerves were greater than my own. She kept furiously pacing around my bedroom trying to impart thousands of pieces of knowledge, until finally, a little fed up, I interrupted. "Priscella, don't you need to get ready too?"

She jumped, "Oh my Gods! I do!" she yelped before running out of the room.

"Do we have any tinctures of lavender?" I asked aloud, staring at Priscella's retreating form.

"I don't think so, but perhaps we should consider making some," Ana commented, looking at Katy and Louisa. I silently agreed, several of our new hires seemed incredibly tense compared to the staff back in Nevremerre.

"I'll get someone to send her some chamomile tea tonight," I eventually decided before throwing myself onto the bed with a sigh. The night hadn't even started and I was feeling drained of all life. I heard Ana usher Katy and Louisa out of the room before flopping down in the bed next to me with a sigh of her own. We laid there in silence for a while before I spoke. "Do you want to go back to Nevremerre?" I asked, haunted by Priscella's story of her staff leaving.

"Yes, no, sometimes, all the time," Ana replied unhelpfully. "See here's the thing, Crown Princess, Dolma is weird, and if I'm really honest, I don't like it. The people act superior and haughty, but some of them don't even know how to read."

"What?!"

"Right, but let me finish. The new staff acts like they're walking on eggshells constantly, and that's beyond annoying. I miss Nevremerre and Charlotte and my other friends, but at the same time, Dolma is a challenge and there's so much I could improve as a housekeeper. There's so much I can learn, and I love working with you Princess. It was harder to leave than I thought it would be, but I still believe it's possible to find happiness here. And, I want to work for it. So, I miss Nevremerre every day, but I have no desire to leave Dolma anytime soon." Relief passed through my whole being. I was honestly terrified to hear her response. Just like Priscilla, I would not stop any of my staff from leaving, but I could not even imagine being here alone.

Chapter 12

The First Dance

We laid on the bed in silence for a while, enjoying the quiet that filled my room, and before I knew it, I fell into a light slumber. I was startled awake sometime later by Mateo knocking at my door and informing me it was time to go. Ana quickly fixed my hair and sent me out. If I was groggy upon waking up, I wasn't anymore. My heels clicked on the stone floor, the heavier footsteps of Mateo and Galileo echoed behind me. My chest heaved with the weight of each hurried breath I took. My stomach was a bundle of nerves. My hands shook slightly by my side, and I couldn't for the life of me think of a single piece of Dolmanian etiquette I had been quizzed on only mere hours before.

It was an unpleasant, but not unfamiliar sensation. I felt this way before many events in Nevremerre: my first Noble banquet, the first time I had to make a speech, my first time opening the tournament. It didn't exactly make my nerves go away, but there was a comfort in knowing I'd felt this all before, that it was only temporary, and that I would survive. Still, this knowledge couldn't stop the surge of nausea that swept through me as I stepped into the small side room where the royal family would wait to be announced.

I was the last to arrive, which decidedly did not help my nerves or the general feelings of awkwardness that filled me when all eyes in the room turned towards me. Harry looked at me and gave me an approving nod before turning back around. Priscella looked, frankly, more nervous than myself. She stood, wringing her hands from the far corner of the door, her eyes roaming up and down my body, probably searching for my flaws. Princess Ollifelle looked at me only briefly before she too went back to staring at an empty wall in front of her. It occurred to me then that I had yet to speak a single word to the young Princess. In my rush to learn about Dolma, and to establish any sort of sustainable conversation with her brother, I had totally neglected to try to speak with Princess Ollifelle. I resolved to fix this in the future.

Finally, I turned towards the eyes of Crown Prince Thomas, my future husband. His eyes stayed on me the longest, but there was a hardness to them, like somehow in the process of becoming a bargaining chip so the people from my home wouldn't starve, I had also become his enemy. He had very purposefully ignored me since the first banquet, and even now, as soon as he met my eye, he haughtily turned his head away. Perhaps, I could have kept fighting for communication, but truthfully, even after two weeks, I was growing weary of fighting for the attention of someone who didn't want to give it. So, I gave up. I had other things to worry about, and a slowly crumbling country to eventually rule and build back together. I was a Crown Princess and a future Queen, I had money and knowledge, I wasn't dependent on a mute Crown Prince to make a difference in my life.

Even with this mindset, I was still utterly alone in the room. However, this time, I realized I was not the only one. Looking around the room, I noticed that each member of the Dolmanian royal family occupied a different corner of the room. There was no eye contact between the other Royals. They each focused on the wall, the floor, anything but each other. Even their knights stood silently around the edge of the room. It was painfully quiet, and I was fairly certain that nerves could only account for two people in the room.

It was awful, and I had no idea how to fix it for the people in the room. I only knew that I would not have the same thing for myself. Instead, I turned to Mateo and Galileo and said, "Did you get letters from home as well?" My voice sounded like a scream, resounded across the silent walls of the side room, but I ignored it, focusing all my attention on Mateo and Galileo.

"I had one for my mother," Mateo said, excitement present in his voice. "She said everyone is doing well, and that my youngest sister has begun training to be a knight! She'll be taking the test in just three years!"

"Oh that's wonderful! Do you think she'll stick with it?" I asked, instantly absorbed in Mateo's words.

"Anica stubbornly goes through with everything she puts her mind to, so I have no doubt she'll pass her test with flying colors when she hits 21."

"Good for her! If she needs any lessons, let me know. I know some great people in the Nera region who would happily go to Casia to teach a willing recruit," Galileo said with a smile.

"Thank you for the offer! I'll write to her tonight to see if she's interested, although she may want to try and do it on our own," Mateo said with a light laugh.

"We all need help now and then," Galileo said sagely, "It's never wise to turn down the hand of help when it could benefit you. Are any of your other siblings knights?" Galileo transitioned.

"Currently, it's just me," Mateo noted, "but Anica and Henry are still too young to choose a career."

"There's no official age to choose a career," I reminded him of the last. "Anica and Henry aren't yet at the age of majority," I clarified for Galileo.

"I see, so what do your other siblings do?" Galileo inquired.

"Are you sure you want to ask?" I teased, "He has nine siblings, we might be here all night."

"Very funny, Crown Princess," Mateo frowned, but his honey eyes twinkled at me beneath his fake ire.

"That's way too many siblings," Galileo said with mock sincerity, "How do you remember them all?"

"We've developed an acronym to keep it all straight," Mateo said seriously. I couldn't hold my straight face any longer and burst out into laughter, and Galileo and Mateo soon joined my mirth.

"Your Majesty, it's time," came a voice from the small side door.

"Oh - I - yes of course," I turned to see Harry stumble over his words, his eyes, and the eyes of everyone else in the room, turned towards me and my knights. "Yes," Harry repeated, shaking his head slightly. "I will go out with Priscella and Ollie, and then when you hear me announce your names and engagement, the two of you shall follow," he said, nodding at Thomas and me.

"Yes, Your Majesty," I nodded back. Everyone else simply nodded in silence. With everyone ready, Harry presented his arm to Priscella who moved out of the room, followed closely by Princess Ollifelle.

The door swung closed and I was left with Thomas and a room full of knights. I didn't bother with filling silence this time, instead I focused on listening to Harry's muffled voice through the wooden door, and slowing the pounding of my heart.

"Princess Avalynn of Nevremerre," came Harry's voice from beyond the door. I moved to walk out.

A warm hand caught my wrist holding me back from pushing open the door. "Not yet," came Thomas' cool voice, gently tugging me back to his side. His hands stayed on my wrist as he intently listened to the door.

"I now welcome your Crown Prince Thomas Rayforth Ecardio Davenforth Carleon and his betrothed Princess Avalynn of Nevremerre," Harry's voice came through once more.

"Now we go," Thomas muttered, and we both walked confidently out the doors. There was a loud round of applause at our arrival that was silenced by the King a few minutes later.

"The wedding will be held 10 weeks from today. All will be invited. And please help me congratulate the future King and Queen of Dolma." Applause rang out again, and Thomas and I waved at the crowd as Priscella had said I should. From there I was dismissed to the waiting crowd of nobles, and Thomas vanished from my side. I was once again left on my own, left to the hungry eyes of the nobles around me.

At least, that's what I thought. Were this Nevremerre, I would be surrounded by nobles curious about their future Queen. I would be peppered with questions about the economy, their territory, and more. Here, in Dolma, I was left completely and wholly alone. At this point, I really shouldn't have been surprised, but I still wasn't quite able to get used to this neglect of their future leader. The nobles did swarm, but they swarmed to the King and the Crown Prince. Priscella, Ollifelle, and I were left to our own devices. For Priscilla and Princess Ollifelle, their ladies-in-waiting soon flocked towards them, and for the first time I understood the need for this, frankly ridiculous, job.

And suddenly, my nerves were replaced by anger and frustration. I was the future Queen of this country. How could no one want to talk to me? For the past two weeks I'd spent most afternoons reading about this country. I knew all of these people were just barely holding up the mansions they were living in. People were starving, their fields were only a few years away from collapse synonymous with the Dust Out, there were no public health measures, and no regulations that could protect the people. In short, it was a mess, and most nobles were part of the problem. They all seemed happy to waste away in the facade of wealth instead of putting in the work to change. It was infuriating.

However, I wasn't like their previous rulers. I was not going to let their negligence stand. I had originally thought this evening was my interview with the nobles where they could learn about what kind of ruler I would be, but since they appeared to have no interest in me, I now had other plans. Tonight was, now, the nobles of Dolma's interview with me. I was going to learn exactly who these people were, if they truly cared about their land or if they were corrupt and needed to be cut out of Dolma's system entirely. I was not looking to create another Nevremerre. That would be impossible, but I could not let the current Dolma last. Even if it took the rest of my life, I would make this country thrive, and let its people live in harmony and prosperity.

To be honest, for all my emotional pep talk from earlier, my talks with the nobles fell into an almost unbearable level of boring predictability. I would bring up their territory, they would look surprised I knew their names. I would ask them questions about their territory, they would bluster through them, giving terribly incorrect answers. Some couldn't even tell me what the main product of their territory was. The level of incompetence was truly horrifying, and dreadfully mundane at the same time.

When I was younger, Mother would tell me stories of knights and people fighting against evil monsters. They were thrilling and exhilarating, but Mother always ended the stories by telling me that the real evil was far more boring. Talking to these Lords and Ladies I finally understood her words. Most of these men and women were painfully boring. Most of them, I realized, didn't cause pain and suffering for their people in their land on purpose. They were just ignorant and often apathetic to the lives of other people. They couldn't answer questions about their territory because they simply didn't care enough about them to learn.

Over the course of an hour, I talked to over fifty nobles, only six correctly answered questions about their territory. Of those six, three seemed genuinely to care about their land, two reminded me of Lord Nicholas in the sense that they would only do what was necessary to keep themselves in comfort, but never go out of their way to help people, and one, one knew exactly what he was doing, and seemed to revel in the pain that he caused.

They're only about a dozen or so more nobles left to talk to, not including the children of these people, and I was already exhausted. "It must be difficult," clucked the fake sympathetic voice from my left.

"Lord Whimely," I acknowledged, recognizing the outrageous volume of blond hair.

"Princess Avalynn," about. "It's such a shame no one has bothered to speak with you for long, but what can be done, you're just a foreign Princess with no power here. It's such a shame they don't know how interesting and fun you are," Lord Whimely smiled.

This, I believe, was supposed to be a compliment. It was comically bad, so comically bad I actually did start laughing. "Lord Whimely," I laughed at his shocked face before composing myself. "I think I understand now how past Queens of Dolma have behaved, or rather how they were raised to behave, but let's be very clear. I am from Nevremerre. I have exorbitant amounts of money, I have been trained in war and combat, as well as all matters of science, literature, math, history, and economics. I have more power in my little finger than some of the people in this room will wield in their entire life. It is not required for me to appease or entertain the people in this room. My duty lies with the people of Nevremerre, Agremerre, and now Dolma, and, I can promise you, there are few more loved in this world than myself."

It was a bit boastful, although definitely not inaccurate. Perhaps, I wouldn't have been so boastful back in Nevremerre, but here I was so fed up with the arrogance that surrounded me. I meant it when I said I did not require the acknowledgment of those here. I made no effort to disclose my position as Nevremerre's possible future Queen, or exactly how much of a salary the King had given me, but I was tired of being viewed as someone with no value other than my physical presence Dolma. It felt good to say that I had more to offer, that I was more than a walking doll. That I was worth more than they could imagine, and not just because of my title, but because of my soul, my spirit, and all the fire, determination, and love I carried inside of me.

With that off my chest, I turned away from Lord Whimely, away from people I didn't know. I had just about reached Lucy, my respite from this foreign land and foreign people, when King Harold called us all to attention. "We will now open the ball this evening. To celebrate their engagement, and their forthcoming wedding, the dance will be opened by the Crown Prince and Princess Avalynn."

I knew this was coming, Priscella had informed me that this was a part of Dolma's traditions. However, unlike in Priscella's life, my betrothed had never bothered to practice with me. Still, I spotted Thomas from across the room and moved towards the center of the floor. Around us the crowd gathered along the outside of the floor, turned towards us, and waited patiently for us to begin. In front of me, Thomas moved forward, meeting me at the center of the ballroom. He cautiously moved to pick up my hand, wrapping his other arm around my waist. I placed my own hands on his arm and shoulder, my fingers flying over the golden embroidery that lined his jacket. Breathing slowly to calm the bundle of nerves that had taken over my stomach, I prepared myself to dance.

Ever so quickly, Thomas pulled me towards him, whispering in my ear, "I'm sorry." I looked at him confused and a bit hopeful that he had changed his mind and would start working and talking with me. Then the music started... then Thomas let go of me and walked over to his lover, leaving me alone, in the middle of a dance floor, amidst the gasps and stares of the nobles and the court.

My mind went blank for what felt like an eternity, but was probably only a few seconds. A million thoughts then bombarded my skull. Should I just retreat? Walk back into the crowd? It was, perhaps, the most appropriate thing to do, maybe even the least embarrassing, but it also felt like a defeat. It was silly of course, how could one be defeated in a battle they didn't even know they were fighting, but I simply couldn't get my body to walk away. So, instead, I did the only thing that I could think of. I danced. The music was still playing and I had spent more than enough time practicing on my own.

It was easy, and once I started any sort of nerves just fell away. It felt freeing, and maybe even a little fun. For a few precious moments I was just a girl dancing to her favorite song. Of course, I was actually a Princess, who had only really heard this song maybe twice before, but one could pretend. When the song came to an end, I finished with a deep curtsey towards King Harold. I was later told that there was a silence between my finish in the applause that came, but the only sound I could hear was the rushing of blood through my veins, and the pounding of my heart.

I only vaguely recognized the applause before King Harold opened the ball to everyone, and I met my next partner, Sir Abel, followed by Lord Marxton, then Lord Whimely, Lord Amerton, and Lord Xander, whom I'd only met tonight. In fact, I had a partner for the entire rest of the evening. And, for the first time since I'd left Nevremerre, I felt optimistic about my life here in Dolma. My optimistic numbness was shattered in an instant as I met the hostile glare of Thomas' lover. Her deadly stare promised pain before our gazes were torn apart as we both twirled away to another partner.

PART TWO

Chapter 13

The Battle of Wills

In some ways, Thomas' abandonment of me the night the nobles came worked in my favor. Now, at least, there were several courtiers who actively chose to speak to me. Not all of what they had to say was kind, but there were at least words coming out of their mouths. Prior to that night the court seemed about as interested in me as they were about the art hanging on the palace wall, that is to say, they simply walked right by me as if I didn't exist. In other ways, my standing in court got a lot worse. Thomas' mistress, Lady Sabine, appeared to have quite the standing among the courtiers, and her animosity towards me only seemed to grow as time went by. Anyone with any affiliation with her was now actively snubbing me at all events. Honestly, I found I just didn't have the time or energy to deal with people who seemed to have no discernible job and chose to waste their money losing bets with each other instead of investing in the economy or their community. I really just didn't have the time to waste on them, so Lucy was assigned to monitor the court, while I focused on the country.

Even working everyday, it still took me another two weeks after the nobles came to get my proposal about the new farming measures to the King and his "agricultural expert". After convincing Harry that my new agriculture plan would be best for his kingdom. Harry arranged a meeting with his "agricultural expert" who I had to convince to do a trial run of my "new methods". Lord Lambaster Eugiene Ademoten, the said "agricultural expert" was an asshole, plain and simple. He was more arrogant than Lord Nicholas, more pompous than a peacock, and more ignorant about agriculture than a fish about a cactus. "Why should we take advice from a woman whose kingdom can't even grow enough food for themselves?" he scoffed. For a brief moment I debated letting another dust out happen, just to watch this man starve. Of course, I could never do that, but by Gods it was tempting.

"As I said before, Lord Lambaster," I ground out, "droughts are believed to be unavoidable natural phenomena. Even Dolma has yet to find a solution to a drought."

"That's because Dolma would never get a drought," Lord Lambaster huffed.

"According to your own records, Dolma has had at least three periods of drought in the past two centuries, one of which lasted nearly 13 years!" I exclaimed.

"There's no need to yell, Princess," Lord Lambaster said condescendingly. "Really, women always get so emotional." Visions of my fist colliding into his face, knocking into his nose with a satisfying crunch filled my head. I never thought of myself as a particularly violent person, but Lord Lambaster seemed determined to change that.

"Are you implying that you don't have emotions, Lord Lambaster?" I said, giving him a falsely sweet smile

"Men, like myself, have the maturity and wisdom not to feel such unproductive things," Lord Lambaster said smugly.

I smiled for real this time, "Well that, Lord Lambaster, is usually called sociopathy. It's a sickness of the mind that is generally considered a poor quality in any sort of leader, as it allows them to abuse and destroy those underneath them. This, eventually, leads to the ruin of all they control. It's clear to me that you are on your way to destroying your country."

"Wh - What? How - How dare you!" Lord Lambaster screamed.

"Now, now, let's - " Harry began.

"No," I cut him off, "You didn't stop him when he was attacking me. You do not get to give him the luxury of pro-tection now that the tables are turned," I said coldly, before turning back to Lord Lambaster. "It's nice to see you express your emotions, that may mean there's hope for you yet."

"I'm not emotional!" Lord Lambaster yelled.

I stared at him. "Do you know what emotions mean, Lord Lambaster?" I asked after a moment. I didn't wait for an answer before continuing on, "Emotions mean you care. I just told you that your current system of farming could kill hundreds of thousands of people, and you didn't bat an eye. I, correctly, insulted your leadership style, and you got upset. This tells me that you care more about yourself than the lives of the people who you are responsible for."

"What you said was just insane!" Lord Lambaster defended.

"No, I presented you with facts and evidence based on decades of peer-reviewed study. Right now you are practicing a willful ignorance, that will lead to a willful negligence, that will kill people. Those deaths will be on your hands."

"It's not my job to feed people!" Lord Lambaster turned to Harry, "Are you just going to let this woman talk to me like that?"

"That's exactly your job," I pushed forward, not letting Harry get the chance to respond. "You are the manager of agriculture. The purpose of agriculture is to feed people. If you don't give access to food for fair prices, you have failed at your job. What else could your job be?"

"To increase the agricultural economy," Lord Lambaster said, although he was sounding a little unsure.

"All right, then here's an economic question for you, how much money will you be making when half of your clientele dies? Of course, there may be a bit of an up charge during scarcity, but when the scarcity ends, if you've managed to get through it without a rebellion - which is doubtful, then you've lost a large portion of your clientele and your workforce. It will take generations to build both of those back up again. Especially if people keep dying from malnutrition due to continued food scarcity caused by labor shortages. There's no way your brief profit increase would cover the generational losses you'd suffer afterwards. And, again, this is only if you can survive the almost guaranteed rebellion that comes with food scarcity."

"There's no way people would rebel. We have guards and the royal knights!" Lord Lambaster said with confidence once more.

"The people outnumber the guards and knights. Not to mention even the Queen's knights have questionable skills at best."

"This is fear-mongering!" Lord Lambaster cried out.

At this point I was a little impressed he even knew the meaning of fear-mongering. "Good. You should be afraid. You have neglected the people you are trying to serve. And, don't think I haven't noticed your lack of regulations on pricing, so that in some areas of Dolma just a few vegetables cost half a week's wages. Which, by the way, are far too low, but I digress. Your job deals with food supply, when the revolution comes do you think you can really get away?"

"You talk as if revolution is imminent," Lord Lambaster almost whispered.

"If people are starving, it is," I replied simply. "Now can you look me in the eye and tell me you have done your absolute best to feed the people of this country?"

"Yes!" Lord Lambaster jumped.

"Then you should be fired."

"What?"

"You're terrible at your job, and if you can't satisfactorily do your job, you should be fired," I said simply.

"I... what? Never in all my life have I been treated like this! You don't need to worry about firing me, I quit!"

"Good," I said.

"What?"

"Do you expect me to care? You are doing a bad job, so either you do better, you get fired, or you quit so I can find someone better to take your place," Lord Lambaster stared at me, then at the King, then back at me. "Your choice," I prompted.

"I... I can do better," Lord Lambaster said.

"Very well, but rest assured, I will be monitoring you very closely. Now, back to my proposal..." I continued on, going over the details of my agricultural plan once more.

"But why should we subsidize the farmers?" Lord Lambaster argued once more.

"Because, if we want this to be successful, farmers need to know the changes we are asking them to make won't negatively impact their profits. Of course, all the research from Nevremerre suggests that growing a multitude of crops and implementing wildlife buffers actually increases profit as time goes on, but as we first make the changes there may be those who struggle," I said, more than a little exasperated with this man.

"If it's going to cause trouble in the beginning, why should we bother changing it?"

Because the current method isn't sustainable!" I cried out, before calming myself once more. "Think about it this way, whether it's in one year or 100 years, your agricultural system will need to change. Would you rather make the change now or when the system has already collapsed and it will take even longer for the soil to be ready to grow healthy crops again? This is a trial project, and I know it will prove to be effective. So, let us change the farming style along the Agremerre border and just see the benefits I know will come."

"Fine," Lord Lambaster finally conceded, "but since this is your idea, Princess Avalynn oh, I'm sure I can count on your monetary support for this endeavor."

I glared at him, "I'm sure Dolma isn't so lacking in gollups that it couldn't fund projects to aid its own country."

"Well it would be difficult to convince the treasury to find something that is so experimental," Lord Lambaster smirked, his ridiculous white mustache wrinkled like a fluffy caterpillar, and I wondered if his facial hair was just as poisonous.

"Considering the fact that this agricultural system has been proven to be effective in both Nevremerre and Agremerre, I would hardly call this an experimental project. Also, doesn't the King control the country's finances?" I said, looking pointedly at Harry.

"Just as Nevremerre has a council, there are people in Dolma that it would be unwise for even a King to act against," Harry said, sitting languidly on a chair to my left as I debated Lord Lambaster and the future food security of this country. I fought the urge to glare at him.

"Exactly!" Lord Lambaster beamed, "Which is why the Princess should fund no less than three-fourths of the project."

"Now Lamby, even I know that is ridiculous," Harry interjected. "This is for Dolma, it can't be mostly funded by a foreigner."

While I was glad that Harry was finally taking a stand in this conversation, I will admit that I was a little upset at being called a foreigner when I was the future Queen. Surely, I could put my own, frankly ridiculously large, budget into this project. I had to remind myself that it really should be the Dolmanian treasury that should fund the whole thing before I got too carried away.

"Dolma will fund fifty percent of the project, and the Princess shall fund the other fifty percent," Harry announced, the order clear in his tone. I opened my mouth to object, but Harry held up a hand to stop me. "Lord Lambaster, you are dismissed. Gather the necessary funds from our half of the required budget, and, tomorrow, you will work with the Princess to create the staff required to convince the farmers to switch their system." This time it was Lord Lambaster's turn to open his mouth in protest. "Since she is supporting half the cost, it is obvious she should also have equal say in the whole proceeding" This effectively shut Lord Lambaster up. "Now leave us," Harry ordered.

We sat in silence as Lord Lambaster stormed out of the room, flinging the doors open exposing the backs of Leonard and Oberon as well as an assortment of the King's knights. When the door finally swung back closed, I found myself releasing a rather audible sigh of relief. Harry laughed at me and said, "You did well with him."

"He was an ass," I glanced at him, "and you were absolutely no help!"

Harry laughed some more, "You didn't need my help."

"No, I didn't, but it would have made things easier. The whole process could have gone smoother and there could have been less resistance from everyone involved," I said seriously.

"I've told you who I was and my desires from the beginning," Harry said simply. "But don't worry, you won't be alone in this. I will contribute a quarter of my own funds to your half of this endeavor, but best not mention that to Lamby. Beyond that, I will make sure your name goes all over this project."

"That's only so you don't have to take any of the blame if it goes wrong," I huffed.

"Now, now Ava, you make it sound like this plan of yours will fail," Harry smirked, a twinkle sparkling in his brown eyes.

"It won't fail," I said with confidence, despite the twinge of unreasonable doubt that had crept into my heart.

"Good. Then let's make sure the citizens of Dolma know exactly who is helping them. I will make you a Queen loved by the people. I will make it impossible for even my idiot son to get rid of you," Harry announced.

"That's not a kind thing to say about your son," I said in response.

"I would not have thought you'd be one to defend him," Harry smirked, "and aren't you supposed to say you won't be driven out so easily?"

"I've had little more than two conversations with Thomas, if you can even call our interactions a conversation. I know nothing about him, and at this point I don't have the time to worry about him. Regarding being "driven out" of Dolma, I would not mind returning to Nevremerre." Harry's eyes widened at my admission. "I won't leave unless I have to," I assured him. "I made the choice to come here, and I will continue to choose to be in Dolma until I am certain that your citizens are set up with all the necessities of life, proper housing, food, access to clean water, health care, and education."

"That's quite a lot you're trying to give away," Harry said, raising an eyebrow.

"It's actually quite little, all things considered," I responded dryly. "Harry, I will not let the people of Dolma suffer as they do now."

"They do not suffer."

"They do, and everyone here has become so accustomed to it they have no idea that there is something better to be had. Even for people as wealthy as yourself, Harry. I will help this country be better, no matter what it takes."

"Is that a threat?" Harry questioned, his face growing cold and stern.

"No, no, it's a promise," I said gently. Harry's face wrinkled in confusion, but he must have eventually decided I wasn't a threat as he relaxed once more. Trusting me so easily was the first poor choice I'd seen Harry make, but I was happy to let him think of me as an ally as opposed to an enemy. Truthfully, I was not unfamiliar with the thought of supporting a rebellion in Dolma. Obviously, peace is preferable whenever possible, but after training with the palace guards and knights, I was so very aware that the Royal army was ill-prepared for a battle. It would take less effort to bring down the palace than Harry could have ever predicted.

Also in my favor, our training sessions had now begun to include several of the palace guards, and more than a few, I believe, now had a greater loyalty to me than to Harry. With all these factors, and with each rude encounter with a noble, I was more and more enchanted by a swift and easy rebellion than trying to change the system that was so entrenched in corruption. But, I had promised Mother that I would wait before making any major changes, and even if I found the court exceptionally annoying, I didn't actually want them to die. Still, I could not get the thought out of my head. So, I simply smiled politely at Harry and excused myself to return to my own safe haven.

Chapter 14

The Children of the
Royal Palace

Much to Ana's pleasure, the Dolmanian staff we had hired had finally grown accustomed to our Nevremerrian and Agremerrian ways. It didn't actually take too long, I noticed, for the staff to adjust. I mean there were still things that shocked them. One notable footman had asked if he'd done anything wrong when I informed him he would only need to work four days a week. Not to mention several other incidents of a similar nature. But, overall, the Dolmanian staff seemed to be adapting quickly and easily to our less strict way of life. There were of course a small number of maids and footmen who thought of the less rigid system in my household as an excuse not to work, but after two of those individuals were swiftly fired, we didn't have another problem. It gave me hope that the citizens of Dolma would react just as well to the other changes I would enact as Queen.

Hope, however, can leave you just as quickly as it comes. I confess it took me far longer than it should have to realize the more nuanced societal problems that Dolma faced. In

179

Nevremerre, the only privilege I had was being the wealthy daughter of a King. In Dolma, I had gained several more privileges I had not even thought to consider. But, when you have a privilege, even unknowingly, it can be very difficult to realize that your privilege exists or that there is something you have that others lack. It took, funnily enough, not my experience, but that of the castle's children to show me just how much privilege I had.

The children of the Dolmanian court had a far different lifestyle than that of my own childhood; although, I suppose my childhood was far from the average. The children in the Royal Palace lived in both an overly strict and a positively wild environment all at the same time. In the mornings and early afternoons they would have demanding schedules of tutoring and instruction, with boys and girls learning vastly different subjects. During this time, every move the child made was monitored and judged, some even receiving physical punishments for small mistakes. Once classes were attended, the children, no matter the age, were let out, utterly unsupervised until classes began again the next morning. It was in these wild, unguarded moments that a steadily growing number of children met me.

It started as mostly whispers behind bookshelves in the library, then cautious observers watching my knights spar on the training grounds and huddled groups spying around corners and running away once my gaze meant theirs. After a few scraped knees and mended bruises, the children stopped running, whispers turned to questions, and some even began learning from my knights. Finally, we ended up where we were today, where at just after 3 o'clock in the afternoon, what could easily be mistaken for a small army would come bursting into my rooms, demanding some form of entertainment.

We had amassed a collection of children from anywhere between the ages of 2 and 15. This initially garnered mixed expressions from my staff. People like Mateo, who had experience with young children, were thrilled, happily playing games and laughing with the ever-growing pack that chose to follow him. My new butler, Kentin, on the other hand, was far less thrilled. He had lofty ideals of propriety and order that children did not fit into. For some reason though, he too had earned himself a series of tiny followers. He never actually complained though, and he seemed to take pleasure in giving his crowd small jobs to do. So, I suspect he liked it more than he let on.

The most surprising reaction came from Miri, who not only already knew several of the children, but was thrilled by the addition of more. While I could go nearly a whole day without seeing my maid/spy, she could almost certainly be counted on to show up when the children arrived. "Children are the best source of information," she replied when I asked her about it one day. "Small enough nobody minds their words when speaking in front of them, smart enough to remember all that was said, and lacking in the social norms that would prevent them from telling it all to you. I've gotten quite the detailed list of extramarital affairs from them, among other things."

I blinked at her "I...what?" I stuttered, unsure what to do with this information.

"Don't worry, you'll see," Miri assured me with a nod, her now black and gray hair bobbing up and down. I briefly wondered how anyone recognized her as her hair and even body shape seemed to change daily. While I never did learn the secret to Miri's shape-shifting abilities, it took less than a week for me to understand her thoughts about children.

My attitude towards children, I confess, was rather indifferent. I certainly didn't dislike them, but I was also trying to, largely single-handedly, restructure the inner workings of a whole government. With the agricultural program now starting, I had turned my attention to the poor quality housing that the majority of the Dolmanian population lived in. Not to mention, I was also preparing for my wedding. All this is to say that I was a little too busy to cater towards the whims and needs of children. So, when the children came, I found myself mostly surrounded by quiet children who preferred to entertain themselves with books, or occasionally a craft project. It was actually a very lovely setup, and apparently also the ideal setting to see the truth behind Dolma's social structures.

"Are people really allowed to marry someone of the same gender in Nevremerre," Lady Irisetta asked loudly, disrupting the comfortable silence of my study.

I stared at her briefly, trying to process her words through the housing bylaws I had been studying. The only sound came from the crackling of the fire heating the room from the early Autumn chill. The other children paused their tasks as well, looking between me and the young teen in confusion. "Well yes, of course. To be honest I'm not really sure why it isn't here," I finally responded. "I really will have to look into that," I mumbled as an afterthought, oblivious to the gaping mouths of the other people in the room.

"But it's impure!" exclaimed Lady Catalina, her dark brown braids flipping around her head as she turned to stare at me.

"Impure?" I asked, startled by the 9 year old in front of me.

"Mhmm," Lady Catalina nodded. "That's what Father said when he saw my uncle kissing the stable boy. He had them both whipped."

Now it was my turn to gape. I could have sworn my eyes popped out of my head as I processed her words. "My mother says it's unnatural," Lord Kisserton said, in his usual high-pitched squeak. "She says people like that should never have been born. Although I don't actually get why," he mused.

Never in my life have I felt less prepared for something than I was to hear those words come out of a tiny 6 year old's mouth. My mind went blank as my brain tripped and fumbled its way through what I was hearing. "Wait, Ki, isn't your father Lord Feris?"

"Yes." I was instantly confronted with the memory of Lucy and Miri gossiping that Lucy had seen Lord Feris kissing Lord Blakely in the corner of the Gambling Hall just two nights ago.

"Uh," I said dumbly into the space in front of me. Where does one even begin in educating these kids on the nuances of gender and sexuality?

"Is it also true that you have a Queen with color?" Lady Irisetta continued eagerly, as if I wasn't still reeling from the fallout of the last question she asked.

"Color?" I repeated cautiously.

"You know, is she," Lady Irisetta paused, looking around the room, "black?" she finally finished, whispering the word as if it was forbidden.

"My mother, the Queen of Nevremerre does have black skin," I answered, still wary. Gasps filled the room.

"I thought if your skin has color you have to be a commoner," Lady Anabell chimed in, her short legs swinging thoughtfully on the couch.

"Where did you hear that?" I asked, aghast.

"Don't know. It's just that I've never seen a noble with color, just servants," she replied neutrally in the face of my shock.

"Well that's not true," I replied, regaining a semblance of my composure. "As you know, Lady Lucy has darker skin, so do several of my knights and Sir Abel. Beyond that, my eldest brother has black skin, and he could become King! So, the fact that there are no nobles of color here tells me that Dolma has some kind of systemic discrimination -"

"What does systemic discrimination mean?" Lord Baderly asked. I paused my rant, staring at the 10 year old and realizing that my words were probably not easily digestible for my child audience.

"Also, if your brother is the eldest, then why isn't he going to become King?" Lady Catalina asked.

"Because Nevremerre is a merit-based monarchy, so all the King's sons compete for the throne," Lady Irisetta said smugly, holding up "A Brief History of Nevremerre," which undoubtedly had started this all. She looked to have only read about a few pages which perhaps would also explain the gaps in her knowledge.

"Perhaps you should finish that book before asking questions, Iris," I sighed before addressing the rest of the room, "As Iris said, Nevremerre is a merit-based monarchy, but the competition is primarily between all of the King or Queen's children, boys and girls. Also, commoners or nobles may enter into the competition if they get approved by the council or if none of the King or Queen's children have the desire or skills needed to rule."

"Including you?" Lord Baderly asked, looking thoroughly shocked.

"Yes. I am a candidate for the throne of Nevremerre."

"Even though you're here?" Iris asked.

"Yes, I cannot legally leave the competition until I'm 21."

"That's so cool!" Lady Anabell jumped off the couch excitedly, "You could be Queen!"

"I'm going to be Queen of this country!" I said incredulously, and perhaps with a little less of the patience one should apply when dealing with children. Clearly, I was better suited for the role of Queen than school teacher. I sighed again before turning back to the children in front of me, "Okay from tomorrow onward, you are all going to get lessons on sexuality, race, and gender equality." There were groans from around the room.

"Don't worry," I reassured them. "they won't be like your other lessons. We will make them really interesting, and you can ask all of your questions, and I'll have snacks made for you."

"Snacks?!"

"Yes, snacks." There were cheers in the room, and I was thankful for having won over my audience. It lasted only a moment though before the heaviness sunk into me. The amount of work this country required to thrive seemed to increase every single day. It was one thing to change the agricultural styles or add plumbing to an area, but how was I possibly supposed to change what was likely centuries of prejudice baked into the country system of daily life?

I sent the children out of the room, and stared out into the fire in front of me. I was completely overwhelmed by the sheer amount of work on my plate. Not to mention surviving the glares and scorn of the Dolmanian nobles, only a few of whom seem to tolerate me, while most were trending towards active dislike, probably due to Lady Sabine's influence. And now, I had to find a way to teach acceptance to a whole country. It was suffocating. It felt like I was drowning. I had no space to breathe, nowhere to go, and I felt alone. My shoulders had a physical ache from the intangible weight they carried, and part of me just wanted to collapse from the stress of it all. I desperately wanted to cry, but nothing ever came. All I could do was sit in the room, watching the sparkling flames of the fire spring and jump up the chimney walls, crushed by the weight of the world around me.

I didn't even hear the door open and then quickly shut as Mateo sprinted in to find Sir Abel. In fact, it took Mateo's hand on my shoulder to break me out of my spiraling trance. He and Abel stood in front of me, Mateo's honey-colored eyes filled with concern as he gently guided me from my desk to the couch. Across from me, Abel's dark eyes were filled with understanding, and a sparkle of joy. Abel's eyes were what grounded me as Mateo hovered over us both uncertainly.

"I'm borrowing Mateo here for a few weeks," Abel said, his voice almost booming through the once silent room. I blinked at him. Abel was, in many ways, a man full of surprises. I always knew I could never be quite sure what he would say next. However, I usually felt that I could cope with his sudden topic changes and unique phrases pretty well. This comment however, was so completely beyond the realm of what I thought he would say that I could only sit there with my mouth hanging open struggling to speak.

"Wh - What? Why? But I want him here," I sounded more like a whiny child than I intended, but I did manage to say something.

Calm as ever, Abel replied, "I do intend on returning him, but I have a project I would like him to work on for me."

"I...what?" In a moment of true self-reflection I had to admit that, in Dolma, I probably seemed like far more of a simpleton than I had in Nevremerre. The sheer amount of times that something in Dolma had stunned me out of any form of sensible speech likely did not instill confidence in my intelligence level. Perhaps, I was less adaptable than I had believed. Forcing myself to calm down and think, I turned to Mateo. "What do you think about this? I will of course allow it, if that is your wish."

"I believe it is best that I work with Sir Abel right now," Mateo replied. My heart sank. I hadn't even realized it until this moment, but I desperately had wanted Mateo by my side. My mind was instantly filled with Priscella's story about all of her maids leaving her. I realized her words had instilled in me a desperate fear that my people would do the same, and I would be unable to do anything to prevent them from leaving. "I believe I should only be gone a few weeks, but it would also be a good time to start training the Dolmanian knights on how to best guard the royals as well."

"I see," I responded. It took all the effort I had to keep him from hearing the lump in my throat. "I hope your work with Sir Abel is productive then."

"Thank you, Crown Princess. I shall return as soon as my task is successful."

"Thank you, Sir Mateo," Abel nodded, "Now if you could get started on your tasks while I meet with the Crown Princess here."

"Sir Abel. Crown Princess," Mateo bowed as he left the room.

Abel and I both watched him leave, sitting silently until the door swung closed behind him, the wood shutting with a soft click. It was only then that Abel turned back to me, "So tell me, Avalynn, what has got you so despondent?"

There are many easy conversations to have with another person. No one has ever struggled to discuss the weather, or sports, or the merits of dog versus cat ownership. It may be difficult to maintain a conversation about these topics, but opening your mouth and beginning to speak about these subjects is very simple. Well, Ari may disagree with me there, but for many, these general topics are easy to discuss. However, speaking of sorrow, of one's fears, and of one's failings is not like speaking of the weather. How do I begin to describe the overwhelming cloud that I am under? What words could I possibly use to describe these feelings that cling inside of me, pressing against my every nerve, threatening to pull me apart? Even if I could describe where I'm at emotionally, how do I tell a person I respect and serve that I am breaking down? And, do I trust that when I fall apart, the man in front of me can put me back together again?

Despite these concerns, there were really only two options: stay in the hellish limbo of my all-consuming emotions, or talk to the man in front of me and hope he can help me feel better. I've never really been one for stagnation, so with a deep breath, I began at the only place I could. "I don't think I can do this. I feel like I'm falling apart. I want to help serve the people of Dolma, but I don't think I can do it on my own," my voice was surprisingly steady, but the words rushed out of me like water behind a dam. I stared at Abel after I finished speaking, silently begging him to save me from the emotions that were crushing me.

"Okay," said Abel with a smile, "I think I can work with that." Relief rushed through me, and for the first time in weeks, a spark of joy filled me as well. I wasn't going to be stuck feeling so heavy forever, someone was going to help me. I didn't have to do things all on my own. As if responding to my thoughts, Abel followed up with, "And who said you were on your own?"

"King Harold is not going to really help me put any of these new policies in place. The majority of the nobles are wholly incompetent. It feels like the task of reforming this entire broken system rests entirely on my shoulders, and everyone else is fighting against me."

"That does not make you alone. Avalynn, listen to me, and hear me now. If you remember nothing else I ever say, remember this. You are never alone. In this physical world you have the support of the trees and the earth and the birds in the sky. The worms under your feet and the flowers that hibernate under the hard winter's ground. This physical world is constantly alive with other beings, so even if there is not another human in sight, you will never truly be alone.

Spiritually, the entire universe is filled with divine, unconditional love you can access at any time. Beyond that you have the support and love of your ancestors, old friends, and beings that get the highest level of joy from helping guide you on your journey of light and love. Finally, you have your perfect soul, your higher self, who will love and support you no matter what you do. If you struggle, make mistakes, or even explore a darker version of yourself, your higher self will always be there for you. For what purer love is there than the love you hold for yourself? You, who can understand and know all of your strengths and weaknesses. The spirits and Gods will always be with you, in this life and the next.

In this moment, you also have the support of all those you brought with you from Nevremerre and Agremerre. I have not been trained to rule as you have, so there are many things I cannot do, but I can help you think with a clear head; I can guide you in times of uncertainty; and I can help you maintain strong relationships with other countries. Lady Lucy can navigate the ways of the court and help diminish those who oppose you. Your knights will keep you of sound body and mind, and your maids will ensure that you never need worry about your food, clothes, or comfort. We will all help you in any way we can. All you need to do is let us know what you haven't the emotional or physical energy to focus. We all have required time to get used to Dolma, and while you were put to work right away, the rest of us have had time to adjust and understand this new place. We are ready now to be of greater use to you. Trust in us, we will take care of all we can. So, please tell me, what would you like us to focus on?"

I thought for a moment. I was reassured by Abel's faith in me and those I work with, but I was still daunted by the sheer amount of work to be done. With my newfound knowledge of the social problems in Dolma, it begged the question of what to do first. Do I first fix the infrastructure or the societal problems, and how do I solve the societal problems? I relayed these concerns to Abel.

"You raised a curious question, Crown Princess," Abel said, switching to my formal title, "but given that you are a Crown Princess, the answer seems obvious. After all, one person alone cannot change societal beliefs."

"I have no intention of allowing bigotry to continue under my rule," I said firmly.

"Hate and fear are not so easily overcome, especially when taught so young. I am not suggesting we let it be, but it will take more than just a few new laws to change generations of learning."

"How long will that take though?"

"Avalynn, before people can truly thrive, they need safety. They need shelter, food, health care, and education. While you create these programs, staff them with qualified individuals of all genders and colors. Educate the youth on the history of Dolma and on its class and race inequities. Inform them of Nevremerre's research on love, sexuality, and gender. Education and exposure are the best tools when fighting ignorance. In order for change to truly be accepted, it must be experienced in a multitude of ways. While change doesn't have to be slow, there is a lot of patience required. All you need to remember is that we will get to a place that we want to be eventually. Have faith that peace, prosperity, and acceptance can all be achieved with time."

"All right, I understand," I said, determination replacing my fears. "I need more nobles and courtiers on my side, and ready to work for this country."

"Consider it done," nodded Abel. "But first, you must go out and ride."

"But there's work to be done!" I exclaimed, once again thrown off balance by his words.

"Life is not all about work. The world is a playground, and no life can be fulfilling without healthy doses of laughter, joy, and excitement. You must find joy in life, Avalynn, especially when there is work or pain making joy difficult. Joy is always around, and you must take the time to seek it out."

"Oh, fine then," I grumbled, feeling more like a child who has to do homework than someone who just got told to have fun, but soon enough it didn't matter as I raced Leonard on horseback down the streets of the capital, Galileo grumbling behind us about safety hazards.

Chapter 15

The Traditions of Home

It was exhilarating, but probably a little reckless as we weaved through the people and vendors that littered Dolma's capital. My laughter rang out over the crowds as Leonard's light curses filled the air as I pulled ahead. A good two lengths in front of him, I came to a stop at our designated finish line at the other end of the city. I was unabashedly smug as Leonard came to a stop, "I win!"

"Dammit, Crown Princess," Leonard said, a wide smile betraying his mock irritation. "It should be considered cheating that you and Kholassi jumped over that fruit cart. You know old Alberta here doesn't jump much anymore!"

"Alberta is only a year older than Kholassi, and you jumped several fences with her on the way to Dolma! You were just scared to jump the cart," I teased.

Leonard opened his mouth to argue some more, when a stern voice cut in, "That fruit cart owner was very upset by your appearance. You both gave him and many other citizens, quite the scare." Galileo's stern voice mirrored his face, causing Leonard and me to look guilty at the ground. Galileo sighed, "While I am aware that you both are expert horsemen, the people of Dolma are not. Please don't scare them."

"You know, if we race more often, people will get used to it," Leonard responded, bravely.

Galileo glared at him. "You are a knight of the kingdom," he shouted. His earlier calm voice deserting him completely, "and you are to be Queen," he said rounding on me, "you cannot go around recklessly -"

"So it's true you are a new Crown Princess," a cool voice came from around the corner, mercifully saving me from Galileo's chastising. As I turned to look at the figure, however, I came to realize his approach was accompanied by a long sword aimed directly at us. Movement on either side of us revealed a group of six other armed men, now circling us. "Pretty little thing, aren't you? Now be a good dear and give us all of your money. I'd hate to send you back with a scar on your face."

"Why?"

"Excuse me? I'm robbing you. This is a robbery."

"I mean, why would you hate to send me back with a scar on my face. Personally, I think I would look rather cool, so why would you hate it?"

"Look lady," the man said, moving closer, "that was a threat. I'm threatening you! What the fu-"

"Now!" I shouted as Galileo, Leonard, and I moved to face our opponents. Mama had always said that in a real fight, one might tense or freeze up, what she failed to mention was how the adrenaline sharpened your movements. My blows seemed to fall faster and stronger. It was an exhilarating high. I finally understood why some of our past rulers got so caught up in fighting in wars. There was no sensation like it. Not that I would ever intentionally put other's lives in danger, I had to remind myself as I stared at the unconscious men before me, but I did now understand the urge.

"What should we do with them, Crown Princess?" Leonard asked, also staring at the slouched bodies of the men before us, and running a hand through his still wind blown hair.

I looked around, noticing a thin woman staring at us from behind the door. She quickly moved to shut it when she saw me, but it was too late. "Excuse me, Madam," I called out.

For a brief moment, I thought she might run away, but she seemed to steel herself before turning and saying, "How can I help you, Your Majesty?"

"Technically, I would be Your Highness, as I am not yet Queen, but you may simply call me Princess Avalynn if you wish. I was wondering if I might borrow your house for an hour or so, you will be compensated, of course," I smiled.

"My house! Whatever for?" the woman asked, her dark eyes widening in shock.

"I would like to ask these gentlemen some questions, and it would be, I believe, more uncomfortable for everyone to do so outside. I can personally assure you of the safety of your person and your personal belongings."

"I... well... all right then," the woman mumbled, seemingly still in a state of shock.

"Thank you!" I beamed, "Here is your compensation," I said, before handing her two gollups. If possible, her eyes widened even further before beckoning us eagerly into her home.

It took two round trips to get all the men into Skai's home. I was a little upset to see Galileo and Leonard carry the men in two at a time while I struggled to bring in just one, but at least I was being helpful. Eventually we managed to get everyone into Skai's living room. While we waited for the men to regain consciousness, we had tea with Skai. She turned out to be the owner of a small soap and incense store in the area. She had quite the wonderful variety of fragrances, and I found myself with a rather extensive load of purchases by the time the first men started to stir.

"What the hell?" came the rather annoyed voice of the main robber, interrupting a fascinating story of the discovery of one of Skai's newer fragrances. Galileo then had to escort Skai out of the room as the man struggled against the rope we had tied him in earlier.

"Hello!" I said smiling. "How's your head?"

"Fantastic," the man said sarcastically.

"Oh good," I replied, blatantly ignoring his sarcasm.

"Why have you taken us here?" the robber demanded.

"I had questions. Like why did you rob us?"

"For money! Why do people normally steal?" he replied, looking at me like I'd grown three heads.

"What did you intend to use that money on?" I followed up.

"I don't know, gold, a fancy cloak, a big house with lots of meat," the robber said, looking around wildly.

"Hmm, it's decided then!" I said cheerfully. "Everyone has two options: go to prison or come work for me! Now, you would have a significantly reduced pay, but you would be able to work for full pay after one year of service. You should be receiving two gollups a month, which is exactly half of what my lowest paid servant receives. You would also live in the palace, where meat is served. I don't provide fancy cloaks, but you can always save up for one. So, what do you think?" I finished.

"Are you crazy, lady?" the main robber asked.

"Depends on who you ask," I replied, thinking of how some of Dolma's courtiers might answer that question. Unsurprisingly, all seven of the robbers agreed to work for me, and soon we were bidding farewell to Skai and hiring a cart to take my new employees back to the Palace. Because I had failed to inform her I was hiring new people, my new hires all wound up under Miri's care. I was a little unsure if this meant I was gaining seven new spies, but at least it would be difficult to steal something under the watchful eye of Miri and my knights.

"Crown Princess! Are you crazy?" came a voice from the doorway, startling me and Lucy, who'd joined me for tea after my adventures in town.

"That seems to be a common question today," I said, setting down my tea cup and turning to face Tullip, the Dolmanian maid who had just burst in. Behind her I could see the anxious faces of several other Dolmanian servants. "I don't believe myself to have gone crazy just yet, so may I ask why you believe I am?"

"You've hired criminals!" Tullip explained, looking desperately at me.

"Of course," I replied, while Lucy said, "Why shouldn't she?"

Tullip looked at me with an expression that clearly stated she believed I had actually gone insane. Before I could try and clarify the matter Chanti's voice spoke up from the corner of the room. "It's a tradition in Nevremerre and Agremerre." All eyes turned to her. "In those two countries, robbing is considered a failing of the King, Queen, and ruling class. So, if a noble is ever robbed, tradition dictates they must redeem themselves by providing the robber with housing, food, and the opportunity for full time employment. They must also look into the reason the robbers were stealing in the first place and try to rectify the problem. During their time working for the noble they stole from, the robber will receive much less than the lowest working wages in the Kingdom, so it is still better to find work if you can," Chanti finished.

"Very good Chanti!" Lucy beamed.

"All she says is true; however, I should add that many rulers in Calvine believe in this tradition as well."

"But what about people robbing for greed?" Kentin, my butler, asked, worry still evidenced on his face.

"Well that does happen, which is why it's tradition, and not law. It's also why the people are closely monitored during their working period," I elaborated, "The knights are making a monitoring schedule as we speak. We'll keep a close eye on the jewelry for a month or so, but in all of the countries that employ this tradition, approximately 72% of all caught robbers, who agree to employment, do not go back into the criminal world."

"It's about giving opportunities for growth instead of punishment," Lucy nodded, returning her attention back to her tea.

"It's okay if you're not convinced," I said, smiling at the still teetering staff, "but please trust that, at the very least we will keep you safe here and please try to keep an open mind to our unfamiliar customs."

"Yes Crown Princess," came a chorus of voices followed by some bows and curtsies.

"People here really are quite fearful," Lucy commented, while I nodded my head in agreement.

Despite what Abel said, my days were still filled with more work than play, but it did feel a lot more manageable. More often than not I could be found meeting with Harry and one or more ministers, trying to convince them to adopt my latest plan for improving their country. It was an exhausting struggle, but my own personal stubbornness did come in handy as I was currently at a 3 out of 3 victory rate. Truthfully, my last plan only succeeded because the expert on architecture quit, but honestly, I counted this as an added bonus.

However, my standing with the nobles was still rather precarious. I'd been informed of at least two poisoning attempts, of which Miri believed Lady Sabine to be involved, but she couldn't find the necessary evidence to use against her. Since neither poisoning attempt even made it to my food, I left the matter with her and my knights. The nobles on Lady Sabine's side continued to avoid or talk down to me, but I did manage to receive the favor of the few competent nobles I had identified at the event at which my wedding was announced, and annoyingly, Lord Whimely.

"You know you really should have seen the look on Lord Castor's face when Lady Shamuses' daughter beat him at the poker table last night! Ha! Served the fat bastard right for underestimating me," Lord Whimely boasted, his legs flung over the sofa, much to the annoyance of myself and the children who occupied my office that afternoon.

"Why you? I thought he was playing against Lady Ursula," asked Iris.

"Well who do you think taught Ursula how to play?" Whimely asked, and a group of high-pitched giggles filled the room, informing me that perhaps my young companions were not as annoyed as I had originally thought. The little traitors.

"Why are you here Whimely?" I sighed, ignoring formality.

"Am I forbidden? But you allow everyone else in!" he whined dramatically, flinging himself onto the sofa once again, to the amusement of the children in the room.

"Are you really that bored with court life?" I asked him, "You know most of the other land owning nobles have gone home; you could do the same."

"Ah, but Princess, that implies that home isn't just as boring as here," Whimely lamented.

"Personally, I find that there aren't many boring places, simply boring people."

"You wound me, Princess."

"Then perhaps you should leave and style yourself into someone more interesting."

"Ah, but then I won't get the information I am looking for."

"And, do tell, what might that be?"

"I hear you are finally hiring some Ladies-in-Waiting."

I stared at this man. "You've been monopolizing my couch for the last two days because of that?"

"Are you actually hiring, Princess?" asked Iris. "Can I be one of your Ladies-in-Waiting?"

"Careful Lady Irisetta, it is said that the salary of our Princess here is only 1,000 gollups a year!" Whimely cautioned.

"And?" I asked, giving him a raised eyebrow.

"Even Princess Ollifelle Analise Elliayah Carleon gives 2,000 gollups a year to her Ladies-in-Waiting, and her annual salary is only 50,000 gollups!"

"Yes, and the King's highest paid servant makes one gollup a month when the minimum amount for a life outside of the palace is at least 1.2 gollups a month. I'm not here to debate with you about the poor financial choices of others."

"Still, how little did His Majesty give you?" Whimely said with concern. "You know, my family does have a large income. I could lend you some."

"Surely my salary is on some sort of public record," I pointed out. "But, for your information, the King pays me highly enough, and even if you were to lend me money, I have no intention of using it to raise the wages of my Ladies-in-Waiting. Provided you don't gamble it away, 1,000 gollups is an excellent salary, and my money is best spent aiding the people."

"Well, I suppose most people do spend a lot of money in the Gambling Hall," Whimely said contemplatively.

"So does that mean you will accept me as your Lady-in-Waiting?" Iris asked. "If I work for you, I won't have to get married immediately!"

"Then I will happily accept you as my Lady-in-Waiting, Iris, but you still have two more years until you come of age in Dolma," I pointed out.

"That's all right, it's more than enough just to say that I will have the position!" Iris smiled happily.

"Oh me too!" cried Catalina, and her words were echoed by the other children.

"Yes, yes, you can all become my Ladies-in-Waiting," I replied, turning back to my work.

"Wait, but Lord Kisserton is a boy," Whimely interrupted.

"Then he can be my Lord-in-Waiting," I replied nonchalantly.

"Could I be your Lord-in-Waiting then?" Whimely asked, peeking up over the couch.

"No, I won't hire you," I answered immediately.

"What?! That's so unfair!"

"Too bad."

"But, could you afford all these Ladies and Lords in-Waiting?"

"I wouldn't hire them if I couldn't afford it," I pointed out.

"You'd be surprised at the number of courtiers who do hire people they can't afford," Whimely muttered. "Well then, how much do you make?"

"Surely you could just look this up on your own some-where?"

"Where? Royal finances are private."

"What?" I said, finally looking back up at him. "but how does the public know if their money is being mismanaged?"

"They don't. They just trust us," Whimely said confidently.

"Well they shouldn't!" I exclaimed.

"Yeah, yeah, whatever, so how much do you make?" Whimely said, pushing the conversation forward once more.

"200,000 gollups a year," I said.

"What?" Whimely said, jumping up from his chair and coming towards me, "but that's what the Crown Prince made before His Majesty docked his salary!"

"Given that I am the Crown Princess, that would make sense. Why'd his salary get docked?"

"Because he didn't dance with you. He only lost 50,000 gollup, so he's still got quite a lot. It'll go back up next year." I noted, with some annoyance, that the amount taken from the Crown Prince completely covered what Harry had agreed to pay for the agricultural plan, but I brushed that aside trying to focus on my work once more.

"You probably also get a lot as the Crown Princess of Nevre-merre," Anabell chimed in.

"I'm not the Crown Princess yet," I commented.

"You have brothers don't you? You won't ever be Nevremerre's Crown Princess," Whimely said.

"Could the people of Dolma please pick up a book about my country just once!" I exclaimed, getting tired of repeatedly explaining myself.

"In Nevremerre," Anabell began.

"No, no, no more Dolmanian nobles get to learn about Nevremerre until they pick up a book and read it for themselves," I cut her off. Around me the children giggled once more.

"You really should read about it, Lord Whimely," Iris said, "It's truly a remarkable country!" A little bubble of pride filled me at Iris' words.

"Fine, I will then," Whimely declared, but he still spent the rest of the afternoon lying on my couch.

It took Whimely three whole days to follow through with his promise to read about Nevremerre. I know this because exactly three days later he came bursting into my rooms yelling, "You could be Queen of Nevremerre!"

His sudden arrival caused quite the stir, and a flurry of swords had to be sheathed once more before I could answer his question. "Yes, as you have already been informed, I am still a candidate for Nevremerre's throne."

"Why haven't you told anybody?" Whimely insisted.

"Well for starters, it's not exactly a secret. How long did it take you before you read that I was eligible for Nevremerre's throne?"

"It was in the first chapter," Whimely replied sheepishly.

"Have you even read beyond the first chapter?" I wondered aloud.

"Well not yet, but I needed to confirm chapter one with you! I will read more," he continued after I sent him a glare.

"Well Chapter One isn't a lie. It's public knowledge, and I can't even get the position for another seven years."

"Oh."

"Oh?"

"You're way more powerful than I thought."

"You don't even know the half of it," Sir Abel jumped in from his seat across the table. "I highly recommend you finish that book, Lord Whimely. But in the meantime, would you care for some tea?" Whimely nodded, silent for the first time since I made his acquaintance, which resulted in a rather lovely tea time.

Chapter 16

The Fallout from Ignorance

Then, war broke out. Or, rather, it almost did.

"When I said I wanted more help and that I would appreciate your help, I did not mean   that you should hide a whole war from me!" I yelled, staring at Mateo and Abel in front of me. "Not that I am not very grateful that you managed to stop any sort of actual fighting from breaking out. I just really would have rather been told."

"In our defense," Abel said, "Mateo did try to tell you first, but at the time you were rather overwhelmed and we could easily deal with it on our own."

"It was war!"

"It was almost war, and, as Mateo cleverly deduced, the soldiers were being lied to and misinformed about the state of the treaty. The soldiers had been informed that Agremerre had broken the treaty, and the Lords had led them to believe that Agremerre lacked the military forces to fight back. By riding out to the Agremerre border himself, he was able to clarify things, resulting in no war, and securing five thousand men willing to testify against the Lords they served because of the misinformation those Lords provided."

"I'm not denying that the outcome is good. Great even, as I'm sure I can convince King Harold to let me fill the seats of the Lords in question. And, I certainly trust your abilities, but please, next time at least give me some sort of warning. What exactly am I supposed to say to King Harold when he asked me why Mateo went down there without informing me?"

"I apologize, Crown Princess," Mateo said seriously.

"Don't apologize! You're a hero who prevented war, just say you'll tell me next time something big happens that you want to handle on your own!"

"Yes, Crown Princess, I promise," Mateo said earnestly.

"It's so hard to be mad at you when you're like this."

"Would you like me to behave differently, Crown Princess?" Mateo asked, a teasing look in his eyes.

"Damn it," I muttered, a warmth creeping up my face that caused me to hurriedly turn around. "I suppose this means you're my knight again."

"I was always your knight, Crown Princess, I was just on loan for a while."

"By the way, our almost skirmish seems to have caught the attention of our neighbors up north. The King of Calvine has accepted an invitation to your wedding. It's unclear whether he himself or a delegate will attend, but they sent a message through Mateo once he halted the Dolmanian army," Abel warned me and I had to turn and face them both once more.

"What could they want with my wedding?" I asked.

"It's unclear at the moment, but it would be best to start diplomatic relations, if possible. If we can avoid war with Calvine - ," Abel began.

"Then my coming here would not have been a complete waste for Nevremerre and Agremerre," I cut him off.

"Avalynn," Abel chastised quietly. I only raised an eyebrow in response.

"Either way, we must make sure the whole court is ready for Calvine's arrival," I continued.

"I have yet to inform King Harold of Calvine's message. I wanted to make sure that you knew first," Mateo informed me. While not necessary at this point, I did feel oddly better to be receiving this information before anyone else.

"Good. I will tell King Harold. No doubt he'll be here shortly. He must be almost done questioning the army commanders." As if determined to prove my words true, Harry came bursting through my doors.

"You, boy," He barked, pointing a finger at Mateo as he stormed inside, "deserve a medal and a prize. What do you want? Do you want to be a Lord? I'm about to have several titles open! And you, Ava, with me. Where is your study? Oh, and you," he pointed at Abel, "bring me my son."

"Yes, Your Majesty," Abel bowed with a small smile.

"Harry, why don't you come with me, and we'll leave Mateo to decide if he wants to be a Lord," I said soothingly, guiding Harry to my office and smiling at a stunned looking Mateo.

"Those damned nobles!" Harry screeched as we entered the room, "They think they can get away with this! Well they've got another thing coming, mark my words."

"I believe you," I replied. And it was true. I had never seen Harry this angry, and I was well aware he was a force to be reckoned with. I was almost looking forward to what his wrath would become.

"I'll have their heads for this," he snarled. I looked at him.

"You'll kill them?"

"Of course, show no mercy to your enemies, Ava."

"Perhaps, but honestly death seems a little tame."

"What?"

"Well, the thing is, if it's just death, then that's the end. I prefer to see them suffer," I didn't mention that in Nevremerre, a death sentence was highly frowned upon, so I tried to resort to other ways to dissuade him.

"What, like torture?"

"No!" I jumped in quickly. "Just take away their title, their land, all their money, and send them to live on their own. They've already lost the support of their armies, so they can't build up power that way. Then if you write an article for the public on exactly how their treacherous actions would have impacted the whole of Dolma, they won't get much, if any, support from the commoners, and finally, tell the nobles that anyone suspected of aiding them will also be investigated for treason and fraud. Oh, and let the children stay here or go with grandparents. They weren't guilty of any crimes and shouldn't be harmed."

"So take away all they love and all their life lines," Harry mused. "I can work with that."

"Good," I breathed, relieved that torture and death were now off the table. "Now, about the Lord positions available, as it was my country almost invaded by your negligence, and my knight who prevented you from losing your country. I would like to be the one to decide who the new rulers of the areas will be."

"As you wish," Harry sighed, "But, I'll put the fear of the Gods in those nobles tonight." He looked rather excited at the thought.

A knock came at the door, "Your Majesty," came Abel's smooth voice, "His Highness, the Crown Prince, is here."

"About time," Harry snapped, "send him in."

The doors pushed open and Thomas walked inside. His face was calm and collected. Although it wasn't blank like his sister's, he still looked not like a person, but like a statue carved from marble. "You called me, Your Majesty," he asked calmly.

"Have you ever been to war, boy?" Harry asked, leaning against my desk.

"No, of course not," Thomas replied, looking briefly confused before his marble mask flew up once more.

"Well, you almost did!" Harry screamed, causing both Thomas and myself to flinch. "That damn mistress of yours sent Lord Feris, Lord Caster, and Lord Waverlion to gather their forces and attempt to attack Nevremerre and Agremerre. I'm sure she thought 5,000 men would be enough. Ha!"

"Lady Sabine did this?" I asked, shocked by this information.

"Well, I don't have the proof, yet," Harry continued.

"If you don't have proof, you can't just accuse her," Thomas said, he looked far more passionate than I had ever seen him.

"Quiet. You're blind when it comes to her wicked ways." This, I thought, was a little dramatic coming from Harry, but he continued on nonetheless, "She likely used her connections at court to bribe and sway those Lords into gathering their forces in the hopes of ending the marriage between you and Avalynn. Your marriage is only a month away, and she wants the position of Queen far more than she could ever want you."

This felt like far too harsh a sentiment not to get involved. "We cannot accuse those we lack evidence to convict," I said gently.

"Don't defend her!" Harry turned on me.

"I don't defend her, but a functional justice system. It does no good to yell at your son over something we cannot prove."

"Fine! But listen here Thomas. I will tell everyone tonight, but make sure that woman hears it. We cannot defeat Nevremerre or Agremerre in battle. They both possess the strongest armies and navies in the world. Should they ever decide to, they could easily take over this entire continent. Look into Nevremerre's history, Thomas, for they were once smaller than Dolma ever was, and now they own the entire western coast."

Thomas looked taken aback by his father's words. In his silence, I stepped in. "You both should know, Calvine's royal family will be coming to our wedding." I proceeded to elaborate on what Mateo had told me.

When I finished, Harry grabbed my desk and looked up towards the ceiling, "May the Gods help us all," he muttered. Before looking at us both and saying, "Tomorrow the three of us will meet to strategize about this. Tonight, you will arrive at the banquet together. Thomas, you will be staying and getting ready here until that time comes." With that, Harry flung the doors open and pushed his way out of the room. Leaving my future husband and me utterly alone.

Chapter 17

The Uninvited Guest

We did not stay that way for very long, as Thomas quickly moved to try and follow his father. However, two knights at the door prevented him from leaving my wing. "Let me out," Thomas demanded, staring at the knights in front of him. While he lacked the intensity of his father, he was somewhat imposing with his looming height. However, to me, he still felt like a child throwing a tantrum.

"Apologies, Your Highness, but we have orders from His Majesty not to let you out," one of the knights responded.

"So I am to be a prisoner in my own home?"

"Technically, this is my home," I pointed out. Thomas did not seem to appreciate my correction, as he huffed before beginning to argue with the knights once more.

"So, have you given more thought to becoming a Lord?" I asked Mateo, choosing to ignore Thomas.

"Would it benefit you, for me to become a Lord here, Crown Princess?" Mateo responded.

"You are a benefit to me in any position you take," I answered honestly. "but this is about what you want Mateo."

"Then I wish to stay by your side, as your knight," Mateo said firmly, and my heart skipped a beat as I smiled back at him. "I meant what I said back in Nevremerre, Crown Princess; there is no greater honor for a knight than serving someone they believe in."

"I -"

"And what do you have to say about this?" Thomas interrupted loudly, standing over the couch.

"Nothing," I replied.

"Nothing?" Thomas echoed.

"Yes. I'm not involved in whatever strange dynamic there is between you and your father, and, as you will surely learn throughout the day, the presence of other people does not deter my ability to work. Plus, maybe, we can finally learn how to talk to each other."

"Fine then," Thomas answered grumpily, throwing himself onto the couch, "but don't expect me to be proper!"

"This is my home, Thomas, everyone is free to act as comfortably as they like. As long as you aren't hurting yourself or others, you are free to do as you please."

"I... really?" Thomas asked me, his clear blue eyes widening with shock.

"Yes, of course," I replied, with a bit of a snap in my voice. "This is a house, not a meeting hall."

"To be fair," Mateo interjected. "I think technically this is still a series of rooms connected to the palace."

I let out a short laugh, "True, but it's home now. Mateo, gather the original group plus Kentin; we need to discuss those new Lord positions."

"Yes Crown Princess," Mateo bowed before leaving the room.

"What new Lord positions?" Thomas asked, sitting up from his reclined position to look curiously over at me.

"Since Nevremerre and Agremerre were about to be attacked, Harry gave me permission to replace the Lords who gathered their armies against my country."

"Do you have some blackmail that I don't know about?"

"This is our third conversation ever, I most definitely have things you don't know about," I said, with only a little bit of condescension.

"Oh, well I guess that's on me then," Thomas replied, playing with the ends of a pillow. "I am sorry about that. Sabine doesn't want me talking to you. I tried to tell her that you didn't want to interfere in our relationship, but she doesn't believe it. I love her, so it's just better to do what she says."

Thomas confessed this more to the pillow than to me, but I suppose it was better than nothing. I still wasn't quite ready to forgive him, or to accept his continued silence. "So, were you just planning on ignoring me for the rest of our marriage?"

There was a tense silence that I took to mean yes. "Look, that's just not possible. At the very least we have to discuss the ruling of the country! We will be leading an entire nation, if we're not on the same page we could harm the people. If Lady Sabine is truly concerned, we can speak only of business matters whenever we meet." Personally, I was of the opinion that you should trust the person you're in a relationship with. Or, at the very least, Thomas could have arranged a meeting with Lady Sabine and me to talk and understand each other.

"I suppose so," Thomas agreed. Oddly, I was even more frustrated by his agreement. Stop being such a pushover! I wanted to scream at him, what do you want in all of this? But I held my tongue, trying to keep this conversation pleasant. Or, at least, I really really tried to. It seems, though, I may have been lacking in self-control.

"Why did you agree so easily? Lady Sabine and I are not the only ones involved in this! You are also a party in this relationship. Stand up for what you want too!" I chastised him.

There was a long wait between my words and his response. A long silence during which Thomas just stared at me, and my cheeks took on steadily pinker hues while I internally chastised myself for speaking at all. My pride refused to let me backpedal on my words, and I ended up forcibly examining the wall behind Thomas's head. It was a rather lovely shade of coral that did wonders to create a brighter atmosphere in the room.

"I would like for us all to get along," Thomas blissfully whispered, saving me from having to continue my mental examination of the room.

"Well then, get working on that because I would like that too," I nodded.

Thomas smiled. It was the first time I had seen him smile, it must have been the first time because I don't think I could have ever forgotten if I had seen this face before. He positively glowed. His near white hair shone around him, and I was reminded of the art that covered the palace walls. It was beautiful, ethereal, and something not to be touched by a simple human like me. He took my breath away, and I didn't mind. After all, everyone loves pretty art on the walls, but it's people who bring life to a home, and only minutes later, Mateo led my people in.

It was a productive meeting once everyone else got used to the living art sitting beside me. He even asked a few thoughtful questions that boded well for our working relationship. Eventually it was decided that Oberon, Hugo, Mateo, and six members of our Dolmanian staff would be sent out to one of the three regions to get candidates for the open noble positions. I was loathe to lose my friends for several weeks, but I trusted these men and the people traveling with them to bring me the people I needed to change this country for the better.

"Your people all listen to you so easily," Thomas commented as he followed me from the living room to my office. I was a bit confused as to why he seemed to attach himself to me, but I was letting it slide as it was at least an improvement from silence.

"I suppose so," I responded, "but they are people who I trust and who trust me, so I think it's only natural."

"I think we have different ideas about what is natural," Thomas said blandly.

"I agree."

"What are you doing now?" Thomas pestered, coming around to look at my desk.

"I'm trying to work on reforming the education system."

"Why?"

"Well, because your curriculum is severely lacking, most girls only go to school until age 8, while most boys only study until age 11!"

"So?"

"Children need a proper education! Everyone deserves the opportunity to learn, and educating everyone leads to greater innovation and culture throughout the country."

"Says who?" Thomas argued, his face growing cold and hard once more. "Some families need those children to work. Who are you to say that education is more important than work?"

"Parents should be making enough that they don't have to rely on their own children for labor!"

"That's simply not possible. Some businesses cannot afford to pay their employees that much, and what about the farmers who need labor for the harvests?"

"If a business cannot afford to pay their employees a living wage, they do not deserve to be a business! And of course it's possible, this is what we are doing in Nevremerre and it works."

"This is Dolma, not Nevremerre, you can't just come in and expect the whole country to change to be like your home!" Thomas said, and I did not even get the chance to reply before he stormed out of my office.

Perhaps I was destined to never actually get along with my future husband. I sighed into my hand, despite what I had told Thomas earlier, this big wing of mine now felt so stifling at just the thought of having Thomas here with me. I stared down at my now only half finished paperwork. There was only one thing to do, I decided. I moved from my desk and set off on my new task. Fifteen minutes later, I walked happily past a still pouting Thomas, and took no small amount of satisfaction from being allowed outside while he was still stuck in my rooms. Followed by Oberon and Leonard today, I joyfully made my way to the training grounds. As per usual these days, the training grounds were filled with knights and guards eagerly learning from Galileo and my other knights.

"Crown Princess," Galileo called out, and the whole field stopped, turned, and bowed in my direction. Now, I like to think that I wasn't power-obsessed or needed the submission of others, but I cannot deny that seeing a field full of men bowing down to me was a thrilling feeling. I think what made it so much more impactful was the contrast between the nobles who gave me rude stares and whispered behind my back, who curtsied and bowed only when other members of the royal family were by my side. Here, these men bowed not out of obligation, but out of trust and gratitude. They accepted me as a leader and as a warrior. With all the drama and the struggle that I had found in Dolma, the knowledge that there were still people who believed in me meant the world to me.

"Please rise," I smiled. "It's wonderful to see you all here. Sir Galileo informs me that you are all progressing wonderfully. Now, I am looking to spar today. Does anyone want to be my partner?" There was a subconscious step back taken by the knights closest to me, that made me laugh a little. Thankfully, however, Sir Julius volunteered. Sir Julius had come a long way since I initially knocked him to the ground after his failed duel with Hugo and Challa. In fact, his lessons with Challa had significantly improved his temperament and overall demeanor. He now also kept referring to Challa as his teacher, even going as far as to bow to him, something with which Challa was incredibly uncomfortable.

Turning my attention back toward the field, I greeted my opponent and raised my sword, "Let's begin shall we?" I was pleased with Sir Julius' improvements. He was far more mobile and his movements sharper than before. I was in no rush to beat him. It was incredibly relaxing for such an active event, I moved quickly around him, giving him tips and instructions as I went. Finally, after half an hour my head was clear and I quickly won our match.

Sir Julius thanked me for my instruction, and I moved on to another partner, this time looking for a challenge. As usual, I found one in Galileo. As the almost champion of this year's Open Tournament, Galileo was a fierce and adaptable opponent. Sparring with him required all my attention and focus. He was light on his feet and better suited to combat my style of fighting. The challenge of it all was thrilling. It took nearly an hour before I collapsed down in front of Galileo's sword. We'd been running about a 50/50 win versus loss record since I arrived, and even with my defeat this time, I was already mentally rehearsing for our next match.

"Your movements were too obvious this time, Crown Princess," Galileo said from his place on the ground beside me. It was an honor to know that after I conceded defeat, he too needed rest.

I gave an exhausted chuckle, "I'll try not to be so easy to read next time." I closed my eyes, letting the cool air hit my tired body.

"I think we're taking up too much of the training ground," Galileo commented, but he, notably, made no move to get up.

"Everything in Dolma is oversized, so I think we can take up this section," I said, also not moving, "And, if they really need the space, they can think of us as obstacle training."

It was Galileo's turn to laugh, "Good idea, Crown Princess."

A sudden shade above me brought an extra chill over my body, and I looked up to see Oberon towering above. "Are you two going to need to be carried back inside?"

"Yes," I responded immediately, while Galileo echoed my sentiments with, "Well that would be nice." Behind us there was a gaggle of snickers from knights who seem to prefer watching us to training.

"Come on," Oberon laughed, reaching out a hand to both of us. Reluctantly, we took his hand and propelled ourselves onto our feet.

"Ana's going to kill us if we don't get you back for a bath," Hugo commented, giving me a once-over while he was fighting some poor guard who seemed to be desperate to land a single blow on my unbothered knight.

"Well I'll be sure to let her know that she's managed to attract the fear of the best knights in the Kingdom," I joked.

"Good," said Hugo, finally finishing his very one-sided match. "I would hate to get on her bad side," he said seriously.

Oberon, Leonard, and I slowly made our way back to my rooms. Sadly, despite my request, I had to walk back using my own manpower. So much for Thomas believing my people followed my words easily. My anger toward the man had all but vanished after my morning spar, so I was feeling quite happy. That is, until I saw him sitting in the exact same place I left him nearly two hours ago. "Surely you have something better to do than sit around on my couch all day," I said incredulously.

"You look a wreck, what did you do?" Thomas asked by way of response.

"Clearly more than you," I replied, taking a warm towel from Lewis, my footman, who just appeared with a sack for the three of us.

"Well, I would do something, but in case you've forgotten, I'm trapped in here all day," Thomas said, eyeing us carefully as we wiped our hands and faces.

"You do know my rooms consist of more than this area, and I know I possess several books and games that most people would consider forms of amusement. Perhaps you could even read about Nevremerre as your father suggested. You will be meeting my parents in just a month's time after all; you should know something about our country," I replied, moving through the room. Once again, Thomas surprisingly followed me through my home.

"I met your father before," he pointed out.

"You saw King Edgar of Nevremerre," I corrected. "My father said he didn't get a chance to speak with you as he was mostly negotiating with Harry."

"Well I must have at least said hello," Thomas insisted.

"Are you sure? You never said hello to me," I pointed out.

"That's different. Your father - "

"King Edgar"

"Right, your father, King Edgar, didn't come to marry me!"

"Well lucky him," I said dryly, walking into my bedroom. To my continued surprise, Thomas kept following me.

"I didn't mean it in a bad way. I don't think you're a bad person to be betrothed to, I'm just not in love with you," Thomas defended.

"Well I'm glad we've established that I'm not a bad person to be engaged to, and, as we've already discussed, I'm not in love with you either. So now that we clarified both of those things, can you please leave?"

"I can't, as you already know, father has banished me to this side of the palace until this evening."

"No, Thomas. I mean can you please leave my bedroom. I would like to take a bath." For the first time, Thomas seemed to notice the room around him, blinking stupidly into the new-found space.

"But why did you take me in here?" he demanded.

"I didn't! You followed me like a lost puppy," I shouted back.

"Oh, right. I should be going then," Thomas cooled down.

"Yes," I agreed.

"You know -" Thomas began

"Out. Bath," I managed ungracefully.

"Wait," Thomas said, quickly turning to face me.

"What?"

"I'm hungry."

"Then, go ask one of my very well-trained and competent staff for some food."

"But what if I want to eat with you?"

"Then starve until I finish bathing," I shouted before closing the door in his face. I turned to find Ana and Miri staring at me from the inside of the room. "I think I liked it more when he didn't talk to me."

"I'll get started on a bath," Ana said sympathetically as I sagged against the door.

"I must say," Miri commented, "he does act differently here than he does in the rest of the palace. I don't think I've ever seen him show that much emotion."

"Perhaps he's becoming more comfortable with you," Ana said hopefully as she took my hand and led me to the bathroom.

"I wish he would become uncomfortable again," I mumbled as I began to undress.

"You don't mean that, Crown Princess," Ana chastised.

"No, no I don't," I sighed as I finally stepped into the blissfully warm bath. I continued my relaxation under the tender care of my two maids. Soon I was being dressed in a long gown by the rest of my maids, and getting ready for lunch. I had to admit my outfit seemed a little nicer than my usual daywear. When I brought this up to my maids, most of them looked away, but Ana was nothing if not honest.

"Your future husband is finally taking an interest in you, we need to start trying to improve his image of you."

"I don't need to dress for a man! And, if he is my future husband, surely he should know what I'm going to look like on a normal day."

"Crown Princess," Ana scolded. "Early impressions matter, and you and Their Majesties originally chose your clothes for your own pleasure back in Nevremerre. We are selecting your clothes today to make an impression, just like your initial outfit into Dolma. Clothes are a representation of you to the people around you, and today we are telling the Crown Prince that you are a competent, desirable, and powerful woman."

"Oh very well then. Thank you," I caved, before walking out the door.

Thomas did, in fact, join me for lunch, although he confessed to having a snack beforehand. It seemed the rest of my staff agreed with Ana, as lunch was also far more formal than we normally enjoyed. Thomas, at the very least, didn't seem to have any issue with this arrangement. He did however go back to his emotionless appearance. It was eerily reminiscent of our first meal together, except this time I didn't have Harry to converse with.

Mother, when we were younger, began our education with an easy phrase, "It's only awkward if you make it." In other words, silent dinners or long pauses were only embarrassing if you believe them to be. Instead, make your silence a deliberate choice, and you will not feel burdened by the quiet. It was a major benefit when dealing with people in Dolma, however, I was having less success with her ideology at the current moment. I blamed Ana for getting into my head about Thomas's visible emotions being attached to his level of comfort. I really didn't want him to feel uncomfortable around me.

"Thomas," I said, breaking the silence, "when looking at Dolma's current labor laws, I was confused on any age labor restrictions you have. Can you explain them to me?" This, I believe, would be a perfectly neutral question. Still related to the government, so Lady Sabine couldn't fault me, and I could get a greater understanding of Dolma's laws.

"I don't know," Thomas responded, ruining my satisfaction of having crafted the perfect question.

"You don't know? What do you mean you don't know?" I blurted at him from across the table.

"Well, I don't know anything about those laws," Thomas replied nonchalantly.

"You are the Crown Prince!" I yelled at him.

"So?"

"What in the Gods' names have you been doing all of this time?" I demanded.

"Well, other things!" Thomas sputtered indignantly, ruining his perfect posture to lean across the table to speak to me. "There are people who can do those things for you when you are King."

"But what if they lie to you? What if you want to change something, wouldn't you need to have an understanding of those laws' nuances? How do you make sure your laws are not outdated or check that they don't now have a negative impact if you don't know what those laws are?" I asked, infuriated by his negligence.

"Well, do you expect me to know everything?"

"When it comes to the laws and regulations that govern your country, yes, yes I do! That is your job. You are the Crown Prince, at any time you could be responsible for the health, safety, and prosperity of all who live here. You should at least know the rules by which you are guiding their lives! I'm not saying you can't have aids," I said, as Thomas stared at me, "or other people can't help fill the gaps in your knowledge, but you should at least have knowledge of the laws you impose on the people."

Thomas stared at his plate, moving his salad around with his fork. "So where do you suggest I start?" he finally asked.

"I have a book of Dolma's laws in my office. You can read that while I work on the new educational proposal," I said.

"All right," Thomas nodded, "but if you're helping me, then I shall help you. Your education plan will get lots of backlash from the nobles. There are many things that you could pass without the knowledge of the nobles, but increasing education for commoners is not one of them. Education is a way for nobles to feel superior. They won't give up that easily."

"So? Education is important; they can't just deny it for people," I pointed out.

"Have you perhaps never lived in the real world?" Thomas asked, incredulously.

"I -" I started to argue back, but Thomas didn't give me the chance.

"Have you learned nothing today? Whether it was Sabine's idea or not, someone was so upset that you were here that they tried to start a war! And they were able to convince three powerful Lords to join them. And, what happens when the next thing they come for is your own life? Or worse, the lives of those around you?"

"We were able to stop the war today, and we discovered the poison attempts before they got to anyone. We can do that again if necessary," I said, but truthfully, I felt a bit scared that harm could actually come to those around me.

"Are you listening to yourself? I admit you've got great people around you, but they're only people! They can make mistakes, or miss things, what if next time you aren't so lucky?" Thomas demanded, and I had to concede he was making excellent points.

"Still, I can't just stop trying to push for positive change just because of the possibility of some retaliation," I pushed on.

"If it truly is that important, then I won't stop you from implementing it eventually, but please be smart about this, wait until you have a better position in court and more nobles on your side. You can't make all the changes you want to see if you're dead. There must be something else you can focus on in the meantime!"

I pondered his words. He was right, and it would be foolish of me to ignore his insights on the matter. I had already noticed the unfounded pride of nobles in Dolma, and I could easily see that pride turning more nefarious, if it were threatened. "Fine, if you've finished eating, then we should go to my study and you can advise me on a better topic for now," I finally decided.

"Let's go then," Thomas agreed, placing his napkin on the table and standing up.

In my study, I gave Thomas my list of things I felt needed to change in Dolma, while I searched for my book on Dolma's laws. "Gods, are you planning to keep anything the same?" Thomas demanded.

"The name will stay the same," I commented dryly.

"This is ridiculous! You are changing the whole country!"

"The country needs changing," I said, turning to face him. "Have you ever seen how the majority of your people live? Because I have. I've been to the houses in the "border" town. I've ridden through your capital city. I've spoken with the people of Dolma, with the staff in the palace, with robbers on the streets, with people in the "border" towns. I have had my staff, knights, and my Lady-in-Waiting bring me as much information as they possibly could about the people in your country, and they are suffering. They are suffering in ways that people in Nevremerre only suffered in our ancient history. Your people work insane hours at incredibly low wages just to avoid starving and to keep a mold-covered roof over their head. You have enough rooms in this Palace to comfortably house possibly the entire city and yet still you have people living on the streets, in utter poverty. Do you think that's okay? To protect the lives of your people, things need to change."

Thomas looked at me, his blue eyes pouring into mine, searching for something. I don't know if he found what it was that he was looking for, but he suddenly turned around and said, "You'll never be able to change it all. Some of these things are unchangeable."

"It may take time, but everything on that list was created by humans, meaning it can be changed by humans too. Everything seems unchangeable until someone changes it," I shrugged, turning back to the bookshelf.

There was silence, and I soon found the book I was looking for on one of the higher shelves. I was moving to get it down when Thomas spoke again, "If you're determined to go down this path, then I would reform health care next. No one will pay attention to the - Gods above, what are you doing?!"

There was a rustle of movement behind me, and I suddenly felt a pair of hands on my waist. "Thomas?" I asked, utterly shocked. There was no response as I was physically picked up and lifted off the shelf.

"What in the world did you think you were doing?" Thomas yelled at me once I was back on the floor.

"Getting you the book you wanted!" I replied, matching his angry tone, although I was more confused than angry.

"You were climbing the bookshelf!"

"Well yes, because that's where the book is," I pointed out.

"It's dangerous!"

"I am an expert climber!"

"That won't prevent you from being crushed by a bookshelf!"

"I won't be crushed by a bookshelf!"

"You don't know that!"

"Fine! Then you can get it for yourself!"

"I will! It seems far safer!"

"Spoilsport," I murmured, sitting down at my desk, "so, health care you said?"

"Yes," Thomas replied, as he sat down on the sofa with his newly retrieved book. "No nobles that I know of pay too much attention to public health. They all have their own private doctors anyways." I sighed, faced once more with the complete and utter negligence of Dolma's ruling class, but started on my health care proposition all the same.

Chapter 18

The Full House

At this point, it had been well over a month since the afternoon child invasion had begun. I was more than used to the small humans who would enter my study. I even began to get used to the inclusion of Lord Whimely every now and then, so it honestly had not even occurred to me to warn Thomas until Anabell, Catalina, Baderly, and Ki came rushing through the door.

"Crown Princess!" Anabell rushed in. Her pink bow was clinging desperately to her blond hair and she ran towards me. "Look what I did," she said excitedly, holding up a small canvas. On it was a painting of the red and gold trees that brightened the world around us at the current moment. Under the trees sat two silhouettes gazing up at the sky above. While clearly still made by someone in the process of learning fine motor control, it was quite the remarkable piece of work for an 8 year old.

"My goodness, Anabell, this is wonderful!" I said sincerely, pulling the little girl onto my lap. "You could be an artist if you wanted to."

"Do you think so?" Anabell beamed at me. "See here," she glowed, "I learned how to do shading. It's still not great, but Governess Tarinell said I did a good job, and she never compliments anybody!"

"That's amazing!" Catalina said, as she moved towards me, followed closely by Baderly and Ki. As I looked up at Catalina, I was suddenly forced to contain my laughter. There, standing in horror in front of the couch was Thomas. He was straight to the sword and still as a statue. It was like he believed that if he just stood still the children wouldn't notice him. Admittedly, it seemed to be working as the children were too busy talking to me to acknowledge him. "Governess Tarinell never compliments me! It's always, "Those arms are too thick", "Tree leaves aren't that red", "Why'd you make their skin blue?"," Catalina said, mimicking the voice of the older woman with a fair amount of accuracy. "It's quite boring to draw landscapes and people all the time."

"Well, in Nevremerre, some people draw in a style called surrealism, in which, I believe, it is perfectly acceptable to draw blue people," I nodded toward Catalina. Turning back to Anabell, I added, "However, many artists also draw in a style called impressionism, where they use very small brush strokes to add depth and light, which looks similar to your style, Anabell."

"Really?" Anabell asked gleefully.

"I wish we got to do art," Ki lamented, sadly looking at Anabell's painting.

"No you don't," Catalina assured him.

"If you really want to learn, Ki, maybe Anabell could teach you," I said.

"Do you draw, Crown Princess?" Baderly asked.

"Not even a little bit," I replied honestly, "I was offered some classes as a child, but I refused in favor of music lessons."

"Lucky," Catalina sighed, "we have to do both."

"Yes, well - " I began, only to be interrupted by a shriek at the door.

"Crown Prince!" Iris' voice called out from the doorway, where she stood dumbfounded. She did, however, recover far better than Thomas, who still stood motionless by the couch. Iris quickly corrected herself with a curtsy. "I greet the Crown Prince Thomas Rayforth Ecardio Davenforth Carleon." Thomas gave a little nod, and then Iris turned to me. She gave another flawless curtsy before saying, "I also greet Princess Avalynn of Nevremerre."

"It's okay, Iris. The Crown Prince is here for the day as well, so please be comfortable," I said quickly. Iris looked a little unsure, but gave me a nod before she too walked over to my desk.

"How was your dance lesson?" I asked, hoping to put her more at ease.

"It was fine. I was partnered with Lord Gallifrey," her nose is wrinkled in distaste. "He's the absolute worst dancer. He kept stepping on my feet! And, neither Tutor Menicants or Governess Lilliana will correct him too much because his father is the expert of agriculture," Iris huffed, looking more comfortable as her rant went on.

"I didn't know Lord Lambaster had a son," I responded.

"Yes, and he's just the worst!" Iris replied.

"So he takes after his father then," I nodded. Iris laughed, fully comfortable in my office once more. With her comfort came that of the other children who had been nervously glancing at Thomas since Iris' entrance.

"Anabell, Ki, Catalina, I have a book on Nevremerre art history, if you'd like to learn more about those styles I was talking about," I said, putting Anabell back down and moving towards the bookshelf.

"Oh, I want to see it!" Anabell jumped.

"I want the pirate story I was reading last time," Catalina exclaimed.

"Where's the one about sharks?" Baderly said, already looking through the shelves.

"Is there a book about Queen Amara?" Iris asked, she had been steadily learning about each of Nevremerre's past Queens, and it seemed the Warrior Queen was next on her list. I went through and found the book everyone wanted, and they went to sit on the couches. Notably, they made quite the wide barrier around Thomas, none daring to get too close.

"Should I get some ink and paper for you, Ki?" I asked the young boy. "You can practice art if you'd like."

"But I don't know what to do," he responded sadly.

"We can teach you!" Anabell smiled.

"Okay then," Ki said happily. I moved the door to get him all he required when a sudden presence stood closely behind me.

"Why are there children in here?" hissed Thomas, next to my ear. I opened the door in front of me and waited until he followed me out into the hall.

"Many children don't have a place to go after their lessons, so they come here," I said, walking through my rooms and gesturing to where kids were doing various activities with my staff.

"What? Why?" Thomas asked, looking scandalized for a brief moment before composing himself as a few of the older children passed by, giving us both a bow.

"Why not?" I replied. "They're not in the way, we have plenty of adults here who enjoy keeping them entertained, and it's probably safer than just having them wander around the palace like they used to do."

"The palace is safe," Thomas insisted.

"I'm currently training many of the palace guards, and I would beg to differ."

"I - who are you to make that determination?" Thomas asked angrily.

"Someone trained by the best warriors in Nevremerre," I snapped back. "What was your military training again?" It did occur to me that my only conversations with my future husband all seemed to end in arguments, but I couldn't seem to stop myself from fighting with him.

"Did you need something, Crown Prince and Crown Princess?" came the dutiful voice of Kentin, his clan of children standing eagerly behind him. It was probably fortunate that his presence cut short our latest disagreement.

"Some paper and ink for my study please. Lord Kisserton would like to draw," I informed him.

"As you wish, Crown Princess," Kentin bowed. After that Thomas and I moved quietly back to my study. Only to run into our next problem.

"I greet Crown Prince Thomas Rayforth Ecardio Davenforth Carleon and Princess Avalynn of Nevremerre," Lord Whimely bowed as we entered my study once more. Personally, I still thought the lengths of people's names in Dolma to be a bit ridiculous, but after hearing Thomas and my name's said back-to-back, my name did start to feel a bit lackluster.

I was pulled from my thoughts by a hand reaching around my waist and pulling me back out of the room. Another hand pulled the door shut in front of us. As soon as the door clicked shut Thomas whirled me around to face him. "What is Whimely doing here?!" he whisper-yelled at me.

I maneuvered myself out of his grasp, "I don't know! He just sort of shows up." I really did try to say this in a calm and mature manner. I really, truly did, but it came out in the same sort of whisper yell he had just directed at me a moment before.

"Do you care nothing at all of your reputation?" Thomas whisper-roared in my direction, "Whimely is a notorious playboy!"

"Why?" I responded unthinkingly, finding nothing even remotely attractive about his curly blond hair, garish style, and, frankly, annoying demand to constantly be receiving attention.

"I - well I don't quite know," Thomas paused in his anger to consider the question. "Wait, that's not the point! He can't just come into your rooms! Do you know what kind of scandal that could cause?" he said, getting back on track.

"Really, Thomas, I highly doubt he's going to ravish me in a room full of children," I said dryly. Thomas's face turned a curious shade of red as he opened his mouth to speak once more.

"I do hope I'm interrupting something," Whimely butted in, his head peeking out of the door.

"Yes, my work, constantly," I replied, opening the study door and going to my desk, "in fact, you both are."

"No don't say that, Princess," Whimely bounced around me. "I assure you, I am the perfect model of decorum."

"You're a nuisance," Thomas muttered, moving back into the room and taking a seat on the couch once more. It seemed highly uncomfortable to sit with such a straight back, I noted. Also observing that his posture was far stiffer than the one he'd exhibited prior to the children's arrival.

Whimely, on the other hand, looked remarkably like a wet noodle as he flung his limbs over any open couch space, nearly hitting Anabell and Ki in the process. "Crown Prince, you wound me," he whined.

"Good," Thomas muttered.

There was silence for a bit, and I foolishly hoped that we could continue our silent work before Whimely dashed those plans once more. "You know, we really haven't seen you around as of late," Whimely said to Thomas. "That Mistress of yours keeps you locked up tight, does she?"

"She, correctly, finds herself to be far more pleasant company than you. I have no intention of neglecting her," Thomas said, primly. It occurred to me that in most relationships bringing up a mistress in front of another person's betrothed would be considered poor form, but given our unusual circumstances, I decided to let this one slide.

"Really? She can't even give you up for one night to spend time with your old friends?" Whimely pestered, although this time I heard the tiniest traces of hurt in his voice. I paused my work to focus on their words. I couldn't really consider this eavesdropping, although the conversation did seem rather private, as they were speaking in normal voices, in a room full of people, and, perhaps most notably, they were speaking in my study of all places.

"Why should she have to?" Thomas demanded, still looking at his book.

"Ever since you started seeing her, you have spent less and less time with the rest of us! The five of us grew up together and this is the first time I'm seeing you outside of a public function in a year!" Whimely said angrily. It was perhaps the first time I'd seen Whimely angry. He wasn't scary in his anger, but it was unsettling to see him without his usual smile. However, if this conversation was anything to go by, I could understand his pain.

"I no longer require seeing friends," Thomas declared, "Sabine is enough." Now, having never been in a relationship myself, not counting a few stolen kisses from people I'd met while traveling around Nevremerre, people I was certain I would never meet again, I was perhaps not the best person to judge another's relationship. However, everything I knew about Thomas' relationship screamed that it was unhealthy. I wouldn't get involved of course. His relationship was really none of my business, so I would simply let him live to make his own choices.

"It's not healthy to cut out friends for the sake of a relationship," I cursed my mouth for speaking, but for some reason it ignored me and kept talking, "and you spend time with your friends not because you need to, but because you want to and because you enjoy being with them. Although there is some fascinating research being done at "The Research of The Mind Institute" in Nibera on the positive impact of socialization on depression and anxiety. They hadn't published their results when I was there last winter, so perhaps they have now," I said sidetracking myself from the previous topic. "Of course socialization likely wouldn't ease the effects of social anxiety. Or maybe it would, a sort of face-your-fears to conquer-your-fears kind of thing. I wonder if "The Research of the Mind Institute" has done any work on that?" There was a silence after that, and I belatedly realized the whole room was watching me blurt out my inner monologue.

"Where is Nibera?" was Thomas' response to my thoughts.

"It's one of the nine regions of Nevremerre," Iris said, proudly. "Surely you know the basic geography of your future wife's home country?" I have never felt more proud and grateful to any child than I had to Iris at that moment, and I couldn't help the small grin that appeared on my face.

"Now hold on," Thomas sputtered, "I bet she doesn't know the regions of Dolma."

"Adelace, Asmeirel, Casimonius, Duegle, and Yaspello," I responded without hesitation. "My entire party learned about it in the week between accepting our marriage and beginning our journey here," I said without bothering to hide my smugness, or to hide the implied question of, "Why didn't you do the same?" Next to Thomas, Whimely gave a little snort, so I turned on him. "Name one other region of Nevremerre, Whimely," I demanded.

Whimely immediately stopped laughing. "Nevre?" he guessed after a long pause. I just stared at him in response. "Well how was I supposed to know? It's not like you have last names to go off of."

"It's literally the first page of "A Brief History of Nevremerre", which I know you've started. Not to mention there are several chapters dedicated to the conquering of each region!"

"Oh yes, my favorite was the conquest of the Mariposa region! The book I'm reading now is on the life of Queen Amara who fought in the initial invasion at 77 years old!" Iris jumped in.

"She can't have lasted long in that war," Whimely pointed out.

"A little under a year," I supplied. "She died in battle at age 78, and is forever known as The Warrior Queen. Personally, I find the life of her grandson, King Archion more interesting. He took the throne after both his grandmother and father died in battle when he was just 19. He then won the war in a year and ruled peacefully for the next twenty years before abdicating."

Iris just shrugged, clearly not as interested in my suggested ruler as she was in Queen Amara. "I'm with Iris," Catalina agreed, "Why would some man be nearly as cool as a warrior Queen?"

"I think he sounds cool," Baderly said.

"Oh, would you like a book on him?" I asked, "I have several here."

"No," he replied bluntly, turning back to "Carnivorous Marine Life".

"Oh, all right then," I said feeling a little dejected. For only a moment, I was transported back to my childhood, where Al would start reading our ancestors' history to Azar and me. Azar would swear that he was sure to be the next Queen Anora, and Al and I would bond over our love of King Archion. It hit my heart like a stampede of wild buffalo, tearing up my barely held together emotions before I was forced to pull myself back into the present. The weird thing about moments like this was despite the pain of the memory, sometimes the hardest part was choosing to return to the present.

This time, the silence lasted longer, so much longer in fact that I was able to get much further into Dolma's hospital system and I was thoroughly engrossed in my work when Whimely decided to interrupt once more.

"What are you reading?" he asked Thomas.

"A book on Dolmanian law," Thomas replied, not looking up from his book.

"Why on the continent are you reading that?" Whimely said, with no small amount of surprise.

"I am the Crown Prince of Dolma," Thomas responded haughtily, "This is my job." Big words from someone who only started reading that book four hours ago, I thought, but quickly went back to my own work. I was determined not to get distracted this time.

"Who would have thought you could do any sort of job?" Whimely teased.

"Now listen here you son-of-a- "

"No! No, no, no! Out! Both of you! Get out of my study!" I yelled, moving up from my desk and pulling both of their collars until they stood up.

"Where are we to go?" Whimely asked, while I pushed them through the door.

"Out," I replied.

"But I can't leave!" Thomas pointed out.

"Thomas, my rooms have five whole floors. Find one and stay. Just get out of my study!" I yelled before slamming the door in their faces.

"Are you allowed to kick out the Crown Prince?" Ki asked, as I moved back to my desk.

"Yes," I responded confidently. "I am his wife, and these are my rooms."

"You're not married yet," Anabell pointed out.

"Close enough," I insisted, before finally getting back to my work.

Chapter 19

The Wrath of King Harold

The rest of the afternoon was extremely productive, especially once the children left for sex and gender education with Sir Abel. I also got news that my public sanitation project was ready to be put into action. Tomorrow, a cleaning staff would clean the streets of waste and within a week cleaning crews would be out in every major city in Dolma. This project came largely out of my own budget, since I insisted that employees be paid 3 gollups a month. Far higher than what the health expert or the King had been willing to pay. I really must do something about setting a minimum wage, but even without Thomas here to say it, I knew that would be difficult to put into place.

Still, victories were victories, even if small, and I was excited to see the streets of Dolma clean and also see the overall improvement in public health. It was nice to see something tangible came out of my new policies. We won't be able to see the effect of the agricultural project until the next harvest, in a year. It would also take several years to expand plumbing and housing development in the capital alone, not to mention out in other cities. It was nice to see something that I could do that would have an immediate effect. Needless to say, I was feeling much better by the time I needed to get ready for the banquet. So much so, I actually forgot Thomas was in my rooms today.

"So what are you - "

"AHHH!" I screamed.

If I could offer anyone one piece of advice, the best response to being surprised by someone or something would be to wait a moment, determine if there is a danger, and then react. When Thomas popped around the corner to talk to me, this is not what I did in my shock. No, I had to go and accidentally kick the Crown Prince, my betrothed, in the shins.

"Ow! Ow! Fuck!" Thomas yelled out in pain as I suddenly realized just what I'd done.

"Oh Gods! Thomas! Thomas I am so sorry! I-"

"Where Is the intruder!" came a loud shout from Galileo followed by all my other knights, swords drawn. At this precise moment, I was 100% willing to drop dead of shame and em-barrassment. I seriously would not have minded if I had simply vanished from the earth right then and there.

"There is no intruder, she just kicked me!" Thomas re-sponded for me, still hopping and holding his right leg.

"Crown Princess?" Galileo asked, looking at me with con-fusion.

"I - I forgot he was here, and he came out so suddenly, I just..." I said, feeling a hot flush on my face as I looked anywhere but at my knights.

"Understood, Crown Princess," Galileo responded, blissfully professional at this moment. "We shall leave you now," he said, motioning for the knights to leave.

Ever unprofessional, Challa stopped by Thomas before leaving and said, "You got lucky, she's got a mean right hook." Challa gave me a wink before he left, and I was sure my face must have been a deep scarlet.

"I really am sorry," I said sincerely to Thomas.

"I think this is going to leave a bruise! Who taught you to kick like that?" Thomas asked, looking more bewildered than in pain at the moment.

"Queen Diana, one of my mothers," I responded automatically.

"Why would she teach you that?" Thomas said, looking even more confused.

"I - well, you'll understand when you meet her," I said, not wanting to have to explain more of Nevremerre's culture today. "I have some things to help with the bruising and with the pain. You better come with me, and I really am sorry."

"Okay, just please don't do it again," he grumbled, hobbling with me towards my room.

"You're really not walking well, would you like me to carry you?" I asked.

"You couldn't," Thomas responded quickly, not even considering the option, and, well, I don't respond well to being told I can't do something. "What are you doing?" Thomas cried out as I put an arm around his back and another around his legs and carried him down the hallway.

"You're too slow walking, and I CAN carry you," I said, definitely too overconfident as I recognized this tall man was heavier than I had predicted. Not that I was going to let that stop me, of course. "And don't move, or I'll drop you, which will hurt far worse than my kick," I said with my last bit of speaking power.

"I doubt it," Thomas muttered, but he did stay still in my arms as I tried to quickly get to my bedroom.

My arms felt like dead weights, but I successfully carried Thomas to my bedroom, and guided him to his sofa. I took much longer than normal getting my medical supplies, hoping to catch my breath without Thomas noticing. I, personally, thought I was fairly successful with this task as I brought over my field medical kit. Thomas was oddly silent as I prepared a green tea poultice to reduce the swelling and bruising. Even with his silence, I could feel him watching me as I filled the bag and let it soak briefly in the hot water I had prepared, before carefully wringing it out. He didn't even speak as I rolled up his trousers to place the bag on the yellowing skin.

"Where did you learn that?" Thomas finally asked, relaxing into the now slightly cool bag.

"Well, my grandmother, the Dowager Queen Elizabeth, taught me about herbs and their healing uses. You'll meet her at the wedding too," I added. "But, I perfected my poultice treatment technique when I worked at the Nera hospital this past summer."

"You worked at a hospital?" Thomas asked, his voice quiet but curious in the late afternoon light of my bedroom.

"Yes," I responded just as softly. "In order to prepare for the drought, my brothers and I were all sent out on jobs to help the people. Since I already had knowledge on herbs, I was sent to the hospital. I was to help keep the people healthy."

"You do a lot for them, your people," Thomas said, his blue eyes meeting my green as I looked up at him.

"Of course. I am a Princess, it is my job and my honor to see my people happy and healthy."

"So you don't regret it, coming here?"

"I will never regret any action I take that keeps my people safe." We stared at each other for a few moments before the door opened and Ana, Katy, and Louisa came in.

"Crown Princess, Crown Prince," Ana curtsied, seemingly unfazed by Thomas' presence. Katy and Louisa looked more fazed, but they admirably followed Ana's lead and curtsied towards the Crown Prince and myself. "It is time for us to get the Crown Princess ready for the banquet. I believe some men have arrived to get you ready as well, Crown Prince."

"Oh yes," Thomas said, "that's what I was going to ask, what are you going to wear tonight? I think we should coordinate. We'll put up a unified front for father's anti-war message."

"Oh, yes," I said, surprised by his initiative, "Yes let's do that. I have yet to decide on what to wear, so if you have a suggestion, I'd be happy to hear it."

"My family's colors are red and black. You should wear red with a bit of black, and I will wear black with a bit of red. Sounds good?"

"Yes," I said, smiling at him. "I think that's a perfect plan." He stared at me for a moment before clearing his throat, "Good, then I'll meet you downstairs later."

My maids were thrilled by Thomas' presence, and as soon as he left I was inundated with questions about Thomas' day. "I heard you fought over lunch," Katy rushed towards me, "but you seem closer now, what happened?"

"I don't know," I sighed. "I'm pretty sure we spent most of our time arguing, so I can't say I know what's going on in his head."

"Maybe he's one of those people who likes to argue," Louisa suggested kindly.

"Who likes to argue?" I demanded.

"Arguably you, Crown Princess," Ana said with a smirk.

"That's not tr-" I paused, catching myself. "Perhaps I should just get ready," I grumbled.

"As you wish, Crown Princess," Ana said, still smirking.

Things went much smoother after that. Ana and Katy talked about the cute knight that worked for Thomas, and Louisa cheerfully told us about the adorable things the children had said to her today. Louisa had a gift for caring for the 2 to 4 year olds that came to us. It usually meant she got afternoon chores off to play with them instead. This suited her just fine, and we often got the benefit of sweet children stories without having to care for the actual children.

So, with a few adjustments to my hair, I was slipped into a gown of deep red. A black ribbon tied around my hair and two bands of dark, almost black, metal were placed around my bare arms. I bid my maids goodbye, and moved down the stairs, the heavy velvet of my dress gliding softly down my legs. I was excited. I had been waiting for the nobles and the courtiers of Dolma to get told off about something. Now, I had wanted the scolding to be related to their poor land management and monetary spending habits, but this was better than nothing. Plus, I really did not want to go to war.

Thomas was already ready when I made my way to the front room. He looked quite striking in his suit of black with a ruby clasp holding onto a black cape behind his right shoulder. Again with his face fixed in a neutral stare, he looked like a gorgeous statue to be shown only in the finest museums. He smiled when he saw me, but it did little to make him look less like art in my eyes. "Are you ready?" he asked, holding out his arm.

I smiled as I took it, "Most definitely."

The walk to the Royal pre-dinner waiting room was pleasant enough, but I found myself irritated by the constant clacking of armor worn by Thomas' four knights. Unlike the knights I've been training for Queen Priscella and Princess Ollifelle, both Thomas' and Harry's knights still wore full sets of heavy armor. It felt rude to comment on it though, so I held my tongue and spoke of my excitement about Harry's speech instead.

Thomas agreed with my statements, "I must admit, it's quite entertaining to watch him express his anger at someone who isn't me. It's far more fun to see it on the other side." We continued in this vein until we arrived at our destination.

"Good! You're here!" Harry barked at us when we entered. "And you look exceptionally put together!" he smiled, "How did you rope him into that?"

"It was Thomas' idea, Harry," I responded.

"Really? Well done boy," Harry complimented, patting Thomas' shoulder. Thomas looked wide-eyed at his father as he turned to me once more. "Is that knight of yours ready to be honored?"

"Yes. Sir Galileo made sure he was appropriately dressed for this evening, although I've yet to see him."

"Yes, well whatever it is, I'm sure he'll be fine. You wouldn't disappoint me, Ava."

"Not on this matter, but I make no promises about other things related to my time here," I responded. Thomas gave my hand a squeeze, looking at me in alarm.

Harry just laughed however, and said, "You do always surprise me, Ava. Now, announce us, and let the show begin!" Harry, dressed in white and gold may have visually matched the beautiful serenity of the palace, but he exited the room like a wild desert storm, sudden, loud, and fierce, ready to reap destruction wherever it moved.

The whole room could feel Harry's energy as they hushed themselves upon his entrance. Behind him, Thomas, Priscella, Ollifelle, and I strove to match his intimidating manner, albeit in a more quiet, dignified sort of way. Like a jungle tiger, able to pounce and tear you to shreds at any moment. "Sit," commanded Harry as he looked at the gaping nobles, his voice echoing across the room for just a moment before there was a rush of shuffled footsteps while people tried to take their seats.

Once everyone was seated, Harry began again, "It seems I have failed to impress upon you the importance of both knowledge and decorum when facing our neighbors. It also seems that the lot of you have failed to learn anything about the home country of your future Queen." There was a teetering in the crowd, but Harry glared at them, causing all movement to stop.

"Had you not been so ignorant," Harry continued, "the events of today would not have occurred. So, let me now educate you on just who my son will be marrying, and who exactly from Nevremerre and Agremerre will be gracing us in just a month's time. There was a pregnant silence in the hall, as everyone waited with bated breath to see just what about my country got their unflappable King so worked up.

From a personal standpoint, I was both thrilled and uncertain. I was dying for these people to know of the power and strength of Nevremerre and of myself. However, at the same time, I did not want my country to be used as a scare tactic. I wanted people to be genuinely curious about my country. To know the prosperity we brought to the kingdom and to learn of the joy felt by our citizens. For the first time, I started to second-guess the plan we discussed this morning. I was tired of being underestimated, but I didn't want Nevremerre to be presented that way. Suddenly, I felt sick, but Harry just kept talking.

"The country of Nevremerre was once tiny, But it managed to amass the strongest army in the known world. Located right next to Agremerre, its closest ally, and owner of the strongest naval fleet in the known world. Both grew to become two of the five largest nations on the continent. Nevremerre's size falling just behind Caperian, and I believe we all know how incredible Caperian's journey was." I actually did not know anything about Caperian, apart from its geographical location, but the room looked far more nervous after the country was mentioned. However, I was still greatly confused as to why any of them were so fearful of a country that they did not even share a border or any trade relations with. I also felt a brief flutter of annoyance that the whole court had learned about Caperian, but hadn't bothered to learn a thing about Nevremerre.

My annoyance quickly turned back to fear and regret as Harry continued, "Nevremerre's army has been the only army to ever defeat Calvine's brutal military. Nevremerre even conquered a section of Calvine's land less than three generations ago. To this day, Calvine still fears them." This was a highly inaccurate statement. The land was given to us by Calvine as a concession of defeat after a war which, according to my great grandfather's journal, Calvine started. Also, it was unclear if

Calvine actually feared us, they just withdrew 90% of their contact with us.

"And yet," Harry pressed forward, "some of you truly believe that your measly armies could win against the warrior nations of the world. Had it not been for Princess Avalynn and her knight, Sir Mateo, this entire country would be gone. Nevremerre and Agremerre would have taken over. None of you would be able to keep your lands, your titles, your money, and some of you may have even lost your lives."

"We don't take the lives of innocents," I jumped in, unable to contain myself any longer.

Harry frowned at me for a moment, but quickly turned his attention back to the nobles. "Yes, Nevremerre doesn't take the lives of the innocent, which of course leads to the question: how many of you are truly innocent? We've taken into custody the three Lords whose foolishness is akin to treason, but I know their folly was financially backed or even instigated by people in this room," Harry paused, looking around the room in the thunderous manner.

"Which is why the Queen, Crown Prince, Princess Ollifelle and myself will be cutting off one half of the salary of every courtier until they can prove their innocence in this matter and their loyalty to me." Gasps filled the room, although most were too terrified to protest. I did note that Harry only demanded loyalty to himself, not the rest of us, but I had never wanted loyalty through fear anyway.

"And now, for those who defied my decisions and chose to take matters into their own hands," Harry paused, and the main hall doors flew open, knights dragged in the chained bodies of the three Lords involved in this ill-planned war. I had to admit Harry's sense of pageantry was second to none. The whole event was incredibly dramatic. I understood the reason and the sentiment behind it, but I can't help but feel this level of fear-mongering was unnecessary and possibly cruel.

The three Lords looked paranoid and their faces seemed frozen in a silent scream. Their eyes moved through the room, but no one else dared to look at them. I found myself drowning in their paranoia. Suddenly everything we decided to do seemed horribly vicious. I forced myself to remember why we were going this far. The innocent lives that could have been lost. The soldiers they had manipulated. My anger returned, and I found I was able to meet their eyes. My own righteous fury blazing through me, my shoulders straightened, and I felt sure for the first time since Harry had started speaking. These men had lied to their soldiers, put armies on the border of Agremerre, and would have ordered them to take the lives of the innocent. Even in the face of their desperation, I was confident that their punishment was deserved. I pushed aside the internal flinch that came through me as the knights pushed them into the ground.

"For your actions against Dolma, you are all being stripped of your title, your lands, and all of your funds. From this day forward you will have only one name, your first. Your children will be allowed to remain at the palace, but they will all lose your last name, which will be replaced with the name Dolma, as a reminder they no longer serve your family, but rather my country. Any nobles who are found to be giving you aid or shelter will be considered aiding traitors to the crown and punished accordingly. This is the decision of the King of Dolma, and will be enacted immediately and completely. So let it be!" Harry declared.

The knights moved out once more, dragging the former Lords out of the room. From there, I was informed, they were taken out to the city and left on the streets, devoid of all possessions except the clothes they wore. In Nevremerre, they likely would have been fine. In Nevremerre there were programs in place to help people find work, housing developments where one could get free shelter for a time, and soup kitchens that helped provide those in need with free food. But, I had to wonder, how long would these men last in the streets of Dolma? Did I perhaps just sentence these men to a slow death? It was more shocking to realize that I was, in more ways than I was prepared to admit, comfortable with this thought. After all, these men were so careless about the lives of thousands of other people, the part of me that demanded justice insisted that they felt the same pain and suffering.

Back in the hall, the nobles were in a state of shock. They spent what felt like hours sitting in silence, watching the doors through which these Lords had just been pulled. Harry looked immensely pleased to see and to watch the nobles struggle and squirm. He let the silence continue for several minutes before demanding their attention once more. "Now, it is of course necessary to reward the man who single-handedly stopped the armies of these Lords. I will honor Sir Mateo of Nevremerre who, as just one man, stopped an army of five thousand." The door opened again and Mateo strode through.

Mateo looked devastatingly handsome in a suit of emerald green, the color of my eyes, I realized belatedly. His allegiance wasn't to Nevremerre or Dolma, it was to me. It was what he promised just a few months ago, down on his knee and the Nevremerre palace gardens. It was what he swore in front of my father along with my party before I left. It was what he demonstrated as he moved confidently towards where Harry was standing, and paused to bow to me before kneeling in front of Dolma's King.

Gods, let me be worthy of this man's loyalty, I thought, as Mateo was given money and land in Dolma. Let my mistakes never be enough for him to abandon me, I prayed as Harry espoused fake virtues that he declared Mateo possessed. None of which could even remotely compare to the virtues he did have, however. How could I have been so lucky to have gotten this man by my side? How could I ever survive if he chose to walk away? Please, please let me be deserving of all he has done and will do for me.

Finally, Mateo had been honored and Harry went to wrap up this whole affair. "Now, in recognition of the mistake we have been saved from, and an acknowledgment of her future as Dolma's Crown Princess, the positions lost today will be re-placed by people chosen by Princess Avalynn of Nevremerre." Gasps filled the room once more, and I wondered if these people would ever stop being surprised. "With all that said, let's eat," Harry finally concluded.

Chapter 20

The Welcome
Day Off

There was a flurry of movement, and a deafening sound of chatter. The voices of hundreds of people dying to gossip about all that just occurred rumbled in the hall. To me it exploded over the room, banging at my skull, chattering my bones, and making it impossible to ignore. I felt the stares of the court crashing into me. Perhaps I could have handled this on another night. I had, after all, survived my lack of a dance with Thomas; the time when I had to tell the nobles of Nevremerre and Agremerre of my leaving for Dolma; and even speaking in front of the crowds for the tournaments. But, for some reason, tonight felt like more than I could manage.

"I'm going to leave," I told Harry, not bothering to wait for a response before I walked out of the room through the side chamber in which the royal family had entered. I must have surprised Oberon and Hugo, my knights for the evening, because I was alone when I finally entered the side room. There was a wild panic that went through me at the thought of seeing another person. Without thinking I ran. I raced through the palace halls, I just wanted a quiet space to myself, nothing else mattered. So, when I finally made it to an empty hallway, one where the only light was through the haunting echo from the shining half moon, I broke down.

Tears wet my face, and I was overwhelmed by the feelings bursting through me. I could only recognize one of the myriad of emotions that enveloped my body and soul. Frustration. Frustration at not knowing why I was like this, why I suddenly hurt so badly. I felt sick to my stomach, as if I could throw up at any moment. My heart was racing, my palms were sweating, and my legs were shaking so badly I had no choice but to collapse onto the floor beneath me. Why? Why was this happening now? What did I do wrong?

Then it hit me. That's what I was feeling - that I had done something wrong. Was I wrong for letting myself be used in a tactic of fear? For just sitting by, while my homeland was painted as war-loving monsters, happy to take away all one held dear? And, if I was wrong, and I had a sinking feeling that I was, what did that mean? Had I become so accustomed to the judgment that was built into Dolma's foundation that I simply let myself comply with it all? Or did I merely give in to the darker part of me that demanded I be recognized, that I be seen as worthy?

Could I even be seen as worthy? The person that had inspired Mateo, Ana, and everyone else to leave their homes, their families, and all that they knew behind, could I still be that person? Gods, was I ever even truly that person? I was selfish and cruel and I couldn't get along with basically any of the nobles here in Dolma, so how in the universe could I be the person who would lead them? How could I be a person who is worthy of all of the trust that my party placed in me? What if I were really not suitable for this role? This whole series of events seemed like nothing more than a divine accident after all. No one had ever actually picked me to rule. I simply checked the bunch of random boxes and had absolutely no control of my own. I never chose to be found by Father, to become Nevremerre's only Princess, the only eligible person to marry Dolma's Crown Prince. I may have chosen to try to become Queen or to go to Dolma, but neither of those things ensured that I could be what the people in Dolma or my party expected and needed me to be. How could I do it? How could I be that person?

"You're a long way from home, Ava," Abel's voice said quietly into the space around us. He gently kneeled down before me, cradling my head between his hands.

"I know," I wailed, "Nevremerre feels like it's on the other side of the world."

"No, Ava, home is not where you are from. It's not a building or region or even a country. It is a feeling. A feeling we get when we are trusting, loving, and living in an authentic version of ourselves. We are centered in our own truth and integrity. It is always with us. We simply must do our best to choose to live in this truth, and to be loving and kind to ourselves when we fail in this. It is choosing to learn and to grow from instances where we fail, and always choosing to pick ourselves back up and put ourselves back out into the world again."

"Gods, Abel, I don't think I can do this." I felt a bit like a broken record, sure I had said this to him before. Every day since I had arrived here, I was moving closer and closer to breaking down. Even now, I felt like this moment was not as far as I could fall. "I am losing who I am, Abel. I let Harry speak of Nevremerre as if it is something to be feared, as though I am something to be feared. And, I wanted that. I wanted to be treated like I was something, even a monster, if I could stop them from acting like I was nothing at all.

But I made a mistake. I can't rule with fear. I cannot do it. It is not me, it is not who I want to be. But, I can't think of what else to do, and I - I am paralyzed that the next time, the next time I mess up, you're all going to realize that I don't have the ability to rule. That I am nothing more than a girl in a pretty dress hiding behind books and the words of others. That I am not mature or responsible, like I'm supposed to be!" I cried out, clinging on to him for some - any kind of support. Any sort of rock I could hold on to to stop my descent into the abyss.

"You're still a child, Avalynn," Abel said.

"No. No," I rejected, pushing him back. "I don't get to be a child. Not here! Not now! I am to be married in a month's time. I am already working on ruling this country. I am not a child. I do not have the luxury of being a child."

"Child is a physical term too. It doesn't just apply to the innocence and freedom childhood allows. There is a reason Nevremerre's age of maturity is 21. It is because you are still physically growing."

"I haven't grown since I was 12," I argued.

"Not just your body, but your mind, your heart, and your soul. Well, it is true that we are always growing and changing on a soul and spiritual level, the most obvious signs of this are in our youth. After all, Ava, whether you know it yet or not, there's still much about the world you have yet to learn. All of which can only come from time and experience. The ability to narrow in and define your own emotions, the knowledge of what situations make you relive pain or loss, even the realization of the knowledge you were lacking can only come with time and hindsight.

One day, your future self will painstakingly heal all that causes you to break now, and with that growth, your future self will look back on you now with infinite love and compassion for all you have struggled through and all you have overcome. As for what we all may or may not expect you to be, I can only say this: everybody in the world perceives you in a certain way, and whatever that perception is, it's none of your business."

"What?" I said, shock overcoming my tears.

"It's none of your business what other people may think of you. It is their thoughts, their head, and you have no business poking your nose into it. All that matters is that you stay true to yourself, that you live in your own personal home. Your true North, if you will. If you believe yourself to have made a mistake tonight, then that is your belief and challenge, no one else is obliged to share it. If you made a mistake, then learn from it and don't ever let it happen again. If, when you reflect on this further, you decide that this was the best choice for you at the time, then smile and move on. There are no true mistakes, Ava, just opportunities to grow and become stronger. Do you understand my words?"

"Yes," I nodded.

"No, you don't," Abel disagreed. "You may understand them here," he said, tapping my head. "But, you haven't yet got the message here," he said, pointing to my heart. "Do not worry, my dear, for there is no doubt in my mind that you soon will. In the meantime, remember my words. Write them down, hang them on all the palace walls, soon they will embed themselves in your heart, and you will become stronger and start to feel whole once more." He paused, staring at me for a long moment, "Now, are you ready to get off the floor?"

His words were filled with compassion and ease. There was no rush conveyed by his gravelly voice. No reason to move until I was ready, he would wait with me, patiently, lovingly, diligently until I chose to move once more. He'd wait with me, even if I said I would never get off the floor again. "Just one more minute," I said softly, looking into his moonlit eyes. Their darkness mirrored the night sky above us, peaceful, calm, and safe from the harsh ravages of the day.

I closed my eyes, leaning against the cold stone wall behind me, breathing in the cool night air. The sharp bite of the early evening stinging my nostrils as I continued to breathe. I waited until my body stilled, my palms cooled, and my breath pushed away my hiccups and quieted my roaring heart. Only after a calm exhaustion filtered through me did I reach out my calloused hand, placing it in Abel's smooth one. "Please help me, I'd like to get up now."

"As you wish, Crown Princess," Abel said with a smile.

Once on my feet, I looked around, finally realizing the predicament I found myself in. "I don't know where I am," I said aloud.

Abel only chuckled, "No worries, Crown Princess. I can see the nervous souls of your knights, and I will lead you to them the same way I found you. I cannot promise the most direct route, but I will lead you to them."

"I trust you," I declared, taking his offered arm. We hadn't even made it down the hallway when I had to lean on his arm heavily, my body weighed down by some invisible force, my only viable option to continue to stumble down the many halls. "I'm sorry for leaning on you so," I apologized to Abel.

"I expected it," he replied, and I hadn't the energy to feel shocked. Instead, a numb echo of the emotion reverberated through me. "People always underestimate the physical toll emotions can have on a body. They can leave you weak, foggy, and clumsy for days or even weeks as our brains focus on sorting out what we just went through. Promise me, Ava, that you will rest tomorrow. No work, no social calls, unless you genuinely desire them. I'd even be happy if you simply stayed in bed all day," Abel suggested, and, at the moment, nothing sounded nicer than sleeping all day, with maybe a break for a novel or two.

"I promise," I agreed, far too exhausted to think of saying anything else.

True to his word, and far faster than I could have managed it, Abel guided me back to my rooms. I gratefully opened the doors, aching to get back into my bed. I was not expecting to be greeted by the feeling of arms around me, "Crown Princess," Oberon's voice rang out against my hair, smooth and comforting.

"That is highly inappropriate," Mateo's voice echoed from behind him.

"Yes, yes, do let the Crown Princess go, Oberon. Remember our job here," Galileo's voice agreed. I, however, disagreed. Oberon was warm. His muscles comforting against me, his height made me feel safe and secure. Plus, I hadn't received any hugs, aside from Abel comforting me after a breakdown, the entire time I'd been in Dolma. I'd forgotten just how much I missed the sensation, so when Oberon began to move away, I simply gripped him tighter, refusing to let go.

"Crown Princess?" Oberon mumbled, confused from above me.

"Please, just a little longer," I basically begged from my place, buried into his blue silk shirt. My only saving grace from this highly embarrassing comment was that I quite literally fell asleep immediately after making it.

When I woke up the next morning, I found myself in my own bed, covered by a wool blanket, still in my gown from the night before, and a soft glow of warm sunlight flitted through the open curtains at the window. Emotionally, I felt better, but physically, I couldn't find even the smallest desire to move my aching limbs. Bed for the day was the only option.

I rung for my maids, letting them care for me and take down my messy hair from the night before. Instead of clothes though, I put myself back into long silk pajamas before instructing my maids to bring all my meals in here for today along with a stack of romance novels. Ana knew my tastes, so I didn't get specific with exact book titles. As they began to leave, I realized I should probably apologize for falling asleep in Oberon's arms yesterday, so I asked them to bring him too.

A few moments later, Oberon knocked on my door. When I told him he could enter, I was startled to find him holding my breakfast tray in one hand and a pot of tea in the other. "You didn't need to do that," I said, rushing over to help him.

Oberon, however, expertly moved himself away, setting everything down on the table between my couches. "It's no matter," he replied, "I enjoyed it. When I was a child, I used to follow around my old butler, copying him as he did all of his work. Although a career in service is not for me, it's nice to get back to your childhood passions every now and then."

I laughed, "And how old were you when you developed this passion?"

"Five," Oberon responded confidently, "I outgrew it by 7 though, deciding I would become a Lord like my fathers. Of course, I later discovered knighthood and I could really never turn back. My sister became the heir instead. I think it's worked out quite well for the two of us," Oberon beamed.

"I think so too," I smiled at him. "I don't mean to hold you up from anything," I said, pushing on to the topic at hand as he sat down across from me. "I just wanted to apologize for falling asleep on you last night, and for having to be carried up to bed." I could feel my face heat up in embarrassment, but I determinedly kept looking at him. With a jolt, I realized that he too was extremely handsome, with light brown skin and dark curly hair that he had grown out a bit since we'd arrived. Not that this made too much of a difference, since it remained in tight curls atop his head. He was muscular, but in a lean way and I was suddenly confronted by the memory of my face in his chest last night. I quickly forced all of this down and in the tightly closed box in my heart as I waited for a response.

"Crown Princess, how could I mind a display of utmost trust!" Oberon beamed, his brown eyes sparkling in the morning light. His full lips showcasing a dazzling smile, and I just stared at him in wild confusion. "In Agremerre," he mercifully explained, "it is believed that falling asleep in someone else's presence is the ultimate sign of trust. This is because to fall soundly asleep you must feel comfortable and safe. You would never fall asleep in front of an enemy, so to fall asleep in front of me, and even more so in my arms, is a sign of trust. I am incredibly grateful to know that my presence makes you feel safe and comfortable. That is, in my opinion, the true duty of a knight, to make all those under my care feel safe and comfortable, sure of the fact that I will protect them from harm, be it from people, disasters, or nature, I will keep them safe," Oberon finished proudly.

"You are a great knight, Sir Oberon," I smiled at him, "I am incredibly lucky to have you on my side here in Dolma. I only hope I can be a ruler worth serving."

"That doesn't matter," Oberon replied, brushing off what was arguably my greatest fear with the same casual ease in which one would push off a bit of dirt from their clothing. "I already knew that I may not always agree with your choices or policies, after all. I certainly never agreed with all that Queen Anora did. But I became a knight, not a Lord. All I really need to know is that you are making the decisions you believe to be the best for the people at the time. You proved yourself in that simply by choosing to come here, and, even though I likely would have done a great many things differently, you continue to show that you make the decisions that you believe best for the people through your work.

We have the same goal, Crown Princess, we both came here to help the people. I do that by serving as your knight, and teaching the guards and knights of Dolma. You do that by coming here and drafting and campaigning for things to change this place. But, honestly, it wouldn't really matter if you did none of those things. You allow me to help people, everything else you do is just a bonus. So I don't really care about worthiness or anything like that. I go where I can do the most good. Getting to work with someone who feels the same is just a bonus."

"Oh," I said. Despite the fact his response was remarkably similar to what I had said to my parents before coming here, I had completely forgotten that my reply could be similar to the reply of others in my party. Or, more accurately, I had never thought there were others who could have had similar reasons for coming here as my own. I had, somewhat inadvertently, placed myself onto a pedestal even in my own mind, and convinced myself that the only reason the people in my party were here was because they wished to be led by me. It was both a tremendous relief and a deadly blow to my ego to learn that my assumption was simply wrong.

I chose to bask more in the relief, however, feeling no need to let my ego become great once more. "I am happy to have your help in aiding the people of Agremerre, Nevremerre, and Dolma. If you ever find or think of a program we can do to give more aid, tell me, and I will help you in implementing it."

"Thank you, Crown Princess," Oberon smiled, giving me a bow, "I will let you rest now."

"Yes, thank you," I agreed, sending him out. Alone at last, I threw myself passionately into a day of doing absolutely nothing.

Or, that was what was supposed to happen. I, at the very least, made it until a little after lunch before Harry came storming into my room, a sheepish looking Thomas in tow. "Ava! We need to discuss Calvine! You should be ready!" Harry barked. I looked up, shaken away from the novel I was reading in the worst possible way. It took me a few seconds to physically adjust to the real world. When I did finally understand Harry's words, I found them to be far less entertaining than my book, so I had an easy job in front of me.

"No, thank you," I responded before turning back to my book. I only had the opportunity to read one more line before I was interrupted again.

"No?" Harry said, his surprised voice leaving a question in the air as he processed my response.

I looked at him then. His mouth hung open slightly, and he had a wild confused look in his brown eyes. Beside him, Thomas looked utterly flabbergasted, at least in his face. His posture was straight and perfect, with his hands placed gracefully behind his back. His face however was gaping like a dead fish. His mouth hanging open and his eyes threatening to pop out of his perfect head. "I'm taking today off. I will not work today. Now, you are welcome to either join me in silent reading or you can leave." There was another long pause in which Harry and Thomas simply stared at me, so I deemed it acceptable to start on my book once more.

"Is that allowed?" Thomas asked, a paragraph later.

Harry followed up with, "But what about Calvine?"

"Thomas, I don't think you've worked a day in your life, so taking a day off is clearly allowed. And, Harry, Calvine will still be there tomorrow. One day will not change much in what we can do anyways," I replied, not looking up for my book, but still realizing I would likely have to start the page again.

"Will you really not discuss this today?" Harry asked, in what, for him, was a rather quiet tone of voice.

"No, I will not," I replied.

"Fine, but you better meet with us tomorrow!" he blustered out of the room.

"Yes, I will see you then!" I shouted cheerfully after him, before restarting the page I was on.

"I meant, are you allowed to say 'no' to father," Thomas clarified into the almost empty room.

"Yes. I just did," I pointed out.

"Right." I got almost through the whole page before I was interrupted again. "Can I stay here?" Thomas asked cautiously. I put my book down to look at him. He stood like carved marble, his body tight and tense he stared at the wall behind me.

"You're welcome to do whatever you wish," I replied carefully, "but would this not upset Lady Sabine?"

"I - probably," he admitted after a moment, "but it's - it's peaceful here."

"If you wish, you can invite her too. I will only be reading, so it might be a good way to get to know each other," I suggested. "Then you could both enjoy the peace."

"I don't think that's going to go the way you think, Ava-lynn." I felt my heart jump at the sound of my name. There really were too few people to call me that for my heart to react in such a manner. "She really doesn't like you."

"Staying in my room is not going to help that," I pointed out.

"I know, I'd just rather not go back right now. She's still a bit angry at me for staying here all day yesterday."

"Why? As you pointed out yesterday, you were quite literally trapped. There were armed knights at the door preventing you from leaving."

"Well, she says I should have found a way, used my power as Crown Prince."

"How exactly does that work against the power of a King?"

"Er - well, I'm not quite sure. I mean of course she's right, she always is, and I apologized, but she's still mad. When she's upset she breaks a lot of things, so it's a bit loud at the moment."

"That is not a healthy way of expressing your anger," I commented, unsure what to do with this information. "Wait, is she breaking your stuff?" I asked.

"Well, yes, she's in my rooms after all," Thomas said, his tone of voice adding an "obviously" to the end of his words.

I ignored his sass, focusing instead on the most pressing matter, "Thomas, that behavior is a problem, especially if this happens whenever she gets mad like you suggested. Destroying people's property is not healthy. You need to set some better boundaries. What happens if someone gets hurt in all of this? Not to mention it's a bit emotionally manipulative. Also what if she breaks something important?"

"Don't worry, I hid everything of significance to me," Thomas said, as if this answered everything as opposed to making it all significantly worse.

"You shouldn't have to hide things from the person who loves you!" I exclaimed.

"Look, I didn't come for relationship advice! Can I stay or not?" Thomas snapped.

"Fine! Fine, you can stay. Just," I sighed, calming myself down. "Just be quiet while I read. You can either get a book from my study or pick something in here from my personal library. Be warned though, about 70% of the books in my personal library are romance novels. So you're not allowed to be judgmental about it."

"If I take a romance novel, does that mean that I can't be judgmental about the book itself or just the presence of the genre overall?"

"The presence of the genre overall," I decided, "I can't force you to like a book."

"Very well," Thomas decided. "Romance novel it is," he said, picking one randomly off the shelf.

Thomas was not silent in his reading, but I didn't mind too much as his shock at the smutty nature of the novel and irritation at the characters' decisions were highly entertaining. It was even more fun to watch him grumpily get up and demand to know where the sequel was. Thus passed an enjoyable afternoon, and even dinner, as Thomas skipped the meal with the nobles in favor of a sandwich tray and more books with me. "Will you still leave, if I can arrange it with father?" Thomas asked me, as he began to head out for the evening.

The question gave me pause. Would I still leave? I wanted to say, "yes, of course," but I found that that was no longer the case. "Will you finish the list of things I want to change?" I asked instead.

"Of course not," Thomas replied quickly. "That list is ridiculous, and most of the things on there can never be changed no matter what you did."

"Then I cannot leave."

"Why?!" Thomas asked, shocked, "because of that silly list?"

"Yes! Because things need to change! Dolma Is suffering, your people are suffering! How would I ever be able to go back to Nevremerre knowing I left them behind?"

"Who says they're suffering? Who gave you the right to say that? You who is always in your study or the library reading about the world, but never living in it. What gives you any right to do a damn thing in Dolma?" Thomas growled at me, stepping into my space.

"What gives me the right?" I echoed back to him, stepping forward as well. "Thomas, I am to be Queen of this country. Not Nevremerre, not Agremerre, but here in Dolma. These people will be my people, my responsibility, and, even if I weren't Queen, they would still be people! They would still be starving on the streets, our streets! They would still lack houses. And they would still be struggling to survive! How could I not help them? I, who have the benefit of money, who has the ability to feed, house, and educate them. How cruel is it to just continue to let them suffer when, I, as a Princess and as a person, I can change their circumstances with no harm to myself?" Thomas fidgeted as I spoke, and I stood silent for a moment before continuing.

"You have no idea how much people suffer, how much brighter and happier things can be. You've lived your whole life like this! Walking around in a gilded cage of luxury, privilege, and ignorance, but I will not and cannot do that. Because, unlike you, I've seen another way in which people could be living, and I know that there is so much more to life than your people are currently getting to experience. Can't you see that by raising up the poorest and most helpless in this country we can only gain greater and higher benefits for everyone else?" I paused for a moment, waiting to see if Thomas would respond to my words. Instead, he stood silently staring at me, and I felt compelled to push on in my tirade.

"You don't have to like me, Thomas. Gods, you don't even have to talk to me, but you will not stand there and tell me, as the future Queen of Dolma, that I have no right to fight for the betterment of this country. Nor can you say that my plans will fail. You do not know me. You have no idea what I am capable of or what I can do. Even small changes can change the lives of thousands, and I can do so much more than small. I am not a doll or a tool of our parents. I am a person, with thoughts and goals and actions all of my own, and you will treat me with respect. The respect that every single person on this whole planet deserves. Now leave this space, and tomorrow, and every day thereafter, do better - for me, for your kingdom, and, most importantly, for yourself."

PART THREE

Chapter 21

The Questionable Threat

Over the next few weeks, Thomas, while no longer avoiding me, looked increasingly uncomfortable in my presence. He was almost overly polite during our discussions about Calvine, and seemed to hover awkwardly around me as I went about my day. Now, he too, could be found in my study each afternoon. The kids got more comfortable with his presence, and Whimely was thrilled, even bringing in more of Thomas' and his childhood friends to my office. I, however, was wondering when exactly my space had become the new hip social event center. I almost wished we could go back to the days when I was ignored - almost.

Still, despite being around me almost every day, Thomas said remarkably little to me. I wasn't entirely sure what to make of this; however, more often than not he would look as though he wanted to say something, but would close his mouth before he got the chance to do so. If I weren't exceptionally busy preparing for more improvements for Dolma and for a wedding, this would have been incredibly annoying. The only benefit to Thomas and the other Lords' presence was that, after one particularly rowdy afternoon, I managed to put them all to work preparing for the wedding. Fortunately, all of Thomas' and Whimely's old friends turned out to be wonderfully competent, giving me more time to deal with other matters.

I still couldn't decide if Harry somewhat villainizing my country was a good thing, probably not if I listened to my gut on the matter. However, I couldn't deny that there were some added benefits. For starters, there were many more bows and curtsies when I walked into a room, and people hid their insults behind whispers. Although who's to say if the whispers were better than outright statements of dislike. At the very least, whispers were easier to ignore, and after all, if you simply speak louder, you can't hear them at all. The biggest benefit, however, came from an encounter with some of the noble parents who, after a month of Abel's lessons, finally discovered that I was teaching their children about sexuality and gender. They were mightily upset by the whole thing, but I couldn't find it in me to care about their "concern" for their clearly neglected children.

"Lords and Ladies," I said when I had enough of their complaints. "In just a week's time, King Edgar of Nevremerre will arrive with Queen Elenore and Queen Diana, all of whom are in a loving, polyamorous relationship. Along with them is Prince Alveron, who is attracted to men. Anything negative said about any of these people or anyone else who travels with them who has sexual orientations that differ from your own or about people who are mis or ungendered will be taken with the highest level of offense. Surely, it is better to educate your children about these things now, before an uneducated comment causes an international incident," I smiled at them.

The faces in the crowd got even paler, if that was possible among the all-white crowd. There were several nods and mumbles of agreement before the courtiers sheepishly retreated. Abel informed me that there were no dropouts from his class and even mentioned a few curious adults looming in the back. Overall, I considered this to be a raging success, even if Harry's speech was the main reason for this triumph.

However, the biggest feeling that ran through me during this time was excitement. My family was coming! All the nostalgia and pining since I'd left Nevremerre turned into a rush of excitement instead. I found myself smiling more and practically skipping down the halls as the day of their arrival approached. And, I was not alone in my feelings. Around me, all those from my party looked far more cheerful, eagerly discussing who all was coming which old friends and family they would get to see again.

It was an excitement foreign to the Dolmanians around us. "Are you really that excited to see your parents again?" Lord Tolbren, one of Thomas' and Whimely's old friends, said in astonishment as he diligently created the seating chart for the wedding and reception. "If I never had to see my father again it would be too soon!"

"Well some of us get along with our parents," I said with a laugh.

"No that can't be true," Lord Zebias said, contemplating the menu options in front of him. "Should the salad be served before or after the soup?" he asked seriously into the room.

"Soup first is considered more formal," Thomas responded back, not looking up from "A Brief History of Nevremerre," which he had finally started to read after pushing Whimely to hurry and finish it. "Are - are they nice, your parents?" he asked, suddenly putting down the book.

"Wondering if the future in-laws will like you?" Whimely joked.

"Of course," I responded, ignoring Whimely, "The King and Queens are very nice to their friends and allies."

"Not to their enemies?" Whimely jumped in again.

"King Edgar and Queen Diana are both knights," I responded, "Both of them have seen active combat against criminals and both of them have killed people who could be considered enemies. As a general rule, I don't find murder to be a friendly act, even when justified. However, I really wouldn't worry about either of them. Honestly, the person you really wouldn't want to anger is Queen Elenore. Mother can be quite ruthless when she wants to be," I added with a smile. It was fun, talking about my family.

"Will we get to meet your family too?" Ki asked from his place on the couch.

"Of course!" I beamed at him and the other children, "I would very much like to introduce you to them!" There was a rush of excited chatter as the children and I pushed aside our readings to talk about my family. It was one of the few things I would happily postpone my work for.

And then, the day came. The day my family would arrive. I woke up irrationally early, far before the near winter sunrise had even begun, far too excited to fall back asleep. It would have been easier to simply wake up and have them here, but instead, I spent agonizing hours waiting for them to show up. Each door opening was met with sharp stares from my party, hoping it was the messenger saying my family was at the front gate. The disappointment in the room was palpable when it was merely Abel or a servant. So much so that a few even apologized for even entering the room. I did feel a little bad that we'd made them feel that way, but I was too much on edge to do anything about it now.

Conversation seemed impossible, so it was essentially an anxious silence that my whole party experienced that morning. Kentin and several other Dolmanian servants helpfully made tea and gave us all supportive smiles. These were appreciated, but gave us nowhere near the relief that the messenger brought when he said Nevremerre carriages were at the gate. I flew down the hall, not caring for propriety as I ran towards the front entrance. The footsteps of my party echoing behind me. I was practically bouncing at the main door when Harry, Priscella, Thomas, and Ollifelle joined us, followed by the rest of the court and servants.

"I've never seen you so fidgety, Avalynn," Priscella commented, placing a slender hand on my shoulder in the hopes of keeping me still. "Do try to calm down. There are many eyes on us here."

"Yes, but be sure to look happy to see your family. This lot should see that you have your family's support," Harry nodded gruffly.

"I do have my family's support," I briefly stilled, confused by Harry's words.

"Right, right. Ah, here they come now," Harry nodded, towards the long drive where several carriages began to appear. There was an instant change in the court. Everyone stood straighter and there was a stiff silence that spread throughout the crowd, ensnaring all around it. The whole court now mirrored the same carved marble appearance that Thomas and Ollifelle almost always exhibited. It felt awkward and formal and wrong. Had it been this way for my arrival, I wondered? I found I couldn't bear to mirror their stillness, so, instead, I eagerly bounced on my toes as the carriages pulled up the long drive.

The carriage hadn't even stopped before Father came bursting out the front door. "My gift!" he cried out, rushing towards me with open arms. Who gives a damn about propriety, I thought as I raced towards him.

"Father!" I cried, flinging my arms around his neck like I was a little girl. I buried my face into his chest as he lifted me off the ground, squeezing me so tightly it was a wonder I could still breathe. But, he smelled like ink and sword polish, and his scratchy beard tickled my face, his arms radiated warmth and comfort and home from their place around me. So, it didn't matter if I couldn't breathe, as long as he was really and truly here with me.

"Put her down, Edgar," Mother scolded.

"Yes, we all want a hug, you can't keep hogging her to yourself like that," Mama agreed, and Father reluctantly set me down.

"If you wanted to hug her then you should have gotten out of the carriage sooner," Father argued, as I rushed into the arms of my mothers.

"Not all of us can safely jump out of a moving carriage, Edgar," Mother scolded over the top of my head.

"Ava!" Azar's voice cried out behind me, but it was Al who got to me first, removing me from our mothers before lifting me into his own arms.

"We missed you!" Al beamed at me as I gave him a warm hug.

"I missed you too," I whispered to him, overflowing with the joy of being near them.

"It's my turn for a hug," Ari demanded. He was taller than when I saw him last, but no doubt there was still more height to come as I was released into his arms, then finally to Azar, who picked me up and refused to put me down while Father and my mothers greeted the gobsmacked court.

It was more than a little funny to watch the formerly serious court stare at us all like we were some sort of fairy tale creatures they've never seen before. Several had their jaws simply hanging open as they watched the scene before them. Even Harry looked utterly dumbfounded, so much so it took him several minutes before he could respond to Father with the official greeting. Eventually, he managed, and my family was invited to a private lunch, just as I had been on my first day.

As we moved inside, I waved cheerfully at the Nevremerre knights and servants I had not gotten to greet from my place in Azar's arms, and I happily watched my party rush to greet their friends. "Where is Carlos?" I asked Azar as we followed the Dolma royal family to lunch.

"Oh he'll come up with Nana in a week," Azar replied. "Father wanted only the best knights with her while she rules as proxy." I nodded, Nana had agreed to take over all official duties so that my family could stay here for three full weeks. Nana would come up for the wedding while several council members divided up the official work for the time my family was away. With still two weeks until the wedding, most guests wouldn't begin to arrive until next week. My whole body was filled with happiness that my family had made an exception to come earlier. I hugged Azar more tightly at the thought.

"So how have you been? What have you been up to?" I asked, happily letting myself be drawn into Azar's tales of Nevremerre. The food distribution was going well, and experiments with different methods of food growth to combat the drought were showing promising results. Mother jumped in to describe vertical farming methods that seemed particularly effective and required far less water. Mama jumped in with a funny story about Azar attempting to water a vertical plant bed, sans ladder, and ending up soaked. I heard laughter fill the halls and I finally felt at peace.

The walk to the lunchroom felt much shorter, but considering my company, and the fact I didn't have to walk, that was probably to be expected. It also didn't escape my notice that the Dolma royal family hadn't said a word and that they looked far more awkward and out-of-place than I had ever seen them. Harry did try to take back some semblance of control once we entered the room, proposing that Father and my mothers sit by him and Priscella at the head of the table, while the rest of us were put together at the end. Azar finally had to put me down, so we could all sit in Harry's assigned seats. I'm not sure what exactly he hoped to accomplish with this arrangement, but the first half of lunch was still just my family catching up. We swapped stories and laughter over the heads of the bewildered Dolmanians, before Mother took pity on them. Actually, pity is not the right word. To be exact, Mother began to interrogate them.

"You must forgive us for ignoring you like this," Mother smiled. Her manners would have one believed she was offering a warm inclusive hand to the Dolmanians among us and clearly they believed that to be the case as well. Harry gave her a small smile, Priscella's shoulders finally relaxed, even Thomas and Ollifelle looked upon Mother kindly. However, those of us familiar with Mother saw a different story. It was in her eyes, the flashing eyes of a predator who had just trapped her prey. I was suddenly very concerned for my future in-laws, but it seemed I was the only one, as the rest of my family watched on with the same predatory gaze. "It's been so long since we've seen each other, we just couldn't help it."

"Not to worry Queen Elenore," Harry smiled, "I'm sure we all understand."

"Do you? I see both of your children here with you," Mother said, her smile still delicately painted onto her face.

Harry, on the other hand, looked quite startled before coughing and adding, "Yes, well Ollifelle will one day be sent to marry foreign royalty."

"How interesting that you're all so willing to sell your children off to other countries," Mama jumped in.

"It's their duty," Harry said quickly, "It helps the country."

"Ah, I see, your diplomacy skills must be awfully poor if your only guarantee of peace and prosperity between your neighbors is purchased through your children," Mother said politely, "Fortunately, Avalynn is quite skilled at diplomacy, so you can go to her when you're struggling."

Priscella's mouth dropped open in shock. Ollifelle and Thomas both looked like their eyes were about to fall out of their heads. Harry floundered for a moment, but Mama cut him off before he had the chance to speak, "I must admit, it's so fascinating how you can keep up such a tradition without revolts. Personally, if I saw that my leader was willing to sell his own children, I would constantly be thinking that perhaps they would choose to sell me next."

"Not to mention intermarriage between only a few countries is likely to end in mental and physical birth defects due to inbreeding," Ari pointed out. Beside him Azar snorted before quickly hiding it behind a sip of water.

Mother, however, just smiled at Ari, "Excellent point, dear, you really do have quite the memory for science."

"Yes, well," Harry stuttered, trying to take back control of the conversation.

"Of course, none of that matters now," Mother said before he could speak. "Fortunately for you, Ava decided to come here, and I will always respect the choices of my children."

"Yes. Well, what's done is done," Harry recovered.

"Come now, Harold," Mother said, a light chastising tone flowing from her thick lips, "If we've learned anything from history it's that nothing is ever truly done. Ripples of the choices made by rulers centuries ago still impact us today, so, as a ruler, can you ever truly be done?" Harry, for just a moment, looked terrified as he stared into the serene face of my mother, who, unlike him, had not once looked uncomfortable or out of control in this conversation. Her pleasant smile was always bright and lovely upon her dark face.

"But, really we can be done with this conversation," Mother said, "We are to be family after all, and I have so many questions for all of you. Now, of course, I have to start with the man who is going to marry my daughter," her stare turned to Thomas, and I heard his quick intake of breath from his spot beside me.

"Oh yes," Al said, his smile perfectly mirrored Mother's as he turned towards Thomas, looking him directly in the eye, "I have many questions for you, Crown Prince Thomas. We are to be brothers-in-law after all. There is much I believe we all are curious about." His words were harmless, but his tone sent a shiver down my spine. I debated jumping in and saving Thomas from my family's probing. However, I have no doubt that if their questions weren't answered here, Thomas would be accosted somewhere else and interrogated. At least in here, there were witnesses and his family to back him up if he answered incorrectly.

"Are you an active reader?" Mother asked, an air of innocence glossed over her words, a stark contrast to the intense look in her eyes as she waited for Thomas' response.

"I have become a very active reader as of late," Thomas responded, hastily, "I was spurred on by Av - I mean, Princess Avalynn's ferocious mind." Thomas gave Mother a nervous smile.

"And what do you mostly read about?" Al followed up, not allowing the intensity Mother had created in the room to falter.

"I have been re-educating myself about Dolma's history and laws," Thomas declared.

"Have you really?" Harry jumped in, looking shocked.

"Hmm, so we can gather that the responsibility to know the foundations of your country are not normally so high on your list of priorities," Mother judged, staring at Thomas once more.

"Well, I -," Thomas began, looking more than a little panicked at where this conversation might be going. For some odd reason, I found myself nervous that he should receive the approval of my family, something that, before today, I had not thought would be difficult to receive. Though I had not much focused on finding a partner when I was back in Nevremerre, too much of my attention being given to working for Nevremerre's throne, I had always believed that my family would love and accept any person I chose. It never seemed in their nature to be harsh to someone I had decided to spend my life with. Yet, their interrogation of Thomas could not be described in any way as accepting.

I had to believe this harsh judgment from my family was a result of Thomas not being someone I explicitly chose, but rather him being the byproduct of another decision I've made. Perhaps a month ago, when Thomas was still distant towards me, I would have enjoyed the pressure he now faced from my family. Now, I found that I wished this conversation would go well. Thomas, after all, was not a bad person. He tried to change where required, he simply had never been told he needed to actively help his country and that he needed to be receptive to all those around him. While I may have thought these things to be natural, I was beginning to understand that they were more likely to be the byproduct of the culture and community one grew up in.

"He is a man of many hobbies, Queen Elenore," Harry jumped in again, removing me from my thoughts, "I was merely surprised he'd picked back up reading."

"It is good to have many talents and exposure to many different kinds of things," Mother accepted, although she still looked questioningly at Thomas.

"Are you at all well versed in any sort of combat?" Mama asked, while she could not match Mother's intense yet calm air, her passion and ferocity brought a different sort of energy to the room. In her eyes you can see the spirit of a warrior, and her muscular body looks poised to strike at any moment.

"I have no training other than the very basics, which I was taught as a young boy," Thomas admitted.

"Do you have knowledge of tactics or command?" Azar asked, the full height and size of him now pointed towards Thomas.

"No," Thomas said after a moment, "I really only know of the history of Dolma's previous military endeavors. With so much peace around us, so much military expertise hardly seems necessary."

"One can never know when the next war might break out," Ari commented, unlike the rest of my family, he was slowly focused on his plate, carefully eating his now organized food. His aloof and disengaged attitude somehow made his words sound far more like a threat than anything else said at the table.

Mother beamed at him, "Right you are, Ari," she said, "We always like to teach our children to be prepared for anything that may come. After all, none of us can really know what the future holds." This too sounded like a threat, although in a more vague way than Ari's words could be interpreted.

Either way, the conversation made Harry so uneasy he followed up with, "You all must be very tired from your journey. Perhaps you should retire to your chambers and we will continue getting to know each other at a later date."

"An excellent suggestion," Father grinned. "It will also give us more time to think of the questions we wish to ask you," he commented jovially.

Harry went pale, "Yes... well, please show the royal family of Nevremerre where they will be staying," Harry ordered a servant, who quickly bowed as my family rose from the table.

"I look forward to our time here, King Harold," Father said. "There seems to be much I'd like to learn about Dolma, and, of course, any opportunity to see my gift is the most important," Father said, kissing my head softly.

"We will get settled, then come to see your rooms, Ava," Mother smiled genuinely at me, "Say in about 2 to 3 hours?"

"Of course!" I beamed at her as my family hugged me once more before they all exited, following the assigned servant.

"Well that went terribly," Harry sighed, throwing himself back into his chair as soon as the door swung shut.

"It really wasn't that bad," I said dutifully.

"For you," Harry scuffed. "I've never felt so inferior in my whole life."

"I'm sure that wasn't their intention," I placated. Harry just rolled his eyes at me.

"Are we bad parents?" Priscella questioned, staring vacantly at the chair Mother had previously occupied.

"No!" Harry refuted right as Ollifelle confidently answered, "Yes." All eyes in the room turned toward the usually quiet girl, who simply shrugged before turning her gaze back toward the empty half of the table.

"I thought you said your parents were nice," Thomas said, turning to me with exasperation leaking through each word.

"They are nice!" I objected.

"To you maybe," Harry grumbled, "You should have at least given us some warning!"

"Just what exactly was I supposed to be warning you about?" I cried, exasperation filling me as well.

"How much they love you!" Harry exclaimed.

"Obviously they love me! They are my family! Honestly Harry, what did you expect?" There was a moment of silence where the entire royal family of Dolma just stared at me.

"Well you're clearly of no help!" Harry declared after a moment. "Go wait for your family Ava, and the rest of us must come up with a new strategy!" The rest of his family nodded, while I stood there wildly confused about the whole affair.

"I really think you are over complicating this," I said uneasily, watching the family move together around Harry.

"I won't lose, Ava!" Harry announced. There were murmurs of agreement from those around him, even Ollifelle seemed to be engaging in Harry's odd line of thinking, "Now out you go!" I let myself be shooed out of the lunch dining room, shaking my head at what was surely a clear bit of foolishness on Harry's part. Still, I would rather spend my time in my own rooms than arguing over a non-existent verbal war.

Chapter 22

The Enjoyable Afternoon

I was in a cheerful mood as I practically skipped towards my rooms. Immediately upon entry, however, I was practically accosted by Whimely, who was followed closely by Tolbren and Zebias. "Your father loves you!" Whimely shouted at me.

"King Edgar," I corrected, "is my father; of course he loves me."

"This is huge for you, Princess," Whimely cried. "No one can ever look down on you now. No doubt people will be far more eager to be on your side."

"Why on the continent would that happen?" I demanded, pushing through the doors and men in front of me into my rooms.

"Princess, don't you see," Whimely hounded me, "with your fa - King Edgar on your side, you have access to all the power and benefit of Nevremerre!"

"I had those to begin with. As a Princess of Nevremerre I have the full backing of my country. King Edgar's love or lack of love has no effect on the matter." I was suddenly highly annoyed by Whimely's words. My power came from myself as an individual and my status as a Princess. It came from the council's and people's trust in me. Why did it require my father's presence for me to be considered strong and worth acknowledging? Everyday in Dolma I felt like I was begging to be recognized and treated like a human and it was infuriating to learn that I could get both of these things only by my proximity to somebody else. Like I was dependent on my father to receive decent, human treatment. Given how the nobles of Dolma treated the lower class, however, I wondered if their definition of human was different than mine.

"Yes, well we know that," Whimely continued, "but now everyone does!" He beamed at me, looking like he just told me the best possible news, but I rather felt like I'd been slapped in the face.

"They shouldn't require King Edgar's presence to treat me like I'm human or respect me for the work I've done or will do," I said seriously.

"It doesn't work that way, Princess," Whimely sighed, "At least not here."

"It should!"

"But it doesn't," Whimely shook his head at me, "However, with this, you can now perhaps come closer to changing us all once again."

"I haven't changed any one yet," I protested.

"That's not at all true, Princess. You've changed us all, far more than you can ever truly know," Whimely smiled. "That's why I like you. You keep everyone on their toes. It's much more fun this way, you know?"

"No. No, I don't," I answered blandly, growing tired of this conversation.

"Perhaps it's best we continue our preparations for the wedding," Tolbren mercifully interjected before Whimely could argue some more.

"Yes, that would be far more beneficial than this conversation," I hurriedly agreed.

"Very well, Princess," Whimely conceded, "but believe me when I say that King Edgar's love for you will be far more beneficial than you believe."

"It's not that I wouldn't appreciate a social boost," I said to Lucy after sending the Lords off to do some work, "but I would rather the public respect me for my own work instead of who my father is."

"You are a Princess," Lucy pointed out, gracefully seated on the lounging chair in her room. "Who your parents are does matter. But I do understand your feelings," she conceded, stretching out her long legs and finally moving towards me. "The people here seem to believe that my gender and skin color somehow affect my brain. I made some progress in changing their minds, and I would hate it, too, if I lost my opportunity to change their thoughts because someone they deemed acceptable "gave" me power," I nodded in feverish agreement as Lucy so elegantly described my feelings. "However, Crown Princess," Lucy continued, "the end goal is not to gain respect for ourselves, but to gain their respect for all those like us, so that no other person would have to fight like we must because of their gender or physical traits. While unpleasant, I can't help but agree with Lord Whimely, this manufactured respect King Edgar has unintentionally created for you will help with our overall goal. Even if we must sacrifice our own pride to accept it."

"I suppose you are right," I conceded.

Lucy put her hand on my shoulder, "I know I am."

"You're so wise Lucy," I laughed, pulling her into a tight hug. "You would have made an amazing High Judge."

"Of course," she agreed, hugging me back, "but this is far more of a challenge! Now," she continued, guiding me back to the lounge and directing me to sit beside her. I relaxed into the chair, and rested my head against Lucy's velvet green dress, "you really don't need to worry about the people. The general public adores you for cleaning the streets. Not to mention, after appointing Lord Hienri, Lady Charmaine Lasteron, and Lady Eloise to their positions in the territories taken from those other idiots, the people in their territories support you wholeheartedly, as do the Lords and Ladies you appointed themselves."

"Well, it was only natural to give them the positions. According to the knights who went to survey the lands, they were the ones doing most of the work anyway," I said.

"Yes, yes, but the point is the people love you, all the soldiers who almost had to fight Agremerre and Nevremerre love you, and the servants and your guards in the palace love you! Worse comes to worst, we simply overthrow those pesky nobles and maybe the King, too, and then take over the country on our own," Lucy smiled down at me.

"That really does sound a whole lot easier, doesn't it?" I sighed.

"Yes," Lucy agreed, "but for now I suppose we can let them live and try to change the country through the legal system."

"All right," I agreed solemnly.

The children came shortly after that, each eager for stories of my family. "King Edgar is massive!" announced Lord Cardinel, one of the kids who usually followed Mateo around. "I bet he could chop the heads off of six men in just one swing," he glowed.

"I heard he can kill a man with just one look," Lord Ebinosi boasted back, trying to use his superior height to intimidate Lord Cardinel. This was rather unsuccessful given the 12 year old had only about an inch over the other boy.

"Well I heard he can remove the spine from your back with just a flick of his hand," came a serious voice from the doorway.

"That's hardly an appropriate lie, Prince Azar," I scolded. I kept my face turned away from the door, however, so he couldn't see my smile.

"Who said I was lying?" Azar injected, moving into the room and crushing me into another hug. "King Edgar is a very strong man."

"However, some things are physically impossible, something you would know if you actually bothered to use that brain of yours," Al insulted as he came into my rooms. "And, let go of Ava, you're crushing her," he said, gently extracting me from Azar's grasp.

"Thank you," I said to Al when I was allowed to breathe once more.

"You seem to be running quite the nursery here," Azar noted, unfazed by Al's arrival.

"Yes, well they don't seem to have anywhere else to go," I whispered to him, conscious of the stares of the other children.

"Then we should make sure they are comfortable," Azar smiled at me. Before he could do so, however, the room was plunged into chaos once more at the entry of my father.

"King Edgar!" a small voice cried out. There were screeches of terror going through the room. Not exactly the reception Father was used to. He looked incredibly shocked and a little sad to see the horrified stares of a room full of children.

"See what you've done," I huffed at Azar, who at least had the decency to look a little sheepish at the mess he created.

"You know you're going to have to fix this," Al said looking pointedly at Azar.

"I know," Azar snapped, before grumpily making his way over to Father. "King Edgar," he said loudly, "the children are eager to hear of your stories as a knight."

"Oh really!" Father said, suddenly bouncing and excited. "Well, if you want to hear stories of knightly heroics you should hear about my wife, Queen Diana. She could even best me in a fight!"

"Really?!" came the excited cries of several children as they quickly lost their fear in favor of excitement at my father's words. He moved to a chair and began to regale them with stories of Mama's warrior days; he also made sure to include Mother's incredible wisdom in coaching Mama. He looked positively delighted to expound on his two wives, and his audience was enthralled by his every word. Azar turned back and gave a smug grin toward Al and me. I had to suppress an eye roll as he weaved his way back to us.

"Told you I could handle it," he smirked.

"Wow, your ability to command a room full of children is truly unparalleled," Al said sarcastically. "Too bad you can only lead those with undeveloped brains."

"Now -" Azar began before I pushed them both out of the room.

"That's enough from both of you!" I commanded, as I pulled them unthinkingly towards my study.

"That's not fair," Azar complained, "You cut me off before I had the chance to retaliate!"

"Given the amount you two fight, I'm sure it will even out somehow."

"Well, we could stop fighting if someone stopped being a pretentious asshole."

"Really, is -" Al began, but I cut him off too.

"No! No more arguing. You only just arrived, by Gods, just please calm down, both of you! Honestly, where is Ari when you need him?" I lamented.

"You know he's been saying the same thing about you recently," Al commented, forgetting his anger.

"It almost sounds like we aren't the favorite siblings here," Azar agreed, and I felt the need to slam my head into the nearest wall. How they could switch from enemies to best friends in a second was astounding... and infuriating.

"Should we be hurt by this?" Al teased.

"Of course not!" Azar joined in, "After all, it can't possibly be true. How could our siblings like anyone better than their trusty, reliable, older brothers. Clearly we must be the favorite, right Ava?"

"How right you are Azar, as the eldest children of the family, it is only our right to be revered and favored, right Ava?" Al chimed in.

"You are both insufferable idiots! I can't believe I missed you!" I said, shoving open my office doors.

"Ah, but you did miss us!" Azar gloated, walking through the doors only to stop upon entering.

Al too stopped upon entering, "And who are these men, Princess Avalynn?"

"Oh just some friends of Crown Prince Thomas," I replied, still moving towards my desk.

"I see," came Azar's gruff voice still by the door.

"Hey, we are your friends, too," Whimely sounded a bit more panicked than normal, his carefree attitude deserting him for some reason.

"Are you now?" I asked, unaffected by his tone, "That's news to me. It seems, Lord Whimely, you mostly just hang around my rooms uninvited."

"I see," Azar repeated. "Well then, Prince Alveron, it seems prudent that we acquaint ourselves with the friends of our soon-to-be brother-in-law."

"Oh, I quite agree, Prince Azar," Al smiled.

"You can't interrogate all the nobles in Dolma," I said, finally catching on.

They ignored me however, "We should introduce ourselves," Al continued. "I am Prince Alveron, Prince and knight of Nevremerre."

"And I am Prince Azar, Prince and knight of Nevremerre." Both of my brothers stood tall, their imposing height and muscular builds filled the room. I found myself once again envious of their innate ability to look intimidating. It was so effective it took several minutes of tense silence before the others in the room finally introduced themselves, their ridiculously long names failing to arouse any sense of dignity or strength in front of my two brothers.

"So, what can you tell us about Crown Prince Thomas," Al said, sitting down between the Dolmanians.

"You know, I really better be heading off," Zebias said, trying to get up and move, only to be stopped by Azar.

"Now where are you going?"

"It really makes it seem like you have something to hide if you leave so quickly," Al chimed in from his spot on the couch.

"That's enough," I finally stepped in, "You're scaring them."

"Come now," Azar pouted, "We are not that scary, are we Ava?"

"Only to idiots," I rolled my eyes, "but they're still afraid, so you will stop."

"Very well, Princess Avalynn," Al conceded.

"Sorry if we scared you," Azar said, sitting down as well.

"We weren't scared," Whimely said, his words still slightly rushed. "It's a pleasure to meet Your Highnesses." His manners at least came through when scared, I noted.

"Sure you weren't," Al smiled, "So Ava, what are you working on?" I happily told Al and Azar about the health care changes I was making. I also told them of my previous projects. They were the perfect advisors, instantly lending a hand. They pointed out flaws in my plans, praised the good, and improved what I was lacking. It felt like being back in Nevremerre, exchanging ideas on how to help the community. The room was filled with excitement and love as we bounced between different ideas and actions we could take to help Dolma. I felt happy and relaxed; it was brilliant.

Not too much longer, Ari, Mother, Mama, and Father came in, led by the children who usually occupied my study. Clearly, Mother, Mama, and Ari had walked in on Father's tales of Mother and Mama and had, wisely, put a stop to it all. Introductions were made, children asked eagerly about my family and home before Tolbren convinced them and his friends to leave my family and me in peace. After that no work could be done. After all, nothing felt more important or vital than experiencing the comfort and love provided by the people I cared most about in the whole wide world. Gods, how I miss them. It was something no mere words would ever be able to fully express, but to have them around me again was the greatest comfort I had ever known.

When we parted hours later it still felt a little raw. I was not ready to have them all disappear again so soon, but it was lessened by the fact that they were just going to a different part of the palace. I would see them again in only a few hours and this time when I walked into Dolma's large Banquet Hall, I would be surrounded by support. Just one of my family members would be enough to negate anything a courtier or noble here could say or do and here I had the benefit of my entire immediate family. I felt untouchable and immensely grateful. I was not alone, or at least I didn't feel so alone anymore.

Chapter 23

The Familiar Pattern

I was still in the process of getting ready when my room was invaded by Dolma's royal family. "Okay, Ava," Harry announced as he walked, uninvited into my room, the rest of his family following closely behind him. "We have come up with a game plan."

"Harry! You can't just walk into my room like that, what if I was changing?"

"Bhah! You only have 10 minutes before you have to leave, I knew you would have been mostly ready," Harry insisted.

"Plus, we checked with your maid who said they were just finishing with your hair now," Priscella clarified.

"Is it nice to wear your hair down like that?" Ollifelle asked, showing more emotion than I'd ever seen from her. "It looks very comfortable."

"Yes, it is. Would you like my maids to style yours the same way?" I asked, hoping to encourage some sort of friendly relationship between the two of us. However, Ollifelle just looked horrified at me. Her brown eyes widening and darting between me and her father.

"Well," Harry asked Ollifelle impatiently, "aren't you going to answer her?" This was not the right response as it only sent Ollifelle into a greater panic, who was now looking furiously between her mother and brother, neither of whom seemed to be of any help.

"Princess Ollifelle Analise Elliayah Carleon," Ana said, coming to the teenager's rescue, "with the cut of your dress, an updo would suit your outfit best, but I believe we could do something so that your hair wouldn't be so tight on your hair." Ana was right, of course, and the combination of Ollifelle's near white hair and pale skin made the tight hairstyle she wore now give the subtle impression that she was bald.

"Well hurry up then!" Harry barked, "We have things to discuss!" Someone somewhere really needed to have a chat with Harry on how he spoke to his children, I thought idly before responding to Harry once more.

"Whether or not things need to be discussed, Harry," I said pointedly, "you have a rather rude tendency of barging into people's rooms unannounced. I highly recommend fixing that."

"Why should I bother? Everything in this country is mine after all," Harry said haughtily.

"That's a great mindset," I said sarcastically, "and totally won't result in resentment from other people. Just tell me why this whole meeting couldn't wait until we were in the side room for the Banquet Hall?" I sighed, not wanting to argue about this now.

"Because your family, the whole reason we need to have this meeting in the first place, will be there!" Harry snapped.

"You're taking my family way too seriously," I surprised myself with this comment, especially considering I'd wished to be taken more seriously by this particular group of people. However, I couldn't deny the truth of my statement. "My family simply wishes to know that I am safe and that I could be happy here. They aren't looking to start an unnecessary war. Just answer their questions honestly, and feel free to ask them questions as well. We may end up finding our two countries could be of use to each other," I said, slipping on my jewelry and letting Miri place my crown onto my head.

"Ask questions... that's a great idea!" Harry jumped. "Listen here, everyone, we must launch our own counter-investigation into Nevremerre. Follow up all of their questions with an interrogation of your own!" Harry said this all with a rather sinister tone, as if he were plotting the downfall of a government. Beside him, his family was all nodding vigorously, like evil henchmen dedicated to the plan. However, I couldn't help but note that they were basically describing a normal conversation. Thinking about the rather pretentious customs of Dolma, and their rather rigid class system, I was beginning to wonder if these people had ever had a real conversation in their lives before I showed up. This may have been an egotistical thought, but I couldn't help but feel like there was some truth to the idea.

With Harry's cunning plan of having a functional conversation settled, and Ollifelle's hair in an adorable side ponytail, with some loose strands framing her face, we were now ready to head into the Banquet Hall. The Dolmanians looked confident and prepared as we walked out of my rooms. This fell in an instant when we ran into Mother and Mama outside of my door.

"Oh Ava, how pretty you look!" Mother's familiar voice rang out as she grabbed my hand to twirl me around, the heavy winter satin of my dress slipping gracefully around me as I smiled at her.

"You both look wonderful as well," I beamed, admiring Mother's tailored gold suit, and Mama's purple velvet dress.

"Thank you, darling," Mother smiled, kissing my forehead before turning towards the Dolmanians. "I wasn't expecting to see you all until later this evening. I'm glad you all seem to be close with Ava."

"Yes, your daughter is quite lovely," Priscella smiled, looking warily at my mothers. "What, may I ask, are you both doing here?" I saw Harry giving an approving nod in Priscella's direction and I had to fight off a laugh at the ridiculousness of the situation.

"I must confess to wanting to spend every minute I can with my baby girl," Mother smiled at me, her dark eyes glistening with tears as she kissed me once more, "We really have missed her, you know."

"Back in Nevremerre, we used to walk down with her for almost every noble event," Mama recalled sentimentally, "and now look at her! Our baby girl will even be getting married soon!"

"Mama!" I blushed, "Come now!"

"You must forgive us old ladies in our remembering," Mother said, fondly patting me on the cheek.

"You aren't old!" I protested with a roll of my eyes.

"See how sweet she is," Mama said to the Dolmanians, "You must be sure to take good care of a sweetheart like her."

"No, no, Diana, she is right, we must both live much, much longer, and prove to these youngins that age is only a number!" Mother declared playfully.

"True. Plus, we simply must get truly old, as I imagine you would look quite attractive as a granny," Mama said with a wink.

"Growing old is only worth it if I can do it with you, my dear," Mother replied before giving Mama a kiss.

I laughed at them both, "If you don't stop flirting we're going to be late!" We moved forward, with me in the middle, linking arms with my mothers.

"And miss Edgar's grand entrance? Not for the world!" Mama declared.

"Yes, he always looks so handsome in his winter wardrobe," Mother agreed. Ever so briefly a pang of jealousy flared through me. What would it be like to have a spouse or spouses who loved me so? I had never been in love back in Nevremerre; that wasn't an issue I needed to deal with. I had time, I could marry whenever and whoever I pleased. Here, in Dolma, my wedding was two weeks away, and while I supposed I liked Thomas, it was most certainly not love. Still, I tried to cheer myself up, I had the love of my family and that of my friends. And, I was happy to work for the people of Dolma. Helping Dolma improve the lives of its citizens was a newfound passion of mine. I was not lacking in love and I could live very happily without it. After all, romantic love was nothing more than sprinkles on top of an already delicious cake, and, having tried some of Aunt Olivia's creations, I knew they sometimes made the cake worse.

We were almost completely down the hall when I heard a rush of footsteps and realized the Dolmanians had not followed behind us. "Do you think we scared them?" Mother asked, noting the sound as well.

"Well, you haven't exactly been kind to them," I pointed out.

"I don't see a reason to be kind to people who trade their children for goods and services," Mother judged.

I, wisely, did not point out that depending on how you looked at everything, Nevremerre could be said to be doing the exact same thing. Instead, I merely said, "Weren't you the one who told me not to rush to do things until I understood more of the culture?"

"Yes, that is because you are to be Dolma's Queen. I am not, so I may safely judge their numerous disasters and oddities from afar," Mother said in a tone that would take no arguments.

"Still, you could go a little easier on them," I pointed out.

"My darling girl," Mother replied, "I am going easy on them." I suddenly had no doubts that this was true, and I also remember that crossing Mother would be a truly terrible mistake. Uncertainty hit me. Perhaps if I were more like Mother my time here would be less difficult. After all, Mother would never lose to the Dolmanian nobles and could likely pass all her projects without even fighting the experts. Yes, Mother would have done well here, but I had truly no idea how to be like her.

"Ava, you must understand, we just want to get to know what your soon-to-be in-laws are like. We want to make sure you have support here," Mama said kindly.

"And if I don't?" I countered. "I won't change my mind now, support or not, there are changes that must be made in Dolma and I want to be the one to help make those changes. So, just be nice," I finished lamely.

"No," Mother replied, "At least not until I get the information I need to help you here. Then, I will act in the best manner to help you."

"Yes. I agree," Mama nodded. "We have just three weeks to help you get everything you want in Dolma and I won't be satisfied until we accomplish it."

I couldn't help but smile at the both of them, "Well right now, all I want is time with mothers like you."

"As you should," Mother nodded, while Mama tackled me into a hug, slowing our progression for just a moment and allowing the Dolmanians a chance to finally catch up.

"What unique dresses you have on," Mama frowned, as Priscella and Ollifelle caught up. "They seem very heavy, can you move at all?" I patted myself on the back for having successfully predicted this conversation months ago as I listened to Mama try to work out the functionality of Dolma's grandiose fashions. Eventually she simply declared that it was useful for hiding weapons and/or bodies, much to the horror of Priscella and Ollifelle. Harry also looked incredibly confused. Thomas, however, appeared to be fighting off laughter, and he gave me a dazzling smile from behind his father when our eyes met.

Finally, in the side chamber near the banquet hall, I was eagerly greeted by all three of my brothers. True to form, father had yet to arrive. The usually silent room became a bustle of activity as Mother fussed over Al and Ari's clothes.

"She shouldn't be so worried," Azar commented beside me, looking very dapper in a blue velvet suit with silver embroidery. "She packed their luggage for this whole trip."

"That's quite a lot of extra work," I pointed out.

"Yes, Al, at least, seemed to feel pretty bad about it, he's promised her he'd get better with his outfit choices so she won't have to worry as much."

"I'm not sure that's his best idea," I said, gazing at his mismatched suit. "He probably should just hire a stylist. It really can't be easy getting dressed when you're color blind."

"At least red and green work well together," Azar nodded.

"And he looks good in both colors," I agreed. The conversation ended with my father's arrival, his purple and gold suit looking like the perfect mix of Mother and Mama's outfit. The three of them gushed over each other and Al and Ari escaped over to Azar and me.

"I like this room," Al commented, "It's nice to just see each other before going out to greet the nobles."

"We should get one in Nevremerre," Ari agreed. Personally, I, too, liked the side room, at least when my family was in it. Usually the heavy silence that filled it was suffocating enough to prefer the judgmental stares of the nobles and courtiers. Ever observant, Ari then asked, "But, why is the royal family of Dolma just staring at us?" Ari made no effort to hide his question, talking at his normal volume. As such, behind him there were several awkward coughs and blushes as the Dolmanians tried to figure out what to do with themselves. Beside me, Azar snorted at the show.

"I'm not sure, but they don't usually talk much when they're here," I tried to answer Ari.

"Oh, well silence is nice too," Ari nodded, and I gave him a smile.

"It's time to exit," Harry called out as his family lined up by the door. Behind them, my family lacked any semblance of order, but, in my opinion, looked just as imposing and cool. This thought must have been shared by the courtiers and nobles in the room, because they all froze when my family approached.

"A rather fearful lot, aren't they," Azar whispered beside me. I was faced with a sudden flashback of Harry instilling an unhealthy amount of fear in the court about my family and country.

"Oh - yes, it seems that way," I stumbled, looking away from him. Soon though, the mingling increased. Afterall, Father was a King and if he could provide money or power, there were several in the room who would push past their fears to get it. The same held true for my brothers, who were soon swarmed by several men and countless women. In fact, the only people still left alone were my mothers and me.

"Well, this place sucks," Mama said, looking over at the crowd surrounding the men in our family.

"Yes, yes it does," Mother agreed with a frown. "Really, what are these people going to do when Queen Anora gets here, or Elizabeth for that matter?"

"They'll probably just ignore Nana," I piped up. "I highly doubt they'll even know who she is, or why she's important to at least two major countries."

"Good Gods, Ava, how can you deal with all of this?" Mama burst.

"Slowly plotting to remove them from power," I said, only slightly joking. However, my mothers both nodded in agreement at my words.

"It's all so white," Mother huffed distastefully, her eyes now on Al who seemed to be getting much less attention than Azar or even Ari. It was odd to watch considering in Dolma's society Al's age alone would be enough to make him Crown Prince.

"Don't worry, I have already made some changes which you will see when more of the nobles come, I have replaced three with incredibly competent individuals, two of whom are people "with color" as the Dolmanians would say. I'm working on getting more competent and diverse people in Dolma's government."

"When more of the nobles come?" Mama questioned, "Are these not the nobles?" I delved into the story of courtiers, although I was still somewhat confused as to their purpose. From there, it only seemed natural to discuss the mess that was Dolma's current governing style. Truthfully, I had never been able to write about the true state of devastation and corruption that seemed to thrive even in the most abundant corners of Dolma. It seemed that to speak of it would be to admit I was struggling. After all the work I went through to convince my family to let me come here, I couldn't bear to let them think of me as anything but successful and happy.

Now they were here. Now two of the most powerful and respected people in all of Nevremerre stood alone, ignored by the room around them, and I could do nothing but tell them of the sheer amount of work I was facing. Despite the initial struggle, the rush of relief that flooded through me when I told my mothers of my problems was instant and tremendous. To share with someone who could truly understand all the nuances of my struggle, yet who wasn't dependent upon me for their happiness and survival was a joyous relief. It was what felt like the missing piece to my soul, and made my world finally click together, so that I was not so unstable. Before either of them had a chance to respond, I was laughing at myself for the foolishness of not telling them sooner. Still, I wondered if they could have ever really understood without being here, and living this awkward moment we faced right now.

"We should just have you leave," Mama said scornfully.

"Oh we can't do that now. She won't do that now," Mother responded for me. "When one is faced with tragedy, one cannot just ignore it. At least, Avalynn can't."

"Mother is right. I could never go back to Nevremerre. I know too much about what's going on here. Once I made the decision to come, the people of Dolma became my people, and I refuse to let them suffer."

"If you truly want your changes to last, long-term, you have a big task ahead of you. It will be about more than just changing policies. New policies with new and better aid and protections for people can really only stay beneficial, if the people who enforce those policies do their due diligence. I have yet to see anyone here in Dolma who seems truly ready to put in the effort required to keep the country running smoothly. I see far more people who will use power, any power, for personal gain," Mother warned. "To change this place, you must also change the people."

"I don't have the ability to change people," I argued back.

"No, you don't," Mother agreed. Despite my earlier protests, I hadn't actually expected Mother to agree with me. Rather, I had expected, as per usual, Mother would impart upon me some new found wisdom and elegance that would lead to the ability to change people. All that was to say I was slightly offended by my own implication that I couldn't change people's minds.

"She just means that no one is responsible for changing the minds of others," Mama smiled, sensing my hurt.

"No. No I don't," Mother frowned, as we both turned to stare at her. Mama looked shocked and gave Mother a pointed stare. "There are definitely people who are responsible for changing people's minds," Mother pushed forward, ignoring Mama. "Avalynn, however, is not the person to do it. It wouldn't fit with her character, and her interference could cause distrust amongst the people. No, Avalynn must be a model for the kind of government they want to see. She should work for the people, and the people must see her working for them. The same goes for the new Ladies and Lords she has hired. People must see their work and they will undoubtedly see their lives improving. They must know it is Avalynn's style of government that is responsible for these changes and they must learn to look at their own Lords and wonder why they aren't doing the same. What we need is gossip and newspapers!" Mother declared.

"Isn't it rather manipulative to only present our story, to only have them see the good in our system? What if this hurts people?" I pointed out.

"All change will hurt someone," Mother told me, "It will hurt anyone who is not ready to adapt, but they will adapt, at the end of the day. The real question is whether the people will be better or worse off after the adaptation? But in this case we have the upper hand because we have the data and the science to back us up. Nevremerre and Agremerre have thrived using systems we have created, and Dolma will too."

"But we're still using the media to manipulate people into thinking our way is right. Surely people should be given the ability to choose which system they prefer without external influence," I argued.

"Avalynn do you believe in Nevremerre's government system?"

"Of course."

"This isn't some opinion we are floating around, Avalynn, the system we are promoting has quantifiable success, while the system Dolma is currently living with has quantifiable failures. And, people will still be free to make their own choice; this is only providing an option. At the end of the day, even if we were to create propaganda for our ideas, Dolma's government will not be the same as Nevremerre or Agremerre; we build our future from our past. Dolma's past will create something entirely new in its governing system. It's our job, or rather your job, Avalynn, to see to it that whatever the new system may be, it functions for the people who live in it and not just for the ones controlling it."

"Besides, Ava," Mama jumped in, "people are being manipulated by the things around them constantly, consciously and unconsciously. If you only ever are surrounded by one thing, then it is difficult to see or experience the world in any other way, but, if you give people options, then they can choose which path to take on their own. Life is about seeing the different paths in front of you and choosing which to take. The wonderful thing about it is that you can switch paths at any time. You will help Dolma get on to a smoother path and we will start by revealing to the whole country just how many other paths exist."

"Okay," I nodded.

"And we will help you in any way we can," Mother said, reaching down and stroking my hair, "So just keep writing your new policies, we will take care of the rest. You will shine as the beacon to lead this country in a new direction. There are many ways for one to change the world, but for change to be permanent and everlasting, all of those ways must work together towards the same goal."

"Come along now, you two," Mama smiled at us, "I see no point in staying at this event any longer." We all agreed, taking her outstretched hands as we left the suffocating isolation of the Dolmanian banquet hall. It was such a loss, I mused as we walked to my rooms; that the prejudices and preconceptions of the Dolmanian courtiers prevented them from making two of the most important connections in Nevremerre. Father rarely did anything without consulting my mothers. No doubt anything the Dolmanians wanted of him now would be doomed to fail. Still, I felt far less defeated leaving the banquet than I had in the past; no matter how many people thought differently. I, at least, knew the power my mothers and I held and it was not something so easily taken away.

I had breakfast with my family the next morning. It was an oddly hostile affair with Mother and Mama only responding to the men in the room with curt, one-word responses. It horrified my father and brothers to no end as they anxiously tried to carry on a conversation. Finally, a distressed Ari cautiously asked if he had done anything wrong. This softened my mothers immensely, and they both apologized to the table.

"I'm sorry," Mother began. "I'm not angry at you, not really, it was just frustrating to watch all of you be easily accepted as figures of power and authority when we, who are technically ranked higher than you, were pushed to the side."

"Not that you all don't deserve the same level of respect as we do," Mama chimed in, "We know you are all wonderful people who work hard for Nevremerre and care about the people. It's just annoying to be considered less than you, when we do the same amount of work."

"I wouldn't say "easily accepted"," Al grumbled, suddenly slouching on to the table, "I had a man ask me whether I could truly run a country with my inferior skin tone. I didn't even know what to say to that! How are you supposed to respond to something like that?" I stared at him in shock.

"That makes no sense," Ari puzzled. "Your skin color doesn't have anything to do with your ability to rule."

"I know," Al sighed, leaning back on his chair. "I don't think you should be here, Ava." he bounced back, staring at me.

"No," I glared at him.

"No? Nevremerre has food now, and we have new methods of farming that will function well enough to feed us if the drought continues. We can keep up the rest of the treaty agreements and bring you back with us without a problem. As of right now, there is nothing Dolma can give us that we can't get ourselves."

"No," I repeated, still glaring at him.

"Why must you be so stubborn?!" Al demanded, now glaring back at me, "This place is awful. They treat you like a second-class citizen, and have given you all the responsibilities they've been neglecting. Just come home. Live well and be happy with us!"

I opened my mouth to argue back, but was cut off by Mama. "Alveron, your sister knows all of that, and if she wanted to return, she knows we would accept her at any time. She is choosing to stay; however, so we will not yell at her over things she understands far better than we do. Instead, we will ask her how we can help, and then we will do everything in our power to turn Dolma into a place fitting of her."

Al stared at her for a moment before turning towards me and sighing, "How can we help you, Ava?"

My family was then given tasks, almost none of which were actually distributed by me. Sticking by her words from yesterday, Mother said I was simply to focus on the wedding and drafting new policies. I did get Ari assigned as my assistant, which was exceptionally helpful. Everyone else was assigned to various tasks by Mother, some of which I wasn't even told the purpose. This seemed very odd considering this was all meant to be done to support me. However, I was soon too busy to think too much about it. With my wedding less than two weeks away, I found myself being dragged to dress fittings, cake tasting, and ceremony rehearsals for hours on end.

"Are weddings always this exhausting?" I questioned Father. Father's job in all of this was to be sure I took breaks, and he had snuck me out of venue preparations to hide in an unused corridor.

"Perhaps here," Father admitted. "It was a lot more fun for me, but for my weddings, I was planning it with your mothers, who I loved very dearly. We were planning our future together, and despite all the work, it was exciting because we were doing it for us. Your marriage is political; this wedding is a show of strength among three nations. It doesn't get to be about you or love. It's a power play the whole world is watching," Father said sadly. He gave my cheek a light pat, "It's not the wedding I hoped for you, my precious gift."

"But it is my life, Father. Not yours," I replied simply.

"I know, my gift, so I will watch it with all the pride and love I have for you."

"Found you," came Thomas' voice from the end of the hall-way, causing me to jump.

"Are you here to take us back then?" I asked, unable to keep the weariness from my voice.

"I'm supposed to," Thomas said, "but I'd much rather hide here with you instead." He flashed me his own tired grin, "I suppose you'll say that's neglecting my duties though."

"Given that I ran away from those duties first, I'm not sure I'm in a position to talk," I smiled back.

"It's okay to take a break from duty every now and then," Father said, smiling at us.

"That's strange to hear, coming from you," I teased.

"Yes, I suspect Elenore gave me this job in hopes of me learning something as well. She's clever like that, your mother." I laughed in response before nodding my agreement with his assessment. "You both run along now, take the rest of the afternoon off, and don't get caught. I'll take care of whatever I can here." He gave Thomas' shoulder a squeeze before walking back to the wedding venue.

"Thank you, King Edgar," Thomas bowed, before he could get too far away.

Father smiled at him, "I mean it, rest now. Guests start to arrive tomorrow, and you won't have any time to relax then. So hide from the world for a bit, and don't get caught!"

We waited in silence as Father's footsteps echoed along the corridor. Once he finally moved out of sight, Thomas held out his hand towards me. "Come, I know a place we can hide."

Chapter 24

The Hidden Room

Thomas pulled me along through the corridors and suddenly I felt like a little kid again. We stopped at each sign of noise, tiptoed and ran our way through the more crowded corridors, hiding from servants and courtiers alike, all the time holding back fits of laughter. Finally we reached a deserted corridor somewhere in the far back of the royal palace. Here, Thomas stopped bothering to hide his laughter or silence the heavy blows of his feet along the stone floors. He squeezed my hand tighter and pulled me into a room at the end of the hall. The massive chamber was clearly unused, the only light came from a dusty window that coated the room in somewhat of a gray haze. White blankets covered what looked like broken furniture, and the whole place was covered in a fine layer of dust. Despite the somewhat lackluster appearance of the room itself, Thomas was smiling at it as if it was one of the greatest world treasures.

"Isn't it wonderful," he beamed, letting go of my hand and moving further into the room. "The Royal Palace is far too big to make use of all the rooms, and we need a massive staff just to keep everything clean, so there are many wings that have been almost completely forgotten about. I found this one when I was 10. I had just been out at my first banquet. Everyone wanted to talk to me, to have me tell my father to get them this or that. I'd been so excited to finally be with the members of the court, but none of them really wanted to know me. They were all far more interested in what I might be able to do for them. Then, they all started following me around. I couldn't go anywhere without being asked for money or a better position, or to meet their son or daughter. It was all too loud and so I ran away. Like I said, the palace is massive, and I found many abandoned rooms. More often than not, I would be found eventually and I wouldn't be able to hide in that spot again. Except here, that is, no one has ever been able to find me here."

Thomas moved over to the window, and began to brush the dirt off the ledge. "I think it's too far back in the palace for anyone to remember it," he mused, before smiling back at me. "It's a bit dusty, but I think I got most of it off the ledge, if you'd like to sit down. We'll be safe here," he nodded, brushing his dirty hand on his trousers before holding it out to me once more. I took it with a smile and accepted his unnecessary help in getting up onto the ledge. Once I was settled, Thomas jumped up onto the ledge, situating himself opposite me.

"You do know that I'll be able to find you here," I pointed out. Though, internally, I doubted that this was true. I had not paid close enough attention to the myriad of turns we'd taken to get here, so I suspected it would be rather unlikely I could find my way back without some assistance.

"That's all right; you don't count," Thomas replied simply.

Despite his words on their own being similar to an insult, I couldn't help but feel this was a compliment and I smiled at him as a growing warmth filled my chest. "Well, then I'm thankful to be one of the few you've trusted with such a sacred space," I responded, turning towards the window. The room looked over a singular tree, its body bare and empty of any color and the ground around it was still lightly dusted with untouched snow from a few days previous.

"Few?" Thomas's voice whirled around me, "You're the only person I've taken here." My head snapped back towards him. He too was staring out the window, his near white hair matching the snow down below.

"What about Lady Sabine or your sister? Or even Whimely? Although, I could see how he might ruin the peace of this place."

Thomas snorted, "Sabine wouldn't see the need in coming to a place like this. Ollie is almost 10 years younger than I, and even if we were close in age, we've been raised mostly separately. One day she will leave, be married to a foreign Prince, as you have been. How is one supposed to become close with someone destined to leave? And, Whimely would disrupt the peace, but that is not why I've never brought him here. As a child, I wasn't sure if Whimely was close to me because he was my friend or if he wanted something from me. If I'm honest, I'm still not sure of his reasons for being so close to me."

"But you're sure about me?" I asked. There was a lot to unpack in Thomas' words, but I found this question slipping out first. It felt more than a little selfish, once the words I'd spoken finally registered in my brain. Surely, I should have comforted him on the merits of his friendship or supported him in creating a better relationship with his sister; those would have been the kinder and better responses. But, now that the question had been asked, I found I could not say anything else until I had an answer. I was dying to know just what this man thought of me.

Thomas' blue eyes met mine as he turned to answer my question and a small smile graced his pale pink lips, "If there's anything in the world you desire, Avalynn, you are clever enough and strong enough to get it yourself."

"That's not fair," I found myself arguing back, "What if I really do need your help for something?"

Thomas laughed, his joy echoing across the dusty room, "Then I will gladly do it because I know that even if I said no, you would find a way to make your plans succeed. The difference between you and the courtiers here, Avalynn, is you're asking me for things you are willing to work to make happen, whereas the courtiers here are looking for lazy solutions to problems they created. Intent matters, and so do one's actions."

"All right then," I accepted before turning back towards the window once more. It was a peaceful silence for a while, as we both enjoyed the stillness of the room around us.

"You can take a lover, you know," Thomas said into the still air, "I won't mind. I would never prosecute you for it."

I sighed against the cool glass window, causing a moment's fog to creep up on the clear surface. I was no longer surprised at the idea of prosecution if a wife took a lover, I knew far too much about Dolma's laws and history now to be surprised by the double standard between men and women. It was, I suppose, a nice sentiment from Thomas, but I wondered if it would really hold true. If Sabine one day asked him to be rid of me, could he really keep the promise he made to me now? And, after his father was gone, would he even keep our marriage, or would I be sent back to Nevremerre all on my own? Nothing was certain in life, which is why I needed to act so quickly to fix all that I could in this uncertain time that I had. And, why I wondered if I could ever trust Thomas' words to me right now.

"I haven't the time for a lover." It was a truthful response, but I omitted the fears of his dishonesty. I wasn't prepared to argue over the ever-changing state of life that held me at the moment.

"Yes, but later or if you ever do find someone you love, then I will accept them. I want you to be happy here," he said quietly.

"Love, romantic love that is, is not a requirement for being happy. I'm happy for the love of my family and friends, I am happy helping Dolma become stronger and I am happy with the love I hold for the way the seasons change or a good book. My life is full and complete now, with or without romantic love," I answered back, a surprising level of indignation in my voice.

"Are you sure?" Thomas asked, quietly and curiously, his words bouncing through the room.

"Of course. Why? Do you not feel you could be happy without Sabine?" I answered back, a little testily.

"Sometimes I feel without her I would be nothing at all," Thomas admitted. "Every trait I have is because of her. If I'm kind, it's because she makes me that way. If I am cruel, it's because that's what she needed me to be. My intelligence is only there because she asked it to be. Any other things I may be are given or taken away by her, so if she weren't here, I wouldn't be anything at all."

"That's ridiculous!" I burst out, and once again I had to berate myself, for surely there was a kinder way of saying what I was about to say. However, it was too late to stop myself now, "We aren't given our traits by other people! Sure, everyone is going to have some idea or opinion about who we are; but just because someone believes something about us doesn't make it true! When you're alone or away from Sabine, you do exist, you don't just disappear! If you don't know exactly who you are in those moments, it's okay; no one is expected to know everything about themselves all the time. That's what life is for! We are constantly growing and changing, so you don't have to know what and who you are in your entirety, but you will always be more than the opinion of one singular person.

Plus, your life isn't about them, it's about you! You get the final, and only, say on what and who you want to be. If you want to be kind, then be kind. If you want to be cruel, then that sucks and you may have to deal with the consequences of being cruel later; but that is your choice to make and you always have that option. You decide what you want to be, and not anyone else!" I finished, panting slightly at the end of my probably unneeded, and likely unhelpful, rant.

"Perhaps you are right," Thomas smiled at me.

"I know I am right," I declared, my inner hopes of being kind and understanding flying out of my brain once more.

"Three months ago, I'm not sure I could have agreed with you. I was positive that Sabine and I had the purest and truest form of love there is, but now I wonder. If I were away for a long period of time, would she forget propriety and jump into my arms as you did with your father, King Edgar? Would she gush over my accomplishments like how your parents speak of each other? She never smiles at me across the Banquet Hall like your family does, happy in the knowledge that I am in the same room as her. To her, I am always doing something wrong; she always has some criticism for me. She doesn't like that I danced with Lady Yelena, even though she's nearly three times my age. She doesn't like that I laughed at Whimely's joke. I should have been with her instead of meeting with my father. It feels as if nothing I ever do will be good enough for her. That no matter how hard I try, I will never be good enough for her."

"I have never been in love," I started, careful about my choice of words this time, "but I have always imagined it to be a partnership, where you support the other and their actions and choices to help each other become who they wish to be. I could never imagine being in love and being less than the other person,-- to have them criticize me rather than to help me grow. I imagine love to be two individuals who choose to be together because every day with that person makes living more happy and fun. Not to say there won't be disagreements or bad days, but at the end of it all, I would feel trusted, supported, and happy with them more often than not. That their presence would add something to my daily life. And, even though I have yet to experience this, the people in love who I have seen, look like what I have imagined."

"So they do," Thomas agreed. "Your parents don't look like they would criticize each other. They always sound so proud of one another and of you and your siblings."

"It sounds like you've been watching my family quite a lot."

"It's hard not to. How can you not look at people so different from anything you've ever seen before? How can you look away at their obvious joy and free and easy laughter? I never realized that happiness, even second-hand happiness, could be so addicting to watch. It scares me sometimes that all that happiness could just go away and leave us all back where we started."

"Of course it will go away," I asserted. Thomas jumped at my words, looking horrified at me now, "No emotion lasts forever. It's not about the joy going away, it's about knowing that even if it does go away, that it will one day come back. That your choices and actions can always bring it back when you are ready for it. It is easy to be happy when you can trust that you'll be happy again."

"But how can you trust that?" Thomas demanded.

"For me, it's experience, I've been happy, I've been sad, I've felt a whole range of in-between, but I know that I'll be happy again because that's what happened in the past. For you, perhaps it's just a leap of faith. You'll just need to believe it for now, and soon, you'll have the experience, just as I do, to trust instead."

"Do you ever think that perhaps we're just too different, that what works in your life will never work for me?"

"There are many things about someone else's life that won't work for me. I will never be as tall as you, I won't ever be able to experience the childhood you've had, but emotions are accessible to everyone, from the highest, most blinding highs, to the deepest, most depressing lows. We all have the ability to feel all of these emotions, so in this, I don't think that we are too different to both experience happiness."

Silence filled the air, and my attention was once again directed out the window as I watched a small brown bird rest on one of the tree branches. "I don't love you," Thomas' voice rang out once more. The bird moved to stretch its wings, flying away from the barren tree.

"I never asked you to," I replied, an echo of a conversation we had ages ago. Thomas nodded, smiling slightly at the familiar phrase before changing the script once more.

"Do you love me?" he asked tentatively.

"No," I responded back, "but I don't dislike you, and I do enjoy our conversations, usually."

"That's good enough then," Thomas nodded.

"Why? Did you want me to love you?"

"Maybe, it's nice to be loved, but probably not. I suspect our marriage will be easier if we aren't in love, and I wouldn't want either of us to have a one-sided affection."

"No. For us, in this situation, I suspect friendship to be the best thing," I agreed.

"Tell me about your childhood," Thomas said abruptly. I could only blink at him in response. Finally, I breathed out, "What do you want to know?"

"I don't know, something, everything. Tell me about your favorite toy, a childhood friend you had, what your aunts and uncles and grandparents were like."

"You'll be meeting most of them soon," I pointed out.

"That doesn't matter," Thomas shrugged. "Your childhood was so different from mine. I just want to know what it was like."

"You've yet to hear anything of my childhood, how would you know it was different?" I teased, but, of course, we both knew he was right.

"Tell me then, so we can compare and I will know for sure," Thomas smiled, his icy eyes looking gold in the late afternoon sun.

"My favorite toy was a gift from Al when I was just five years old," I began. Thomas was a captive audience, curiously asking questions and laughing at all the right moments. It was easy to talk like this; so easy I hadn't even noticed the sun go down; or that I'd never got to ask him any questions about his own childhood.

"I suspect we'll have plenty of time for that later," Thomas said when I told him this, lifting me off the ledge and holding out his hand so I could follow him through the palace once more. Grabbing his hand, I nodded in agreement. He was right, as his wife there would be plenty of time to ask questions.

Chapter 25

The Backup Plan

Harry was furious when we both finally arrived in the side chamber before dinner, or at least, as furious as one could be with my family watching over him. He really could only make slightly passive-aggressive comments about the importance of a bride and groom being actually present while the wedding is rehearsed and final selections were going on. However, his anger didn't seem to reach either of us. I, for one, was quite content with how my afternoon had played out, and it seemed Thomas agreed with me.

Dinner turned out to be more of a strategic meeting than the usual noble meet-and- greet, but perhaps that, too, was to be expected given that the next week was to be filled with the arrival of nobles and monarchs from all over the continent. Some of these meetings were going to be more exciting than others. Anora and Nana would arrive in two days time, bringing Carlos along with her. Charlotte and Dame Elise, my former maid and her knight girlfriend, and Murphy and healer Autumn, my friends from the Nera hospital, would be coming as well. The Matron of Nera hospital had sent me a lovely letter wishing me luck, but informing me that she was needed at the hospital. Aunt Olivia, Uncle Octavian, and Uncle Octavian's family would arrive with some council members tomorrow and I could only hope Lord Nicholas wasn't with them. However, we were also expecting Royals from Andaluca, Experion, Abethy, and Calvine. Out of all the eleven nations on the continent, seven of the nation's monarchs would be present at my wedding. Needless to say, tensions were running awfully high, and Thomas and I were both sent to bed early by a still irate Harry.

Despite his anger last night, it was actually a blessing that Harry had sent us to bed early, as for the next three days I was run ragged hosting welcoming parties for all the many, many, many guests who arrived for the wedding. I was hardly able to speak with Anora, Aunt Olivia, Nana, or anyone else before I was pulled away to the next guest. Suddenly, I was even more grateful Father and the others had come early or I likely wouldn't have seen them much at all. I bowed and curtsied, meeting Queens, Kings, Princes, and Princesses whose goodwill and cooperation were vital to maintaining peace, but even with them I was unable to converse for very long. I hadn't even made it to my actual wedding yet and I was already exhausted.

It wasn't until two days before my wedding that I was actually able to slow down. It was ironic really, I thought, as I sat in a private lunch, that the arrival of Calvine's King, Queen, and third Prince would prove to be a blessing. Being so close to war with Calvine meant we could not just say a simple hello before moving on. No, with Calvine we would need to establish a repartee, to see what they might think, and to determine if an attack was truly imminent. Or, really, Harry did. I got to use this time as a much-needed break from my overworked brain, which was still struggling to distinguish the Queen of Andaluca from one of Dolma's ladies from the Princess of Abethy -- all light-skinned women with brown hair who blended together in my mind. It probably wasn't fair for anyone, given that I also fit the same description, but there were just so many new faces.

"You've made many changes since Princess Avalynn's arrival," King Olivender said. I couldn't tell if it was simply him being from Calvine or if it were intentional, but the man had an incredible talent for making everything sound sinister.

"Yes, well the Princess has added a great deal of value to our country with her expertise," Harry responded gruffly. "So far, her changes have seen great results.

"Yes. I can see that," King Olivender mused.

"Has your winter seen much snow this year?" I asked the Calvine royals. The question was innocuous enough, but it did serve a purpose as greater snows in Calvine usually led to more water for both Nevremerre and Agremerre. Dolma got most of its water from mountain ranges in Experion and from rainfall.

"More than last year," Queen Clarion said with a small nod. "I don't think Nevremerre and Agremerre will face a drought again next summer." I felt a spark of panic fly through me at how quickly she picked up on the intent behind my question. I soothed myself quickly however, confident in the knowledge that if she were smart enough to pick up on the subtext behind my question, she was smart enough to know attacking any country with the benefit of Nevremerre'a and Agremerre's military was a bad idea. With that in mind, I easily made it through the rest of the stilted lunch conversation. With little I needed to say, I actually felt much more refreshed after the meal.

Dinner that evening was a grand affair, with all the guests having now arrived, Thomas and I were plunged into the center of attention. I had not been so popular at a dinner since I'd been in Nevremerre. Despite my resistance to dinners like this one back in Nevremerre, suddenly having people to talk to me again was much more fun than I'd remembered. Clearly, the lack of conversation at Noble Banquets was affecting me more than I had thought. I was almost shockingly cheerful through-out the evening. I was fascinated by all the monarchs and the different governing styles they spoke of. I was enthralled by stories of their culture, their thoughts on royal weddings, the crops they grew, the jobs they valued, and so on. Logically, I knew that the fewer neighbors Nevremerre had, the easier it was to keep peace and trade abundant. But, I couldn't help but be a little sad that we could not experience all the new and diverse places I was now learning of.

It felt far too soon when Priscella pulled me away, and an-nounced to the crowd that, per Dolmanian tradition, I would spend tomorrow preparing for the wedding unable to see any-one, but female family members and maids. Sadly, I bid good-bye to the friends and the new people I had been speaking with and told them I hoped to talk more after the wedding. Although, I doubted I would actually have the time.

"Don't look too down, child," Priscella hummed as she walked me to my rooms. "You'll be glad of this time alone come tomorrow. You'll be able to use the day to rest and enjoy your freedom before it leaves you on your wedding day."

"I don't see why a marriage would mean leaving my freedom behind," I countered.

"Perhaps not in Nevremerre, but it's more difficult here. Married women have rules to follow here."

"So do unmarried women," I pointed out, once again upset at the treatment of women in Dolma.

"Yes, but those rules have never applied to you. They will now," Priscella said, giving my hand a pat.

"You make it sound like it's some sort of trap."

"It is," she paused for a moment to look at me, "but perhaps you'll manage to find your way out." Priscella kept walking, pulling me further towards my rooms. With a soft smile, she kissed me lightly on the cheek, "I'll see you in two days."

Back in my own room, I pondered her words. Truthfully, Priscella's marriage did look like a trap. Neither she nor Harry seemed particularly happy with the arrangement. Divorce, I knew, wasn't an option in Dolma, especially not for a King and Queen. I wondered if I had the ability to make my marriage any less miserable, or if Thomas and I would be headed for the same fate. Now that the wedding was so close, I felt an immense pressure of nerves build from inside of me. That, along with Priscella's words, really did make it feel like I had only one more day of freedom, one more day to run away from this madness.

Try as I might, I couldn't find it in me to fall asleep that night, and oddly that made Priscella's initial words come true. I was grateful not to have to socialize beyond my female family members, as I was far too tired to carry on a decent conversation. It was a strange mix of comfort and anxiety as I was bathed, massaged, slathered in all sorts of lotions and oils to prepare for tomorrow. I was physically relaxed, but an emotional disaster, until my mothers and Nana finally arrived.

"Sorry we're a bit late, Ava dear," Mother said, giving my forehead a kiss. "They almost wouldn't let Charlotte here in, but we wouldn't just leave her behind."

"What? Why ever not?"

"Never you mind, Crown Princess," Charlotte said, giving me a hug. "Let's just get you ready for tomorrow." She moved away with Ana and some other maids.

"Nervous, my dear?" Nana asked, moving towards me and resting a wrinkled hand against my cheek. I just shrugged in response.

"I was so nervous before marrying your father," Mother jumped in. "I just wanted everything to be perfect, but the moment I saw him, walking down the aisle, I knew it already was perfect."

"That's very romantic, Mother," I laughed, "but it's slightly different when you're not marrying for love. I feel as if it's my last chance to escape."

"I have five different escape routes mapped out right now," Mama jumped in, "We can leave now and no one will be any the wiser! I can get you out of the country before nightfall." Mama was looking seriously at me, her eyes unblinking as she grabbed my shoulders. I knew then that she was absolutely serious in everything she had said. One word from me and we'd escape back to Nevremerre and no one would know until tomorrow.

"Avalynn, you must always remember this," came Nana's soft voice from beside me. "You can always change or reverse the choices you've made. Even here and even when there are rules saying you shouldn't. If you ever wish to leave Dolma you can. We'll figure out how to get you a divorce, or we'll sneak you out of here and bring you back to Nevremerre where we will declare your marriage invalid and you can live the life you wish. Nothing is set in stone, dear girl, and rules are only man-made constructs to serve the good of the people. And if they do not serve the good of the people, they are no use following."

Instantly I felt lighter. I wasn't trapped, I could leave at any moment, and it was all up to me to decide what I wanted to do. "There's no need for escape just yet, Mama, but I promise to contact you if there ever is."

"As long as you know, but if that time ever comes, I will have you out of here within a week," Mama insisted.

"Yes, Mama," I smiled. The maids came in then, shortly followed by Aunt Olivia and a mountain of cupcakes for us to enjoy. How she managed to convince the cook to let her spend the day before my wedding baking, I will never know, but her thunderous laughter was infectious as we were pampered and polished for the remainder of the day.

"Edgar would be sorry he's missed this," Nana said idly, as we drank lavender tea by the fire, the early night moon picking up on her silk robe, bathing her in silvery light.

"He and the boys," Mama agreed. "They would have liked to spend the day with you, too."

"King Harry was adamant about this tradition," I sighed, "Apparently in Dolma it's considered bad luck for the bride to see any man the day before the wedding. Fortunately, I'll get to see them again tomorrow after the ceremony."

"Still," Mother continued, "You're his daughter, I'm sure he would have wanted to spend this time with you as well."

"Plus, he would have enjoyed the manicure and pedicure," Aunt Olivia chimed in, wiggling her purple fingers.

"Father gets those anyway," I pointed out, "but I know what you mean. If we were in Nevremerre, I could have Father and all the boys with me right now."

"You could torture Al with proper skin and hair care," Mother laughed.

"Or, more likely, confuse Ari by the sheer amount of stuff to be done to prepare," Mama chuckled in agreement.

"Yes, but I, at the very least, I'm glad that we get to spend this time together," Nana nodded. "Tomorrow, Ava, you will become a Crown Princess, I believe that is what we should be celebrating instead of a wedding. Tomorrow, you take your next step in becoming a Queen. And, what a glorious Queen you shall be. What a fine Crown Princess shall the people of Dolma gain."

"Here, here!" Mama exclaimed.

"To the Future Queen of Dolma," Mother smiled, raising the teacup beside her.

"To the Future Queen," the rest of the room chorused back, beaming at me, and with that I was sent off to bed. Sleep came far easier than it had last night, and I woke brimming with excitement. Nana was right, today I was one step closer to achieving the goal I had set for myself at just 11 years old. Today, I would become a Crown Princess.

Despite all the preparations done the day before, it still took me hours to get completely ready, and I wasn't allowed to look at myself until everything was done. Or, at least, not if I didn't want a harsh scolding from Ana and Charlotte who had set that rule. Of course, I had absolutely no intention of ever going against any rule made by these two women, so I simply sat, only somewhat impatiently, and waited for them to finish their work.

When it was finally time to see myself, I took my own breath away. I felt stunning, my hair twisted up behind me, save a few locks gently curled around my face. My gold crown sparkling in the afternoon sun. Its twisted branches made me look like the Fairy Queens I had only heard of in the fantasy stories from my childhood. My dress felt like it was flowing around me, embroidery on the sheer fabric gave the appearance of flowers floating along my arms. Behind me, my back was completely exposed before a long train of white satin was delicately laid several feet behind me. My cheeks and lips were softly dusted in a sort of pink color, and gold earrings and necklaces hung from my body, each finished with one singular long pearl, looking like frozen teardrops along my skin.

"Oh, Princess," Ana whispered into the heavy silence of the room. I did not know what to say. I felt like I was in a dream or a fairy tale, almost inhuman. I felt dainty and delicate, but also powerful and dangerous at the same time. What do you say when you've been changed into something mythical? And could there ever be words strong enough to thank the people who made you that way?

I could only smile at them, trying to keep the tears from my eyes as I attempted to telepathically communicate my love and gratitude. "Come now, Crown Princess," Ana said, reaching out to take my hand, "We must get you to the wedding hall." behind her, Charlotte nodded, a few tears falling from her own eyes. In lieu of words, I kissed them both on the cheek, and only once when I was almost out the door did I turn and give my meager "thank you."

Galileo met me at the door, as a bride-to-be was only to have one knight to escort her to her wedding. This, I was told, would decrease the number of men who would see her before the groom. It was also, as I pointed out to Harry on numerous occasions, incredibly ridiculous. For starters, they now guaranteed that my walk from my rooms to the wedding hall would be my most vulnerable time, meaning I could very easily be attacked on the way to my own wedding! And, there was also the fact that this could all be avoided if Dolma allowed female knights.

Harry, however, was not too keen on my statements, insisting the Royal Palace was safe enough without extra knights (this I found odd, as every member of Dolma's royal family had at least four knights with them at all times), and stated he wasn't ready to even indulge the idea of female knights. Apparently responding with, "You better learn to indulge it before Queen

Diana, knight of Nevremerre arrives," was not helpful and I was sternly told to just have one knight. Galileo and Miri worked to place spies along the hallway despite Harry's objections. And, I doubted he would learn of their actions.

"My Queen," Galileo bowed as I walked into the entryway. It was all so quiet with all other people who live here already out and stationed either in or around the wedding hall. I hadn't realized how familiar the noise and bustle of my rooms had become.

"I am not Queen yet," I told the bowing head of Galileo.

"Not yet, but soon," he responded, standing up straight once more.

"You make it sound like you're going to kill King Harold," I joked.

"Only if you command it, my Queen," Galileo responded seriously.

"Best not say that to anyone else," I said after taking a brief pause to assess his words, "I don't need my head knight arrested for treason."

"They'd never be able to catch me," Galileo said confidently, holding his arm out to me, "but I shall do as you ask all the same."

I smiled as I took his arm, allowing him to escort me through the seemingly empty palace halls. "Thank you, sir Galileo," I whispered to him.

"It has been, and always will be, my greatest honor to serve you, my Queen," Galileo said, his voice echoing along the corridor.

"I'm still not yet a Queen," I pointed out.

"Oh, but you are, for you are my Queen, and you have been since the moment you accepted me in your party to Dolma. With each day, I find your position as Queen only grows stronger. Rest assured, my Queen, I will not address you as such in the presence of others, but I look forward to the day when your official title matches the one I know you to be in my mind."

"You've always been so good to me. All of you."

"It is easy to serve and trust someone who also works for and trusts you," Galileo replied simply. "It is easy to serve you."

At last the wedding hall approached us. "Are you nervous?" Galileo whispered to me, conscious of the looming crowd within.

"No," I said honestly. "This is only one step towards creating a life I desire. I am excited." Galileo nodded at me then.

"I wish you luck, Crown Princess," Galileo bowed as two female servants opened the door to the side chamber I'd be waiting in before my entrance was to be made.

"Thank you, sir Galileo," I said as I disappeared into the empty chamber, hearing the strong click of the doors latching close behind me.

Chapter 26

The Dual Vows

I was once again struck by the oddity of Dolma's customs as I stood in the windowless room, pitch black, except for a few tall candles placed on a small table to my right. In Nevremerre, a person about to be married would wait with their family or friends before walking out towards their spouse who would be walking towards them from the opposite direction. They would meet in the middle of their walks and declare their love before the Gods. The audience would be filled with people the couple cared about, shouting their love from their seats. Here, I was to wait alone before walking to where Thomas already stood. The eyes of nearly a thousand people all looking at me. At least, we would be observing the Nevremerre traditions of being surrounded by nature and of declaring our intentions on our own. I don't think I would have appreciated having to listen to one of Dolma's few priests speaking on the sanctity of marriage before we wed. From somewhere beyond my black and orange room, a clock struck 2 o'clock and the doors around me flew open once more. It was time for my wedding to begin.

When you are a kid, you imagine your wedding a certain way. I was no different. I imagined my wedding to be like all the weddings in Nevremerre: outside, a small event of only close friends and family, the crowd yelling out their love for me, and a person I loved walking towards me. And, really, I wasn't attached to all those details, it was simply just all that I had ever known. But now, walking indoors, in a silent hall, filled with hundreds of people, towards an unmoving statue masquerading as a human, it felt weird. No other word quite fits.

I wasn't disappointed, I had helped plan this. I wasn't missing Nevremerre or longing for some love I had left behind. No, I was fine with this wedding. Grateful, even, that I was not stepping into the cold winter air and instead, got to see the picturesque halls of the Dolma Royal Palace overgrown with plants, flowers, and vines that had been carefully cultivated in the greenhouse for the past three months. The hall looked positively magical in the mix of green and white and my dress was able to keep me warm in a way that would have been impossible with the current snow.

Yes, my wedding was beautiful, but it was oh so very weird. So wildly unfamiliar to my subconscious and it was unsettling being such a departure from what I had unintentionally learned as a child. I was honestly feeling like I was having a mental breakdown as I moved down the aisle, unsure of how to process the world around me. But, when I reached Thomas, he grabbed my hand and I had a grounding point. His physical presence helped my mind from flying away.

"Today we come in the presence of you all and with the blessing of the Gods to join our lives in marriage," Thomas' voice slipped gracefully through the well-rehearsed words, his face smooth and placid. He looked calm and unbothered by the proceedings around him. He spoke out to the audience in front of us, not even as much as glancing at me. It, oddly, made me feel steadier, and I followed his lead, my voice echoing through the hall.

"We will now recite the vows of our marriage. In these vows we hold together our partnership. We set and reveal our combined goals, and we make the promises by which we shall hold each other accountable in our future."

Thomas moved then, grabbing both of my hands and turning me toward him. His icy blue eyes showed the first signs of anxiety and I felt his grip around my hands tighten. A sudden wave of understanding coursed through me. We were now reaching the part of the ceremony most unfamiliar to him. I felt certain the same weirdness that had just flooded my body now coursed through his. I gave his hand a gentle squeeze and sent him a soft smile.

Deviating from our initial plan, I spoke now, giving my vows first. "In this space, with the blessing of the Gods all around us, and trusting in the reverence of the fabrics that weave this world together: Time, Life, Magic, Nature, and Wisdom, I come to bind my life to this man, Thomas Rayforth Ecardio Davenforth Carleon. With our marriage, I promise partnership, that I will work with you to accomplish our goals and to strengthen this Kingdom." The words rolled easily off my tongue.

It was easy to make these vows to Thomas, as I knew these vows were not for Thomas, but rather vows I made for Dolma, for the people of Dolma, as their future Queen. "I promise to always work for our success and to look for solutions to any challenges we may face. I promise to always be compassionate and understanding when faced with your weaknesses and I promise to cherish and celebrate your strengths. In this life, with all the power I hold, I will always work to grow, to become the highest version of myself I can be, and I vouch to use this growth that I gain and the knowledge that I carry to increase and expand our prosperity, peace, and joy. This I vow to you, to all here today, and with the understanding and blessing of the Gods all around us."

Silence hung in the air for a moment, punctured only by the sound of my own breath. Then, Thomas' own voice broke through, his eyes focused only on me, piercing and filled with an emotion that I could not name. They hooked onto my own and I could not look away. "In this space, with the blessing of the Gods all around us, and trusting in the reverence of the fabrics that weave this world together: Time, Life, Magic, Nature, and Wisdom, I come to bind my life to this woman, Avalynn. I vow to you today that I will always strive to know, acknowledge, and understand your strength, intelligence, compassion, and power. I promise to confide in you my honest thoughts, feelings, and opinions on the world we live in, and I promise to work with you as what we are: partners, rulers, and equals in all things. You are my friend and my lifelong companion and I will always strive to deserve the trust and wisdom you grace me with everyday. I will push myself as you do to be the highest version of myself I can be, and I promise to use that growth and all my learning to support you in your goals and dreams. Together, we will create a relationship and a country that thrives and is filled with joy; this I vow to you, to all here today, and with the understanding and blessing of the Gods all around us."

Our voices chanted together as we finished the ceremony, "In all times, throughout all our life, death, and life again, with magic in the air we breathe, surrounded by the nature this world has blessed us with, and with the present and conscious wisdom from this and all our lives, I bind myself to you today knowing that I will choose to spend the rest of this life and this time with you. Today I choose to marry you. Today we are married."

Applause broke out from the crowd around us, and we walked together back out of the hall. "So that's it. We're married," Thomas said, sighing with some relief as we rushed to the side chamber adjacent to the Banquet Hall where we'd see our parents before going off to greet our guests.

"Yes," I replied, entering the room and turning back towards Thomas, "We are married." We stared at each other for a long moment, processing the absurdity of it all.

"So, now what?" Thomas asked eventually. He looked so dreadfully confused, and his normal hardened face softened like that of a lost puppy. I didn't mean to laugh at him, I really didn't, but seeing him standing there looking so lost, I just couldn't help myself. I burst into a fit of giggles. "What? What did I say?" Thomas said, a startled look in his eyes as I continued to laugh. "Ava! What did I say?" A smile was on his own face now too, as my mirth continued. Eventually, Thomas joined in my laughter, pulling me towards him and giving me a large hug. He was softer than I imagined, and warmer. It was easy, sometimes, to forget he was human, but here, in his arms, with both of us shaking from relief and laughter, he seems more alive than ever.

Slowly, our laughter stilled, but Thomas kept me in his arms. "I'm glad it was you," he whispered into my hair. "Despite being with Sabine, I always knew I would have to marry for political reasons. I'm not saying it was right and I'd like to change this custom for our children, but it was what I knew. It was what was expected of me. I didn't think there was any way to avoid it. So, I'm really very grateful it was you I got to marry. It makes it so much easier that I get to marry a friend. I know a marriage like this isn't what you expected, so I'll promise you now what I should have promised when you first arrived. I will try to be a good husband. I will try to be someone you can always trust and rely on. I will help you with your impossible goals, and together we will make Dolma stronger. Please just tell me if I'm doing anything wrong." Thomas pulled back, his hand sliding gently onto my arms, cradling me out in front of him. "I... I would like you to be happy."

"I will be," I assured him with a smile. "No individual is solely responsible for the happiness of another," I continued, echoing Nana's words to me a long time ago. "And, a relationship works both ways, even arranged relationships. You must be sure to tell me if there's ever anything I can do for you too."

"There could never be."

"There can and there will be. We are in this relationship for a long time, Thomas; there are bound to be disagreements or challenges. You must tell me what you need, too, or else how ever am I supposed to help? Or even to know that you are struggling?"

"All right then, we will tell each other of any issues we have."

"It's a deal." Thomas beamed at me, the dazzling bright smile I'd seen only a few times before.

"I'm glad you are my wife, Crown Prince Avalynn Carleon," Thomas bowed before me.

"Thomas -" a bang filled the room causing me to jump.

"Avalynn!" Father cried, pulling me into a massive hug that lifted my feet off the ground. "You look so pretty," he sobbed, and I felt his hot tears against my exposed shoulders.

"Edgar, put her down. You'll ruin her dress," Mother scolded, dabbing her own eyes with a purple and gold handkerchief.

"But she does look so pretty," Mama wailed, joining Father in an all-consuming embrace. Her tears now joining Father's as they slid across my skin. While this whole display made me feel very loved, it also made me feel rather suffocated. I was, after all, quite a bit smaller than the two people crushing me between them, and it was getting rather difficult to breathe, or to move at all for that matter. Still, my slow suffocation wouldn't end, "And now she's married," Mama said tearfully, holding me even closer, and squeezing any remaining air from my lungs.

"Yes, dears, but now you're crushing the poor child. Do let her breathe," came the cool refreshing voice of Nana followed by the sweet release of Father and Mama. I immediately gasped as air once again filled my chest, and I was able to breathe.

"Now look what you've done," Mother sighed, gently rubbing my back as I regained a normal breathing pattern. "Honestly you two are so dramatic!"

"But she's married!" Father blubbed, from a safe distance this time.

"Yes, and the goal is to see her live after her wedding," Azar teased, patting Father on the back.

"Like you were much better," Al pointed out, "You sobbed like a waterfall throughout the entire wedding, ruining both Ari's and my handkerchiefs, I might add."

"I'll wash them!" Azar protested indignantly. Al just ignored him, walking over to me instead.

"You really do look beautiful, Ava, and I thought your vows were very fitting as both a promise to your husband and the country," he said, kissing me on the forehead, and beaming at me. I smiled back. Of course Al would have understood my dual-sided vows. A warmth rushed through me as I moved to hug my observant and caring older brother.

Azar turned to Thomas, "Welcome to the family!" he smiled, pulling Thomas into a hug. Azar, as per usual, was perfectly comfortable with this, and perfectly oblivious to the panic and confusion that flashed onto Thomas's face before he awkwardly patted Azar on the back. "Now you'd best be careful now," Azar said seriously as he pulled away, "If you hurt my sister, she'll kill you."

"I will not!" I objected furiously.

"It will likely be slow and painful, too," Azar nodded, ignoring me.

"I'm not going to murder my husband!" I cried out moving towards him.

"And she'll never get caught."

"Damn it, Azar!" I yelled, trying, unsuccessfully, to push him away from Thomas. "I'm not going to murder anyone just because they hurt me!"

"Oh yes, she's far more likely to destroy everything you care about," Al jumped in.

"Al!" I cried out. "I won't do that either," I said looking seriously at Thomas, internally begging him not to listen to the taunts of my ridiculous brothers.

"Don't worry, Prince Azar, I am well aware of the cruelty my wife is capable of," Thomas replied back, giving me a mischievous smile.

"Thomas!" Betrayal flooded through me as I heard Al and Azar laugh behind me.

"Isn't it rude to upset a bride on her wedding day?" Ari asked from behind me, looking curiously at my brothers and me.

"Yes!" I exclaimed, gratefully walking over to my younger brother and placing a hand gently on his shoulder. "Of course my favorite brother would be the one to stand up for me," I said, looking directly at Al and Azar.

"Hold on now!" Al gasped.

"Steady on, Ava!" Azar said, placing a hand over his heart dramatically.

"And you're not much better," I glared at Thomas accusingly.

"Just making nice with the in-laws," Thomas smiled, throwing his hands up in the air and a gesture of mock innocence.

"At my expense?" I glared.

"I have a much easier time believing that this was all really at your expense, darling," Thomas sauntered over to me, "If you hadn't been smiling this whole time." Thomas' blue eyes sparkled as my hand flew over my mouth.

"Yeah, so Ari's not really your favorite brother, right?" Azar said, putting his arm around me.

"Of course not," Al replied in my stead, "Clearly I'm her favorite brother."

"You?!" Azar exclaimed.

"I am older," Al said calmly.

"You don't get to be the favorite just because of that!" Azar shouted.

"But I'm the only one Ava said was her favorite," Ari pointed out, interrupting them both.

There was a slight pause as Al and Azar both turned to look at him. "Now -" "You see -" they both started at the same time before Father gave them a quick yank at the back of their shirts.

"Come now, we should have some decorum at your sister's wedding," Father said seriously. He was met with questioning gazes for most everybody in the room, "Ehm, Harold, is it not time we go out to greet the guests?" Father sheepishly deflected.

"Oh, yes! Quite right you are," Harry agreed, beckoning to a page who quickly began announcing my two families to the waiting crowd next door.

Finally, Harry's voice reached over into the room, "I now present to you the bride and groom, Crown Prince Thomas Rayforth Ecardio Davenforth Carleon and Crown Princess Ava-lynn Carleon of Dolma!" There was a thunderous applause as I walked out on Thomas' arm, looking out at the crowd below.

Chapter 27

The Dance of Kings

It took less than five minutes for me to determine that greeting guests at one's wedding was an exhausting affair. Thomas and I stood at the back of the room while a seemingly endless line of people came up to congratulate us. There was a series of never-ending pleasantries with people I'd barely met; and the people I actually did want to talk to were shooed away far too quickly, in order to get through the whole crowd. By the end of the line, we'd been standing for nearly two hours, and my feet were aching. The only real benefit was Lady Sabine was also rushed, so she didn't have the time to hurl any of her usual veiled insults before a servant hurried her away for the next guest. I was so hoping we'd gotten past her anger at me marrying her lover, but her glare told me that this was not the case. I optimistically hoped that this was all simply the stress of seeing the person you love marry another, but I had the sinking feeling that we'd never really get past this.

"If I never have to speak to another person again, it'd be too soon," Thomas confided as we collapsed into our seats for the ridiculously extravagant twelve course meal that was to come next.

I nodded fervently in agreement, "How is it that all the worst people got to speak with us the longest?" I complained.

"Because they were all the people with zero respect for the line behind them," Thomas sighed, as I let out a small giggle. "Who knew weddings would be this exhausting?" Thomas continued. "It's only 4 in the afternoon and I'm already exhausted. Father's lucky I'm not falling asleep at the table, how I am expected to stay awake past 10 is insane."

"I agree, we should have scheduled in a nap."

"A wedding nap, now that's a brilliant idea!" Thomas gave me a tired smile, "And now, of course, we are expected to talk to each other for this entire meal, or else we might give off the impression we don't like each other and won't be a good King and Queen! It's too much! Not that I don't enjoy talking with you," Thomas hurriedly added, "It's just -"

"I know exactly what you mean," I rescued him, and he gave me a relieved smile in return. "Do you think anyone would notice if we just mimed communication?" Beside me Thomas started opening and closing his mouth.

"Do you think it worked?" he asked a moment later.

I laughed, "Well maybe, but you do look a bit like a dead fish. I'm not sure I'd be able to keep a straight face."

Thomas laughed out loud, "Perhaps that's all the more reason to keep doing it."

Twelve courses was ridiculously long, a complete waste of food, and an excellent time to recover from the stress of the wedding. It took over two hours to eat, but during that time Thomas and I were to be left alone, sitting at a table in the center of the room to be watched by all. This was less awkward than it sounded and Thomas had, at some time over the past three months, become someone easy to talk to. Plus, he felt similar to myself about the whole ordeal. We shared stories of our childhoods or, in my case, spoke of the friends I had invited to the wedding. It was not perfect and I still felt as though a wedding nap was in order. However, I did feel more refreshed by the time the tables were put away, and the hall set up for the dancing.

We followed an old Nevremerre tradition for the ball we were about to host: the couple would not dance together until right before they were to depart for the evening. For us, our dance was planned for 10 in the evening. I was very unsure of how I was going to dance for another four hours, but it would seem I'd have to survive somehow.

"Here dear, drink up," Nana's voice washed over me as she handed me a teacup. "Quickly now, you'll have to open the ball with your Father soon." As a general rule, I always listen to Nana; throughout my life it had simply become the most reasonable option in any given scenario. So, even though I had no idea what she gave me, and even if it tasted bitter and heavy, I chugged the contents of that tea glass down. Nana smiled at me, "It will take a few minutes to kick in, but that will keep you going for the rest of the evening. Also, I've sent some balm to your new rooms this evening, put it on before you go to bed, it will help with the ache in your feet."

"Thank you, Nana," I almost cried, overwhelmed with gratitude over her simple actions.

"No time to thank me, Songbird, they're waiting on you," she said, gently nudging me to where Father, Thomas, and Priscella stood on the edge of the dance floor. "We'll talk more later, my songbird. Tonight, I suspect you will be in too high of demand for a proper conversation."

Accepting her words, I moved toward Father. Holding his hand out to me, we moved onto the dance floor and got into position as we waited for the music to begin. "When you all were small," Father spoke to me softly as we began to move to the first notes of the music, "I imagined many moments about your future. My favorite, perhaps, although it really is hard to choose a favorite when you had yet to do any of what you imagined, was that I knew that one day I would get to dance with each of you at an event in which you were the star. Now I did not know if this would be your first ball as a competitor in the Knights Tournament, your wedding, or perhaps your coming of age ceremony, but I knew I would have this dance with each of you." His voice was quiet as he spoke, his gentle rumble reverberating close to my ear.

"I knew that it would be my greatest pleasure, as your father, to use these moments to loudly reminisce on some of the greatest stories of your childhood. Stories I collected earnestly and deliberately as I watched you all grow into the people you are today."

"It was on purpose!" I gasped, thinking back to Al and Azar's dances with Father these past two years.

Father grinned at me, "Of course, my gift. I do most things on purpose. It's very useful for being King." He paused his speech for a moment, looking down sadly at me, "I had a great many stories for you, too, you know, but I don't think I can tell them here. You see, an important part of these dances is that I always imagined them happening surrounded by friends, our country men, and people who supported us. But that is not the case here, in this country, in this wedding, at this time. Anything we say that is loud enough for the room to hear could be used as ammunition against you, and I will never give them something they can hurt you with.

So, I will not fulfill my dream of telling embarrassing stories of you while we dance today. Instead, I want you to remember that even if I can't say the words, I am thinking of you as I did your brothers, as I will with Ari. I am thinking of the child you used to be and comparing it to the adult you are now, and I am filled with so much pride and love that it feels as if my heart will burst. For you were a wonderful child and you are now the most wonderful and remarkable adult. It has been my greatest joy to see you live the life of your choosing, even if I am far away. I love you with all I have, my precious gift."

"Oh Father," I whispered, desperately trying to keep the tears from falling down my face. "I know I chose this, and I don't regret it. I really don't. I think I can do so much good here, and that excites and inspires me. I know I made the best choice for me and everyone else," I paused, considering my next words carefully. "But I miss the life I could have had. I wanted to be a knight, to win the Introductory and the Open Brackets. To fall in love and marry the person I loved, to be Nevremerre's Queen."

"You could still be Nevremerre's Queen."

"No. No I can't. You've seen this place, Father. I don't have the time required to get this country to Nevremerre's standard. Most of Dolma either fears Nevremerre or believes us to be savages. I will need more than just a few years to fix the perceptions and problems I've found here. Did you know they almost didn't let Charlotte serve me today and yesterday? At the time, I didn't have the ability to focus on the reason why, but now the ceremony is over, I know the answer. It's because they believed her to be male because she was born into the wrong body. I must fight for Dolma to become more open, more accepting, to care more about its citizens, and to weed out the corruption that thrives here. I cannot do that and rule Nevremerre, and I cannot subject the people of Nevremerre to people who will not even treat them as humans.

One day, I hope, my efforts will succeed and Dolma and Nevremerre could successfully merge, but I doubt it will be in my lifetime. At least right now, I must be taken out of contention for Nevremerre's throne. However, I believe that I may still need the power that comes from King Harold and others in Dolma believing I could still inherit Nevremerre's throne, so please exclude me from contention only when it is time to choose a ruler."

"I understand," Father said after a beat of silence, "and I confess I believe your decision to be the right one for now. But, the future, Ava, is still uncertain. I am not yet convinced that we need to take you out of complete contention for the throne just yet. We can discuss it more when that time approaches. Until then, Ava, remember this," Father said, coming close to me once more as the music began its closing notes. "Just because this life isn't the one you imagined, does not mean it can't be happy, so please, my gift, be happy."

"Yes Father," I smiled at him. Around us, music was re-placed by polite applause and Father gave me a deep bow before Mother replaced him as my partner. And as the night continued, Mother was replaced by Mama, then each of my brothers, and then my friends. Nana's mystery drink worked wonders, and I still managed to have the energy to dance with Carlos, who practically threw me around the floor. Friends were replaced by Dolmanians, who were replaced with foreign-ers, who led me to start a waltz with none other than the King of Calvine.

"This is a very well done wedding, Crown Princess," he began, his voice sounding a little sinister for what should have been a compliment.

"Thank you, we work to make it a pleasing mix of both cultures."

"Yes, Nevremerre's ability to command cultural and diplo-matic relations is something to be envied."

"It is something we put a great effort into," I tried to smile back, growing increasingly uncomfortable.

"Yes, had Calvine worked to foster the same relationships, perhaps we would have conquered Dolma by now."

"What?" I blurted out, then internally winced at my blunder.

"You must be aware that we were considering attacking Dolma, as that is partially the reason for your wedding after all."

"Well of course I am. I simply hadn't expected you to talk of it so openly."

"Yes, well it would be foolish to do such a thing now. Even had Nevremerre and Agremerre not agreed to lend their support, my spies tell me you have already begun the process of reforming this gilded wasteland. No doubt it will become harder and harder to take over."

"It would be quite incorrect for me not to make the country I will one day rule the best it could be," I replied cautiously.

"Yes, you would think that." This, I thought, was a rather rude statement from someone who just met me two days ago, but it seemed wise not to comment on it. "Still, it's our own fault. If we had improved our diplomatic relations with Nevremerre and Agremerre sooner, perhaps you would have come to us with your drought struggles, and Dolma would have been in our hands. Surely you don't deny that the people would do far better with us ruling them."

Privately, I agreed with the sentiments, but that too would not be wise to say aloud. Instead, I settled on, "As Calvine has never sent out ambassadors, I know too little of your country to make an official judgment."

King Olivender smiled for a moment. "That will change," he declared. "I will not allow my country to lose out on an opportunity like this again. I will talk with the Kings and Queens of our neighboring countries and have our ambassadors placed in every court."

"That's quite an interesting proposal," I said, a little shocked.

"Calvine learns from its mistakes, Crown Princess," King Olivender said simply. He pulled me towards him, lowering his voice as we continued our waltz. "You may not know about us, but I know about Dolma. I know the struggles of the foreigners and a woman like yourself will face here. When our ambassador comes to this Palace, know this, should you ever wish for a dramatic change in your life here, Calvine will support you. With you, Crown Princess Avalynn Carleon, I will happily negotiate a deal, whether you desire revolution or escape, you can have the power of Calvine at your side." The dance came to a close and King Olivender quickly pulled away. "I congratulate you on your wedding, Crown Princess," he finished with a small bow.

"Thank you for your words, King Olivender," I curtsied back. Our eyes met for just a moment before he nodded and turned away.

Harry was beside me in a flash, "Well, what did he want?" he asked, roughly maneuvering me into position for the next dance.

"You know, you're supposed to ask before you grab someone to dance," I sighed.

"So you won't tell me what he said," Harry retorted, his eyebrows wiggling in impatience.

"He wants to place an ambassador in the courts of Dolma, Agremerre, and Nevremerre, and he congratulated me on my wedding," I finally said once the music had started.

"He should be talking to me about that!" Harry huffed. Mentally, I knew Harry was only slightly older than Father, but in moments like these, and with his ice blonde hair, he reminded me of a crotchety old grandpa.

"I think he was planning to," I placated. "He was just telling me that our treaty made him realize Calvine would benefit from more relations with other countries."

"I'm sure it did, that old git."

"He's younger than you."

"I'm younger in spirit!" I only stared in response. "Well, he can't invade us now, can he?" Harry grinned once more. "Not without suffering a heavy loss. Gods below, we might even be able to invade Calvine now," Harry whispered to me.

"Neither Nevremerre nor Agremerre would agree to that and it's not part of the treaty," I pointed out, "and it's not exactly a wise move either way."

"I know. I know, but it's nice how the tables have turned. Besides, you're my daughter now, you should be more supportive."

"I'm plenty supportive when you don't want to do stupid things."

"Don't be smart with me now."

"Isn't my brain the reason you brought me here?"

"True enough. Fine, I'll let you have this one, as it is your wedding day and all."

"Thanks," I deadpanned.

"Not to worry, sarcasm can't affect me today. Calvine will not be attacking, my intellectual genius has paid off once again, and you have married my son in an event that all guests will speak of for generations to come. You and Thomas behaved perfectly! What a triumph this day has been."

"It's not over yet."

"Just one more dance. All you must do now is dance with my son, and this public display is done." Around us the music stopped once more. "Good luck, Ava," Harry smiled as he walked me over to where Thomas was standing.

Chapter 28

The King's Child

It was eerily reminiscent of that moment all those months ago, when Thomas had left me alone in the middle of the ballroom. As if reading my mind, Thomas picked up my hand and pulled me into position. "I won't leave you this time," he promised. "It was wrong of me to do that the last time."

"Then why did you?" I asked, not ready to grant forgiveness quite yet. "You apologized last time, too, so you knew what you were doing was wrong."

"Yes. Yes I did, too. I believed if I danced with you, Sabine would leave me."

"Will she leave you now?" I asked, starting to pull away from him.

Thomas held me close to him, "We are Crown Prince and Crown Princess now. Duty must come first." Behind us the orchestra started to play once more.

A beautiful waltz echoed through the hall, all eyes focused on us once more. "That's quite a change in thought and I'm not sure it's true. My parents love each other quite dearly, and they also rule wonderfully."

"Your parents are also married and they rule a country together. Sabine will not be ruling with us and Sabine is not my wife."

"I've never been against you having a lover," I pointed out, despite the hypocrisy of Thomas being allowed to have a lover and not me.

"As long as she doesn't get in the way of our duty," Thomas accurately refuted me. "Because part of my duty is an arranged marriage, it's more difficult to add love into the equation."

"But not impossible."

"You're much more of an idealist than I initially realized," Thomas said while we twirled around the room.

"Ideals are what allow us to create a better world," I defended.

"Perhaps," Thomas smiled, "but that's not something to discuss right now. While not originally part of my beliefs, I confess I now believe duty should be placed above love."

"How can you possibly have changed your beliefs so much?"

"I've been given the evidence I needed to change them. Plus, I am not so sure that my beliefs were actually so different. Not initially anyways."

"And what of Lady Sabine?"

"You know, I wonder," Thomas began. "Before your parents had arrived I would have sworn that we had the truest form of love there is. However, after seeing how your parents interact with each other, I think perhaps I was wrong. I suppose we never really get to see love here, most everyone here has married for political gain or financial gain or for some reason other than love. It makes it difficult to recognize love when you are dating someone. Watching your parents, I know what love should look like. It's obvious when you watch them talk, look, or even just exist together and how they love you and your siblings. It's so easy for them, so safe. I don't think my relationship with Sabine has ever been like that."

"So are you breaking it off with her? "I asked, unable to hide my surprise.

Thomas looked at me. "If I confess something to you now, can I ask that you don't give me advice. I will tell you, and then I would like to dance in silence, to leave what I'm going to tell you for me to solve on my own."

"Of course, if you wish."

"I am a coward, Avalynn. I'm not a brave man. I know I should part with her, but I find I'm too afraid to do just that. I told you once that everything I am Sabine gives me; you told me that was nonsense, and, intellectually, I know you to be right. But, emotionally, I am too terrified of becoming nothing to let her go just yet. I need to find a way to become something again."

"And you think you will be able to find that while you are still with her?" Thomas gave me a judgemental look. "It's not advice or judgment," I quickly added, "Just a question."

Thomas sighed, "I don't know. The trouble is I'm much too scared to move forward and I know too much to go back to where we were before. I'm frozen and I can't seem to find a way to take any step." I nodded this time, following my promise of silence as we continued our dance. "Fine," Thomas said finally, a touch of impatience coloring his voice. "Say what you want. Silence doesn't much suit you anyways."

I fought back a grin, "I only want to say that, one day, when you thaw out and choose to make a move, I will support you in your choice. And, I think you will unfreeze sooner than you think."

"Perhaps you'll be right once more, Crown Princess," Thomas bowed to me as our dance came to a close.

We then said a quick goodbye to the crowd as we finally exited the Banquet Hall. We followed a servant to where our new joint rooms would be located, just slightly down from where the King and Queen resided. It was only when we walked into the deserted rooms and the door swung closed behind us that the full extent of my exhaustion caught up to me. With a large sigh, I collapsed against the door behind me, sinking to the floor.

"That will make it harder to get to bed later," Thomas pointed out, his voice hovering above me.

"I don't care. I couldn't move now if I wanted to!"

To my surprise, Thomas sank down beside me, his head sinking back against the wooden door. "Me either," he confessed with his eyes closed.

We sat soaking in the quiet, and I tried desperately to not fall asleep. Instead, I forced movement as I slipped off my shoes. The relief I felt at the action was positively euphoric and a moan escaped my lips as I flexed and wiggled my feet in the cold air. "That good, huh," came Thomas' groggy voice from beside me.

"I'm not sure there is any shoe that's designed for nearly eight hours of constant use," I mumbled back. "Do you think we could just sleep here?"

"If only," Thomas laughed breathily, "but we still must have our first night."

"Our what?" I said, jolting into a more upright position. My mind fumbling for what part of this ceremony I had possibly forgotten.

Thomas' eyes flew open as well. "Avalynn," he said cautiously, a confused look in his eyes. "We are the future King and Queen of Dolma, we are expected to have children, and to start that..." Thomas began to blush a little before he cleared his throat and pushed on, "that process tonight."

"Well sure, but why must we have biological children, and even if we did, why must we start tonight?"

"What would we have if not biological children? And the people need to know the crown is secure, that there are plenty of heirs to take over, so we must begin as soon as possible."

"We could adopt," I pointed out in frustration.

"An adopted child cannot become King," Thomas said dismissively.

"Why not?" I demanded angrily, "I was adopted."

Thomas' eyes went wide and his hand flew out over my mouth, stopping me from speaking. "Don't - don't say another word. We can't talk about this here." There was a panic and desperation in his tone that gave me pause, and I silenced my usual comeback. Slowly, I nodded against his hand.

Thomas immediately let go of my mouth, and he looked frantically around the room. Even sticking his head out of the door and looking down both sides of the hall. "No one is there," I reassured him. "Not even the servants are allowed to be here until morning." A blush crept over my cheeks as I finally realized why that was supposed to be the case. Thomas didn't respond to my comment, however, and instead gently helped me to my feet, picking up my shoes as well.

"Come with me," he said, moving quickly through the much larger set of rooms until he made it to a large door that opened to the largest bedroom I had ever seen. Our bedroom. My face felt hot once more, but I pushed that aside and followed Thomas into the room. He placed my shoes on a nearby vanity before turning back to me. "Is the door closed?" he asked, his voice low and serious in the candle-lit room. I nodded back, a little confused as to why he was asking such an obvious question. "Securely?" he pressed on.

"Yes Thomas," I finally replied. "I have closed the door securely," I added, marginally annoyed by the line of questioning.

Not fazed by my annoyance, Thomas just said, "Good," and ran his hand through his hair. "What exactly do you mean that you were adopted?" he asked finally.

"Well, what do you think? It's not exactly a complicated term. My father found me, alone, in a boat along the Nevremerre coast line. After a search that failed to find my parents, Father adopted me," I huffed.

"So you don't carry the King's blood?" Thomas asked.

"No. I am not his biological child," I said, thoroughly irritated.

"Avalynn," Thomas chided. "This is serious. No one here must ever know you are adopted."

"What? Why?" I asked, calming down a little at the severity of his tone.

"Dolma believes in blood purity. The idea that the blood in your veins is what makes you what you are. Nobles are nobles because they have the blood of nobles. Kings will be Kings because they have the blood of Kings. It's this mindset that keeps our class structure alive, and before you say anything, I'm well aware that the class structure is on your list of things to be changed. Clearly, your biological parentage doesn't actually define you, but there are many here who do believe this. If it were ever learned that you were adopted, at best, you would lose any power or respect they may have given you, and, at worst, they might demand your execution."

"My execution!"

"Yes. They'd say you tricked us by claiming to be a King's daughter when really you were not."

"But I am a King's daughter!"

"I know. I know that Avalynn, but that's not the belief here. There would be a backlash if it were ever discovered you didn't share King Edgar's blood. So much backlash even my father wouldn't be able to control it. I know it's ridiculous to you, but I'm begging you to trust me here and keep your adoption a secret. You can ask any Dolmanian about blood purity and you could easily prove what I am saying to be true."

"It's okay," I sighed, "You don't need to beg. I believe you." I fell down onto a stool by the vanity where my shoes now sat. Mentally I flicked through my party, trying to determine if anyone would have said something about my birth. I quickly dismissed this idea though. In Nevremerre, my adoption simply didn't matter. It was only ever really discussed on my found day, and that wouldn't happen for several more months. "It does explain a lot about the rigidity of Dolma's class system."

"I'm sorry," Thomas whispered, sitting down on a cushioned bench by the foot of the bed.

"You are not solely responsible for the creation of Dolma's class system," I said, wearily.

"No, but I will help you end it."

I looked up at him, his determined face meeting mine, confident and bolder than I had ever seen him. "You're right, things need to change here. I will help you do that."

"Okay," I breathed, I was so incredibly sure he meant the words he spoke it nearly took my breath away. I took a moment to refocus, "Now what of children?" I asked, pulling us back to the original topic.

"I don't believe we can change the minds of the nobles and the public that quickly," Thomas said slowly, "I think we will need biological children, at least to start, but I don't ever wish to make you uncomfortable, we can start having children when you're ready."

"And when you agree, too. We are married, it is a choice we make together," I nodded. "I have no intention of sleeping with you while you are still in a relationship with someone else," I said bluntly.

"Of course. We can discuss this again after I "unthaw" as you put it," Thomas agreed. "For tonight, we will simply fake it."

"Fake it?"

Thomas got up and began to move around the room, "Our marriage is something that everyone is watching and that several will wish did not occur. They are looking for reasons to invalidate it. Everyone from my father to different nobles, to foreign dignitaries will have sent spies tomorrow to ensure our marriage was consummated. Fortunately, we can fake the proof they're looking for." Thomas pulled back the white sheets, and took off his shirt, using a paper knife he pressed along the inside of his upper arm until a few drops of blood hit the sheet. "There, now they will see what they're looking for."

I gaped at him, "I remember hearing about that old tale as a child. You can't tell me people here still believe that a woman always bleeds during her first time having sex? That's nonsense."

"What?" Thomas blushed, "But this is expected."

"I am reforming your entire medical system," I exclaimed, in exasperation. "You do know that's medically inaccurate! And also occasionally a sign the man is a bad lover."

"Is it really?" Thomas asked, "Well it's still considered real in Dolma, and in most of the countries we border. But, I guess we'll be correcting that soon."

"Also in Nevremerre, people aren't required to be virgins before they marry. What would you have done then?"

"You are going to serve our country by bringing the knowledge and determination needed to change our broken systems. I will of course try to learn, but I don't have that knowledge yet. I don't know what's been done in Nevremerre and Agremerre to help those countries thrive. I do have knowledge of Dolma though, and all of the strange and weird customs that matter here. So I would have done what's necessary to help you stay here. Until I learn more, we will work as a team. You as the person with the knowledge of how we can change, and me as the person who will guide you through the oddities of Dolma. Please trust me to deal with the Dolmanian customs and norms as I trust you to change our poor policies and laws."

"Very well," I smiled at him, "I will trust you. But, did you have to bleed on the bed before we slept on it?"

Thomas blushed. "It - it needed to be there before the staff comes in the morning." He eventually decided. We both stared at the bed for a moment, "We could maybe cover it with the top sheet and sleep under the duvet?"

"Let's do that," I agreed. We quickly got ready for bed, and Thomas cleaned and replaced the paper knife before pulling the top sheet back up the bed. Slowly I blew out the candles around us until just the silver moonlight filled the room.

"Avalynn," Thomas' voice broke the midnight silence as we climbed onto opposite sides of he bed. "I meant what I said at our wedding. I mean to support you, for us to be a team that works together for the betterment of Dolma. I am on your side here."

"Then, starting tomorrow, we work together to change this place," I said, watching his inky figure from the other side of the bed.

"Yes. Tomorrow, together," Thomas agreed drowsily as our breaths slowly evened out and we fell into the greedy hands of an exhausted sleep, desperate to prepare us for the battle to come.

2.5 Years Later

"You must push, Crown Princess."

"I am pushing!" I cried, yelling rather unjustly at the poor nurse, but when one was experiencing the pain I currently felt, yelling was just about the only thing I could do.

"Oh I wish my mothers were here!" I cried out again.

Nana's soothing hand caressed my face and cheek. "They'll come as soon as they can, they weren't to know you'd go into labor a month early, and you wouldn't want your father here. He'd be an absolute mess - your brothers too, no doubt.

"You knew!" I panted angrily, between occasional screams. "You had a vision, which is why you're here now! So you should have just brought them along!"

"Now is not the time to be yelling at your Grandmother," Priscella said from her spot on my other side. "You must focus, Avalynn," she said kindly.

"Augh!!" I screamed as another contraction came over me, as I tried my best to breathe normally.

"Very good, Crown Princess. The head is almost out now, you must keep going!" the nurse urged.

"I don't think I really have a choice in the matter!" I screamed, as my insides were torn apart. I belatedly remembered Carlos suggesting no one ever have children and I suddenly found my-self agreeing wholeheartedly. I was slowly being dissected and ripped into pieces to bring this child into the world. Of course, I had loved the child immensely during the past months, and I would love it infinitely in the future. But, it was rather difficult to remember all of that now.

"Just a bit more, Crown Princess," the nurse called, as I screamed out once more. Another cry met my own this time, as the sound of my baby's voice hit the air. At this point I couldn't help but sob uncontrollably at the sound. "There, there, Crown Princess. You'll meet him in a moment, you must continue to push for now."

"So it's a boy?" Priscella asked excitedly, moving towards the nurse.

I didn't let her go, however, holding her hand tightly in my own. "Please don't leave me yet," I sobbed. She hesitated slightly before nodding and moving back over to me.

"We're right here, my songbird," Nana cooed, "We'll be with you as long as you need us." And I did need them, several more minutes of pain followed before I was finally able to hold my child. He was red and wrinkly, but I was already so proud of him. The pain still flitted through me as my body recovered from the trauma of it all, but Nana and Priscella were there, and my precious child was with me too.

"You've done it, my dear," Priscella said, kissing my head, and then the baby's, "You've made an heir. Everything will be easier now. You are the mother of a future King. People will have to respect you now."

"The people already respect and love me," I said wearily.

"Yes, they do," Priscella agreed, "but now the nobles will have to as well. You don't have to worry now, you will be considered a true Crown Princess. You've done your duty. No one can treat you as less now."

"You're wrong," I said, looking at my beautiful son, "This will change very little, for I will still do things the nobles fear or resent. Perhaps they will not say it to my face, but they will still think it. I have not changed after all, I will still keep working. My duty as Crown Princess and later Queen is to help the people, regardless of any children I have. My duty as a mother is to love my child unconditionally and ensure he has what he needs to thrive. Really, the only difference between the two roles is who my work is directed towards." I smiled before looking at Priscella. "The Dolma my son will grow up in will not be the same as the one his father and grandfather have lived in. Dolma has changed and will continue to change. I will make sure of it."

Priscella hummed beside me. "I will tell the King and Thomas of the news," she nodded before taking the maid and heading out of the room, leaving my Nana and me alone with my son.

"Songbird," Nana began, looking seriously at me now. "Since it will take Priscella quite some time to move through this grand palace to where the men are, I must impart upon you some rather important news. While I did have a vision that my new great-grandson may be born early, that was not the only reason I came to Dolma so soon. I have a message for you, my dear, from Queen Anora of Agremerre. A message I think it vital you read now."

"Of course Nana," I said, looking at her in confusion. She nodded and with the skill of an expert transferred my son into her own arms, while handing me a letter.

"Read now, my songbird."

I hadn't the thought to argue with her as I took the sealed letter and opened it.

My Dearest Avalynn,

The neat scrawl of Anora filled the page as I began to read her letter.

I have heard the pleasant news that you are expecting a child of your own any day now, and I wish you all the best in that process. I can only hope that your delivery is far less stressful than my own. At almost three years old your Goddaughter, and my little trouble maker is certainly living up to her birth as a source of mischief in this world. But, even if she is a wild thing now, she is already showing compassion and wit that will make her a strong Queen of my country, should she wish it.

The problem I face now should have been something I resolved sooner, but there have been a great many other things to focus on these past few years. Now that I am no longer the mother of a newborn, now that Agremerre's drought has successfully ended, and considering the tragic recent events that occurred in Maychula, I must now think of succession for the throne of my country. Genevieve is clearly the next heir, if she decides to take that path, and my will states as much, but Genevieve is still so young. That is why, my dear girl, In the event of my death, or an inability to rule, I have made you Agremerre's heir until Genevieve comes of age.

The documents have already been signed, sealed, and set into motion. You have already been approved by the High Judges, and being over 21 now, you are legally able to be Agremerre's Queen. I apologize for thrusting this position upon you, but as Queen of Agremerre, I must do what is best for my country. As a mother, I must do what is best for my daughter. You are both. I trust you as my daughter's Godmother to guide her well should I not be here, and I trust you as an Nevremerre-educated Crown Princess who has already made moves to grow and change a culture I thought unchangeable. My people still love you for your sacrifice in going to Dolma, and they will happily accept you as a ruler. You will make an excellent Queen of Agremerre, if only temporarily, and you will make an excellent role model and caretaker of my daughter.

With that, I wish you the best of luck with your birth and newborn, and I look forward to conversing with you again soon, Crown Princess Avalynn of Dolma and Agremerre.

Love,
Queen Anora of Agremerre

*Avalynn's journey continues
in "The Kingdom We Rule".
Expected release in Fall of
2022*

Acknowledgements

A big thank you to everyone who helped me create this book. The cover was designed by the amazing and talented Jen Leong. Check out more of her incredible art at www.jern-inc.com. The maps were the work of my wonderful mother, Julie Nelson. Thank you also to my editors, Julie Nelson, Tim Nelson, and Diane Peterson Mathis. Finally, I am immensely grateful to all of you who have read and enjoyed this book. You have helped me bring my dream to life--literally--this story came to me in a dream!

About the Author

Halle Clark grew up in Phoenix, Arizona. She moved to Scotland to attend the University of St. Andrews and graduated in 2020 with a degree in Honours Biology. She currently lives on a 36-acre ranch in Pagosa Springs, Colorado, where she working on her next book, the final book in this Trilogy. She also works part time at a local animal hospital. Her hobbies include reading, playing with her dog, and flying through the air as much as possible.

www.ingramcontent.com/pod-product-compliance
Lightning Source LLC
Chambersburg PA
CBHW070200120726
47909CB00001B/187